*To Debra,
Enjoy!*

The White Witch's Daughter

Book One

J.C. Wade

J.C. Wade Originals

Copyright © 2023 J.C. Wade All rights reserved

Second Edition

J.C. Wade Originals, LLC

ISBN 9798986485768 (pbk)

ISBN 9798986485751 (digital)

Printed in the United States of America

No portion of this book may be reproduced in any form without written permission from the publisher or author, except as permitted by U.S. copyright law.

Contents

Dedication		V
Prologue		VI
1.	Chapter One	1
2.	Chapter Two	22
3.	Chapter Three	45
4.	Chapter Four	60
5.	Chapter Five	83
6.	Chapter Six	99
7.	Chapter Seven	118
8.	Chapter Eight	138
9.	Chapter Nine	168
10.	Chapter Ten	191
11.	Chapter Eleven	206
12.	Chapter Twelve	225
13.	Chapter Thirteen	257

14. Chapter Fourteen	275
15. Chapter Fifteen	296
16. Chapter Sixteen	312
Epilogue	322
Acknowledgments	325
About Author	326
Also By	327
Excerpt from A Conjuring of Valor: Book Two	330

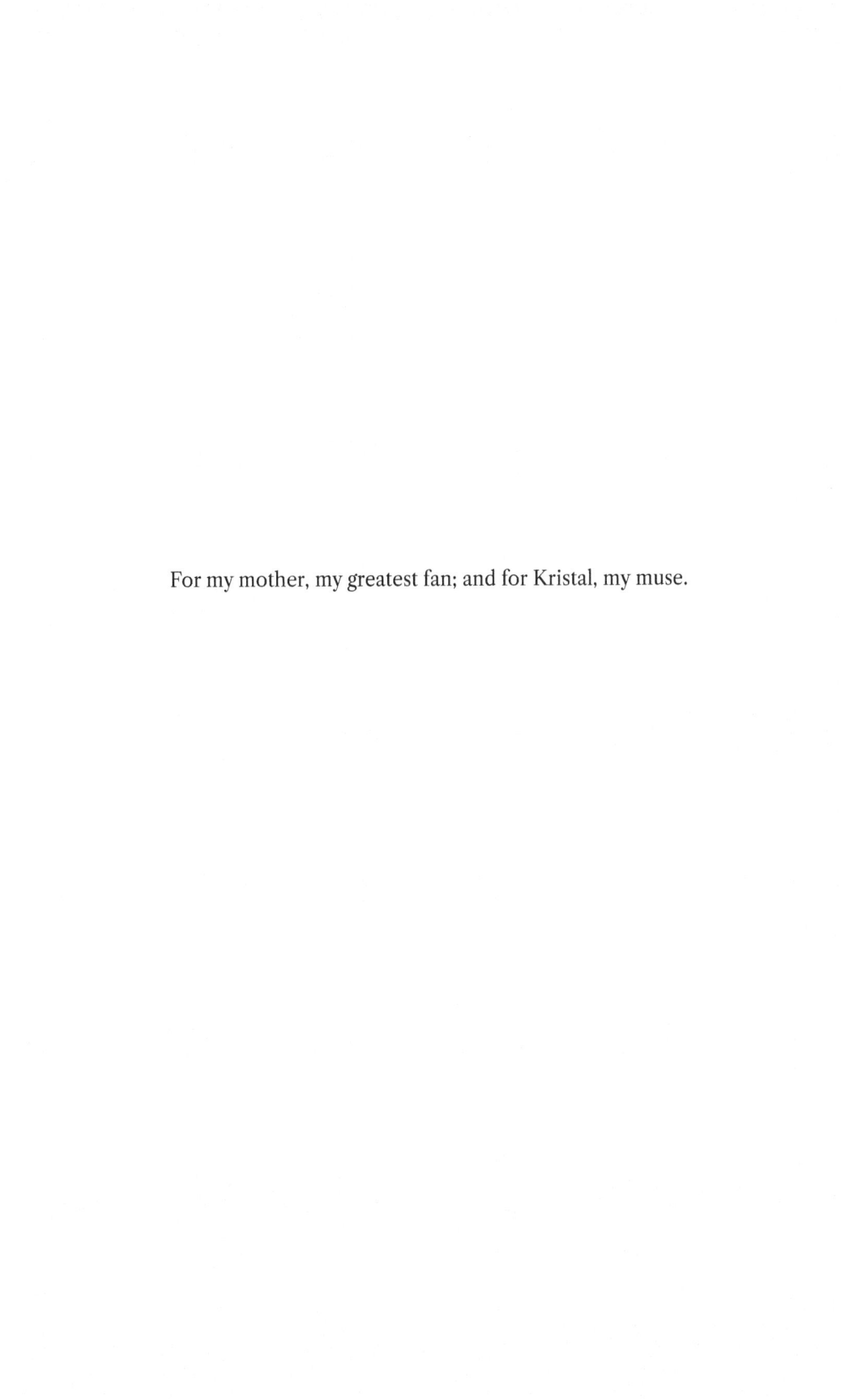

For my mother, my greatest fan; and for Kristal, my muse.

Prologue

Following the deaths of the Scottish king Alexander III and his only heir, Margaret, Maid of Norway, a council of twelve—the Guardians of Scotland—was created to name the new ruler among the clans. The council, seeing the division among the people on whom they felt should rightfully rule, feared civil war.

In an effort to waylay conflict, the Guardians called upon their neighbor and supposed friend, King Edward I of England, to act as an arbitrator between rival petitioners. At Berwick Castle in the year of our Lord 1292, King Edward, looking to acquire a loyal vassal, named John Balliol as the new king of Scotland.

Coerced into recognizing King Edward as the Lord Paramount of Scotland, in addition to excessive demands for men and money to fund his expensive war against France, Balliol was left with little choice but to rebel. Scotland sought a mutual defense pact with King Philippe IV of France, thus inciting King Edward's anger.

The Scots launched a failed attack against England in 1296, to which King Edward retaliated, sacking Berwick-upon-Tweed and killing over ten thousand people.

Chapter One

Carlisle, England

April 1296

Edyth pressed herself against the wall in the darkened hallway of her childhood home, her satchel clutched tightly against her breast. She could hear the whispers of the remaining servants in the buttery as she tried to remain out of sight.

"I dinae see one reason tae call her a—"

"Shh! Diven't say the word, Mira! Tis a sin, I tell yeh, tae blaspheme so."

It was Agnes, a kitchen maid, and Mira, the household's matronly chatelaine.

"Well, saying it or no don't make it true!" Mira hissed. Edyth easily could picture her in her mind, Mira's fists bunched up on her ample hips and her wobbly chin jutted out defiantly in reaction to Agnes's willingness to believe the rumors.

"Still, I'd no' like to hear the word spoken here. What if Edyth takes after her mam, eh? I caught her watchin' me with them cat eyes o' hers. She could be doin' the devil's work. Me 'ead 'as been aching—"

"Nonsense!" Mira barked. She could have smiled at the chat- elain's defense of her. "I've known 'er since she was nowt but a wee bairn, Agnes. Edyth ain't no more guilty than her ain' sweet mam. Twas nowt but a scandal. And look what talkin's done! First 'er mam hangit and disgraced, then her dear faither murdered in the street. Edyth needs our care, no' fear, and certainly no' finger pointing!"

Agnes grunted. "Well, I'll not stay in this house, true or not, Mira. If it's true what they say about Lady DeVries, then there'll be evil in these walls. And even if it's nowt but lies, there be those that believe it, and they will cause harm here. Ye mark me words, nowt but sorrow will come tae this house."

Edyth had heard enough of this talk for the past week to last a lifetime. Fighting the panicked whispers of heresy and witchcraft was like trying to catch smoke in your hands. What had been said against her mother in treachery had spread too fast to dispel. First, a quick and unfair trial, ushered in by the hands of the malicious Father Brewer, then a pronouncement that her mother was to be hanged for her crimes against God and the church, then last, her father—her dear father—had been stabbed in the street as he had fought the crowd in the town square where her mother had swung.

There had been chaos in the large crowd, and no witnesses had come forth. Edyth could still hear her town's people—people whom she had grown up around, people she had loved—chanting and screaming to "kill the witch" as her father was swallowed up in the churning crowd. His murderer was still unknown and free.

The thought of it made her belly burn with rage.

With no way to avenge for her parents' murders, she had little choice but to flee herself, now that the townspeople's attention had been turned to the remaining member of her family—herself.

Marcum, their steward, had already warned off a crowd of angry men who had pounded on the door. A frothing crowd had come, demanding Marcum produce "the white witch's daughter," as though they didn't know her name. Indeed, they'd known her these past eighteen years, had watched her blossom into a woman grown. It was easier for them that way, she supposed. If she had no name, she would be easier to kill.

It wouldn't be long now before a mob's bloodlust would end in yet another person's life in an effort to protect her. She couldn't stay holed up, afraid; she couldn't stand to see another drop of blood spilled.

Edyth stood erect now, clothed in her father's too-large hose, shirt, and tunic, and stepped out into the haze of torchlight that lit the corridor. The two servants were just out of sight, around the corner, but she could still hear them whispering to each other. Edyth wished she had time to gaze about her, putting to memory her childhood home, but Thom was waiting for her in the stables.

Edyth entered the hall to her left, a once comfortable place full of cherished memories of her mother quietly embroidering and her father's thorough tutelage on all the subjects he prized. Edyth flung open her mother's sewing box and picked through it as quickly as she could: a bone needle, thread, and a long strip of leather. Edyth paused as she fingered a bit of blue ribbon before pocketing it. It was worthless as far as necessities went, but she loved the color; it was the same blue as her mother's eyes.

A loud bang resounded from across the yard, making Edyth jump. She whipped her head around in time to see Mira rush in.

"My lady, Edyth!" Mira gasped, eyeing her strange manner of dress. "There are villagers outside again. They're growing unruly. I don't know how long Marcum can hold them off this time."

Edyth rushed to the heavy trunk that held her parents' treasures: books. She grasped her mother's red leather tome full of hand drawn pictures of herbs, roots, and flowers. It was a book made for the sole purpose of saving lives; such a tool would have only condemned her further if it had been found. Edyth shoved it into her satchel, next to the neatly tied squares of linens holding dried herbs and blinked back tears. Her lovely, poised, and gentle mother was gone, buried next to thieves and adulterers.

Edyth wiped at her eyes and searched the room. She hesitated for only a moment when her eye fell upon her father's handmade reader, evidence of his daring nerve to teach his daughter to read and write, among many other subjects—some of which even her mother disapproved of. Edyth decided she couldn't part with the heavy black script of her father's hand and tore a handful of pages from the binding before stuffing them inside her mother's book. Edyth turned on her heel and abruptly ran into Mira, whose eyes were welling with tears.

"My lady, please don't be foolish. Why are ye dressed so?"

Edyth strode past the woman she'd known as a second mother and opened a box on the mantle. She pulled out her mother's money purse and pocketed it as well. "You know I can't stay, Mira." Even as she spoke, she heard angry shouts from outside the gate.

"Dinnae leave so, Milady. Marcum will see us safe."

Edyth's eyes fell upon the chess board she and her father had used so often and picked up the white queen from her father's side of the board. It hadn't been polished; it still held his smudged prints from their last game together. The sense of loss threatened to overcome her once more, but she swallowed it away. She took her handkerchief from her sleeve and wrapped the queen in it, careful not to wipe her father's mark from it, and placed it in her satchel.

"Thom has drawn me a map to cousin Meg." She was proud that her voice hadn't wavered.

"Scotland?" Mira gasped and then crossed herself. "Edyth, nay! King Edward has taken Berwick. We're at war!"

"Aye, but war is upon us in Carlisle, and it is our own that attack! I cannot stay here. There is no life here for me."

"Ye shouldnae have said what ye did about Father Brewer, Milady. Yer mother always warned ye about yer wicked tongue—"

"Perhaps you're right," Edyth interrupted, forestalling the woman. She didn't want to hear it. What she'd said was true. The man *was* a liar, and worse, she was certain he *would* burn in hell, just as she'd said. She shook her head to rid the image of his smug, fat face as he hissed lies about her mother, lies the townspeople had swallowed whole, for who would believe her mother over a priest, a man of God? It was easier, she supposed, to believe her mother a witch and a heretic than to believe what Father Brewer had done to poor Annie.

"But Scotland!" Mira protested. "Why not...why don't you...there's the baron's family. Perhaps they—"

"No," Edyth said flatly. She didn't have time to argue. Marcum's voice was still raised against the men in the yard, and Thom was waiting. "My family name is forever tarnished. The baron of Wessex is dead. There will be no more petitions for my hand, and that suits me well enough. I can have a life with Meg that I cannot have here." Edyth pressed her hand against the satchel resting on her hip; how was it that her entire life could fit into a single bag?

The shouts were louder now. Mira clutched Edyth's arm, her eyes wide with fear. The buttery door flew open and banged into the wall. Mira let out a shriek and clung so tightly to Edyth's arm that she was sure to leave marks. It was Thom, the young stable master. He'd only had the role for a year now, after his father had died from being thrown from a horse. Although he was but a handful of years older than Edyth, she'd always looked upon him as much older. He had an old soul, her father had once said.

"Lady, you must come. Now!"

Edyth pulled her arm from Mira, clutching her satchel to her chest, and followed Thom through the buttery and down the stairs toward the kitchen at a dead run.

"Marcum has been overrun, milady," breathed Thom once they'd reached the back door. "There are about eight of them. He...he couldn't hold them off."

Fear swelled within her. That, and something lately new: hate. She'd never known the emotion before, had never experienced the burning rage that was now coursing through her. "He's...they killed him?"

Thom nodded, his eyes dark. "They're sure to be outside the front door by now." Thom handed Edyth a straight, heavy dagger. "Take this. Use it if you must."

Edyth nodded, wondering if she could.

"Let me go first, Milady. Wait here." Thom pushed the door open a fraction, just enough to peer through, and when he saw no one, he met her eyes. He opened his mouth, an apology written there.

"Don't," she said; she didn't think she could bear to hear his apology for what part he had played in this, their current hell. Emotions warred behind his eyes, but with a curt nod, he slipped out.

Edyth waited impatiently. Mira tottered in, out of breath and red faced. She clutched onto Edyth once more and sobbed. "My dear Edyth. My dear child."

Edyth hugged the buxom woman and kissed her graying hair, her nerves jumping, her legs wobbly. There were no words. How could she tell the woman who had loved her all her life goodbye? How could she thank her for the endless smiles, the warmth she exuded, the love she shared? She was all that remained of her childhood. Edyth's eyes stung, her heart breaking anew.

If she could open her chest and live without her heart, she would tear it out at the root and be done with the pain.

Thom opened the door and beckoned Edyth silently. Mira sobbed all the harder but let her arms drop from around Edyth's shoulders. Thom shushed her harshly, and Mira had the good sense to silence her fretting. Her shoulders quivered with silent tears, her apron clutched to her mouth. *It was time.*

"Don't forget your hat," Thom reminded her. "The moon is bright, and your hair will give you away."

Edyth did as he bid, cursing her ugly orange hair for the thousandth time. And then with one last look at Mira, she stepped out the door.

The air was chilly, the sky clear. The sound of wood splintering in the distance made her jump.

"That'll be the front door," whispered Thom. "Run to the stables. I'll follow you."

He awkwardly pulled a sword from the scabbard at his waist. Edyth's worry intensified. She doubted if Thom had actually ever used a sword—at least for its intended, deadly, purpose—and knew that if he was engaged in a fight, he would surely lose.

But she couldn't think about that right now. She ran forward, stumbling over her own feet before righting herself. The stables were only fifty yards from the cold storage door and thankfully not in sight of the front of the house, but if someone decided to search elsewhere for her....

Her heart raced, her feet sliding in the cold mire the spring thaw had caused as she ran for the stables. A shout, a crash of steel on steel, a grunt.... Edyth dared to look over her shoulder and saw Thom grappling with Hugh, the smithy's son. Thom had blocked a heavy blow from Hugh and was scrambling backward to reset himself for another attack.

Edyth couldn't bear to watch. She ran the distance to the stables, entering into the inky blackness without caution. Edyth knew the way to Harris's stall and didn't need a light. It was better this way; she didn't have time to say goodbye to her mare, and not seeing her would make it easier. Thom had said the distance was too far and the country too rough for the poor old girl and had insisted she take her father's destrier, Harris. He knew her well, but neither were accustomed to each other.

Edyth felt her way in a rush, bumping into buckets and tripping once over a line of rope that had tangled around her ankle. She cringed at the noise she was making; she could feel the horses' nervousness at her frantic movements. Her eyes adjusted as she neared Harris's stall. Thom had prepared her as best he could. There was only so much Harris could carry on his back and still hold Edyth.

Edyth forced herself to calm and held her hand out for Harris to sniff. She couldn't keep it from shaking. "Come on, boy. I need you to fly for me."

She entered his stall; he jerked his head back and she grabbed hold of his bridle, stroking his nose. "You're my only chance," she whispered. She led him out of the open stall and clambered up onto his back, riding like a man for the first time since she was just a girl. She nudged him forward, and he took up like a jackrabbit. She had to hold on to his mane to keep her seat.

Harris tore through the stable doors, past a raucous crowd surrounding what was most assuredly a dead body. A sob caught in her throat at the sight of the man who had died so she could escape. *Thom.*

"Go, Harris," Edyth commanded, tears clouding her vision. "Steal away!"

Edyth rode hard and fast, her head bent low over Harris's strong neck. She didn't stop until his flanks heaved and his mouth foamed.

Perthshire, Scotland
A heavy fog had lain low on the land as the Ruthven warriors had mounted their horses in the early morning dark. The usually bustling village had been quiet and still as they'd left, gone even before the tinkers had set up their shops on the low street. By the time they'd made it to the River Tay, the fishers' schooners were just casting off their ropes and heading out to the lightening horizon to the approval of the gulls. The reek of rotting fish was sharp on the wind, and Ewan's eyes stung, even as he filled his lungs with the homely scent.

Seeing his home again after so many years away, first fostering with his uncle and then in France soldiering, felt strange. He thought that, at any moment, he'd wake to find himself ankle deep in the mud of the Loire River beds once more, fighting for his life. He wasn't sorry to have left those shores despite the grief that had met him at home. Malcolm, the earl of Perthshire, was now dead and he, Ewan, found himself thrust into a different battle altogether.

He'd missed his father's burial by a week, to his disappointment, but despite the loss, he was glad to be home again. His mother needed him in more ways than she was prepared to admit, and his sister needed a firm hand, as always.

He'd left home as all noble sons did, at the age of seven, to foster with his uncle in the Campbell lands. At the age of twelve, once his fostering days were over, his future had lain before him like a bright beacon of honor, but at that time, he knew nothing of how glory was really won. He'd dreamed only of leaving his father's house and his mother's loving grip to become a man in his own right—a man in truth, like his father and his uncle.

The honorable future he'd dreamed of as a lad no longer hung before him, vivid and ripe for the picking. Instead, he was met with intrigue and secrets, guile, and fear. The politics his father had so cleverly maneuvered his family through were now solely his responsibility, and he felt the full weight of them. Their king, John Baliol, had run for sanctuary to God-Knew-Where while the English bastard Longshanks tightened his hold on them.

He'd had a missive waiting for him on his return from France, demanding the house of Ruthven pay more English taxes to, no doubt, pay for Longshank's bloody, ongoing war with France—the war his father had demanded he fight in. And yet all those long months, his father had been playing both sides: paying Edward in silver while paying Phillipe in blood.

However bad things appeared, his brother was with him in all things, thankfully. Iain was canny, and together, they might survive the war with their lands intact. It was more than Longshanks' damnable taxes that occupied his mind, however. His father's longtime friend John Scott in the lowlands had called for aid. So close to Berwick, John was having considerable difficulty keeping the swarming English off his lands. He'd lost his only son and half of his retainers when the garrison had been sacked. Unable to protect himself properly, Ewan agreed to bolster the Scott's dwindling numbers by supplying the man with more fighting men.

The riding had been slow in the wee hours due to the fog. The twenty fighting men he'd brought with him had slowed their journey even more, but there was little he could do about either. They were quiet and experienced enough that he could not complain. He'd sent his messenger ahead to Dundas and Hay to let them know of their plans and anticipated reaching the Dundas holding by nightfall. Traveling so far into the lowlands offered him a rare opportunity to speak to his neighbors about the coming storm of violence and political intrigue that was about to unfold. It was something his father would have done and Ewan, so green and inexperienced in such matters, dreaded even the slightest misstep lest he thrust his family into dishonor and ruin.

Iain was ahead of him, riding beside Graham, the massive tracker. He would keep Graham with him, and perhaps Fingal, as they headed home from Scott territory. Fingal, his lead bowman, was small with a face like a rat, pointed and twitchy, but for what he lacked in physical appeal, he made up with skill. He and Graham, along with Iain, would be enough, he thought, to safely reach home should anything untoward happen.

The light was weak, the sky covered in dark, billowing clouds that threatened rain. Indeed, rain was already falling in the distance so that the Ochill Hills appeared to fade and run off the landscape much like ink from a dampened page.

Ewan urged his horse forward and caught up to his brother and Graham, who were deep in conversation. The width of the road wasn't wide enough to accommodate three horsemen, so he was forced to wait behind them until the trees thinned enough for him to pass them.

"Land is everything," said Iain emphatically. "If we lose our land, we lose all."

"Ye cannae think tae side with that whoreson, Longshanks," replied Graham, "even if ye get tae keep yer scraps. What good will it do ye tae keep yer lands but no' be free?"

Iain shook his head, his wavy brown hair lifting in the breeze. "I've no wish tae be tied to the English crown nor more than you, but we best step canny," replied Iain. "Our father has already signed the Ragman Roll. Our hands are tied."

"What Malcolm did and what yer brother will do are two different affairs," said Graham dismissively. "Ewan can choose to be his own man."

"Iain is right," said Ewan, gaining their attention. They turned in their saddles and nodded to him with respect.

Graham went rather pink in the ears, no doubt embarrassed to have been speaking so freely about his laird. "Milord."

"We must look at all options before declaring openly against the English," said Ewan. He looked to the sky and rolled his right shoulder, which had bothered him ever since the battle at Blave. "But more to present," he said, squinting at the angry clouds, "if we hurry, we can reach Dundas in a few hours and possibly stay dry."

Graham scratched his bearded neck, lifting his chin to the heavens. "Mmph," he agreed. He leveled one ice-blue eye at Ewan, framed by neat blond brows. He'd lost the ability to open his right eye when he'd been on the wrong end of a horse at the tender age of nine. Ewan didn't think the eye was gone, just useless, but he'd never asked. The loss of Graham's eye did not hinder his abilities as a tracker in the least, but it did make him shy away from shoeing horses.

"The lads will thank ye if they can get tae the holding dry," Graham agreed in his soft tones. Graham's size and his voice had always seemed at odds to Ewan, but he'd never heard anyone sing more beautifully. Like a bird, Iain had said, and Ewan couldn't disagree.

Iain nodded and raised his fist. "Oy!" he cried, signaling his want for the men's attention. With a quick spur, his horse bounded forward. "Quickly, lads, if ye dinnae wish tae be drookit!"

Despite their efforts, by the time they reached the Dundas holding, the rain had found them and they were wet through. Muddy splatters covered them from head to toe. Ewan's feet had stuck in the sludge of the stable yard as he'd dismounted, but the worst of it seemed to be over. A light drizzle spat down upon them; pigs rooted in the mud, oblivious to the rain.

A stable lad had squelched over and taken his horse, which was all too eager to be led away into the shadowy utopia that awaited it. "Welcome, Lord Ruthven!" called the feminine tones of Lady Anice, second wife of Robert Dundas, from the stone steps leading into the holding. "You are welcome."

Ewan bowed deeply and ascended, reaching for her hands. They were small, almost like a child's, and pink with cold. "My lady," he said, bending to kiss them, "thank you for your hospitality."

Her shy smile reached her hazel eyes, sooty with long lashes. He'd danced with Anice as a lad once in Edinburgh. He'd thought her beautiful then, but she was even more so now. "The years have been kind to you, Lady," said Ewan, smiling. "How have you been faring, being chained to that nyaff Robert?" he teased.

Her laugh chimed lightly, but she did not answer. Her eyes had strayed to Iain, who was now standing beside him. "Lady," said Iain, bowing neatly, "we thank ye for your hospitality."

"You are, all, most welcome," she said with a curtsey. "Please," she said, turning and motioning to the door behind her, "let's get out of this driech weather. My man will escort your men to the garrison barracks."

The men courteously stomped the majority of the mud from their boots before entering the dark anteroom. They shook their heads like dogs, sending droplets of water flying. Two torches burned brightly, dazzling Ewan's eyes. The arrow slits on either side of the doorway kept the room cold and blustery. The room itself seemed to breathe as the wind gusted through the openings, making the torches dance and shadows swing.

A nervous lass appeared beside them, offering them linen to dry their faces. "Please, sir," she said, holding out her towel to

Ewan as though he were a wild animal and prone to striking. He thanked the lass, who presently appeared as though she wanted nothing more than to shrink into the wall and disappear.

Grateful, he wiped his head and face, and then smiled as he returned the proffered gift. This only seemed to alarm her further. Startled, she nodded mutely and jerked the rags from their hands before bouncing a quick curtsey, her face in flame.

"Robert is eager to see you," said Lady Anice, her eyes following the girl's escape with barely concealed exasperation. She paused as though debating what to say. "She came to us from Berwick. She is still learning that she has a place here with us."

Ewan nodded his understanding. "We, too, have gained a widow and a son."

"So far north?" asked Lady Anice, her surprise evident.

"They were searching out family," said Iain as way of explanation.

"I see," answered Lady Anice, nodding her understanding. "We have four and ten refugees ourselves. Poor dears." Her pretty mouth pressed into a frown at the mention of them. Lady Anice waited as they discarded their swords and heavy surcoats into servants' waiting arms. She motioned them forward with a sweeping arm, and they were, all three, led by a torch-carrying, chain-mailed soldier.

"My husband is with Sir Gilbert in his rooms. I'm afraid you've missed supper, but I will have something sent up to you. Do ye care to change or freshen yourselves further?"

Ewan shook his head. "No, but thank you, lady. I won't keep your husband waiting."

She nodded, the seed pearls on her crispinette winking merrily in the torchlight. "As you like. They're waiting for you above stairs. I'll go see to your meal. Alexander will bring you to my husband's rooms." After a quick curtsey, she turned down a torch-lit hallway and disappeared, her slippers silent on the stones.

"This way," directed Alexander in a bored, flat voice, his chain mail chinking and clinking in rhythm as they walked in companionable silence until they reached their destination.

The room was large and comfortably fitted with furs and rushes. There was no fire in this room, much to Ewan's disappointment, but there was whiskey, which was almost as good.

"Lords Ruthven!" called a boisterous Robert, bounding from his chair. "You *are* welcome!" he said. "Come, take a nip and wash down the dust from the road."

"The dust has long been washed away," said Iain good naturedly. Robert laughed—he was always ready with a laugh—and welcomed them in, his arm thrown wide to usher them to their seats. Ewan remembered liking him even as a lad. It was hard not to like Robert, but he knew better than to assume his smiles were genuine. He was as cunning as a she-wolf.

The table was laden with horn cups, a few rolls of vellum, some quills, and a stoppered inkwell. The seats were high-backed and hard but not uncomfortable. Ewan settled himself as best he could, wet through.

"You are acquainted with Sir Gilbert Hay, I trust?"

"Yes," said Ewan succinctly. He remembered seeing the man once in Perth, but more so, he recalled messengers carrying missives emblazoned with the Hay crest to his father.

Sir Hay stood and bowed neatly, his black pointed beard touching his chest. He'd always reminded Ewan of a skeleton, with deep-set eyes and wan skin. His cheeks were sunken, his bony wrists protruding from the sleeve of his sark, but his eyes were keen and alight. His father had once said that Sir Hay missed nothing and often said even less.

"I trust your family is well," said Gilbert in a voice like the wind, before regaining his seat. The tip of his long nose was pink from drink, Ewan noticed, and was gratified. He hoped the drink might loosen his tongue a bit.

"Yes," said Ewan, "quite well." He accepted a horn cup with a tot of whiskey from Robert. "My sister Cait is as lively as ever, and Mother is doing as well as she might."

"Mmph," said Robert, nodding, suddenly sullen. "I was sorry to hear of your father's passing. He was an admirable ally and even greater foe."

"He was a clever man, your father," said Gilbert. He raised his cup and took a sip in salute. "We could use his guidance presently."

"Ewan can offer his assistance, I'm sure," said Robert with an appraising look. "He is his father's son, after all. And you, Iain," he added politely, raising a cup in salute.

Iain nodded. They all took a sip and sat in silence a moment, eyes roving.

"I see you received our message," said Iain, indicating Gilbert Hay's presence with a nod in his direction. "Thank you for your willingness to meet so abruptly."

Gilbert's benign smile slid from his face. "Oh, yes. I was happy to receive it. I agree, we need to discuss our next move now that King Edward has invaded."

"I have lands in England, tied to my wife's line, of course," said Robert, looking into his cup. "I would not like to see them confiscated. Nor my holdings here, mind."

"My father already signed the Ragman Roll four years ago," said Ewan with a shrug. "There is little room or choice left to me."

"Ah," said Gilbert, leaning forward in his chair. The candlelight was mimicked in his dark eyes, making them appear as though they were spotted with stars. "For all intents and purposes, so are we. We were all left but little choice to subscribe to the tyrant. Publicly, we are his." His long, spiderlike fingers folded themselves together on the tabletop. "You should know this better than anyone."

"Yes," said Robert, interested. "How was France? I heard you fought bravely."

"It was war," said Ewan, rolling his injured shoulder out of habit more than pain. Ligaments popped and caught on scar tissue as he rotated his arm, but it did little to alleviate the pressing ache he felt there, always.

There was a soft knock on the door, and upon Robert's word, two servant girls entered carrying trays of food and drink. They laid them before the men and curtseyed respectfully, asking if they needed anything more. Robert dismissed them with a flick of his hand, his rings catching the light from the candles. The platters of food were laid with an assortment of cold fowl and cheeses that made Ewan's mouth water.

"Please," said Robert, motioning with his hands that they should eat. He himself stabbed a piece of spiced meat with his dagger and took a bite, all the while talking around his food. "Baliol was left little choice than to rebel against England with that little attack on Carlisle, but his strike has cost us Berwick." He paused to swallow a mouthful of food, his eyes roving over the platter for his next target. "That, and Baliol's openly regarded mutual defense with France," he continued, settling on a drumstick. "He should have been far more private in who he chose as friends, but we can learn from his errors." He paused to swallow and gestured to the food. "I trust you don't mind me having a wee bite, hmm?"

Ewan didn't think he needed to point out that it was his, Robert's, food, and therefore he didn't need permission, but he shook his head, saying, "By all means."

"I really shouldn't," confided Robert, patting his round belly, "but I can't seem to help myself." He cleared his throat and took a quick sip of his drink before settling into his chair more comfortably. "Now," he continued, "I don't think Baliol will be able to stop Edward outright. He is weak, which is precisely why Edward backed him. He's controllable," he said, emphasizing his words with a shake of his drumstick.

"Agreed," said Iain, taking cheese for himself. "Baliol is not a strong leader. We cannot have a king chosen by England, but what are we to do? We squabble and fight over whose right it is to rule, and now we are invaded."

"Too true," grunted Robert, pouring ale for everyone.

"What do you propose?" asked Ewan, accepting the ale with a nod of thanks. It was dark and rich and very welcome.

"This is a delicate matter," intoned Gilbert softly. "We cannot take direct action, but if you will agree to follow our lead, we will have the best chance of keeping our lands and titles intact while we await a stronger leader."

"You want us to agree to a pact?" asked Ewan, leery. The last thing he wanted to do was get himself embroiled in a treasonous contract when he had no guarantee that they would uphold their end of the bargain. "What do you have in mind?"

"Nothing as of yet," said Robert, making small, plaintive motions with his hands, "but we know Edward will not stop at Berwick. He will push his army north and take what he might while he can. The time will come—soon," he added, pointing his dagger at Ewan to emphasize his words. A piece of pigeon clung to the tip, shining with fat, "when we must fight, but we must do it together, as one, or we will fail, just as we did in Berwick."

"What he means to say," said Sir Gilbert, "is that we cannot rebel until we have a strong candidate for useful king, one that will unite the clans. Until that happens, we must wait. Do not mistake me," he said, his deep-set eyes burrowing into Ewan, "for I mean no such offense, but you are young and untested. Youth can be hasty when prudence is needed. We are the wiser here. Accept our gift of knowledge and follow our lead. Now is not the time for King Edward to take notice of you."

Ewan digested this information as he ate. He agreed with them. Division among the clans had caused this mess, but should he trust these men wholly? Who was to say that they were not trying to use him in some elaborate plot? And how could he trust these men would know the right time to stand and fight? Ewan took a drink and looked each man in the eyes. "I will not make any bargains this night. I must think and ask more questions."

"A wise choice," said Sir Gilbert, sitting back in his chair, a thin smile of approval on his skeletal face.

Robert chuckled and swallowed his most recent bite. "Didn't I tell you, Gilbert? He is his father's son, no doubt."

"Tell me," said Iain, pouring himself some ale, "how do your refugees from Berwick fair?"

Robert nodded mutely, chewing industriously. "They are well enough," he said finally, his food gone. "Mostly women and children scared out of their wits, but a few lads nay old enough to fight."

"I currently have a dozen such people under my care," said Gilbert. "Why do you ask?"

"We've gained one such widow and son," explained Iain. "So far north?" asked Robert, his brows raised in surprise.

Iain nodded, replacing his drink onto the table and explained.

"The woman had something...*odd* to say about the garrison leader there. Do ye ken him? William the Hardy of Douglas?" At their affirmation, he continued. "She claims that 'er husband believed the Douglas tae be in league with the English. Her husband said that the Douglas played us false."

Robert grunted, his lower lip pushed out in contemplation. "Could be," he said. "William is a canny man. It would not surprise me if it were true. His manors in Essex and Herefordhire were forfeit after his arrest last year. With Baliol's weak rule, he would see his favors would be better suited with Edward." He sat for a moment, thinking, and then broke from his momentary stupor to say, "His Scots holdings will be dangerous to cross right now. He'll be defending them against his neighbors' anger, no doubt. Ye best step warily there, lads."

Iain caught Ewan's eyes at that remark. They would have to cross those lands to get to the Scotts clan, and it was unlikely they would do so in secret, seeing as how they had twenty fighting men to transport. The alternative was three days' journey around the western border of their lands, which he wanted to avoid. The Scotts were in dire need.

Ewan ate his dinner relatively mute, listening instead to their predictions on where Edward would strike next. It was a long time before he was able to lay his weary bones down for rest, but sleep was evasive. His mind was too busy with questions and possibilities.

They left early the next morning despite Robert's insistence they stay. The men, accustomed to riding hard for lengthy periods of time, had pushed their horses the majority of the day, but by midafternoon, they all, horses included, required rest. It was just as well. Ewan hadn't yet decided whether or not to push through the western lands of clan Douglas or go around, and they were at the cusp of the border as it was.

"What's your decision?" asked Iain privately after Ewan had dismounted. The men were talking and laughing quietly among themselves at the river's edge. The sun was high and the shadows short, but it was cold and blustery after yesterday's heavy rains.

"I think we should push through Douglas lands," said Ewan rummaging for his waterskin. The holding was far to the east, and John was desperate for men. "I'd hate to waste three days when we can be there tonight," he said.

"Agreed," said Iain, walking beside his brother toward the water. "I'd like to see how clan Douglas will greet us if we stumble upon them. Their reaction will be truth enough of the Hardy's loyalties."

Ewan nodded, frowning slightly as he thought. "True enough, Iain, but this time, we gamble with more than our own lives."

Iain clapped his brother on the back, almost hard enough to send him staggering. He caught himself and shoved back at his brother. "I'm a great gambler, so long as I have other peoples' money to spend," remarked Iain. "We will get there tonight. Besides, I have a mind to visit John's sweet niece if she's still at the keep."

Ewan scoffed. "What makes you think she'll deign to see you this time?"

Iain waggled his eyebrows. "I am persistent, am I not? She cannot withstand all my charms forever."

"Or you could get your nose broken for you a second time," suggested Ewan, darting away as his brother swung a playful slap at the back of his head. "Come," he said, laughing, "let us fill our skins and be on our way. Your lady is waiting."

Chapter Two

Despite Edyth's dramatic getaway, the rest of the night was wholly uneventful, if not uncomfortable. She'd stopped at some point in the middle of the night when she dared not push Harris further. Aside from her own fatigue, Harris had been heavily sweating and frothing, and with little moonlight to go by, there had been an ever-increasing chance of mishap and injury.

Dark places—hollows among the trees, the feet of the mountains to the east—had seemed even darker still, lending to her already active imagination. Hidden eyes of beasts and men had seemed to await her in each gloomy shadow, making Edyth tense in anticipation, worry for nothing, and shiver with fear.

But the body can only endure so much suffering before complete collapse, so she'd chosen the high ground, well away from the river to better hear an enemy's approach. She'd pulled on Harris's reins, who at that point was all too eager to rest, stumbled to her hands and knees, and lay still in a heap, unable to move. She hadn't really had time to weep over her losses, and she hadn't time now, but she wished she could.

Crying would help make room for her to sort out her feelings, muddled as they were, but no tears would come.

She didn't eat; she doubted she'd ever been hungry again. Instead, she used the last dregs of her energy to wrap the animal fur from the back of her saddle around her cloaked shoulders. She slumped gratefully against a granite outcropping spotted with flat, leafy lichen that glowed softly in the dim light. Something about the rock's ancient, solid presence, so steady and unmovable, gave her comfort. It sheltered her as well as loving arms might have.

Sleep had proved elusive. Not only was the night blustery and cold, but her nerves were beyond frayed. Her body felt heavy, weighed down with sorrow and fatigue so intense that she wondered if, in the morning, she would rise right out of her cumbersome body and simply leave it behind.

Each time she closed her eyes seeking rest, however, she saw her mother's feet swinging and her father's gray, pallid skin as he'd lain on the wooden, scrubbed table in the cold storage room, the angry rent in his flesh born from an unknown blade, puckered in a fatal kiss. And she saw beautiful Annie, Thom's sister—the start of all their troubles.

Edyth wondered absently if beauty was a punishment from God. Beautiful things were so often ruined through wanting.

She shook her head to rid herself of the haunting images that would plague her for the rest of her life and looked to the heavens, but not to pray. She hadn't prayed since it had happened. The thrumming chord that had connected her to God had somehow snapped, the melody now discordant and broken.

God had proven suddenly—cruelly—inconstant, but the stars...the stars would not change. She scanned the sky and effortlessly found Cygnus, Aquila, Ursa Major, and her once-favorite, Orion, with whom she now realized she had much in common. His was a story of love stolen away by death. And Edyth was Artemis, doomed to live without.

Edyth would have sworn she hadn't slept, except for the fact that she'd awoken with a start just before dawn. Two squirrels twittered angrily with each other, obnoxiously protesting some injustice done, chasing and jumping from dangerous heights. She rose with great difficulty, noting with some asperity that she hadn't parted ways with her clay tabernacle. Apparently, there was still more she could endure. The human body had an amazing ability to function on virtually no sleep, little food, and much too much heartache.

Roll replaced, she took a long drink from her waterskin and then removed Thom's map, which was rolled neatly in her satchel. Previous plans whispered about the day before with Thom, accompanied with a flurry of flight, she'd escaped with her life and hadn't given any real thought, had ignored—the *how* of the journey ahead. The goal had been to, quite simply, put as much distance between herself and Father Brewer's cohorts as she could.

But now that she'd escaped and the dangers from her recent past were miles behind her, a new and terrifying danger awaited her. In theory, she knew how to get to Meg, but now that it came to the actual practice of it, she faltered.

If she'd had time, previously, to consider the enormity of the task—to cross vast expanses of unfriendly territory using a map drawn by a stable master who hadn't left Carlisle since he was twelve—she would have, of course, endeavored to find some alternative solution. She might have written to her cousin; she could have arranged for escorts, perhaps. But she hadn't had time, and she was utterly alone in the world.

Edyth frowned at the map, seeing it for the first time. She held it tightly, both to avoid it catching the wind and flying away as much as to keep her hands from trembling. Her fingers ached with cold, but her heart felt colder still. The path that lay before her wasn't really a path at all. There was a circle that she assumed was a lake, several crisscrossing lines labeled as old Roman highway, some rounded lines that were meant to be hills, and an *X* marking where Thom thought the MacPherson clan resided.

An imaginary fracture in her resolve, which had started the night of her parents' deaths, lengthened and splintered like fresh ice over a pond. She knew, above all else, she must remain calm, however wearisome or futile the task, but it was proving impossible.

Her father had taught her that having a cheerful heart was better than courage, for it sustained the bearer far better and longer, but she didn't think she could ever conjure such a feeling ever again.

Thom had shoved the map into her satchel the night before with whispered instructions to watch the sun, head north, and stay off the roads. He'd said he'd never gone so far as Meg's clan but that there would be some who could help guide her with the glaring caveat that she'd "best be choosy" on who she spoke to. And she'd simply nodded like the great mongrel she obviously was, too preoccupied with gathering her chosen belongings for the journey to ask important questions.

How on earth was she to know who to trust?

Edyth swallowed the bubble that had formed in her throat and looked once more to the sky. The stars were mostly gone now, but she could still see Venus, the morning star, in the purpled eastern horizon. Artemis was industriously occupied in her eternal occupation of pulling the curtain of darkness away from the earth to reveal the dawn.

Edyth carefully rolled the map up and attempted to force cheer into her heart. It wasn't as if she were wholly unprepared. She had some money for lodging, if needed, and a dagger for protection. Thom had even insisted she take a short bow for hunting, though it had been quite some time since she'd used one. She'd only ever killed one thing in her life—a fat gray squirrel—but she'd cried and regretted it immediately. She was determined, however, that she would use it again if she had to. Aside from that, though, she had more accomplishments than fine embroidering and curtseying skills to boast of, much to her mother's mortification. Not that climbing trees or spitting to a target would be helpful in the least.

Edyth sighed and pulled her hat down to her ears, ignoring her fear. If she could not count on any of her virtues, she could at least rely on her faults. Her mother had called her stubborn and foolhardy on enough occasions; if she could not be brave, then at least she could be stubborn.

Edyth mounted Harris, thinking once more of her parents. And now Thom. If nothing else, if she never made it to Meg, the least she could do would be to honor them in the only way she could. She would die well, if all else failed.

It was with these grim thoughts that she rode west, down the hill, then turned north at the river, going as fast as she dared before the stars faded completely. The air was still and hushed as it is only in the early twilight hours of the day. No breeze stirred the limbs; no birds yet called to one another as though snow, not open sky, covered the ground, blanketing any sounds into hushed silence.

The ground was soft with the spring thaw, muddy in the low places, but Harris was sure-footed and strong.

There was an unnamable something within her that told her to stay off the road to the east, and so the going was long and interrupted often with impassable landscapes—rivers too deep to cross, crags too steep to climb, and dark forests she didn't dare to enter.

The hours were marked by the changing shadows as Edyth rode. Twice Edyth spotted a crofter's hut, burned to char and ash, in time enough to give it a wide berth. She didn't want to chance meeting anyone, dead or alive.

Only a few weeks ago, the brutal Scots had raided the outskirts of Carlisle, they being a persistent and formidable canker to their lands and people. Cattle had been stolen, houses burned, and people killed. Seeing the blackened homes of her father's crofters made her stomach turn sour. Enraged, she'd spurred Harris on, giving a wide berth so she would not witness any further evidence of the destruction.

And this is where she was headed—to cross all the miles between England and Meg filled with such horrors—to live among brutish men. Men who took without care, killed without thought. Men, she realized with a jolt, like those she had lived among all her life, and it hadn't mattered one whit that they'd once been cared for by her family.

Feeling lost within herself and thoroughly heartsick, she looked back over her shoulder. The land was open here with forest filling in the low places where the hillocks met. Large boulders dotted the landscape like crumbs fallen from a giant's plate. Would she miss this, her home? No, she didn't think so. The only pieces of England she would carry in her heart were those that her parents now rested in.

Her life had changed so suddenly, so abruptly, that she had no notion of her next step. What was she to do? She'd been brought up as a lady, knowing full well what was expected of her. And at the ripe age of thirteen, she'd been promised to the Baron Wessex, fulfilling her lifelong expectation of marrying well for the sake of land, title, and riches.

She had known as soon as she'd met the man that she had not wanted to marry him, but young maidens did not have the advantage of choice. Thankfully, their union had been postponed due to the baron's absence. He was fighting in the king's campaign against the French and had, therefore, been unable to wed her, not that she'd minded. She'd always felt a little guilty for wishing he'd die in battle, and then she'd suddenly be free. She'd said many prayers as a penance for those thoughts.

And now God had granted her wish of freedom, but it had come at the ultimate price. And now what? Her life was her own to choose freely the path before her, but she could not see a way. She could perceive no purpose to her life now aside from putting one foot in front of the next. But there was Meg. Meg was all she had left of family. Perhaps with her, she might find a bit of herself again. Meg had always known how to cheer her up or, at the very least, distract her from her woes. A great storyteller, Meg was bound to dream up an ending for this, Edyth's great tragedy, and help her shape it into reality.

Hours passed. The landscape changed, the sun grew hot, and she had to stop at a stream to refresh; she forced herself to eat and felt sick after. On she traveled. Getting back on Harris had proved to be rather difficult; her limbs were stiff, her hands raw, and her backside surely blistered. She gritted her teeth through it all until she became numb once more, keeping a keen eye out for telling features that might give her a clue to where she was on Thom's map. Still nothing spoke to her, but she forced her fears away, drawing on her stubborn nature, watching the sun.

Once, her ears had tricked her into thinking that she'd heard people's voices, and she'd pulled out her dagger, hidden herself and Harris as best she could, and waited. After what felt like a long time with her heart in the throat and no foe in sight, she replaced her dagger, her fingers cramped from squeezing the handle so tightly. She'd had to try half a dozen times to replace the dagger, her breath short.

It was several hours later when the sun was sinking toward the western horizon, casting a golden hue through the boughs of the trees, that she finally stopped.

Below her was a wide valley with a few visible patches of freshly turned earth, a snaking pillar of smoke from what she assumed was an unseen cottage, and the bright green of freshly budded leaves. She could almost smell the woodsmoke and taste the gravy-soaked bannock she imagined would be there.

No, it would be best if she backed up from the ridge and found a low place to make camp, where her fire wouldn't be spotted. In the morning, she could continue on and try once more to get her bearings.

Edyth looked around her at the black pines and leaf mold and shivered. A dirt floor of a stable would be better—and welcome—to another night of cold rocks under her back and constant worry of danger lurking in every shadow. It wasn't the rocks or even the cold that bothered her. Really, it was being utterly and inescapably uncertain that made her heart stutter. Was she even going in the right direction?

She pulled out Thom's map again but this time without the expectation of hope at finally seeing something telling. The valley could very well provide her with what the map could not, she reasoned. Someone was down there, a family perhaps that could lead her in the right direction. Her uncertainty would be eased. Was it worth the risk?

What if, instead of finding a family, she found that the fire belonged to some vagrant? He could rob her or kill her. Edyth hesitated and looked to the sky.

No, perhaps she shouldn't stop at all. The stars would be out in another two hours at least, and she could use them to help guide her north through the night. She could, that is, if she wasn't utterly spent. And she had to think of Harris as well.

Edyth hesitated and looked behind her once more, hating the thought of wandering, unknowingly, forever in the darkening forest. Envisioning countless days of ambivalence, wandering in doubt, she made up her mind. She was careful to wind her way down the steep slope and had made it near the bottom before necessity demanded that she dismount to pull her bow out of the roll at the back of the saddle.

Edyth had been tutored by her father and her neighbor friend James in the sport of archery, but it had been well over two years since she'd even picked up her bow. Her mother had disapproved of the unladylike sport and demanded that she dedicate more time to the feminine tasks that would appeal to the baron. If only she'd disobeyed!

Edyth had to use all her body weight to string it, which took several tries and left her breathless in her exhausted state. Then she slung it gracefully over her shoulder and onto her back. Next, she tied her quiver of arrows around her waist, enjoying the familiar feel of it, much like a well-worn shoe.

Not knowing what she would find or how she would be received, Edyth wanted to project an image of lethal strength and self-sufficiency, instead of appearing like a rabbit that had been run down by a fox.

A beautiful thicket of budding birch met her at the bottom of the hill. She could smell freshly turned earth, and her fears lessened slightly, reassured. These people, whoever they were, would be farmers, not brigands ready to pounce on her.

Finally, after several minutes, she cleared the trees and saw two women, bent over neatly tilled rows of earth, planting seeds. Edyth exhaled a breath she hadn't known she'd been holding. She'd overheard Agnes tell a kitchen maid once that Scottish men stole women from enemies as they would cattle. She'd heard other stories, too, that had made her face burn red, and her stomach grow tight, but there were no men here that she could see. Fortune was on her side. At least for now.

Edyth nudged Harris forward, relieved at the outcome. The two women righted themselves quickly upon noticing her, but Edyth could not yet make out their faces clearly enough to guess their thoughts. One woman stretched backward and placed her hands on the small of her back, kneading it. The other stood still, much like a scarecrow, her fist wrapped tightly around the shaft of a hoe.

The small cottage, not far from the field, had a stone foundation and a thatched roof in poor repair. There was an outbuilding on the far side of the house but no sign of beasts or men. A few chickens scratched near the door but scattered and squawked as the door was flung wide on its leather hinges.

A young girl flew out, her brown skirts swishing around her ankles. She stopped on a command from one of the women and retreated back inside just as quickly as she had come, her eyes wide with alarm.

Edyth made her way over to the two women slowly but halted as soon as the scarecrow righted her tool and took a defensive stance. Edyth, assuming they were afraid that she was a man, removed her hat before dismounting. Her long plait fell heavily down her back, straight as one of the arrows in her quiver. She bowed as neatly as she could and tried to smile politely, though her knees felt watery.

"What's this?" asked the scarecrow, her eyes narrowed. "Who are ye, and why are ye come?"

Edyth straightened herself and took a steadying breath. "I saw your fire," she said, gesturing unnecessarily to the smoke snaking its way into the sky. "I was hoping for a place to stay for the night."

The two women looked at each other, then back at her. The silence stretched on.

Edyth cleared her throat. "I seem to have lost my bearings. Tell me, where am I?" she asked, fumbling for the map she'd placed in her shirtfront. She unfolded it and offered it toward them, but they didn't move to take it. Holding it there between them dumbly for several more seconds, she finally let her hand fall. She fought the urge to wipe her palms, which were now sweating profusely onto her hose. "Who is lord over this land?" she tried.

Edyth thought they'd stand there forever, glaring at her before the shorter, dark woman who'd kneaded her back spoke, her eyes narrowed in clear disdain. "No. Ye cannae stay here."

"I don't want to cause you any trouble," said Edyth. "I'm only passing through and could use a soft place to sleep. Maybe in your stable, there?"

The tall, tawny woman who so resembled a scarecrow gave her companion a "hold on" look that gave Edyth hope.

"I can pay," said Edyth, laying a hand on her satchel as if it were proof of her sincerity.

"Eh?" said Scarecrow, her eyes following Edyth's motion. "I have coins," said Edyth. "Silver."

At this the women paused, glancing at one another in silent communication. Apparently, prejudice could be overlooked with the proper enticement. Edyth knew that silver would be a rare commodity to these women, who most likely traded in everyday, useful items. Still, silver was always useful.

"Show us," said the plump woman, her dark eyes alight.

Edyth hesitated, not wishing to show them the entire contents of her purse but also afraid to appear as though she was hiding something from them. After a brief inward struggle, Edyth pulled the purse from her satchel and moved it in a way so that the contents clicked together. Without waiting to see if this gesture was evidence enough, she returned the purse and laid a hand over the leather flap that closed the satchel.

"And you will leave at first light?" confirmed Scarecrow, her eyes darting from Edyth's hand on her satchel to her face.

"Oh yes," said Edyth, nodding. "I don't wish to be any trouble. I give you my word."

The shorter, plumper of the two scoffed disgustedly and said, "The word of the English isnae worth much these days." Edyth's mouth tightened, thinking of the stolen cattle and burned homes in Carlisle but said nothing.

"Dinnae fash o'er it, Raddah," said Scarecrow, making little dismissive motions with her hands. "I'll take her in and get her settled. You finish here."

Edyth followed the tall, slender woman through the dooryard. A few chickens came running from the shade of a scrubby bush nearby for something to eat, but the woman ignored them, muttering something under her breath as she brushed one aside with a hole-ridden boot.

The windowless room was dark and stuffy but welcoming enough. The stone hearth was large and blackened with soot; a pot hung from an iron hook, which was suspended over the fire, bubbling in a homely fashion that made Edyth feel less like an intruder in a strange place. From the smell emanating from it, Edyth supposed dinner would be porridge; her stomach growled at the thought of something hot to eat, even if it was gruel. A swath of gray wool was strung across a portion of the one-room home, presumably hiding the sleeping area. A sturdy looking table, laden with a clay ewer and an assortment of wrinkled winter apples, stood on the opposite wall of the hearth.

"Get on with it then," said Scarecrow, exchanging her working apron for her slightly cleaner kitchen apron from a peg by the door. She motioned for Edyth impatiently. Moving her satchel from her hip to her lap, Edyth sat on the three legged stool the woman had indicated.

Industriously using her apron to pull the pot away from the fire, the woman ladled a goodly portion of dinner onto a wooden plate, where it oozed wetly into a formless shape before she plopped it down in front of Edyth. Porridge, just as she had suspected. Nothing had ever been more appetizing, and her mouth filled with saliva as she gazed upon it.

"You said you had coin," stated Scarecrow matter-of-factly, her brown eyes intent, her open palm waiting. The lines of her hands were dark with dirt so that it looked like little brown rivers flowed over them.

"Oh yes," said Edyth, immediately rummaging through her satchel and removing her mother's embroidered pouch. It held a small handful of coins, but certainly not a fortune. She pulled on the drawstring, feeling much like a mouse that had been spotted by a hawk. As the circle of fabric opened and Edyth sifted through the contents with a forefinger, she could feel the woman's eyes heavily on her. Indeed, the woman seemed to scarcely breathe as Edyth pulled out a silver penny and placed it in her dirty, rough hand.

"I thank you for the fine meal," said Edyth, meaning it. She pulled another penny from the purse. "And for a roof over my head."

The woman's fist closed like a trap; it disappeared into the folds of her skirt, her eyes still fixed on Edyth's money pouch as she pulled it closed and deposited it back into her satchel. Edyth hesitated, not sure if now was the best time to discuss the map.

"Why are ye dressed like a lad?" asked a small, tentative voice. Edyth suddenly found a pair of large, round eyes in a pale, round face looking up at her from under the table, one small hand clutched around a corn husk doll.

"Well, hello," said Edyth, smiling softly at the little girl. She was very frail; the bones on her wrists stuck out sharply from the ends of her dress sleeves. While it was clear she was well cared for and mostly clean, Edyth found her to be far too thin. She had no shoes, but that wasn't so uncommon among the peasant folk.

"Oh," said Edyth, looking down at herself as though she was unaware of her attire. "I have very far to travel, and riding a horse is much more pleasant this way."

The girl, about seven, Edyth guessed, stared at her too-large sark and woolen hose, a smudge of dirt on the side of her nose. "My da had clothes like yours," she said, her voice soft.

"Elspeth!" hissed Scarecrow, motioning with her head to leave off. "Go see tae the chickens, lass, and be quick about it."

At this the girl marched to the door and threw it open, glancing over her shoulder at Edyth, her wide eyes full of questions.

Scarecrow busied herself at the hearth, swinging the pot back over the flame. She ladled something wet into a horn cup and placed it in front of Edyth with a slice of stale bread.

Edyth nodded her thanks and used the bread to help load her wooden spoon. It wasn't exactly what she'd hoped for, but it was creamy and warm. She ate it heartily, grateful that she hadn't had to roast a squirrel or frog over a fire.

The woman stood, watching Edyth with disapproving, pursed lips for a moment before muttering none too quietly about Edyth being a godless heathen. She took a rag from her pocket and wiped her neck. "Ye'll sleep in the hay, out yonder," said Scarecrow, indicating with her chin in the direction of the stable. "As soon as ye've finished yer meal, ye can see tae yer horse."

Edyth nodded, feeling guilty at just leaving Harris so abruptly. "Yes. Thank you. Can you tell me where I am? I have a map, but it means naught to me." Edyth took a last bite of the stale and now-sticky bread, wiped her fingers on her sark in a markedly unladylike fashion, and rolled out Thom's map.

"I came from Carlisle," said Edyth, indicating the bottom of the map, thinking it wouldn't matter if they knew where she'd come from. "Tell me, am I in Scotland yet? I need to get to MacPherson land."

Scarecrow's eyes showed her surprise. "Oh, aye, yer in Scotland, lass, but the highlands are far. And dangerous," she said, looking suspiciously at Edyth once more. "Though I suppose for an English lass, ye think ye'll have Longshanks' soldiers paving the way for ye right enough." Scarecrow's lips pursed tightly, her hands clutching her rag hard enough to make her knuckles turn white.

Edyth opened her mouth to counter this remark, shaking her head, but didn't know what to say. It was true that King Edward had invaded, but Scots had struck Carlisle first. And perhaps that wasn't such a bad thing for her, after all, now that Scarecrow mentioned it.

Meg was far and the way dangerous. Would it be so terrible for her to encounter English soldiers? While she certainly didn't wish to be in the thick of battle, she had a quick, romantic vision of a gallant knight escorting her through dangerous landscapes to Meg's doorstep. And who better than an Englishman to take pity on her very English self and chivalrously escort her to Meg? She would likely not get such concern from a Scotsman. Not if Scarecrow and Raddah were the standard by which she would be received.

Edyth bit her lip, thinking of Thom's warning about staying away from people as much as possible. English soldiers might force her to return to England, out of harm's way, and she couldn't let that happen. "Surely there aren't any English soldiers near," said Edyth, suddenly wary.

Scarecrow glanced at her from the corner of her eye as she picked up Edyth's empty platter. "Only the rare deserter now and again. The bulk of 'em will be at Berwick, I expect, with yer murderous king."

Edyth's lips tightened as she fought back the urge to retort. Instead, she said, "Is that where all the men have gone? To Berwick to fight?"

There was a clatter as Scarecrow bumped into a vacant stool; the wooden plate rolled and wobbled across the floor before settling against the stone of the hearth with a thump. The woman uttered an oath and righted the stool, her hands fluttering to her forehead. "Ye should tend tae yer horse now, English," said Scarecrow.

Feeling as though a weight had been lifted from her shoulders as soon as she exited the hut, Edyth ventured into the dusky light of the stable yard.

The stables, while rather small, boasted two stalls and a hayloft, all of which were devoid of hay. Edyth frowned at what was to be her bed: a pile of molded, manure-strewn rushes. Harris had been left outside, where he had rummaged for what spring grasses he could find. She'd seen to his hooves and brushed him down with a comb she'd found in a stall. At least there would be roof over her head, she reasoned, watching the rising moon. She didn't have much time before full dark, and she still needed to fill her waterskin.

Hastening her steps across the empty yard, she caught sight of a white apron in the kale yard. With a thankful heart, she noticed it was the girl, Elspeth. She had just located her cat. The girl crooned to it softly, hugging it to her chest, ignoring its mewling protests.

Edyth hastened to the girl, her lips tugging into a soft smile at the forced show of unwelcome love Elspeth was determined to see through. "What's your cat's name?" asked Edyth, squatting so she could scratch behind the kitten's ear.

The girl shyly returned the smile and proudly displayed her prize, hind legs pumping empty air.

"Cat," said the girl. The kitten's cries grew louder still, and so Elspeth drew it against her chest once more, whispering into its flattened and agitated ears.

"I'm in need of water," said Edyth, displaying her waterskin as evidence.

Elspeth nodded and looked behind her at the house briefly before whispering, "Come, I'll show you. Mam willnae be too keen on me being out with ye, but I'll show ye and come back quick like."

"Thank you," said Edyth, feeling an uncertain kinship with the girl. There was something about Elspeth—maybe it was the ease in which she chose to disobey her mother—that reminded her of herself at that age. Memories tumbled about in her mind, quick and incomplete at the thought, making her heart constrict of its own accord.

"There's a wee spring over there, in the trees," said the girl, pointing with her chin just as her mother had. Elspeth set down the kitten, which quickly escaped around the corner of the house, its gray tail high.

The ground was lumpy with dead grasses and sprinkled with crumbled bits of brown leaves, but there was a well-trod path to the right filled with the shadows of twilight. Once they reached the path, the going was easier and Edyth said, "I don't wish to cause you trouble. I can find it on my own, I think, if it's at the end of this path."

Elspeth chewed her bottom lip and then blurted, "Are ye gonna murder us in our beds?"

Edyth was so surprised she stopped dead in her tracks. "Of course not," she sputtered, shocked.

Elspeth nodded knowingly. "I didnae think so, but me mam and me auntie were arguing over it in the house, so I thought I'd just ask." The girl shrugged, unconcerned.

"Why would they think such a thing?" asked Edyth, completely taken aback.

Elspeth had started walking again, wiping her nose with the heel of her hand, but Edyth had seen how the girl's eyes had darkened before they were hidden from her view. The trees were growing denser now on the path, and the light lessened considerably. "The spring is just here," said the girl, indicating a pile of stones stacked neatly at the head of a bubbling stream of water. The water looked black in the dark copse, but it smelled fine, so Edyth filled her skin and took a few sips. It was good.

"Why are ye alone?" asked Elspeth. Her face appeared all the more pale in the darkness, like a second moon in the night sky. "Me mam says that only a lady who's an outcast or a spy would travel alone...and dressed as a lad, no less. Are ye a spy, then?" she asked, her eyes wide with something akin to excitement.

Edyth couldn't help but smile. "No, not a spy. What I said is true. I must travel to my cousin in Scotland."

"But why are ye alone?" she asked, her eyes looking like dark pools in the low light.

Edyth hesitated. She didn't feel up to telling anyone the truth of it but couldn't think of a suitable lie either. "I suppose...I no longer have a home," she stated simply.

Elspeth seemed interested. "What's become of your home? Did soldiers come and burn it down?"

Edyth shook her head, wondering about the horrors the girl had seen in her short life. "My parents...they died." Her heart seemed to stop at the words, and it was with effort that she took her next breath. "I have no home left to me."

Elspeth nodded at this, looking curious but accepting of these facts, which Edyth appreciated.

"My da is deid," said Elspeth with a sigh. "And me brother, Hamish. And me uncle, Robert." She said it so plainly, just as she might discuss the weather. "When the soldiers came and took all our kein and sheep awa, they took the men too. The laird brought us back their bodies but no kein or sheep."

Elspeth looked so very pale and thin. A strong wind would surely carry her away like a leaf. How could one so frail carry such a burden?

"I'm so sorry," said Edyth, her heart aching anew. "Truly, I am." She touched the girl's shoulder, sharing her grief.

"Me mam says the English will come and take what's left. Is that true?" she asked, a note of worry lacing her question.

"No," Edyth answered automatically but faltered despite herself. Once upon a time, she would have believed the best of her people, but that had died along with her parents. In truth, she did not know.

She doubted there would be anything here soldiers would want anyway, so said nothing more.

"We best hurry," said Elspeth, already starting down the path toward the house. "Me mam willnae miss me for long."

"You go ahead," said Edyth. "It will be better if we go separately." Elspeth nodded and doubled her stride.

By the time Edyth made it down the path and had deposited her waterskin in her saddle bag, Elspeth was nowhere to be seen. Harris was nosing through the inedible rushes along the dirt floor of the stable, uninterested in Edyth. A dove was nested somewhere in the eaves, its homey cooing breaking the silence. She pulled out her map once more and frowned. She would have to speak again to the women, despite her genuine desire to avoid them. Thinking of speaking to them put her stomach into knots for some reason, but there was nothing for it. She'd have to grit her teeth and get it over with. *They're just farm folk*, she said to herself.

The only indication that the house was occupied was the faint light flickering in the spaces around the door. She could hear the muffled sounds of conversation from inside but could not make anything out. There was some shuffling and murmurs, and then the door was thrown open at her knock, the steely eyes of Raddah greeting her. "Good e'en," said Edyth, stopping herself mid-curtsey. She straightened herself and cleared her throat. "You've said the way to the MacPherson clan is far. I have little hope of getting there on my own, especially with this," she said, handing the woman her map.

Raddah took it and unrolled it, her eyes bouncing over the page, then settling back on Edyth. After what appeared to be an internal struggle, she finally motioned Edyth in with an impatient hand and shut the door behind her. Elspeth was sitting by the hearth, darning some hose in the firelight while her mother stood over her shoulder, presumably giving instruction. The room was hot and stuffy and smelled of sweating bodies.

"What now?" asked Scarecrow. Her hardened face looked eerie in the dim light. Half of her face was illuminated, showing the weatherworn wrinkles around her eyes and mouth. The other half, the side that was nearest to Edyth, was contrasted in shadow so that her eye was a pool of darkness, her cheek sunken.

"She wants help with this wee map," said Raddah, flapping Thom's drawing in the air.

Scarecrow's thin lips disappeared. Elspeth's needle hung midair, her mouth slightly agape as she turned her head to watch the proceedings. Edyth noticed she looked like she'd been crying.

"It'll cost ye," said Raddah with a quick bob to her head, as if encouraging herself. "Aye. We've fed ye and sheltered ye where we might, but if ye want more from us, ye'll be paying."

Edyth bit her lip. While it was evident that these women desperately needed money, so might Edyth. It was all she had in this world, aside from the meager things strapped to Harris's saddle and what she'd brought with her in her satchel. On the other hand, paying them would most likely be the quickest way to end the evening. And she was quite tired and sore and desperately wanted to lie down.

Edyth reluctantly nodded her ascent, hoping she was making the right choice, and fished out her coin purse from her satchel. It clanked and chimed as she pulled the drawstring open, and when the circle of fabric once again revealed its contents, she chose another silver penny.

"Nay," said Raddah, "we'll be wanting more than yer pence." Her hands were fisted on her wide hips, her shoulders raised in a way that made her appear to have no neck at all.

"You'll get what I think your directions are worth," said Edyth coolly. Quite suddenly, her temper raised to the surface without warning, like a snake rearing to strike. *The nerve of this woman....* She fisted her purse in her hand, watching the silent conversation now taking place between the two women. Her face burned with the heat of anger. Their eyes seemed to say nothing good at all, thought Edyth.

"Ye'll no' make it on yer own," said Raddah, a steely glint in her eye that Edyth did not like. "Ye'll be fodder for yon soldiers, whichever way ye go. Ye'd best give us what we ask and be glad of it."

"You said there were no soldiers near," said Edyth, her eyes turning to Scarecrow, accusation heavy in her voice.

Scarecrow shrugged, indifferent. "It doesnae matter tae me where they are, so long as they're no' on my doorstep."

Edyth exhaled sharply through her nose, squeezing her purse so tightly one of the silver pieces' sharp edges, no doubt clipped, bit through the fabric and into her hand. "How much are you wanting for simple directions then?"

Raddah's beetle-black eyes shone bright with the promise of payment. "We want it all, English."

Edyth's mouth fell open, aghast. She sputtered slightly, then said, "No, directions are not worth—"

"No directions will get ye tae the highlands, no matter how fine," said Scarecrow. She looked as though she had a bad taste in her mouth. Robbing someone blind didn't taste as sweet on her tongue as it so obviously did to her companion, Edyth thought sardonically.

"It's no wonder the Scots have gained such a powerful enemy as King Edward," said Edyth, her temper riled so high that she ignored her internal voice of caution. While it was clear that they could overpower her—there were three of them to the one of her, after all—she could not stop herself. Her fingers tingled strangely as her irritation surged.

"Greedy, false, brutish people they've said...I hadn't wanted to believe it, but here is the truth of it, staring me in the face. You'll make such needless demands of me when I have done nothing to deserve it! I simply asked for directions. Nothing more! And you want to rob me of all I have!" Edyth's voice, which had started out with a waver, grew in its strength and volume so that by the end, she realized she was shouting.

Elspeth was now standing, her worried eyes darting between her mother and her aunt, her hands worrying her skirts. "Mam," she said, her voice high and reedy. "Auntie...surely ye willnae steal from her."

"She's a spy!" hissed Raddah, her eyes narrowing, spittle clinging to her bottom lip. "Now haude yer wheesht, lass, and stay out of it."

"I am no spy!" said Edyth, indignant. "What valuable information could I possibly gain from a pair of abandoned, bitter women?"

Raddah shook her head much like a bull about to charge, her face contorted in rage. "Ye'll not speak to me so!"

"It's the truth!" shouted Edyth, standing a head over the woman, her body strung taut like the string of a bow. "You have conveniently contrived a story to ease your conscience, but you know it's a lie."

"She told me her family's dead!" shouted Elspeth, wailing in fear now. "I asked, and she told me she's no' a spy!"

Scarecrow waved a hand at her daughter dismissively, her face red. Her eyes were wide and frantic, like a caged animal. "Raddah," she rasped. "Raddah," but did not move to stop her.

Having quite enough, Edyth made for the door, but her path was blocked by Raddah's stout frame. "You'll no' be leaving here with that coin, Lassie. English coin is as good as any, and I dinnae think I'll regret taking from one such as you."

"Da wouldnae do it!" shouted Elspeth. Tears streamed from her eyes as she pulled on Raddah's arm.

"I said shut *up*!" roared Raddah, and she turned and struck Elspeth hard across her face. She fell with a shocked whimper and cowered, holding her cheek. Scarecrow stooped to her daughter, hissing angry words through her teeth.

Edyth had two choices, she reasoned. She could give them the money and flee with her life, or she could try and escape with both. In the momentary distraction that Elsepth had caused, Edyth sprang into action. Swiftly stooping to grab the three legged-stool she'd sat in only an hour ago—had it really only been an hour? —she swung it by its feet as hard as she could. The seat struck Raddah across the shoulder, causing her to stumble but not fall. She glared at Edyth, a noise like a growl rumbling in her chest and squared her shoulders, ready to strike.

Raddah was a sturdy woman, but the adrenaline surging through Edyth made her stronger. She swung again, just as Raddah pounced, and hit the woman above the ear. There was a sound like a whip cracking as the stool broke to pieces. Raddah fell to the floor, the judder from the hit still singing in her bones.

All her life, Edyth had hated the fact that, when the flames of her temper were fanned into a rage, they would inevitably leap their bounds and spread through her like liquid fire to fill her, then, finally, spill forth in the form of tears. Angry and hot, the tears were going to come; she could feel her face flush, her eyes sting. She took several heaving breaths, Elspeth's sobs ringing in her ears.

Scarecrow fell upon her sister, her breast heaving. "Look what ye've done!" she screeched, mopping the blood from Raddah's ear with her apron. Their piercing cries seemed to double and redouble in her brain, bouncing around in an echo that made her head want to split in two. "Ye clatty chancer! Get out and to hell with ye!"

Edyth didn't need to be told twice, but her legs didn't seem to want to cooperate, and she stumbled out the door. The night was cool against her heated skin; she could feel the breeze kiss her enflamed cheeks as she fumbled across the yard and tore open the stable door.

Harris didn't object as she hastily resaddled him even though it felt like it took twice as long to do it. Her fingers were numb and scrabbling; she couldn't get enough air. She couldn't breathe. And then she was on Harris and kicking him too hard in his flanks, her hands shaking so violently she let go of the reins and fisted her hands in his mane.

And then he was carrying her away while she sobbed into his neck, not caring where she went.

Chapter Three

She couldn't begin to sort through her feelings; they were like a tangled briar, clinging and full of thorns. She didn't know where one thought ended and another began. Anger and then grief cycled within her. Why had they done it?

She didn't understand. She had been hated—hunted—by the villagers in Carlisle because her mother had been falsely accused of being a heretic and a witch. Edyth had simply been guilty by association; her mother was culpable simply because Father Brewer had said so.

Yet somehow, Edyth had understood the fear associated with the lie against her mother. She'd seen bloodlust before. She'd seen and felt the reactions of her fellow Englishmen when the Scots had attacked, burned, and thieved. She'd even seen it aimed at petty crimes in the square. And she'd seen what it could do, how it could ravish and ruin lives. But Edyth didn't understand Raddah's immediate distrust and hatred of her.

Flashes of Raddah's angry, hissing demands flashed in her mind. There had been so much blood, like a spring of water weeping from a rock. Edyth winced. Her wrist was hurting from the blow she'd struck, and she found that as the time passed, it was becoming harder and harder to ignore.

Underpinning the hurt and anger coursing through her was an overwhelming feeling of inadequacy. How could she ever make it? She had failed the first true test of her journey. Thom had warned her to stay away from people, and she'd broken that rule at the first opportunity. She had no instincts for this, let alone any practical knowledge of how to go forward. She was cold and scared and, worse yet, didn't have any idea of where she was.

Edyth angrily wiped her tears away with her shirtsleeve, forcing several deep breaths, and looked to the stars. North. Always north. But the heavens were overcast and silent.

Harris was slow and tired as she was, but she would not stop so near the cottage. On she rode until her body was shaking with nerves or cold, she didn't know. She was high on a ridge now, the forest too sparse to her liking. The wind whipped and whistled through the boughs, the needles of the pines *whooshing* like a great wave on the ocean. No, it was not far enough. She must keep going.

Harris braved his fatigue long enough to reach the next ridge, and cover or no, she knew she must let them both rest. With a great effort, she slid from his sturdy back and walked him deeper into a copse of birch saplings, alders, and pines. The leaves were mere buds, but the ground was mossy and beckoned to her. Every effort seemed to cost her. Her body ached, and her breathing labored. Somehow she managed to unsaddle Harris and tie him to a tree before she unrolled her bed of furs and collapsed.

Sleep was swift but unsettling. She dreamed of her father's cries, her mother's terrified eyes as she has swung in the square, bulging and frantic, and of Raddah's nightmarish head, rolling across the floor, hissing, "Spy! She's a spy!"

Excitement surged through Edyth, jittery and thrilling. At first glance, she thought she was seeing a riverbed, long since dried up and void of life, but as Harris crept closer, she realized with a jolt that it could be her salvation. It was wide and made of large, flat stones that fit together perfectly. *A road.* And not just any road, built and used by villagers. It was a Roman road, engineered to outlast time. She knew it in her bones.

Edyth fumbled for her map but came up short, forgetting for a moment that she'd lost it. She'd given it to Raddah and had left it in her escape, along with any hope she'd held that someone would offer kindness.

She brushed the thought aside, knowing that it didn't matter. A road...*this* road meant that she would most assuredly find a proper village. It meant she could pay for a room in a public house. It meant a hot meal. It meant she could finally get her bearings and find Meg. It was almost enough to make her forget about her aching muscles, save for the warning Thom had given her to stay off all roads. A road was a twin blade, dangerous yet beautiful. It meant travelers or soldiers.

Avoiding it, however, had its own dangers. If she obeyed Thom's warning, she would wander through the woods, replaying the same, mundane task of watching the sun, never knowing where she really was or how far she'd gone. Without a road, she would be hard pressed to find her bearings and was sure to fail.

Edyth thought of Scarecrow and Raddah. She'd ignored Thom's tenet to stay away from people unless absolutely necessary, and look where that had gotten her. Edyth bit her lip, her stomach in knots, and looked down the path. It was open and benign. The sun was high, and it washed the road into a white ribbon that disappeared around a bend. Birds chirped in the trees around her.

Harris bent his head to the ground, nosing for spring grasses, ignorant of her wrestle. Rubbing his neck absently, she said, "What do you think, Harris? We'll most likely only come across traveling villagers, surely. We'd be sure to hear a throng of soldiers before we saw them. We could hide in the woods until they passed."

She took a breath, giddy with the potential danger—and equal salvation—of her choice and pulled her hat more securely around her ears, taking care to tuck in her plait. *I won't ever get anywhere sitting idle.*

Before she could change her mind, she urged Harris forward with a soft click of her tongue, the ringing of his shoes on the stones resounding as brightly as the cold sun.

◈

The sun was close to setting; purple and blue-black streaks of clouds colored the sky. The wind had shifted, and the air turned colder still. Ewan shifted in his saddle uneasily and rolled his shoulder. Cold always made the ache worse. They still hadn't yet made it to the Scott keep, though he thought they were close. Graham had seen sign of men and, because they were on Douglas land, could not chance ambush, Ewan had given the order to wait while his scouts had canvassed the area and reported back. Perhaps he hadn't needed to take the precaution; there were twenty-three of them, all fighting men, after all, but he couldn't risk any one of them being injured or killed.

As it was, now several hours past the time they'd anticipated arriving, and they were still on Douglas land. At least he thought they were. It had been many a year since he'd come this way. They could not ride quickly in this light, and they could not stay and make camp.

"Go canny, lads," said Ewan, steering his steed through two trees. The burn they'd already had to cross twice had snaked its way across their path once more. It was swift but shallow. Large rocks jutted up from the steep banks, but he saw a place, at the bend of the river, where the rocks were small, sitting like turtles in the silt. They could cross there, before full dark, and be at the Scott keep within the hour.

"We cannae be far from the Scott keep now," said Ewan, dismounting from his horse at the river's edge. His men were following suit, and just as he'd grabbed his horse's reins, the familiar swoosh of an arrow being let loose rent the air. It thudded and twanged, embedded deeply into a tree.

"Arrows!" shouted one of his men. They scattered like mice, leading their horses behind trees, pulling swords, and ducking for cover.

They waited. Ewan could hear his heartbeat in his ears. His hands flexed on his sword, waiting, but no more arrows came.

"Show yourselves," shouted Ewan, his eyes roving the darkening trees beyond the river.

"Ye're on Scott land! Uninvited!" replied a bodiless voice from somewhere in the opposite tree line. "State yer business!"

Iain huffed angrily. "Scotts! Ye damn fools!" He stepped out from behind a tree and pointed his short sword to the arrow embedded therein. "Ye shot an arrow at my face!" Iain cried, indignant. "That's a fine welcome!"

"If you're the manky sons of bitches that're gutting me cattle, then yer no friend o' mine!"

Ewan stepped out, his hands shaking with unspent energy. "John?" asked Ewan, forcing his nerves to settle. "Tis I, Ewan Ruthven. We'd thank ye kindly if ye dinae skelp us afore we're fed."

There was a pregnant pause, then a booming bark of laughter, followed by a rustling of brush as four men stepped out from the cover of the trees. "Welcome!" said a short, excessively hairy man, his arms thrown wide. His teeth shone brightly in the weak light, his black beard hiding the rest of his face. "Ye should have said so!" wheedled the man in good humor. "I thought ye might be the scunners who've been stealing away me sheep and cattle."

Ewan's men grumbled and put their swords away.

"If ye'd use the eyes in yer head, ye might have seen we've no such beasts among us," said Iain, leading his horse into the water. "Who's been reiving yer stock, man?" he asked, clasping hands with the man and then pulling him into a hug. They pounded each other's backs and exchanged jibes as the water swirled around their calves.

"We're glad ye're here," said John, slapping Ewan on the back as he joined them. They exited the water together onto the opposite bank, and Ewan motioned for the others to follow suit.

"We're in desperate need of ye," said John. "I thank ye."

"So your letter stated," said Iain. "We came as soon as we could." "We've been tracking some bandits and want to be catchin' 'em afore they get awa'. We could use yer help. They've been slaughtering our cattle in the fields, leaving 'em to rot in the sun. We found two beasts this e'en and have been tracking the *cacans*."

"Do ye think it be the Douglas?" asked Iain, looking back across the river. The Ruthven men were crossing the river, the dappled, golden light from the sunset patterning their bodies so that parts of them appeared dark with wet, while other parts glowed as flame. They were talking among themselves, their voices a humming undercurrent to the swift waters.

John shook his head. "Our position is precarious this far south. Berwick is'nae far, and the English have dared tae cross our borders more than once. We've killed any we've found, o' course, but that doesnae mean we havenae missed a few. Still, it could be the Douglas, but I dinae think they would waste the meat."

Ewan agreed. It sounded more like the English were doing all they could to torment the Scotts, even wasting precious cattle when they could be using them for themselves. Idiots, the lot of them.

John whistled, and a man emerged from the thicket deeper in the forest, leading the Scott horses. "Will ye ride with us?" John asked Ewan, his breathing heavy. John was a stout man and built like an ox. "Thomas!" he called, his deep voice booming the command. The man who'd held the horses made his way over, leading John's horse.

"Aye, we'll help," said Ewan, mounting his own horse.

"I didnae expect ye so soon. I see ye cut across Douglas territory," said John, motioning with his chin in the direction from which they'd come. "Did ye meet anyone?"

Ewan shook his head, taking his reins in hand. "No, we didnae, but I've heard that the Douglas isnae tae home just now."

"Mmph. Thomas, take these men to the keep," John said, indicating the Ruthven fighting men now remounting their steeds. "We'll continue on."

"How far ahead do ye think they'll be?" asked Graham, his interest piqued. "I'm in a mind tae stick my sword into something English."

John frowned, thinking. "Well, we need tae get back on their trail since it was you we started tracking 'bout five miles upriver, but I'd say they'd be closer to Armstrong land by now."

"We'd best hurry then," said Ewan, looking at the fading light. "Lead on."

Edyth placed the larger twigs she'd gathered onto the fire and warmed her hands. The sun was gone now. She'd been lucky enough to stumble upon a river and had tried her hand at hunting some food. She scoffed softly, remembering her dismal attempt. She'd spent more time chasing her lost arrows than finding things to shoot, and so, after three misses (two birds and a squirrel), she'd given up. Edyth looked at her ration of food: four oatcakes, a half loaf of bread, a hunk of cheese, and two apples left. She wouldn't go hungry, in any case, now that she'd found the road.

Before long, she was sure to find a public house where she could buy food and rest in a bed. She certainly couldn't rely on her lacking bow skill to feed her. It had seemed so much easier when she was younger, shooting with James in the forest behind the mill. She'd matched his skill at ten, at least.

The sun had gone completely now, and shadows from her fire danced upon the forest. Edyth eyed the small fire she'd started and followed the smoke up into the sky. She realized, suddenly, how foolish it had been to build a fire, alone as she was. She had been so intent to eat and to warm herself in the cold night air that she hadn't thought twice about her actions. Now, however, she worried.

She looked around her and into the darkened trees beyond the small light her fire afforded. She looked over at where she knew Harris stood near the stream, merely a dark shadow against the even darker forest. Her uneasiness grew. She would just have to be cold. How foolish of her to light a fire, especially being so close to the road. She'd taken care to go deep into the woods, of course, and she hadn't seen anyone all afternoon, but it was still a chance she should not have taken.

Edyth stood and made her way carefully to the stream. She filled her waterskin and washed her blistered hands, which stung uncomfortably in the frigid water. She would use the firelight to ready her bedding, and then she would put it out with the water from her skin. The wind blew, erupting goose bumps along her body, and she tried not to think about the temptation of keeping the warm, crackling fire. Once her hands were clean, she scrubbed her face and neck.

She filled her cupped hands and drank her fill, the coolness of the water in her belly making her shiver all the more.

Edyth had just stood when Harris snorted and pranced nervously. Her senses sharpened, and she stood as still as stone, her eyes roving in the dark. The water trickled behind her, the fire crackled, and shadows danced. Harris whipped his head back and blew. She went to him and grabbed his bridle, trying to calm him. He made her feel slightly better now, somehow, being at his side, but as she scanned the dark and shadowy forest around her, she noticed the sudden absence of crickets and the unnatural silence that had settled over her little camp.

She held her breath, holding still, her nerves frayed. The hair on her arms sprang to life; her heart beat wildly. Had those women sent someone to find her, to execute the English lass they'd so openly hated? Edyth let go of Harris's reins and slowly lowered her hand to the dagger at her waist, all the while eyeing her bow and quiver only a few paces away, resting against her pack.

You're a damn fool, she chided herself, trembling.

She had to remain calm. She had to keep her wits about her. She tried to swallow, but her mouth had gone dry. Her hands shook, the grip on her dagger growing slippery with sweat. A twig snapped somewhere to her left, and she whipped toward it, her body tense. She pointed her dagger in the direction the noise had come from, wishing for a sword. Wishing for her father. Harris pawed at the ground and blustered, prancing and pawing on the spot.

"Shhh," she said to Harris, only halfway paying attention to his movement. "It's probably nothing...a—"

There was a whooping shout, a rustle of tree limbs, and then several men were suddenly there in her camp. She tried to count them. Four? No. Six. Too many for her to even hope to escape from unscathed.

They moved slowly; in the firelight, their sarks glowed like the moon. Edyth backed full up against Harris's side, her dagger held up as a warning.

"Look at our luck, Will," said a man, his lascivious eyes roving over her form. "We was just thinking we needed to sate our thirst."

Someone snickered as they inched nearer. They were English. Their accents gave them away immediately. Deserters? They all carried swords. The man speaking had a sword at his side and a dagger tied to his leg with a leather strap. His teeth were bared in what she assumed was meant to be a charming smile, but it made her stomach clench uncomfortably.

"Leave me be," said Edyth, her voice raspy even to her ears. She cleared her throat; it felt as if her very heart was lodged there, restricting her breathing.

"You invited us here," said the sneering man, gesturing toward the fire.

Edyth grimaced inwardly.

"You will not lay a hand on me!" Edyth demanded, flashing her dagger in his direction, sounding far braver than she felt.

"She's English!" said another man who stood near the fire. He was holding her pack. He held it up and turned it over so her belongings fell and rolled upon the ground. Another man had picked up her bow, examining it with keen eyes.

"What's an English chit doing in a man's clothes?" one man asked.

"I'm more interested to know why she's so far from home. And all alone too," said the leering man.

"I could ask the same of you," said Edyth stiffly. "Deserters, are you?"

Edyth watched from the corner of her eye as another man walked the perimeter of her camp. He stopped near the fire and began to rudely eat her rations of food. Edyth's lips tightened in anger. *I hope he chokes on it.*

"What have you got in here for us, wench?" said the man who had dumped her pack. He was short for a man—about as tall as she was, she'd wager—and had dark features. He pushed the toe of his boot through the items littering the ground and stooped to pick up her satchel. "Coin?" He rummaged through her satchel, tossing out the things he thought useless.

Of course, they were worthless to him, but to Edyth, they were everything. She held her breath and watched as her mother's medicinal herb notes and her father's letters were carelessly tossed to the ground. At least he hadn't thrown them into the fire. Next, he pulled out her handkerchief with, she knew, the chess piece still marked by her father's fingers. She didn't want him to touch it. She didn't want his mark to erase what she held so sacred. He unfolded the white linen and looked at the white queen nestled in the kerchief, puzzled.

I have some coin!" she shouted, distracting him. "In the leather pouch...there on the ground."

The man dropped the chess piece and cloth without thought and picked up the pouch she'd pointed out. "Ah!" he said, delighted, but after dumping the contents of her purse into his hand, she saw his mouth twist in disappointment. "What is all this rubbish?" he asked, motioning to all her belongings. He didn't wait for her to reply. "This is it? This isn't enough to buy me and my men ale. What are you doing traveling so far from home, alone, and with so little money?"

"I...I'm not alone," she lied quickly. "My father is hunting. He...he'll be here soon."

He pocketed the money and scowled at her. "What kind of father would leave a helpless daughter all alone in the wild of Scotland?" he asked, looking her up and down, his head turned to the side. "Nay," he said, seeing through her lie. "Mayhap you've got some sort of treasure hidden on you." He stepped over her pile of bedding and strewn belongings and walked closer to her.

"Don't...don't come any closer!" said Edyth, holding her dagger at the ready, but the man merely smiled.

He looked her up and down. Edyth's skin crawled. Suddenly, without warning, he lunged for her, his hand closing around her wrist so she could not strike. Edyth growled in frustration. Harris, agitated, moved away from the commotion toward the cluster of trees nearest the river, blowing and huffing. She missed him immeasurably. "Oy, you'll be sure to share her with the rest of us now, Anthony!" called a man Edyth couldn't see.

Anthony wrenched the weapon from her hand and handed it off to a man who had materialized at her attacker's side. Edyth tugged on her arm and twisted her wrist in his fist, keeping her eyes trained on him, but he held fast.

"We'll all take turns, Will. It's not so often luck turns our way. We'll all get a taste." Someone guffawed. Anthony smiled.

Anthony's muddy-brown hair was cropped to his shoulders, hanging in dirty strands. His tunic was stained and hung low over his breeches. He smiled smugly at Edyth, his steely eyes glinting in the firelight. Edyth's breaths were coming quickly, her mind reeling. There were so many of them and only one of her. There was no way she could escape. She wanted to cry, to scream, but she knew there wasn't anyone near who could help her.

"My family," said Edyth, an idea forming in her mind quickly. "They have money. If you but let me go, I can get you the money you desire. Whatever the amount. Just let me go."

He pretended to ponder it and then shook his greasy head. "I think not."

Edyth's mind raced. She looked around her wildly, searching for some magical means of escape, but no ideas came to her.

Suddenly his free hand clamped onto the back of her neck, and she was yanked into him. His wet, stinking mouth crushed onto her own, and she instinctively bit down on his lip. He cried out and shoved her to the ground. Before Edyth had a chance to scramble away, he fell to his knees at her side and tried to grab hold of her wrists again, but she kicked out at him. She caught his neck with her heel and scrambled to her knees. She could hear the others jeering at the entertainment. He coughed and swore, but someone had hold of her again. She was dragged to her feet, her arms held tightly behind her back by two strong hands.

"She's a lively thing," someone said appraisingly. More laughs.

Edyth thrashed in her captor's arms, but it only caused her shoulders to twinge and ache. Anthony's face came into view. He smiled and brushed an errant lock of her hair from her face, his tongue darting out to wet his bloodied lip.

Edyth was frantic with fear. She couldn't get enough air.

He bent to kiss her neck. "No!" she cried, shying away from him. He bit the soft flesh where her shoulder met her neck and pushed her to her knees.

"Two can play this game, chit."

"Please," she pleaded, tears filling her eyes. She was unceremoniously shoved onto the ground, the smell of wet earth filling her nostrils. Edyth didn't even have time to push herself up. He flipped her over as if she'd weighed nothing and tore at her father's shirt. It ripped open along her shoulder, exposing tender flesh. Edyth clawed and kicked frantically, screaming in rage, and was rewarded with a fist to her cheek. Stars appeared before her eyes, and she blinked to clear her vision, but still the stars remained.

She hesitated. Maybe it was best if she passed out; yes, then she wouldn't remember anything. He moved to kiss her, and she turned her head away in disgust. His breath reeked of whiskey and rotting teeth. She pushed her hands against his chin, deflecting his pursuit. She screamed again as loud as she could and tasted blood in her throat.

A strong hand slipped around her neck, squeezing tightly, cutting off her cry with a gurgle. He tugged on the laces holding her breeches closed. Her vision began to blur. Edyth's eyes rolled. Despair filled her. It would be over soon. The world spun and swam before her, the dark pines above her swirling strangely as he tugged at her clothes.

Suddenly he let loose, and blissful, cold air entered her stinging lungs. Her vision returned, foggy and splotchy. She gasped and coughed, her limbs shaking; he had only let go of her neck to fiddle with the ties on his soiled breeches. There were hoots and shouts of approval from his men.

Another shout rent the air—a scream that raised the fine hairs on the back of her neck—and then Anthony fell against her, a dagger protruding from his eye socket. Edyth's own scream had lodged in her throat as she scrambled out from underneath him, dizzy and confused, holding her hose up with one hand. She wiped her attacker's blood from her face and neck where he'd slumped against her, her horror reaching new heights.

It was chaos: more shouts, but this time they were accompanied with the steely clangs of swords. Edyth could only think to escape. Looking around for Harris, she whistled as loud as she could, but it only came out as a winded sputter. She stared momentarily in disbelief at her defenders. They laughed and jeered as they fought, smiling grimly and speaking words she could not understand.

Pulling on the ties of her hose and fastening her clothing with fumbling fingers, she searched for her bow and quiver of arrows. She stumbled to them, discarded only a short distance away. Notching an arrow, she backed up against a tree to take aim. There was a frenzy of fighting, a blur of action. Edyth pulled her bowstring but hesitated, her previous misses giving her pause.

She was so mesmerized by their swift and powerful sword strokes and the rhythmic burr of their tongues as they spoke to one another that she didn't notice one of the wounded English crawl her way. His hand reached around her ankle and pulled.

She inadvertently let loose of the arrow and screamed in fright. The man's head was bleeding, and he appeared to have a gaping hole in his leg, but he was still strong enough to make Edyth lose her balance. The force of his pull felled her. He intended to exact some form of revenge upon her, apparently, because he scrambled toward her, spitting curses.

Edyth kicked and screamed. He had his arms around her knees now. She flailed and pounded her fists against his head. She pulled his hair, grunting. She felt quite mad, but her efforts were rewarded. Her knee hit his chin, and his arms slackened just enough for her to kick free. She crawled away and stood, tripping over her own feet as she went.

Without thought, she mechanically picked up a nearby rock and threw it as hard as she could at his face. She didn't wait to see where it hit him but was satisfied when he grunted in pain. She spotted a discarded sword several paces away. Running, she slipped in the mud, but she finally reached it and hefted it. It was short and very heavy. Too heavy for her, really, but she used all her strength to swing it over her head and down in an unstoppable arc to where the man was now scrambling toward her. Just as he reached her feet, the heavy sword sliced into his back with a sickening, crunching thump.

She cried out, just as the man did, and then vomited atop him. A sob burst through her. Her hands were shaking uncontrollably. "Sweet Mary, pray for me," she cried, turning away from the gruesome scene. Before she could so much as take two steps, a sharp pain blasted through her head, and the world went black.

Chapter Four

There was a fluttering of wings in the inky darkness. They rustled and settled faintly, a whisper in her ears. The wind blew—cold and cutting—and then suddenly, she could see. The darkness had faded in degrees so slowly that it was almost like watching the sun rise. One moment the world was black and empty, and then quite suddenly, the scene appeared, fully blossomed and rich in color.

There was a field, mud-churned and bloody, by the feet of horses and men. It rolled and dipped so that the light shone brightly on the high ground, illuminating sparks of glittering, winking helms. The low ground lay shadowed and secretive, though Edyth knew, without seeing, that dead men lay there. A stream cut through the middle of the battlefield as though God himself had drawn his finger in the sand, dividing it as he once had the night from day.

The wind gusted, rushing in her ears. A standard snapped and flapped against its halberd, its end stuck crookedly into rent soil. A blue-and-yellow emblem winked in and out of her view: three sheafs of wheat and a single word, *Fuimus*, it said. *I exist.* She did not know who claimed this ensign, but sorrow filled her at the realization that they were, all of them, dead.

Swiftly, a cloud of ravens eclipsed the sun. Scores of wings fluttered as they fell upon the field, pecking and cawing at the feast before them, fighting among themselves. One near her fell like a stone from the sky and landed at her feet onto the chest of a man. He had been pinned to the earth with a pike. She hadn't seen him before, but he appeared now, bloodied and struggling for breath. Edyth stared at him, wanting to help, but she could not move. She could only watch, helplessly, as his mouth moved, forming soundless words around the puddle of blood that had pooled therein.

A great ripping noise rent the air, and Edyth's eyes wrenched away from the man's dark-blue eyes to see the ensign, torn from its staff, as it was carried away in the wind. It fluttered and turned in the air, then fell onto the blood-soaked earth.

Suddenly her vision darkened, and she felt as though she was falling, tumbling like one of the birds, in an endless, starless sky.

She awoke with a jolt, pain pounding in her skull. She fisted her hands in the sheets, squeezing her eyes shut against the throbbing torment that had settled in her head. Her heartbeat was frantic; she could feel it at the base of her skull, thudding vigorously, relentlessly. She lay still for a long moment, willing her breathing to slow; she focused on it now. It whistled from her nose. In. Out. In. Out.

Dully, slowly, the dream ebbed away into the recesses of her brain, and she registered the small clues of her surroundings: woodsmoke and lavender, a lumpy, wool-stuffed mattress, and finely spun linen against her skin.

She sat up and immediately regretted it. Clutching her head, she lay back down, and waited for the blinding pain to subside.

She remembered the wood and the men who had assaulted her, she remembered the sickening bite as the sword she'd wielded had pierced flesh, but she could not remember how she'd gotten here.

Who had come to her rescue? Had she been found by some noble, chivalrous English soldiers, hunting deserters? She couldn't know until she got out of bed and found someone to talk to, but talking could be dangerous.

She would be immediately known for an English lady as soon as she opened her mouth. If she had been rescued by English knights, they may force her back to English soil, seeing her unfit to travel in a war-torn land, *which is altogether true*, she thought wryly.

There were some clans, she knew, that were loyal to King Edward. It was possible that she'd been rescued by one. Would they hold her captive, "safe," from the travails of war so that she could not leave? While this outcome wasn't too grievous to be borne, it still was not her desire. She wanted to get to Meg, to the only family she had left in this world.

Edyth bit her lip and tried to sit up again, this time much more slowly. The pressure in her head changed shape, but the flash of blinding light did not come as it had before. She sat in the darkness of the draped bed, breathing heavily, thinking.

If she were rescued by loyal Scots, she could only imagine one outcome. A Scotsman would most assuredly ruin her and leave her for dead. She'd heard stories of their wanton, barbaric customs. They stole women as they did beasts, robbing innocents of their virtue. Fear filled her at the thought. She would be used and passed around from person to person, kept as a slave and forced to perform depraved acts. Why had she come? She'd been a fool to try. Tears pricked her eyes, and she pressed the heels of her hands to them as though to dam them.

She saw Meg as she'd seen her last when they were twelve. They'd shared their secrets under her coverlet, her chestnut hair fram- ing her pale face. She'd always been jealous of Meg's hair. *Orange hair*, she'd told Meg, *was, truly, a terrible curse to bear.* Meg had sighed dramatically. She'd hated her brown eyes. *Boring brown. If only I had green eyes like yours...*

They'd pretended to be women grown, married to princes. They'd dressed up in her mother's finest gowns and pranced through the house, ordering people about. They'd stolen sweets from the kitchens and played pranks on James. Meg had pushed him into the miller's pond, but he hadn't minded. James had vowed to marry Meg one day, and they'd giggled over his doe-eyed expression. So much had changed. She needed her friend. Meg was her only chance of happiness, of belonging. Of family.

Not knowing what to do but feeling that she needed to move to take action in some small way, she scooted to the edge of the bed and fumbled to open the heavy, bottle green drapes. A rush of cool air hit her and snaked up her bare legs; she shivered uncontrollably and then winced as every muscle in her body protested the movement. It was still daylight. Streaks of sunlight filtered in between the slats of the shutters over the window, painting the floor in golden stripes. Edyth wondered how long she'd been here.

Her body felt heavy and fatigued, sore in places she hadn't previously known existed. She was dressed in a shift, worn and soft and not her own. Her feet dangled over the edge of the bed, inches above a large black fur. *Bear?* she wondered, her mind latching onto things of little consequence. The fire against the wall was small and smoldering, banked to burn slowly. The embers glowed, pulsing in rhythm to her breathing. The wooden floor was strewn with rushes and lavender, a painful reminiscence of home. Her mother's rooms had smelled the same, sweetly pungent, and her heart constricted at the memory.

Edyth looked to the other furnishings, trying to distract her senses. There was a table at the side of the bed that held a stub of a candle in a clay pricket, a basin and pitcher of water, and linen for washing. So much she saw, until the door opened. She froze, staring, like a deer catching a dangerous scent, as a stout woman with graying strawberry-blond hair entered. She was carrying a tray of what looked like crockery. Edyth hoped it was food. They locked eyes, and the woman smiled as though coaxing a kitten from a corner.

"Good e'en to ye, mistress," said the woman, happy surprise evident on her round face. "Yer awake now, and that's somethin' to be thankful for," said the woman, striding across the room and pushing the tray onto the table. The ewer and basin made a rude sound as they were forced to the side by the edge of the tray.

"There now," she said, straightening up and looking Edyth over. "I was right worrit for ye, with a cut on the back o' yer head the length of me fist, but we set ye tae rights, we did. How are ye feelin' this e'en, lassie?" asked the woman, reaching a plump hand toward her forehead. Edyth let the woman touch her, her eyes wide with confusion and fear. She'd been cut?

Edyth raised her hands to feel her skull and realized with a shock that her hair was far too thin and light, a good portion of it being shorn away. Her jaw fell open in disbelief, a small mewling sound of distress escaping her. Her hair, which had, the last time she'd been awake, been down to her waist, was now drastically changed. The majority of her hair, under what had been kept on her crown, had been shorn off to the scalp. It fell above her shoulders, like a boy.

"Now, now," said the plump woman in soothing tones. "We had tae stitch ye up, and yer hair was interfering, it was. Tis better not to let yer vanity get in the way of yer healing, aye? It will grow back, more quickly than you'd think."

Edyth knew she was right but could do nothing to assuage her vanity. Her fingers tenderly canvassed the curved line of stitches that started at the base of her skull. The cut was long, about four inches, she would guess, the hair shorn so short that it stood out stiffly around the wound.

"Wh...what happened to me?" Edyth croaked, her throat thick with emotion and disuse.

The woman eyed her for a moment, but not unkindly. "Ye dinnae remember?" She shook her head solemnly, her sharp brown eyes peering into Edyth as though searching for confirmation that Edyth's brain had, indeed, been addled.

The woman sighed and frowned. "I cannae be sure. Himself dinae tell me, but it looks to me as though someone tried to brain ye with an ax or summat." She raised a hand to Edyth's forehead, the smell of kitchen fire in her skirts. "Still no ague, praise the saints," said the woman, her kind brown eyes smiling. Her hands settled briefly on Edyth's cheeks, appraising her.

"Now," said the woman, turning back to the table, "I've brought a wee bit o' help with me." The woman opened the crockery lid and proudly displayed the bowl to Edyth. Leeches.

Edyth waited patiently, trying not to show her dislike of the creatures, as she pulled what was left of her hair to the side to allow the woman access to her wound. Her mother had used leeches in such cases as well. Her job had been to bring them home once found, but never had she been obliged to use them herself. Edyth closed her eyes, not from pain but in an effort to avoid the questioning eyes of the kindly matron. She certainly didn't want to answer any nosy questions.

Edyth felt the woman move away after a moment, and she dared to peek. The stout woman bent and busied herself in the large basket by the fire. The logs she placed therein did not catch right away, and she watched benignly as the woman muttered under her breath and poked at the coals with an iron. Giving up on that unsuccessful attempt, she instead got to her knees with a voluble creaking of joints and huffs to blow forcibly on the coals. They bloomed with renewed heat, from black to orange, and then a flicker of flame licked to life. "There now. That's better," said the woman after a log caught.

She got to her feet in stages, propping her hands on her knees first and then straightening up with a grunt. She then walked smartly to the end of the bed and bent, disappearing behind the mattress and drapes. She returned to Edyth carrying a chamber pot nestled in the crook of an arm and motioned for Edyth to stand with the other. "Come now, lass. No need tae be discomfited."

Edyth did, indeed, feel discomfited to a large degree but knew that she would need help with the necessary task of emptying her bladder. Scooting more closely to the edge of the bed, she slid onto shaky legs. The woman gripped her arm firmly with her free arm and nodded reassuringly. "That's a good lass," she said.

Once finished, the woman helped her back into the bed and then threw the contents of the chamber pot out the window. "I'll get ye summat to eat, lass, and tell Himself that ye're awake. When I get back, I'll take the wee barnacles off yer wound." She winked at Edyth in a commiserating way and left her without a backward glance.

Edyth couldn't help the small smile she gave in return. Despite her being a potential Scottish foe, she liked the woman very much. She settled her back against the pillows, trying to ignore the strange tickling sensation the leeches caused.

Now that she was alone again, her mind returned to more sinister possibilities. Who was "Himself," and what would he do with her? What would he say? More importantly, what should she say in return?

It wasn't long before the woman returned, as promised, bringing broth and bread, followed by a slightly taller man, who was, Edyth couldn't help but notice, just as round through the middle. He waited patiently as the matron completed her business of seeing Edyth rid of the leeches. They were fat and round, glistening in the light from the window.

The man's near-black, wiry hair stood out at all angles, his beard twisting and curling down his chest. He had patches of gray at his temples and just under his bottom lip that made him appear statelier and somehow less like a disheveled haystack.

He had beautiful green-gray eyes that squinted continuously as he observed his matron's movements. Edyth did not know why, but something about him did not seem as terrifying as she had envisioned. In fact, under different circumstances, she could probably like him. That is to say, if he were not a murdering Scot, and she not his enemy. Something about his presence bespoke of a hidden, jovial nature, but Edyth knew better than to assume appearances matched temperaments.

Now finished with her task, the matron curtseyed, tray and leeches in hand, and left the room. The door closed with a soft thud, and Edyth was left alone with the man, her nerves frayed to new heights. The silence in the room buzzed in her ears as they stared at each other, he standing with his beefy hands behind his back, and she with her own hands gripping the sheets under the coverlet.

The silence could not have been long, but when he finally cleared his throat and spoke, she felt that her nerves had been about to unravel completely.

"I'll not keep ye long," he said with a rumble, his voice reverberating in the small space between them. He turned, searching out the chair near the hearth, and returned to her bedside. "I ken ye've had some trouble, and I willnae ask ye to spend much time, but there are questions that must be asked and answered. I've me people to mind, aye?"

Edyth nodded her understanding. He had an easygoing manner that beckoned her senses to settle and unwind, yet she knew he was also a lord and keen to keep his interests his own. He would not accept lies, and somehow, she knew that he would know the difference.

"I'm Robert Scott, Lord of Buccheuch, and I'd welcome ye as a guest in my home."

Edyth swallowed, her lips pinched together tightly. She knew that name. Buccheuch was not far from Berwick, and it was only a little farther to Carlisle.

"Thank you," she said softly, letting out the breath she'd been holding, feeling disappointed in how little distance she'd actually covered. It was no wonder, really, traveling as she had, wandering the forest. It would be very difficult, indeed, to get to Meg, if she made it at all.

"What is yer name, lass?" he asked, his keen, green eyes kind and interested. Although the size of his body—and his voice—should have made her all the more terrified, she could not muster fear. Perhaps she was just too tired to care, but she felt herself start to relax her hold on the bedclothes. She felt the tense lines of her body relax more fully into the pillows. She decided, quite without realizing that she had, to speak to him.

"I am Lady Edyth DeVries," she said, "Lately of Carlisle," she added on an exhale. There, it was out, with no way of going back.

He did not react as she'd supposed he might, with anger or even surprise. He did not appear delighted to have caught such a prize either. His face was, instead, an indiscernible mask, which did not comfort her in the least. It would be better if she could read his thoughts, for they would dictate her actions.

"What are the blessed circumstances that bring ye to my land, Lady Edyth?" He leaned forward, his hands folded, his elbows resting on his knees. His heavy brows were raised in question, waiting. They said, quite frankly, *I am patient, and I will wait, and I* will *get an answer.*

Edyth bit her lip, unsure where to begin or even how much she should say. Considering the damning nature of her mother's death, she thought that telling as little as possible was in her best interest. No one would trust the daughter of a witch. She would be ruled evil, immoral, or simply unlucky.

"I had to leave my home...after my father died," she stated, thinking quickly. It wasn't a lie, nor was it the complete truth, but it was as much as she felt she should say. "I am traveling to my cousin who is married to a MacPherson. She is all the family I have left to me." She could not keep his gaze and looked to her hands.

His chair creaked loudly as he considered her. After a beat, he cleared his throat and said, "You, a lady, and traveling alone?" Edyth dared to meet his eyes, seeing clearly the question written there. "Ye have the speech and bearing of a lady. Do ye deny it?"

She shook her head briefly, immediately regretting the action as the stitches pulled her skin uncomfortably. "Yes, the circumstances are somewhat...well, they're rather difficult to speak of. My home was given a new lord, appointed by King Edward, and I had to leave immediately."

"Surely this lord would allow an escort for such as you," he said, motioning toward her with his broad hands. "Or if he were as grudging as ye claim, he could certainly have given ye time to get news tae your family in the highlands."

Edyth shrugged, unwilling to say more. "I left in haste and did not wait for the new lord to arrive. He does not know of me, nor I of him," she added. "Perhaps I was too hasty." Edyth repressed a sigh, feeling like things were going sour rather rapidly. She pinched the bridge of her nose in an effort to stop the unrelenting headache pounding in her skull. She could see his questions, but something within her would not let her speak freely of her sorrow.

They sat in silence, his eyes surveying her in a way that made her want to squirm. Finally, he said, "When we found ye, ye were wearing a man's clothes. Do ye care tae explain that, Lady Edyth?"

Edyth took a deep breath, thankful for the change in topic. "Yes. Yes, I wore my father's clothes in an attempt to appear less... feminine," she said, shrugging slightly. "I thought that if

I had to travel alone that my way would be easier as a man, but it did not prove helpful in the end."

He nodded at this, apparently accepting the explanation. "We found yer fire," he said, sitting back in the chair once more, crossing his arms across his massive chest. Black, coarse hairs covered his forearms where his sleeves had been pushed back. "We'd been tracking some bandits, and when we saw the smoke, we thought it would be them."

He paused here as though waiting expectantly for something, but Edyth didn't know what to say. *Yes, she'd built a fire. Yes, she'd realized how stupid she'd been. No, she was not properly prepared to defend herself.* She felt ashamed of herself suddenly, as if in building the fire, she'd let her father down.

Robert rubbed the tops of his knees softly, his short fingers splayed wide, looking uncomfortable. "I hope we weren't too late for ye, lass," he said, his mossy green eyes meeting her intently. Finally she understood.

"I wasn't...that is to say, I was not harmed, aside from my sensibilities." Heat bloomed up her chest and into her face. She had to look away. The fire crackled in the silence as she avoided his keen eyes. "Thank you," she said finally, still avoiding his gaze that seemed to see through her. "Thank you for saving me from them."

Lord Scott stood and picked up the chair. He moved it back to its spot by the fire saying, "Not at all, lass. I should be thanking ye for the fire. Without it, we wouldn't have found the bast—them." He walked toward the door but stopped before opening it as though he'd just recalled something he'd forgotten. "I have a guest here, presently, who lives in the highlands. Would ye like to speak tae him about an escort?"

Edyth blinked, feeling stupid with shock. That was it? No more questions? And he, with his lands in jeopardy of confiscation by King Edward's vast army, would show an Englishwoman this kindness? It did not make sense.

She opened her mouth, her heart leaping with relief at the unexpected sympathy, and stuttered, "Yes, I...of course. I could never repay you, but you would have my thanks."

He bowed very slightly to her at the door, looking suddenly full of sorrow. "There are many that are displaced by this war, Lady Edyth. We will, all of us, need each other."

It was two days later that Edyth received the good news. She'd been standing at the window in the cool spring air, feeling properly fed and rested and not a little anxious to be on her way, when there was a knock at the door.

It opened upon her command, but instead of the matron Agatha, it was a man she'd never before seen. He was quite tall, easily well over a head above her own unusual height, with short, curling hair the color of freshly tilled earth. But more striking was his attire. This man wore no trews or hose. Instead, a billowing swath of muted greens, grays, and golds wound around his body in a cloud.

And he had *naked knees*. She realized suddenly that she was staring and jerked herself out of her stupor, her eyes wide. She'd seen Scots before, men who had come to speak with her father and conduct business, but they hadn't dressed like this.

So much she saw until she spotted her satchel gripped in his hand.

"Oh," she exclaimed, grateful surprise flowing through her. "I thought my possessions were forever lost to the forest." She crossed the distance between them and grabbed the bag from him, only remembering to curtsey after he bowed.

"Thank you," she said, meaning it, feeling quite awkward. Her bag felt heavy and familiar, the soft, supple leather as good as any silk to her mind. She held it to her bosom, wanting to go through it immediately to catalogue all that was there or missing, but she could not. It would have to wait.

"I hope ye're feeling well, lady," said the man, a smile playing at the corner of his wide mouth. "Yer pack is with yer horse in the stables."

"Harris!" she exclaimed, happier than she could remember being in recent memory. "Wherever did you find him?" Somewhere in the recesses of her mind, her mother's voice chastised her for her lack of social propriety, but she couldn't muster up the strength to care.

"He wasn't far. We brought you both here together."

"Oh," was all she could say. A raincloud seemed to settle over her, dampening her buoyed spirits. So he'd been there. He'd been one of the men to rescue her. She felt...exposed and a little ashamed, though she could not say why.

"I am Laird Ewan Ruthven," he said with another short, polite bow. "I understand that Lord Scott spoke of me to you."

She looked at him then, fully, for the first time, he, her supposed salvation. His large dark blue eyes kept his secrets but were not unkind. He was long and sinewy, muscled like a soldier. Surely he could protect her and bring her safely to Meg.

"Are you the...will you be escorting me to my cousin? She is a MacPherson."

He bit his lip and a dimple formed in his left cheek, pulling her eye. "Aye, but I cannot bring ye there straightaway. I must return tae Perthshire first, but I can bring ye to your cousin as ye desire."

Edyth nodded, trying to sift through her thoughts, which were scattered and slippery. While she felt relief at being shown such kindness, it was belied by a leery suspicion. Should she trust them, these conspiring and important men? Could she afford not to?

"Yes, it's my desire," said Edyth simply, trying to avoid looking at his knees.

"I ken that Lord Scott spoke with ye," he said, "but I have some questions of my own, if ye dinnae mind."

Edyth felt her spine stiffen. More questions? And most likely those she could not—or would not—answer. *Here is the thorn in the rose offered me*, she thought. *Now I will learn what he will gain from helping me.*

The man—Ewan, she reminded herself—rolled his shoulder stiffly, a slight grimace on his face, looking around the room. "I can see ye only have the one chair here," he said. "Please, will ye sit a bit while we speak?"

Edyth pursed her lips and shook her head, still hugging her satchel to her chest as one might a talisman. "I'd rather stand, thank you."

He nodded, his eyes narrowing slightly as he surveyed her. "As ye like," he said, her stomach flipping strangely as she met his gaze. She looked away, unable to hold his eyes.

"I can see that ye're distressed, lady. I only mean to ask about how it is we found ye as we did, alone and in considerable danger." He walked the few steps over to the fire and warmed his hands, giving her a respite from his intense gaze.

"I've already told Lord Scott about why I left home," she clipped to his back. Her hands were beginning to sweat, and she had to readjust her hold on her bag.

"Aye," he said, rubbing the stubble on his chin with a long forefinger; the familiar scratching sound brought to mind images of her father, and she shook her head slightly to be rid of the ghost. "I ken what ye said tae him, but it's me who's got to take ye, aye?"

Edyth's lips thinned, unsure. On the one hand, it was only logical for him to want to know who she was. She wondered the same about him, after all. Could he be trusted? Raddah and Scarecrow had assumed she had been a spy, so he, too, must assume the same. But if that was so, what could she say to waylay his fears?

"Lord Scott and his matron are the only kind souls I've met since leaving England," she said, taking the offensive. "It saddens me to know he now thinks of me as an enemy."

Ewan shook his head, his lips pursed. "Lord Scott and his people have suffered greatly in recent weeks." He pushed off the mantle and picked up the flint laying thereon, flipping it one-handed in an arc. "His heart is softened by remorse," he continued, "and he doesnae have it in him tae pressure you. He has lost much." He paused, staring into her as though he could divine her thoughts. "He doesnae deem ye as an enemy, lass. Nor do I," he added with a soft lift of a shoulder. "But I would like tae ken who it is I'm traveling with, aye?"

He replaced the flint onto the mantle just so, so that it was square with the corner of the wooden beam. Edyth could feel the weight of his stare but could not meet his eyes, coward that she was. She felt her heart soften slightly of its own accord, seeing her own losses and the imagined losses of Lord Scott. *And Elspeth*, she reminded herself.

"Ye say we're the first kind souls ye've encountered," he continued, "but ye should ken, lady, that those wretches we saved ye from in the wood were no' Scots."

Edyth nodded. "Yes, I know," she said, her tone softening to match her heart. Her feet were growing tired of standing and she wished she hadn't refused the chair. She shifted her weight and let the satchel dangle from her hand, seeing the mounds of earth that now covered her parents. Who had Lord Scott lost?

She sighed, weary, and said, "Both English and Scottish people I've encountered have shown little regard for life of late, milord. I only say we are enemies because of the aggression of the Scots to my own fair city and now King Edward against your people." She shrugged, feeling a weight settle over her heart at the memories playing in her mind. "I have no ill will toward Scots," she said. "Indeed, I want nothing more than to wash my hands of England."

Ewan showed his surprise, his eyes distant, though they were trained on her. The sunlight played on the waves of his hair, much like sun on the sea. She could see all the colors that made it—chestnut, roan, gold, and russet. The colors rose and fell in the curving waves that fell over his ears and his forehead.

She felt her cheeks burn suddenly as she realized that she was staring again. And perhaps, more so, at her frankness. She had a bad habit of speaking when she shouldn't and, often, saying the wrong thing. It was a flaw in her now made worse. After everything she'd been through, she found that her words were harder to hold within her. Staring, though…that had never been a problem before.

"Ye say," he continued, clearing his throat, "that ye dinae wish tae be English?"

"No," she said, shaking her head. She forced herself to meet his eyes again. "I've discovered that my countrymen are…." Edyth trailed off, not sure what to say. She'd wanted to say murderous. Bloodthirsty. But then she thought of Thom and Annie. Mira and James. She knew she couldn't include them in her estimation. "My people have committed great injustices," she finished lamely, knowing she wasn't being direct, "to many people. I wished to leave them."

Ewan frowned, his eyes on his boots. "So ye came to Scotland. Are ye sayin' ye wish tae be a Scot, then?" He met her eyes, one fine brow raised in question.

"Mayhap I do not want to belong to any one people," said Edyth, her eyes watching the shapes that played in the fire. "I have not known much kindness in either country." Her voice was soft but full of feeling. She set her satchel down by her feet and smoothed the folds of her borrowed woolen skirts with her clammy hands, weary to her bones.

She thought he'd deny her slight on his own people, but he only said, "Why, then, did ye come? The way is dangerous, and as ye say, people have been unkind."

"I...I seek refuge," she said with a slight sigh, hoping he could see without the telling. Hoping he could see that she was not dangerous, only a frightened maiden who needed a place of refuge as keenly as she needed air.

He shook his head, unwilling to accept such a simple answer. "But to leave yer kin as ye have, to steal into a warring country, and ill prepared at that, to seek refuge...*here*," he said, moving his hand in a way that she took to encompass Scotland as a whole. "Lady Edyth, I must confess that I cannae see the logic. Why would a lass such as yerself seek to find refuge among clashing swords?"

"My cousin Meg is a MacPherson—"

He waved his hand at her, dismissing her explanation. "Aye, as ye've said, lady," he interrupted. "That doesnae explain why ye left yer home in a hurry, without waiting for an escort from the lord of Carlisle, nor from your family." His voice and eyes softened then, seeing her apparent discomfort. "There's something yer no' telling us, and I, as the laird of my people, cannae bring ye with me in good conscience, until I ken what it is yer no' saying."

Right. It made sense to her. She understood his position and did not blame him for it. In fact, she was grateful for his openness. It was refreshing. But understanding him would not ease the discomfort she knew she would have to endure in the telling.

She looked to the fire, seeing images rise and fall out of the flames, Annie's beautiful, tear-stained face as she was carted off, whisked away from the only home she'd ever had. Father Brewer's face contorted in anger, refusing the accusation. Her mother—her strong mother—brought low. Her father's face in death, still and waxy and so unreal.

Feeling rather faint, she moved the step required to reach the chair, holding on to the back to stay upright. Ewan was at her side in an instant, his strong hands gripping her arms as he helped her to sit. Worried eyes looked into her own, blue and as beautiful as a summer's day.

"Are ye well, lady?" he asked, sounding concerned. "Here, take some water," he said, hurrying to the ewer by the bed and returning with a cupful. He tried to help her take a sip, but the horn cup bumped against her teeth, and water spilled down her front.

"Damn," he said, apologetic. He withdrew a handkerchief from his sporran and made to dab at the wetness on her breast but then stopped abruptly, realizing his mistake, and handed it her. His cheeks burned a lovely shade of pink that made Edyth smile despite herself. She wiped at the spots with his handkerchief, mumbling a dismissal, "Quite all right."

She held his handkerchief in her hand, solemnity returning to her like a mantle. She was to the point in her explanation where mere words brought physical pain. What could she say to him that might ease his mind? What could she say that would confirm her innocence? What else could she say but the truth? Any lie or any missing pieces to the story might cause further suspicion. And if she wanted his help—and she did, desperately—she did not want to anger him with falsehoods.

Not that she could think of any lie to explain her sudden flight. But aside from that, the thought of lying about what had happened seemed to be a violent injustice to her parents' memories. Could she lie? Could she diminish the cruelty that had ripped her life apart?

Her heartbeat quickened in her chest at the mere thought of the retelling. She didn't want to reopen her carefully bandaged heart, still so raw, but she thought, perhaps, that if he knew the truth, just maybe, he would understand and still agree to help her.

After what felt like a very long time, she said, "I...it is difficult for me to speak of it, but I understand that I must."

Nodding his understanding, Ewan said, "I will no' speak until ye've finished, tae help with the telling."

Edyth frowned into her lap, her mind busy trying to cut the connection it shared with her heart. She tried to school it to stay unemotional, to state the facts as they were, but even now the threat of tears prickled at the back of her throat. She cleared them away, or attempted to, thinking that this man wouldn't be accustomed to weeping females, though she didn't know why it mattered to her. She only knew that her pride did not want him to see her cry.

Edyth took a deep breath, assuaged by images that she'd tried for weeks to forget. They came without thought, without invitation, as ruthless as a swarm of wasps: Father Brewer's wet mouth spitting accusation, his quavering finger pointed at her mother's kind heart, members of the crowd shouting their assent, accusing, lying.

A mob, once started, is hard to dispel. Its disbandment is costly and exact. People want blood, so long as it belongs to someone else. And then an image of her father swam in view, and oh, how her heart hurt anew; her unsteady, undone heart, a traitor to her desire to stay unemotional, shuddered and quivered within her like a caged bird.

Already her throat had grown thick, constricted with waiting tears. "My cousin does not know of my sorrow, nor that am I seeking her aid." She wiped at her eyes, turning her head toward the fire as though she might shield her weeping from his view. "I am no longer safe in England," she continued. "My mother was accused falsely of a crime and tried unfairly. She..." her voice faltered. The tears were coming faster now, falling from her cheeks to spatter upon her lap. She squeezed them tightly closed and waited for the tears to recede, biting her lip to try and ground herself to the pain of it.

When she felt she could, she added, "My mother learned of a grievous sin committed by a man of God. When she confronted him, he twisted her words and turned the people's hearts against her. She was hung by her own people—my people—for a crime she did not commit." Sniffing, she roughly wiped her wet cheeks and clenched her fists hard in her lap. "My...my father was m-murdered in the street by the...by the same." Her voice broke and her chin wobbled, the view of the carpet dissolving into a formless splatter of color.

She couldn't look at him; she wished he would leave so she could cry in earnest. But now that she'd started to speak, it was if a dam had been broken, and her words tumbled forth with no regard for who this man was or what he might think of her. "My mother...she wasn't allowed to be buried in the churchyard. I couldn't separate them. I didn't think it right..." Covering her face with her hands, Edyth could not hold back the sob that ripped from her throat, her shoulders shaking. "S-so I buried my father next to her, among the thieves and...and...." She couldn't continue. Her words fell away even as she felt his arms lift and enfold her.

She did not protest, though if she were in her right mind she would have never allowed such liberties. Still, she felt no ill intent from him, and so she imagined his arms as those of her father and wept against his chest, her breath catching and her body trembling.

She didn't weep for long, she didn't think, but her head felt cloudy and her eyes puffy when she pulled away, realizing with a jolt that she was seated atop Ewan's lap. She had no memory of this change, but now she felt the panic of having shared too much as large, warm hands stroked her arms and back in comfort. She leapt from him, her legs as awkward as a new foal, and apologized.

Her face was hot, and her tongue thick. She wanted the floor to swallow her whole. She wished he would leave. She was afraid to look at him, to see the pity she imagined there.

Or maybe she would only see a confirmation of what he knew as English cruelty.

"So you see," she said, swallowing her emotions with great effort, "my home is no longer my own. The accusation against my mother followed me. The mob demanded my adjuration; I escaped with my life and little else."

He stood and moved to her, standing far too close for comfort. She wiped her face with his handkerchief, avoiding his gaze. Fingers lifted her chin, and she found his eyes. She didn't know what she saw there, but it was not unkind. His eyes were glassy from the heat of the fire.

"Lady Edyth," he said, his voice soft and kind, "I ken it was difficult to speak of such things, and I thank ye for yer trust in me." A large hand reached out to touch her shoulder, but he stopped himself, thinking better of it.

She nodded absently, realizing that until this moment, she hadn't yet cried for her parents; she hadn't had a moment to spare for grieving until now. She didn't know if she felt any better, but she didn't feel worse.

"I apologize—" she said, her voiced muffled. She straightened her spine primly. "I don't mean to be speak so informally with you and..." Here she gestured to her flushed, wet face, embarrassment welling within her.

"Ye needn't be embarrassed, lady. I'm sorry for the pains ye've endured, but ye must understand why I needed tae learn of your purpose here."

Edyth tried to smile ruefully, but she couldn't muster the strength. "S-so now what do you plan to do with me?" she said with a hiccup. "Will you help me get to my cousin?" She worried the wet cloth in her hands, trying not to appear too desperate.

"It would be my honor," he said. He bowed formally and took her hand. He kissed it, whiskers prickling her skin. "I had plans to leave on the morrow, but I ken ye had a nasty hit to the head. Is that too soon for ye? We canna stay long," he added quickly. "King Edward will be moving to strike soon."

Edyth nodded, ready to see Meg. "Yes...yes, tomorrow."

Upon opening the canvas pack that had been brought up to her, at her request, she was delighted to see her mother's herbal journal and the sheaves of paper her father had written on for her. She leafed through the book and found her mother's bone needle still neatly piercing the vellum. She lovingly stroked a few of her father's penned words before closing the book and continuing her search.

She found her coin pouch and opened it, hoping that the white queen had been stowed in it, but it was blaringly absent. She was surprised, however, to find more money than she had brought with her. They must have mistaken some of the English men's money for her own, which meant they had searched their bodies.

Edyth fished through her satchel twice more, holding her breath. When she didn't find it, she hastily dumped her pack out onto the floor and fell to her knees to sift through her belongings: her brush, soap, a line for fishing, some stockings for the cold days and nights, a few bits of cat gut thread and dried herbs, and a flour sack with only an apple and a dirty piece of cheese left. Her heart's desire, however, the white queen that still held her father's print, was no longer with her things.

Edyth knew it had been dark, and to the Scotsmen who had saved her, the chess piece—if they had even spotted it—would have seemed trivial. Edyth tried to tell herself that it was only a trinket, that the queen was, indeed, petty. But in the end, after cataloguing her items one by one, she felt defeated. She couldn't help the tears that brimmed in her eyes as she thought about the unpolished rock that had still held a bit of her father. *Stop it. You're alive.*

She picked up her father's page and traced his heavy script with the tip of her finger.

A cruce salus. From the cross comes salvation.

He'd been teaching her mass in Latin. Edyth hugged her knees to her chest, the book pressed to her heart, thinking of his face. She would draw her parents as soon as she could, before their features softened and blurred.

Tomorrow she would truly be on her way to Meg. Maybe God hadn't forsaken her after all.

Chapter Five

The morning had come early. It felt as though she'd only just fallen asleep when she'd been roused by a servant to dress. She'd woken easily and without complaint, despite her lack of sleep. There was a strange, buzzing current that ran through her veins that had prevented her from relaxing fully.

Lord Scott's wife, Mairi, had insisted she take the borrowed woolen gown with her and had even pressed a rich, green cloak onto her as well. She'd been so overcome with their generosity after experiencing so much contention that she'd found she couldn't stop saying "thank you," much to the lady's irritation.

As it was, she now found herself standing in the stable yard, boots weighted down with mud, while she waited for her horse to be brought to her. It had rained heavily in the night, part of why she'd been kept awake, she thought. The clouds were merely spitting now, though, wetting her face and clothes with a fine mist of water that beaded up on her woolen cloak and exposed skin. The ground, however, was heavily saturated and sucked at her feet as she walked.

The sky's hue was changing subtlety, from the midnight blue of predawn to the periwinkle that announces the sun's arrival. The lonely sound of geese called from above, though she couldn't see them. It was still dark, and the yard cluttered with shadows, but she could see the shapes of people moving, working, and making ready.

A man exited the stable with Harris. It was like seeing an old friend. Harris was a beautiful dappled gray that made him appear as a ghost in the dim light. She felt a broad smile curve into existence as he nodded his massive head in greeting. The man who had his reins on the other hand did not appear to be in such good health. He was limping and had a rather disgruntled expression on his face as he tugged on Harris's reins.

The man stopped suddenly and struggled to pull his boot out of a rather deep, sucking bit of mud in the yard. Her smile faltered as she watched the man struggle to free himself, tugging on his knee with both hands. In doing so, his kilt, which was already blowing in the wind, climbed high enough to expose a glaringly bright bandage on his thigh. Edyth looked away so as not to embarrass either of them and wondered why men would wear such inconvenient, revealing garb.

Having won his freedom, the man was now at Edyth's side, breathing rather heavily for such a short walk. He leaned his head against Harris's neck, his eyes closed. She waited a few heart beats, and when he still did not open his eyes, she grew alarmed. Indeed, she thought he'd actually swayed on his feet, though it could have only been the wind in his kilt.

"Are you quite well, sir?" asked Edyth, alarmed. She moved to touch him but then stopped herself. She touched Harris instead, taking in the man's appearance with growing concern.

"Aye," he said, lifting his head, his eyes half closed. "Tis but a touch of the ague. I've had worse, lady. Here," he said, standing straighter with apparent effort," I've brought ye yer horse. Tis a fine beast."

"Thank you," said Edyth, eyeing the man for more signs of sickness. It was too dark to see his eyes properly, but even in the dim light, she could see they were bloodshot. "He's been a good friend to me," she said, rubbing the velvet of Harris's nose.

"Shall I help ye up, then?" asked the man. He did sway then but steadied himself, his hand on Harris's withers.

Edyth didn't want to offend, but she rather doubted he'd have the strength to do it. In fact, he looked as though he just might fall over if the wind gusted any harder.

Edyth eyed the distance from the ground to the saddle dubiously. While she'd become rather good at mounting Harris on her own, she'd been doing it in men's hose. A skirt was another thing altogether.

"Well," she said, not knowing what social propriety dictated she do in this instance. "I suppose if you insist." Edyth looked around the yard in desperation. She spotted the man who had spoken to her yesterday, Ewan, arms full, exiting the stable, but she wasn't sure if she wanted his help either. She felt exposed and embarrassed by her tears yesterday and wasn't ready to face him.

The limping man sidled over to her side of the horse. He motioned for her to come closer. "Here now, lady. Place your foot here," he said, bending over and lacing his fingers together. "Dinnae fash, Lady. We've all got mothers and sisters. Let's get on with it," he said, apparently assuming she was uncomfortable with riding in a skirt or showing her ankles or some such nonsense. She'd never understood what made women's ankles so sacred.

Edyth lifted a heavy boot and shook it to try and loosen the brick that had formed around her foot, stalling.

"A little mud willnae bother me, neither. Come now," he said again, moving his hands together in a way that communicated his impatience.

Not wanting to cause him physical strain but also unwilling to embarrass him, she placed her manure and mud-encrusted left boot into his waiting hands.

"Iain!" someone shouted, just in time. Turning, she spotted Ewan, squelching his way over to them, his kilt swinging and blowing in the breeze. Edyth found herself being rather annoyed at all the bare limbs on display. She hastily removed her foot, relieved.

"Iain," he said again upon reaching them, "Fingal wants to know was it you who took his—" he stopped speaking, getting a decent look at the man's state. "Ye look like hell, Iain!" he said empathically. "Didn't ye see Agatha?"

Iain straightened from his crouch and waved a hand in dismissal. "Aye, I just left her. She gave me a wee tonic to drink. I'll bide."

The look on Ewan's face said he didn't hold to the same belief. He ran a hand through his curling, wayward hair. It was disheveled from the wind and stuck up at odd angles. "I think perhaps...aye, well, there's nothing for it." He eyed the limping man with a sort of frustrated long-suffering that Edyth knew well, being on the receiving end of it countless times. "Damn," said Ewan, looking between the pair of them, "I didn't want to, but I think we'll have to go through Douglas again."

Iain's spine stiffened, coming to full attention. "Do ye think that's wise?" he said, motioning with his head none too discreetly in Edyth's direction. He grimaced, holding a muddy hand to his aching forehead.

"We've no other choice," said Ewan, exasperated. "If ye'd gone to Agatha like you were told to when we first.... Bah," he said, shaking his head in dismissal. "I havenae the time. Iain, we cannae afford a whole three days' journey out of our way...maybe more," he added. He was looking at Edyth now, his lips pressed thin in a disapproving way she did not feel she deserved.

She raised her eyebrows in question, her pride ruffled, but he said nothing and looked to the sky. "We're already starting later than I'd like. Can ye ride?" he asked.

Iain scoffed, clearly affronted. "*Can I ride?*" he repeated, his voice dripping with scorn.

Ewan, looking rather dubious, said, "Mmph. I dinae need tae be looking after ye as well."

The remark took her by surprise; she felt it in the pit of her stomach, like she'd been punched. "There's no need to grouse at the man," said Edyth, quite forgetting herself. "Or me," she added, angry. "It's not my fault he's ill."

Ewan shared a glance with Iain that she couldn't read. Iain almost smiled, a corner of his mouth quivering upward, but then he caught her eye and she wondered if she'd imagined it.

"I can ride as quickly as any man," she said, jutting her chin out in defiance. "You won't have cause to coddle me, if that's what you meant." She had no idea if she actually *could* keep up, but she didn't like his assumption that she couldn't. *Stupid man!*

His blue eyes narrowed into a look of confusion and then, apparently realizing his insult, said, "Forgive me, lady. I dinnae doubt yer abilities. I only mean, the way is dangerous, and my divided attention could cause a gross error. You *are* my responsibility," he added, pulling on calfskin gloves. "I would see you safely to your cousin, but I cannot if you are dead."

Edyth didn't know what to say. What he said was true, she realized, but she didn't have to like his manner.

"You must ride close. Fingal will bring up the rear," he said, hanging a waterskin onto her saddle. "You must obey orders immediately and without question. Is that understood?"

Edyth nodded, her unease building. Into what trouble were they bringing her?

"Good," he said, and then he grabbed her around the waist and all but threw her onto Harris's back. She let out a yelp of surprise but settled herself more comfortably in the saddle.

Her skirts made it uncomfortable to ride astride, but she tugged them up to accommodate the position, grateful for her father's hose to keep her exposed legs from the elements.

"Lady," Ewan said, nodding brusquely, and then he turned to Iain. "We must be off," was all he said before turning on his heel and stalking off toward his own horse. "Mount up!" he shouted over his shoulder.

"Crabbit ejit," muttered Iain. "He's only worried, aye?" He watched Ewan mount his horse, shaking his head in disapproval. "Ye best keep yer eyes sharp and yer ears pricked, lady, if we're going through Douglas."

"What is Douglas?" she asked. She found herself thinking of the dagger currently housed in her boot. "Should I string my bow?" Iain did smile then, letting out a wheezing sort of laugh that caused a coughing fit. When he was finished, he wiped his mouth with the back of his hand and asked, "Who taught ye tae shoot with a bow, Lady Edyth?"

Edyth, bewildered at the question, answered, "My father encouraged the sport, though it has been some years since I've practiced. Why?"

He nodded, a smile still on his face. "No reason, but haps next time ye have the chance, think twice afore ye loose."

Edyth searched her mind for the last time she'd used her bow and, quite quickly, she recalled the panic of the night in the forest. She'd been keen to help her saviors; she'd forgotten all about the arrow she'd loosed when the man had attacked her.

"Who?" she asked, grimacing, already knowing. "Who did I hit with my arrow?"

Iain shook his head, the soft smile still gracing his face, and then he bowed, his arms splayed wide. "If I die," he said upon straightening back up, a twinkle in his eye, "it will have been an honor to have caught an arrow from such a lady."

He laughed at Edyth's expression and then coughed again, his shoulders heaving.

"My lord," said Edyth, her face hot. Mortification filled her. "I didn't mean...a man grabbed me and I loosed. I am truly sorry."

"Iain," barked Ewan, steering his chestnut destrier toward them, "has the ague affected your hearing?"

"Dinnae fash, lady," he said, sobering at once. "I dinnae mean ye discomfort. We must ride, but we will speak again." And then he was limping away toward the horse the servant held for him.

Edyth pulled her cloak more tightly around her shoulders. The cold pierced through her, her stomach in knots. Not only was she beholden to these men for saving her in the forest, and now for escorting her to Meg, but she'd seriously injured one of them. She thought she might be sick.

Edyth gathered her reins, watching the back of Ewan's head as he led the way out of the stable gate. Hating that she was a burden to him, she also knew she could not get to Meg without his help.

Edyth steered Harris behind the limping man, Iain, thinking how silly it had been for her to feel so optimistic when she'd woken only an hour ago. The unknown danger ahead of them sent goose pimples up her arms and she shivered. She glanced behind. The keep was a dark, foreboding mountain in the early morning light. She hoped that Lord Scott could hold it.

She could hear the water long before she could see it. What had started out as a faraway sound, much like that of wild windstorm pushing through a forest, had grown into a dizzying roar. Despite the horses' sure-footed advance, her anxiety grew with each slippery step Harris took on the narrow trail cut into the side of the ridge. She'd seen glimpses of the white, frothy water far below them through the trees and was glad to be far away from it, but knew in her bones that with one misstep, she would tumble down through the treetops and fall into the white-capped water.

The air was full of moisture; dewy droplets formed on Harris's neck and ears and upon her own arms and hands as though she were walking through an unseen cloud. The thick broom and trees prevented her seeing far, which aggravated her nervous condition, but she found solace in the steady, grim-faced men around her. They didn't show any signs of distress as their horses navigated the switchback trails, sliding in the muddy turns, nor when Graham's horse tripped over a loose rock that nearly unseated him.

They took it all in stride and in silence, not that she would be able to hear them through the roaring in her ears. Still, it was a comfort to see their lack of concern. She'd caught Ewan's eyes a few times on their descent as he looked back to check on her. It comforted her just as well as anything. She thought she'd even managed a weak smile at one point.

After what felt like a lifetime, with her heart lodged in her throat, they finally made it to the bottom of the mountainside; she felt undone and boneless. Edyth let out the shaky breath she'd been holding and looked around, flexing her cramped hands. She never wanted to traverse such a steep hill atop a beast again. Still, she'd made it without a whimper and was rather proud of herself.

The water was slower here, with swirling eddies breaking up the green-brown surface. Dead leaves and sticks floated by that had been plucked from their resting places by the swollen river.

The men dismounted, speaking softly to one another. Ewan cast an uncertain look at the water and shook his head. He mumbled something to Iain while Graham tightened the straps on his saddle. "I've never seen it so high," she heard Ewan say.

"But it's the only place to cross," said Graham.

Edyth's heart skipped a beat. *Surely they didn't mean to swim across.* Edyth dismounted, and her legs nearly gave way when her boots hit the spongy riverbank. She craned her neck in all directions, searching for a ferry, but without luck. She was certain the water was far too swift and deep—not to mention bitter cold—for her to swim across. She swallowed hard and approached Ewan, who had pulled out a length of rope from a saddlebag.

"Sir Ruthven," she said quietly, casting a glance at Fingal as he brushed past her. She didn't want her cowardice to be overheard. "How do you mean to cross this river?" she asked, leaning toward him intimately when he did not look up. Had he heard her? She had tried to keep the abject fear from her voice but wasn't sure if she'd done it.

Ewan's hands did not still on the rope as he unwound it. "Ye've done well, seated atop the beast all the day. I expect ye can sit on him just as well wet."

"I-I've never ridden a horse in the water," she said, her voice betraying her. "I cannot swim well...."

He looked fully at her then. His nearness and the intensity of his gaze sent a thrill through her. She'd never known anyone to have such deep blue eyes. There was no gray—no silver specks sprinkled about as stars in the sky—but flecked with a still-darker hue of blue. They drew her in.

"Ye've naught tae fear, lady. I'll see ye safely across." The thrum of his voice seemed to drift through her and she felt slightly giddy. She shook her head in an effort to regain her presence of mind.

"I cannot agree, sir," she said, her eyes darting to the water as though it might suddenly grow an appendage and snatch her up. "I'm not an accomplished swimmer. I-I'm quite afraid of water, especially a river so swift."

"Do ye ken I've a sister, Lady Edyth? She'll be about your age, I'd expect."

When Edyth shook her head, slightly bewildered at the mention of a sister, he continued on. "Cait—that's my sister—Iain, and I, we would all swim regularly at a fine spring no' far from our home. I say swim, but she'd always stick the shallows and chase minnows and the like. She'd throw mud at us too."

Edyth waited for more in the story and opened her mouth and shut it twice before finally saying, "Er...that's a very fine story, Sir Ruthven, but I don't see how that pertains to the current situation."

"Please call me Ewan," he said, bending at the waist and pulling on his heavy hauberk until it fell with a jangle of metal over his head and onto the ground. "Brothers can be rather vexing for little girls," he said, slightly red faced. He shoved the hauberk into a canvas bag, his eyes sparkling. "Especially brothers who throw their sisters into swimming holes." He tied the bag onto the back of the horse and rested his elbow upon it, a smile gracing his features. "Cait learned that with the right reward, she could indeed swim. If it's true for Cait, I'm almost certain it'll be true for you."

Was he teasing her? How different he was from the kind man who had comforted her yesterday! He was! He was laughing at her!

Her feelings must have shown on her face because he took her cold hands into his very large, warm ones.

"Pay me no mind, lady. It is how I cajole my Cait into good humor." He looked intently into her face, his blue eyes serious again. "Forgive me for saying so, but this"—he gestured toward the water with his chin—"is a mere trifle compared to the other feats you've already bested. I've never seen such bravery as yours the night I first spotted you in the glade, fighting off those English soldiers.

"This is a simple crossing," he continued, stepping closer. His voice was low and intimate; she could feel his breath upon her cheek, and she felt her heart quicken in reaction to his nearness. She took a useless, gulping breath to try and calm her racing heart.

"Ye've crossed enemy lines, traveled alone, fought for your honor and won. What is a river compared to all else you've overcome? It's naught but another thread in your hero's story. You will cross here and come to the other side victorious. Do not doubt your abilities, Lady Edyth, for I certainly do not. And remember, even if ye cannae swim, we *can*, and we will see ye safe."

She was probably blushing if the heat from her face was any indication. While his words certainly appealed to her pride, her nerves were not so easily assuaged. But she thought that perhaps he was right. Perhaps she should trust herself more. With a squeeze of his hand, Edyth left him reluctantly and stood beside Harris, staring across the wide expanse of water to the other side.

The opposite side was full of broom and tall, straight alder trees, newly budded in bright green. A trail snaked up the bank and wound to the right and out of sight. Water as dark as tea covered the roots of the trees and bushes, pulling forest debris away, stolen just like her breath. The comfort of Ewan's promise wavered. She swallowed hard and forced herself to unclench her fists.

"I'll tie yer horse tae mine, lass," said Fingal in his quiet, graveled voice. He peered at her with squinted eyes as he fastened a thin rope to Harris's bridle. He was her height with a small yet sturdy frame that hinted at sinewy strength. "D'ye nae mind the burn a bit, lassy. Gird yer skirts if ye've a mind to. The water will fill them and pull at ye if ye dinnae."

Edyth must have looked like a rabbit caught in a trap because Fingal cocked his head to the side, his bottom teeth embedded into his upper lip. After a heartbeat, he took a deep breath as though preparing himself for some disagreeable task and motioned to her skirt with his hands, sweeping them up in the air as though he were winnowing grain. "Yer skirts, lassy. Get 'em up."

Edyth shook her head in confusion and yelped when the older man took matters into his own hands, quite literally. Taking two large handfuls of skirt from just under her knees, he commanded she hold them up in her hands. Using a rather muddy booted foot, he nudged her feet farther apart with a grunt.

Edyth could feel her cheeks burning.

"Dinnae fash, lady," called Iain, letting go of the horse's hoof he'd just been inspecting, "Fingal only likes ugly, fat women, so yer quite safe."

Fingal snorted and said something in return that she could not discern. While she was quite ignorant to Scots speech, she knew an insult when she heard one, but to Edyth's surprise, Iain laughed heartily and placed a large hand on Fingal's bony shoulder in a commiserating way. "Kind o' ye tae offer, *mo shíorghrá*, but I must say I'm busy just the noo."

Fingal gave Iain an exasperated look and then shoved the rope into his friend's chest, forcing him to take it. Fingal stalked away, shaking his head.

"Is he very angry?" she asked Iain, watching as he bent to inspect another horseshoe, wondering at their banter. Edyth thought their manners very strange.

Iain, looking rather pale and glassy-eyed, shook his head. "He's no' angry. Our insults are only in jest." He paused here to catch his breath, leaning on his horse for support. "He was telling ye tae tie yer skirts up so that the water doesnae drag ye off of yer horse." He closed his eyes, breathing as though he'd just run half a league. "Do ye ken how it's done?"

Edyth frowned, her concern growing. If he'd looked under the weather this morning, that was nothing to how he looked now. "Yes, I know how," she said absently, moving closer to feel his forehead with the back of her hand. His fever was very high; she could feel the heat coming off him before she'd even touched him.

He opened one bloodshot eye at her touch. "I'll bide, Lady Edyth. In fact, I'm thinking I might take a wee dip tae cool meself."

She smiled weakly at his joke. "That's not a bad idea."

Her momentary distraction from the task at hand came to an end as soon as Fingal returned with his horse and tied the other end of the rope to his saddle.

"Leave off yer shoon," advised Fingal as he checked the tightness of Harris's saddle. Edyth noticed that his own boots had been removed and placed carefully on the back of his horse. Her nerves immediately escaped beyond their boundaries. She thought Ewan was going to take her across.

"Fingal is the finest swimmer among us," said Iain softly. "Like a wee fish."

Edyth nodded, biting her lip. Removing her boots, she handed them to Fingal to tie onto the back of her saddle and went about the business of girding her skirts. At least the bunched-up fabric between her legs would keep her knees from knocking together, she thought wryly. Lord, she'd never been so scared in all her life. Her mouth had gone completely dry and her hands had grown slippery with sweat.

Before she was ready or could even protest, however, she was seated atop Harris, who didn't take kindly to being tied to the horse in front of him. He tossed his head in disapproval when Fingal's horse wandered a little too far forward, forcing Harris to follow. Her tension must have been palpable, for the steed wouldn't hold still while she watched Ewan and Iain enter the water.

Muttering absently to Harris, she watched in nervous anticipation as Iain's horse followed Ewan into the water. Both men had removed their boots, and for good reason. Their horses surged into the river, blowing and struggling against the current; the muddy water lapped at the men's calves, and they weren't even close to halfway across the expanse of the river.

Ewan called out encouragement to his steed, pulling on the reins to encourage the horse to turn against the stream. The water was swift enough to pull them farther downriver, away from the trail. His efforts weren't rewarded, however, as the horses were swimming now, the water up to the men's hips. Edyth thought her heart might beat right out of her chest.

"So much for dry shoon," murmured Fingal. They watched as both men clung to their horse's manes, legs outstretched behind as they floated alongside the swimming horses.

Edyth held her breath until they were able to reach the other side and caught footholds somewhere in the thick broom that swallowed them up. Blowing and shaking their manes, the horses emerged safely. So much she saw between the limbs of trees, and then before she was ready, Fingal was nudging his steed forward, pulling Harris in tow.

"Hold tight, lass," said Fingal. He needn't have told her. Her fingers were already aching from the death grip she held on Harris's reins.

The rush of the river was loud but not loud enough to drown out the fears racing through her mind. The water was swift enough, and the bed rocky enough, to cause Harris to stumble. He righted himself quickly enough, but Edyth's fears intensified. She could see in her mind Harris balking at the task or tripping in deeper water so as to carry him—and her with him—downstream. He would unseat her; the cold would suffocate her.

Such were her thoughts that by the time the frigid water touched her toes, she found herself balled up on the saddle, tense and unsteady. Someone shouted at her from the bank to relax her legs, but through her panic, she couldn't. She tried, but the water stung her feet and legs.

Desperate, she pulled on Harris's reins, winning her an angry snort. She couldn't avoid the water. It was up to her thighs now, chilling her to the bone. Her feet and calves tingled unpleasantly as they numbed. Alarmed, she realized she couldn't feel her toes at all. It hadn't taken any time at all to lose the feeling in her extremities.

The water was so swift that it pulled on her as her bunched up skirts filled with water, tugging her bottom off the saddle. She should have taken her dress completely off. It was pulling on her, heavy and burdensome. Panicked, she cried out, clinging to the reins, as her bottom was pulled off the horse completely. Harris lost his feet and began to swim, snorting and twisting his neck as the full weight of Edyth's body pulled on the tethers. She was sinking! She gulped for air just before the water overtook her.

Her entire body burned in the shocking cold. Somehow, she'd let go of the reins. She couldn't feel her hands! Her skirts were heavy and *everywhere*, trapping her flailing hands, floating in front of her face. Her left leg hit something hard, a slimy boulder by the feel of it, but she couldn't feel the bottom. Her chest felt as though it were on fire. She couldn't see anything but a sort of inky blackness.

The current carried her swiftly, turning her and pushing, and then miraculously, it spit her out of the water just enough for her to reach the surface. She gasped and sputtered, flailing her arms to stay afloat. She saw Fingal upriver through blurry eyes, maneuvering his horse downstream. She heard someone shouting, and then the water overtook her once more. Her dress was so heavy and she was so cold. Her arms didn't seem to work properly.

A sharp pain seared her skull as Fingal reached her. Somehow still atop his steed, he took hold of her hair—the only part of her that seemed to float—and reeled her in. He took hold of one arm, his jaw clamped in a grimace at the effort. She grabbed onto Fingal's waist, coughing and sputtering, gasping for sweet air. He was shouting at her, but she couldn't spare the effort to decipher his words. She rested her head against the stranger's thigh, shuddering.

Chapter Six

She couldn't stop shivering, even wrapped up as she was in a large plaid Ewan had given her. She sat, dazed and shivering on a fallen tree as Graham, Fingal, and Ewan made camp. They'd moved farther east to avoid the masking roar of the river, but the men spoke in hushed tones and had an air of nervousness they hadn't had before. It was clear to her that they were not yet out of danger.

Iain was slumped against the same tree, his head covered by a similar looking, quivering blanket. He'd fallen against the tree and had shut his eyes as soon as they'd dismounted. He hadn't moved since. Her guilt weighed on her.

Edyth bit her lip, considering. While she wasn't her mother, she did have *some* knowledge of herbal cures and had helped her mother tend to a wide variety of injuries. Would they welcome such ministrations, though? Would they think she was a witch? Looking at Iain shivering, his pale skin seeming to pulse with heat, she decided it didn't matter what they thought. If he died because of her, she would never forgive herself.

She looked about her, but no one was paying her any heed. Graham was unsaddling the last horse, and Fingal was feeding his steed something from a leather bag, its nose buried. She did not see Ewan now, but she knew he was walking the perimeter of their makeshift camp. With no one watching, she crouched in front of Iain and, hesitating for only a breath, lifted his damp kilt.

The cloth tied around his muscled thigh was dirtied with dried blood and yellowed with pus. The wet knot in the fabric proved too difficult for her to untie, so she borrowed the dirk at his waist and carefully pulled the knot apart with the tip of the knife, watching his wan face for any sign of objection. She ignored the thought that she might be invading his privacy and unwrapped the injured leg as carefully as she could.

Edyth gasped at what lay underneath. The puckered wound was blue and black from bruising, but what concerned her most was the oozing pus that poured forth when she gently pressed her fingers against the swollen skin. Iain groaned when she'd touched him, but he did not open his eyes. He was burning up, his eyes roving under his eyelids, his breathing fast and shallow.

Edyth did not hesitate. Repressing a groan as she stood, her legs stiff, she wobbled to her saddle across the clearing. The outer saddlebag was mostly wet through, but her satchel, which had been tucked inside, had helped to keep her items from complete ruin. She was relieved to find that her mother's journal and her father's lessons had only gotten wet on one corner, the writing in both preserved.

Ewan appeared suddenly, making her jump. His shirt was wet through so that she could clearly see the muscled expanse of his chest, shoulders, and arms. She'd never seen a man built so solidly this close up and so...bare. It left her breathless, but she couldn't look away. Despite a wet kilt and clinging sark, though, he didn't betray any sort of discomfort.

"Lady Edyth," he began, his demeanor troubled. He helped her to rise, a strange current running through her at his touch. "There is much I must say to you."

He frowned, looking at her small hand in his, and she wondered if he felt the same queer sensation.

"Your hand is like ice," he said, the worry line deepening between his brows. "Are ye well, lady?" he asked, searching her face intently. He chaffed her hand with his own, engulfing it in warmth.

Edyth stared at their joining. How could he be so warm when she, herself, was chilled through? The tendons of his long hands jumped as he softly squeezed her hand, hinting at their power. They were soldier's hands, accustomed to gripping heavy weapons, to fierce, brute strength that demanded his opponent to yield. Yet now they were also tender and gentle, and they set her heart to racing. "I...I'm worried for your brother," she stammered, looking past him to the other side of the clearing where he still lay. "But I am well enough."

Ewan followed her gaze, his lips pressed into a thin, bloodless line. "Yes. As am I. This is one of the things we must speak of. We are not safe here, but I did not account for the river being so high. I fear he's worse now. We must ride again soon."

His eyes returned to her face; his concern clearly written there for her to see. Pressing her hand gently before finally letting it go, his eyes shone with worry. "I regret taking you this way. I must apologize for breaking my promise to you."

"Your promise?" She couldn't seem to recall anything of the sort, her brain seemingly replaced with stuffed wool. She shook her head in an effort to clear it.

"Aye, I promised that I would see you safely across the burn, and yet I...you nearly drowned." He took a breath through his nose, his lips pressed tightly. The window into his thoughts closed as he looked to the ground, his eyes hidden behind sooty lashes. "In my haste to get Iain home, and you with him, I took a chance that has cost ye both. I must ask yer forgiveness."

Moved, Edyth wanted to touch him, but she stopped herself. They were not familiar enough with each other to warrant such intimacies, regardless of him only just warming her hands, but she did understand his feelings. She, too, felt the keen sting of being responsible for another's distress.

"Sir Ruthven—"

"Ewan," he reminded her.

She smiled slightly, conceding. "Very well. Ewan. I recall that you promised to see me safely on the other side, which I am. I regret that you didn't promise to keep me warm or dry, but if you want to make that promise now, I will hold you to it."

Ewan's grim mouth curved up at one end, amused, his thoughts open to her once more as his eyes came alive with what she took to be relief.

"You don't need my forgiveness. Though I'm wet and chilled, I am alive and all the closer to my goal. I'm in *your* debt," continued Edyth. "If anyone needs forgiveness, it's me. Iain told me that I'm the cause of his wound."

His brows shot up in surprise, but she pressed on, not wanting him to interrupt her. "It wasn't by design of course, but still, *I am* to blame. I would like to help, where I can."

She only hesitated for a moment, and then she held her mother's journal up for him to see, choosing in that instant to trust him further. He took the book with a questioning look and leafed through it, pausing to read here and there. "You're *bana-bhuidseach geal*. A witch."

She flinched at his words, snatching back the book. "These are medicines. Herbs!" she all but hissed, feeling very vulnerable indeed. "I am no witch." Her hands clutched the tome tight enough for her knuckles to turn white. She didn't want to show her fear, but she felt suddenly very foolish for having shown this man—a man whom she thought might be a friend—something so dangerous.

Ewan held up a hand, forestalling her. "Be still," he said softly, stepping close enough to touch her wrist with two long, straight fingers. "Tis no evil thing to be *bana-bhuidseach geal*. This is fortunate, indeed. Please," he said, holding her gaze. "Show me." He lifted the trembling hand that held the book, his brow raised in expectation.

Edyth surveyed him warily. *Was this a trick?* She wanted to trust him. She wanted to help Iain.

Trust me, he seemed to say, though no words were spoken. He waited patiently, without coaxing. Reluctantly, she loosened her grip and relinquished her mother's journal, swallowing her fear. She watched as his eyes roved back and forth, reading, his fingers leafing through pages.

"What do ye recommend for an injury such as Iain's?" he asked, his velvety voice working some sort of magic on her. He turned the book sideways, looking at a rather long image of a weed drawn over two pages. Two sheaves of parchment fell to the forest floor, scrawled with the heavy black hand of her father. They both stooped to retrieve them, their heads close together.

"In nominee Patris et Filii et Spiritus Sancti," Ewan read, his eyes full of questions. He handed the pages over to Edyth, an expression on his face she could not decipher. She stood abruptly, chewing her lip. "Do ye ken what these say then?"

Edyth nodded, feeling culpable. Would he reject her completely now? Would he punish her as a bride of the devil as her own mother had been? But he said nothing. His eyes returned to the herbal without further comment.

"Ye've a fine hand," he said finally after what felt a very long time.

She shook her head. "It was my mother's. It's her hand, not mine. I'm not a real physic. She—" Edyth broke off, biting her lip as Ewan's sharp eyes caught hold of her own.

He lowered the book, his eyes gone soft. "This is your mother's work?" he asked, offering it back to her. "Your mother was condemned for this?"

"In part." She nodded and took it, her fingers lighting upon his own that sent a shock up her arm and set her heart to racing. She cleared her throat, ignoring the feeling, and opened the book, turning pages as she looked for medicines she knew. "She was a very talented physic. People from our village came to her for everything. I helped her many times, though I am not as skilled as she is...*was*." She took a shaky breath and showed Ewan the page she had found.

"Do you know this herb...or this one?" she asked, pointing to the drawings.

When Ewan shook his head, she said, "Yarrow and garlic will pull out the sickness in his leg. I have some dried herbs—or they used to be dry—but fresh is better."

"It's too early for yarrow, and I've no garlic with me." He looked worried. He bit his lip, making a dimple appear in his left cheek.

"We'll use what I have, but I must have hot water. Will you build me a fire?"

Ewan looked to his brother and then back to Edyth, indecision written upon his fine features. "We are in danger here and a fire will bring any Douglasses nearby straight to us. Can it wait?"

"I can't say," she said helplessly. "I wish I knew. I looked at his wound and it worries me. If I wait too long, it could kill him."

Ewan's brow furrowed in worry. He seemed to war within himself and then he said, "Do what ye can for him. Quickly." He turned abruptly from her, his mouth set in a stubborn way and set about gathering sticks.

Edyth found the yarrow wedged in the bottom of her satchel and pulled it out, the corner of her mouth tucked in. Most of the herbs were dry, but some were damp, the linen bags turned see-through. She made her way back to Iain, passing the men as they questioned Ewan's actions.

"Ewan, a fire? Nay!" said Graham, his one eye roving around the clearing. "We're still a good ten miles away from the border."

"I ken that well enough," said Ewan, placing the twigs he'd gathered into a pile. "Iain is unconscious and fevering. His leg needs immediate attention. The lass has herbs that can help."

Graham and Fingal both looked at Edyth, their curiosity evident.

"Ye ken I wouldnae tarry here, nor start a fire, if it could be helped."

Graham made a sound like air leaving a bellows. "Then we cannae stay here after a fire, Ewan. I saw signs of someone taking this trail not very long ago."

Ewan nodded, busy arranging the twigs and sticks. He twisted a handful of long, dry grasses together in a practiced manner and then paused, looking up at his men. "We'll tend tae his leg and then go canny through the night." He met Graham's eye, steely and determined. "I willnae risk his life or his leg, Graham. I won't."

Fingal made an indiscernible noise in his throat before picking up and breaking a rather large stick against his knee. "We'll have tae tie the lad tae his seat, Ewan. He'll no' be able tae ride on his own as he is."

The rest of the conversation was lost to Edyth as she mentally reviewed what was to be done. She inhaled the little bags holding her herbs, sharp and pungent. They reminded her of her mother's workroom, full of hanging flowers, stems, and branches, bowls of roots and fungi. The smells were familiar and comforting but also melancholy. Edyth sighed and put her cheerless thoughts from her mind, tending to the task of cutting cloth from the bottom of her sodden chemise for Iain's binding.

"I've started the fire. What aught will ye be needing from me?" asked Ewan, crouching down to her level.

"I need water boiled to make a poultice."

Iain moved, his head rolling in an effort to hold it up. He shivered and Edyth adjusted the plaid more tightly closed around him.

"He's waking" said Fingal unnecessarily.

"Lady Edyth is a *bana-bhuidseach geal*," said Ewan, drawing Iain's glazed gaze.

"What other talents are ye hiding from us?" rasped Iain, his eyes drooping, but Edyth saw the effort of a smile on his face.

"Oh, a great many things," said Edyth quietly, feeling his forehead and cheeks with the back of her hand. "Most of which are too embarrassing to mention."

"I would...hear," he panted. The corners of Iain's lips twitched, and he closed his eyes.

"You need to rest, Iain," said Ewan, frowning in concern at Iain's exposed leg. "We will be on the move again as soon as the lass binds yer wound. I'll see tae the water," he said.

She reached out a smudged, cold hand and touched his knee; naked as it was, she did not feel embarrassed. Only a heaviness filled her. "It grieves me that I am the cause of your suffering."

Iain opened his glassy eyes and shook his head, rolling it along the fallen tree supporting him. "Dinnae fash, lady. I've had worse scratches."

An hour later, Iain's leg was bandaged, and he sat precariously atop his horse. Ewan had taken Fingal's advice and had tied him to his saddle, mostly to keep him from falling on his head should he slide off. There was also the danger of him being knocked off by a tree branch, and he too slow or weak to prevent it.

They were silent, save for the jingle of tack and the squeak of leather, as they made their way warily through the dense forest. They were on a narrow trail that wound through hillocks steeped with holly and broom. There were no birds or squirrels about, adding to their nervous state.

Edyth followed behind Iain, and Fingal took up the rear, as usual. Every time Iain grunted in pain as his horse navigated a difficult incline or splashed jauntily through a trickling brook, Edyth's regret increased.

Graham, a good tracker, was the first in the procession, followed by Ewan. Graham was communicating to Ewan using hand signals, none of which Edyth understood. They would stop randomly at a sign from Graham and Ewan would dismount with the giant, looking closely at a broken branch or bruised leaves. They would whisper to each other, their expressions grave, then remount. Sometimes they continued to follow the trail, and other times they forged their own, pushing through clinging vines and knotted branches, slowing them further.

Exhausted from the day's events, hungry, and sore, the desperation of their situation engulfed her. She saw villains around every bend and tree so that the tension in her muscles sent spasms through her. She held her tongue, though, too afraid of the risk should she utter a sound.

The sun was on its way toward the horizon; Edyth guessed there were only scant hours left of light when it happened. They'd come upon a game trail covered in dead leaves from the previous year. The leaves being crushed by their horses filled the air, making her wince at the noise.

A piercing war cry rent the air. Harris bolted at the noise, running off the trail and into the wet, clinging branches. Edyth fought with him, looking wildly around her as more shouting and screaming erupted.

It was chaos. Four—no, five—men had emerged from around a bend in the trail, twigs sticking up from their clothes and hair in a wild array. They had long swords strapped to their backs, winking over their shoulders, their short swords drawn. They charged, running toward them from the east, screaming at the tops of their lungs.

Edyth's heart jumped somewhere to the vicinity of her throat and stuck there.

Ewan had reacted quickly, drawing his own sword with a metallic ringing that sent a chill down her spine. He circled around and grabbed Iain's reins, but her view was blocked now by Fingal, his leg touching hers. "Keep close tae me," he growled, drawing his bow in the blink of an eye. He loosed an arrow with a *whoosh*, his long hair lifting from the draft.

Swords clashed, men shouted, and then Fingal was swearing. Something was very wrong. She spurred Harris forward without thought, pushing him through thick, clinging branches, and emerged back onto the trail. She immediately saw the trouble.

Ewan was struggling with Iain's horse in the middle of the trail. He could not fight and protect Iain at the same time. With one hand, he held Iain's reins, and in the other, he swung his sword, lashing out at a large man who had just pulled the long sword from his back.

Iain's horse wasn't having any of it and reared, screaming, forcing Ewan to let go. Iain was still unconscious, his body jumping and bouncing with the movement of his horse.

"Take the horse! Go!" Ewan bellowed, swinging viciously to block the man's attack.

Her body reacted without thought, and before she knew it, she had spurred her heels into Harris's flanks and was rushing toward the fray. An arrow flew over her head as she stretched her hand out for Iain's horse.

Edyth leaned as far as she dared, bouncing precariously on Harris's back, and swiped at the fallen reins. They slid through her hand, and she fumbled with them, her fingers catching the ends just in time. She grasped them tightly, her fingernails digging into the palm of her hand, and flexed her foot in her stirrup, trying with all her might to stay in the saddle. With a monumental effort, she righted herself and spurred Harris forward, pulling Iain's horse behind. It jerked its head, pulling on the reins, which bit into her raw skin, but she held fast, pulling with all her might.

Into the forest they ran, branches whipping her in the face, pulling on her hair, and snagging her dress. Her breath was ragged, her heart beating a frantic rhythm. Thick woods and brush forced her to circumvent them, slowing them down, but Edyth had no choice. She glanced back and saw that Iain was leaning heavily to one side, both arms dangling toward the ground. She could not stop, but she slowed, looking for a place to hide.

She spied a dense patch of holly a short distance away, thick and high enough to hide their horses. It was as good as she was likely to find, she decided, and made her way to it, all the while thinking of the others. What would she do if they were killed? It was all her fault! Ewan had chosen the more dangerous road in favor of the time they would save. He wouldn't have chosen this road if she hadn't shot Iain. She bit back a groan of anguish at the thought and chewed her lip, listening for any sign of what was happening. In the distance, she could hear the steely clangs of swords and shouts.

She dismounted and went to Iain. Twigs snapped under her feet and she winced at the noise, afraid. She looked wildly around her, as still as a statue, waiting for someone to pounce, but nothing happened. She took a few deep breaths, trying to calm her heart, and went to Iain, stepping carefully. He was semi-unconscious, the muscles in his face twitching in discomfort. His eyes rolled under closed lids.

"Iain," she whispered, trying to lift him. He was far too heavy.

His horse shifted and huffed.

There was nothing for it. He would just have to hang there until she had some help. Her hands shook as she fumbled for the dirk in her boot. She held it in her hands, her eyes darting around her, as she contemplated her circumstance.

Iain stirred, grunting, before collapsing again against his steed. His noise sounded like a trump to her ears in the quiet wood; Edyth held her breath. She waited impatiently, imagining all sorts of horrible things that may be happening.

The distant sounds of battle continued, but the sound of a horse screaming in pain made her drop her dirk. Swearing, she picked it back up and, thinking better of it, replaced it in her boot. Her bow would be better here. She rushed to Harris and pulled her weapon out from its place behind the saddle.

She had to use all her body weight to string it. It took her three tries to get the job done, but finally she caught the string to the notch at the end and strung it. She pushed hair from her eyes with a shaking hand and nocked an arrow, trying to control the fear she felt racing through her body.

Edyth couldn't see anything from where she was behind the thick holly, so she quietly moved to the edge of the thicket, where the leaves were a bit sparser, to peek out and await Ewan's return.

The sounds of the battle hadn't completely quieted, but Edyth heard something much closer, which caused her heart to beat all the faster. The sounds of long-dead leaves being crushed underfoot filled the space, alarming her of someone's approach.

Two men's approach, she corrected, both armed with swords. They were following the obvious path she'd taken through the forest, which led right to her hiding spot. They had no horses that she could see. One man motioned to the other, sidestepping a deep track. He pointed right to their hiding place. Edyth's heart hammered so hard in her chest it hurt.

Harris, who was not used to battle, must have felt the tension from Edyth because he pranced nervously and bumped into Iain's horse, who swayed and slipped even further in his saddle. He would fall to the ground in just moments and could be trampled if the horses, already uneasy, bolted. Edyth knew she had to act fast. She pulled on her bowstring; the quiet sounds of stress it made in her ears seemed overly loud, even with the scraping of swords ringing in the distance.

One of the men held up a finger and then pointed to the holly. She had never calculated taking a man's life before. Yes, she had killed the English brigand with his own sword, but that had been uncalculated. Defensive. Now as she aimed her arrow at the nearest man's heart, indecision warred within her. Was this a sin? Her arm felt the strain of holding the bow tight. She couldn't hold it much longer; her forearms burned with the effort to hold steady. She let out her breath as she'd been taught, anchoring her hand to her cheek.

The man motioned for them to continue forward, only twenty yards from their hiding place now, centered in the small clearing. She had to act now.

Now.

Her fingers relaxed; the arrow whipped through the leaves that hid her, then soared through air as if in slow motion. She watched it, breathless, as it found its mark deep in the first man's neck. He sputtered wetly, clawing at the arrow as he gulped for air. Falling to his knees, the man slumped onto his side and, after some desperate spasms, lay quite still. Her heart was lodged in her throat. She forgot to breathe.

But there was no time to think. No time for anything except to nock another arrow. As Edyth fumbled for another, her fingers cold and trembling, one of the horses grunted with effort. She turned just in time to see Iain's saddle slide sideways on the horse, his weight being too much for it. He fell with a thud onto the ground and lay like a rag doll, legs and arms akimbo, but she could not spare even one more second on him.

The other man was running in a crouch toward the horse's noise, his sword held to the side with both hands. Edyth's chest hurt from the ceaseless pounding within; her ears roared with blood. Her fingers ached from gripping the second arrow so tightly. Moving to a better position, she pulled the string and expelled her breath, keeping her eyes locked on her target: the beating heart of a man twice her size.

Her arrow hit his right arm. The man stopped short, nearly dropping his sword, but then his crazed gaze locked on her own through the glossy leaves. In her effort to get a better shot, she had inadvertently exposed her left side to his view.

He was running at her now; he would pounce onto her in mere seconds.

She backed up, out through the thicket, and abandoned her bow, fishing instead for the long dagger Thom had forced upon her. She produced it just as his face, red with anger, burst through the holly. The point of her arrow was grotesquely protruding from the back of his arm. His grim face registered a moment of surprise at finding a lone woman and a crumpled man, but it did not stay his anger.

She knew she would die. There was no way she could defeat him. But if she was to die, she would do it well, like her mother. She jutted out her chin, determined not to beg or cry.

Her last hope, she pinched the pointed end of her dagger in her fingers and flung it at him. It whipped through the air, end over end, even as he stalked forward. Edyth staggered backward and bumped into Iain's prone form.

She thought her heart might quit entirely when the man deflected her dagger easily with his sword. The sound of clashing metal rang through the forest as her dagger soared out of sight.

Don't panic. Think. Iain had a sword, but she knew she wouldn't be able to wield it with any accuracy. He had a dirk, though. She'd used it earlier to untie the knot around his leg.

She fell to Iain's side at her feet. Heat radiated from his crumpled body, but she could see the glinting end of a dirk protruding from his boot. Her hand had only just grasped the end of Iain's dagger when the man was upon her.

He grabbed her shoulder, flinging her around to face him. In the same instant, Edyth put all her might into swinging Iain's dirk into the man's side. She felt the sickening sensation of blade on bone as she drove it under the last of his ribs. The man roared, his face mere inches from her own. Spittle hit her face. She tried to back away and tripped over Iain's legs.

The man fingered his wound with shaking fingers, blood spilling freely from between them. His gaze snapped to hers. He was wild with anger, his blue eyes cold and fierce. The world was all quiet for one eerie second, and then he pierced the silence with a shrill war cry that made the hairs on the back of her neck stand on end.

He lifted his sword; Edyth flinched. She would die here. Mira, Meg...they would never know what had happened to her. But instead of being run through, her head jerked back with savage violence when the hilt of his sword struck her heavily just under her left eye. Stars danced before her, and then the breath left her as he crumpled on top of her, their legs entangled across Iain's prone form.

She was dazed. What had happened? Edyth scrambled out from under him, frantically kicking and pushing. Her cloak was caught underneath him, but she was able to tug free with a mighty effort and crawl away. She tripped twice but kept fumbling forward. Away... away.

From somewhere far off, she heard someone crying. When she glanced over her shoulder, to gauge the distance from her attacker, Edyth saw, instead, his motionless form, still atop Iain, the handle of a second dagger protruding from his back.

Edyth only then realized, as she scanned the thicket and saw Ewan taking great strides to her, that it had been her own cries she'd heard and that Ewan had saved her.

She had no control over her body. Her hands shook violently as she tried to wipe off the blood that was smeared across her hand and down her wrist and onto her skirts. The tears would not stop. The world was washed away, the lines blurred and fuzzy. She felt weak; her head seemed to float above her body in a strangely detached way. And then before she knew it, she was in Ewan's arms.

Edyth grasped onto his shirt, trembling like a leaf.

The thrum of his voice was muffled...far away. She was terribly cold. She burrowed into him, wishing she could disappear altogether. His body was hard and rigid, his arms like the bands of a cage encircling her, but she did not feel safe.

Rough hands ran over her limbs, her back; he turned her this way and that, tossing her cloak from her to expose any wounds, but her injuries were not visible. His hands snatched at her wrist, bright with blood. Fingers like hot irons branded her skin. "Not mine," she mumbled, her tongue thick. "Not mine."

"I thought there were only five." He pulled her to him again, her ear pressed to his chest. She could feel his heart beating a quick rhythm under her cheek, like a bird's wings fluttering in a bush. He swore then, trembling along with her. "I thought there were only five. Iain?" He swallowed, squeezing her more tightly at his silent question.

Edyth shook her head against his chest, sniffing. "He lives. He fell off his horse."

A sound, not unlike a sob, escaped Ewan. "Thank God." He gently pushed her away, his blue eyes nearly black with rage or maybe fear. "Are ye hale, then, Edyth? Have ye been hurt?"

Stupid with shock, she simply shook her head and wrapped her arms around herself. "I don't...no," she stammered. "No, I'm not hurt."

His expression suddenly darkened, and his strong fingers grasped her chin. He turned her head to the right and bit out a curse. "Ye *are* hurt," he said, touching her cheek. He made a sound of regret in his throat. "I'm afraid that knot will split open."

Edyth fingered the large and very painful lump under her eye where the man had hit her. It was hot and puffy, but she didn't think broken. "It could have been much worse," she said, her own voice sounding very far off.

Fingal and Graham tumbled just then through the holly, looking bewildered but unharmed.

"Are ye well, lady?" asked Fingal, throwing down the bow that was slung over his shoulder. "I saw a man felled with an arrow."

"Iain?" asked Graham, eyeing his friend worriedly.

"The strap holding him broke, and he fell," Edyth informed them. She was trembling so badly her teeth clacked together.

Graham and Ewan removed the fallen man and straightened out Iain's body to a more comfortable position.

Placing an ear near Iain's mouth, Ewan's face relaxed. "He's breathing," he announced, his relief apparent.

"Check for breaks," Graham suggested, peering down on Iain with a critical eye.

Unsteady and unwilling to stand any longer, Edyth slumped to the ground. Her raw, blistered palms were covered in the stranger's blood, staining them to match her soul. God had already proved his dislike of her. He'd taken her family, her home, and any friend she'd ever had. And now she'd committed the most grievous of sins. Did that mean that she would be separated from her family, even in death? Her parents had been innocent, but she could no longer claim the same.

"I counted only five horses," said Graham, breaking through her thoughts. "I dinnae ken where the other two came from. I am sorry, lassie. Truly."

Edyth shook his apology away. "These men had no horses." She then told them what had happened as best she could, her throat dry. "That's a braw lass," said Fingal. He nodded once, in approval, and she looked away.

"Let's get some water down these two and gather our wits," said Ewan, picking up Iain's fallen plaid. He draped it over his brother once more, his face grim. The other men moved about her, gathering, assessing, speaking softly, but she paid them no heed. Her mind was in a fog, her heart as heavy as it had ever been. She could not stop seeing the arrow plunge into the man's neck. She could still hear his sputtering, desperate attempts for air. The blood on her hands was sticky and pungent. She thought she might be sick.

Ewan pulled the daggers protruding from her attacker's back and wiped the blood off onto the man's trews, glaring.

"They must 'ave split off afore we crossed their path," said Graham gravely. "Taken a different path tae ambush us."

"Aye," Ewan agreed.

"Are ye well, Edyth?" asked Graham, crouching into her view. His very blue eye searched her face benignly. "Ye look a might bit pale," he said in a conversational tone as though merely speaking of the weather. He reached over to pull some leaves and twigs from her hair.

"How do ye 'spect she feels, Graham?" asked Ewan.

Graham didn't show he was upset by the barked question. He simply offered her the waterskin, tipping it into her mouth so she could drink. She swallowed automatically, the cool water making her shiver anew. Graham helped her to clean the blood from her hands as best she could with what was left in the waterskin.

She watched as Fingal walked over and retrieved the Douglas man's sword. He lifted it high, examining its edge.

"Dinnae fash, Milady," whispered Graham. "We've had a right difficult day, but we're braw, all. We'll be across the border before ye know it."

Ewan approached and squatted near Edyth's side, his fierce demeanor softening as he addressed her. "This is my fault," he said, his voice quiet, solemn. "I willna leave ye again, my lady. I swear it." And then he replaced her lost dagger into her boot, his mouth in a grim line.

"Why are we sharing a horse?" asked Edyth moments later as Ewan climbed into the saddle behind her. He lifted her so that she was better settled between his legs and carefully wrapped his plaid around them both.

"My horse has fallen," said Ewan, tucking the edges of the soft cloth under her legs. "The Douglas's horses ran off, and I dinnae have the time or inclination tae hunt them. I hope ye dinnae mind sharing yours."

Edyth shook her head, feeling numb.

"Lay yer head, lass," he said, the low timbre of his voice sending a shiver through her. "I'll see ye safe."

Chapter Seven

Edyth was awoken by a soft nudge on her shoulder. The cold air snaked its way under her fur and the blanket covering her. Her skin erupted into a riot of goose pimples that seemed to burn with the cold. She hadn't thought it possible to be more uncomfortable but life—as of late—was proving her wrong in all its facets. She wearily ran a hand through her tangled hair so she could better see the person who'd awoken her and repressed a groan that blossomed in her throat. She ached all over.

"Milady, wake up. We must leave."

Her eyes narrowed, trying to focus her bleary vision in the dappled light, but her left eye was nearly swollen shut. She could tell that, though they were under a canopy of leaves and intertwined branches, the sun was much higher in the sky than it ought to be. She remembered Ewan's face in the dark, speaking to her as he'd helped her from the horse, his mouth moving without sound. She must have slept very late indeed.

"We must be off," he said again, his white teeth flashing bright in the dim light. "Ye were so tired ye didnae even wake when we made camp," explained Ewan, helping her to stand.

Everything was already packed up except for her things. She saw Iain standing nearby, leaning heavily against his horse.

"I must see to Iain. Has his fever broken?" Not waiting for an answer, she walked over to her patient, her muscles stiff and aching, to peer up at his pale face. He opened his eyes and gave her a nod. "Your medicine is helping, lady," he said, his voice a rasp.

She ran a hand over his brow, noting that the fever, while lessened, was not gone.

"Ewan replaced the herbs not long ago. He thought it best tae let ye sleep. I hope ye dinnae mind him going through yer bag. He saw where ye'd stored them," Iain explained.

"Oh," she said, looking over her shoulder at Ewan, who was rolling up the furs on which she'd slept.

"I hope I haven't caused you all to be late, tarrying here on my account."

"Wheesht," said Iain, "we all needed rest. Me most of all," he said conspiratorially. Then after a pause, "I've learned that ye saved my life. I mean tae thank ye."

She shrugged, feeling uncomfortable. She hadn't considered that she'd saved his life, only that she had killed. Swallowing, she said, "Seeing as how I'm the cause of all of this, it is I who should be thanking you."

Iain placed a hand on her shoulder, drawing her eye to his. "Nay, lady. Ye're no' the cause. Dinnae think it."

Edyth shook her head, a riot of emotions coursing through her. "Because of your wound, which I caused, we took a more dangerous route. It *is* my fault."

"What of the evil that resides in the Douglass's heart? Is that your fault as well? He would have cut you down, then me, defenseless." He nodded, a significant look in his eye. "Ye've saved my life, Lady Edyth, and I will be grateful to ye for it, regardless of yer misplaced guilt."

The sincerity of his words comforted her slightly, and she pressed his hands, her eyes drawn to the kilt covering his injury. Edyth wondered about Ewan's attempt at the poultice but chose not to ask to inspect his efforts. They'd already wasted so much time letting her sleep.

"It's time tae mount up," said Ewan, holding Harris's reins. "Do see tae yer ablutions, Edyth, and we'll be off."

A half of an hour later, she'd readied herself as best she could, grateful for the chance to better scrub the dried blood from her inflamed hands in a trickling, frigid stream. They'd fed her some oats and water in a cup, promising better fare the next time they stopped, and helped her to mount.

Her muscles had protested returning to Harris's back, but Ewan was warm and comforting, and before long, her muscles eased enough to forget their pain. Ewan kept up a steady stream of questions related to her wellbeing, which had both annoyed and endeared her.

He'd told her earlier that they'd crossed onto Livingstone the night before, which bordered his own land on the south. He'd pointed out unfamiliar plants, giving her their Gaelic names, which she tried to repeat, but the vowels were slippery and unusual from her own dialect, making him laugh a few times. He was a patient teacher, though, and she found herself relaxing enough to speak more openly with him.

Now as it was, the sun was high, and the clouds had parted well enough to burn off the perpetual fog that covered them. She could better see the bright greens and yellows of spring that helped to lighten her heavy heart. Something about Iain's sincere thanks and Ewan's comforting presence helped to shift her mind away from her own pain.

"Thank you," said Edyth, smelling a white flower Ewan had plucked for her.

"For what do I deserve your thanks, lady?" he asked, his thighs flexing as he directed Harris over a rocky outcropping. "Ye've had quite the adventure since leaving home," said Ewan, "and I regret that I've added tae yer discomfort. I'm sorry for the suffering I've caused ye." The thrum of his voice vibrated against her back, warming her further.

She shook her head, which was resting quite boldly against the broad expanse of his chest. "It seems we both suffer from misplaced guilt," she muttered, feeling only gratitude for Ewan's escort, river crossings, and ambushes aside.

He cleared his throat and then said, curiosity evident in his voice, "Ye told me that ye wished to belong tae no king, yet I must know, after all that has befallen you, if ye are happy with yer choice. Do ye wish now that ye had stayed home? You'd be dry and far less traumatized, at least, and not at the mercy of strangers."

Edyth thought about his words, staring at the trail ahead but not seeing it. While she might not have fallen in a river and nearly drowned, she had no guarantee that she would be dry or even safe had she stayed in England. She would be as a beggar, surely, and under the perilous care of the church. Father Brewer would ensure her death. She was sure of it. In fact, though she could not prove it, she suspected that he had been behind the continued attacks on her home and person. She was even more sure that had she stayed in England, she would currently be buried near her mother and father...or imprisoned until she confessed. And imprisonment was far worse than death, to her mind.

The word *home* did not set comfortably in her mind, at least when associated with England. That spot of land would forever be stained with spilled blood. "Home" had left *her* when her parents had died and those whom she'd thought had loved her had turned against her. She would not find a place in England, no. She hoped to find a place in Scotland.

Ignoring his question, she spoke her heart, which she found surprisingly easy with Ewan, even after so much betrayal. With him behind her, her face hidden from his view, she felt as though she were in confession, masked and safe from judgment. "Ewan," she said, using his Christian name. She'd used it before because he'd insisted, but now it felt different. Something between them had changed. They were friends now, instead of forced acquaintances.

"I must be cursed," she said, thinking about her recent past. "I don't know what sin I've committed to displease God, but he is angry with me." Her voice was small and full of regret. "I mean...I've killed since, which is enough to cause damnation, but before this all happened, I was innocent."

He made an interrogative noise in his throat and readjusted his plaid around them more securely, re-tucking the ends beneath her thighs, one end of the plaid tucked under the opposite leg, and so the same with the other, so they were cocooned together. "Ye think it a sin tae protect yer own life? Or that of another?"

Edyth bit her lip, thinking of Ewan saving her from that man in the forest with his dirk. "No, I suppose not," she said. "But I feel as though I've done wrong. I feel...soiled by it."

She felt Ewan nod, his chin brushing the top of her head. "That's a sure sign that ye've a good heart and a clean soul, lass" said Ewan with authority. "That feeling ye describe—being soiled— it fades o'er time." She felt him stretch and roll his right shoulder, pushing her forward slightly. "My father told me, before I left tae fight in France, that the only way through the shame of taking a life was tae live yer own well. With honor. It's a sort of payment...justice, for what ye've taken."

"Like making amends?"

She felt him shake his head, pausing as though searching for the right words." War is a damn filthy business. The men ye face are just as scairt as ye are. The others around ye help tae keep yer feet planted where they belong, which is a blessing in and of itself. They wouldn't likely thank ye for turning tail and running off, no more than you would care for being left alone on the field. But when the command comes, and ye must kill or be killed, ye cannae think about yer principles on morality. But it's what comes after that takes the most courage."

He was silent for a long while, and Edyth imagined that he was somewhere else, reliving some scene. She waited patiently, not wanting to press him. Finally, she felt him shrug as though casting off a shroud. "Well, what I meant tae say is that if ye find that ye're one o' the few left standing, there'll be ghosts. There will be plenty of time tae think about what ye've done in the name o' some unseen king afterward. Ye lose a part o' yerself in battle, and the bits that are left... they are what ye must build your life upon thereafter. I pray, God, that what's left of my soul is worthy of the lives I've taken."

They moved in silence, and Edyth knew, with a conviction she did not understand, that Ewan was a good man. "What if your broken bits—your soul—is sullied. Deemed unfit for God or family or whomever?"

Ewan took a deep breath, his chest expanding and pressing against her back. "Well, I cannae say what will happen for all men, for I can only speak of my own soul. I didn't always feel that I was worthy of my life. Why did I live in place of another mother's son? But I remembered what my father had told me, who knew something of war. Have ye ever seen a house built without a foundation?" he asked.

She had. Several of the crofters, in their haste to build a place for animals or for themselves, before weather turned poor, built right upon the ground. Without the careful stacking of fieldstone and mortar, the structures were constantly susceptible to vermin and flooding. The walls were often pushed to and fro by the harsh winds that blew down the valley as well. Before long they would fall down completely.

"It is the same of people, aye? Ye take what's good of yerself, and ye build upon it as ye would the foundation of yer home. Ye patch yer life back, bit by bit, until yer foundation is whole once more. Otherwise, those that have no foundation, they crumble and fall and often turn to things that distract them from themselves for a time."

"Distractions?"

"Drinking, gambling, whoring, and the like, begging yer pardon," he added, in deference to her delicate sex.

She shrugged and asked, "So you must choose honor—live for a purpose—to show that you respect those you had to kill?"

"Aye. It shows that they died for a purpose, and no' so some fool can return home tae drink himself into oblivion. It's yer life for theirs, so ye must live what time ye have left well. The alternative is to live a useless life, to crumble and fall. I had to choose how I would live my life."

"You chose to build." It wasn't a question. She could see the fruits of his choice plainly before her. Edyth didn't feel as though the brigand she'd felled with the borrowed sword had been living a life of good works, and she couldn't begin to make a judgment on the Douglas men who had fallen at her hand, but she wanted to believe that *she*, at least, had lived an honorable life up to now. She thought of her parents then and her choices. Would they feel honored? She hoped so. What would her father have said if he had seen her choices? She hoped he would be proud, if not unashamed.

"How—" she cleared her throat and tried again, "how long before the ghosts leave you?"

He sighed; she felt the breath stir the hair on the top of her head. "I dinnae ken. Some will stay with ye longer than others, but it *will* get easier tae abide them."

They rode on for a way in silence. Edyth hardly noticed the changing landscape as they climbed, her mind far away.

"Why would ye say ye're cursed?" asked Ewan after a time, bringing her back to her original question.

She took a deep breath, not sure of the words. "Isn't that the way of the world?" she asked, cocking her head over her shoulder so her words would reach him more easily. "God punishes us in our fallen states. He shows mercy to those who love him best and doles out punishment to those who do not love him enough."

"Ye have a strange view of God, lass, but what crime are ye to have committed? Have ye murdered or robbed? Have ye committed adultery or forsaken the sick and hungry?"

Edyth's brow furrowed at his questions. She supposed she hadn't murdered those men, strictly speaking. No, she hadn't done any of those things, yet she *was* cursed. Why else had her parents been taken from her in such a violent fashion?

Perhaps it was that she was strong willed and hadn't always honored her parents' wishes. Didn't God love those who honored their parents in such a way? She'd vexed her mother greatly at times. Nor was she always humble and teachable. Indeed, her mother and father had said she was stubborn more times than she could count. She felt the burden of the sin on her shoulders every day. Perhaps if she'd honored them as God had intended, then she would still have them. Unsure how to put voice to her burden, she said, "What of the curse of Eve? Every woman is punished—cursed—with the pain and anguish of carrying and birthing children. If I'm punished for Eve's sin in the Garden of Eden, wouldn't God also punish me for my parents' sins, in addition to my own?"

Father Brewer had called her mother a "wanton bride of the devil." Surely God would never favor a daughter of such a woman. She continued, "I have neither robbed nor forsaken the lowly, yet still I am punished. Why does God hate women?" she asked, feeling the force of her emotions in her words and was surprised she did not feel embarrassed by her boldness. "I have done all I've ever been told to do. I attended mass, I confessed, I prayed—I don't understand." She sighed sharply, her frustration evident.

She felt Ewan shift, ducking his head as they passed under a low branch. His body pushed hers forward as he did so, and she felt the broad expanse of his chest connect fully with her back. She closed her eyes, imagining it as a hug. It felt like ages since she'd been touched. Her heart ached for connection. For acceptance.

"I don't think he hates any of his creations," he said in her ear, making little goosebumps appear along her neck.

"How can you say so?" she asked, twisting her torso to look him in the face. He was very close and smelled wonderfully of outdoors and something wholly male that she could not define. She lowered her voice, her face heated from their forced intimacy. "What of the curse of Eve? What of the female plight to be owned and at the mercy of her husband? God has placed us beneath men, and I cannot account for it."

Ewan considered her, his mouth turned down in a frown as he thought. She turned back around, sure that he would have nothing to say against her argument.

"If ye are cursed for being a woman, then so am I for being a man." At her scoff, he pressed, "A man must give an oath of homage to a king he may or may not love. He is bound as his vassal and must offer his life, property, and heirs to his lord. I have bled in France for a king I do not love. Is this a curse from God?"

She'd never considered such a thing. Men were those with rights and privileges she would never have. Yes, they had to go to battle, but women had the burden of waiting, which she'd always considered far worse. Action was always preferable to idle worry in her mind.

"Isn't the king's claim to the throne given by God?" she asked, choosing a new line of attack.

When she felt him nod, she continued, "If a king is appointed by God, then were you not fighting for a holy purpose in France? We are commanded to love God. Service to your king is service to God."

"I do not believe that all of man's ambitions are God's will. The king, in his greed, has stretched his hand beyond his rightful place. I believe he will be held accountable for the lives he's wasted. Scotia is nae full of heathens. Nor is France, so how can the king's purposes be holy? He is fueled only by greed."

"What if God is greedy?" she asked boldly.

"If God is greedy, wouldn't he cease to be God? How could God command us to be something he is not?"

Edyth did not know. Her thoughts bounced around in her head; she had more questions than answers, and so she fell silent. If the king was in error—who was supposed to have been called by God himself—then could Father Brewer also be wrong? His acts and lies disgusted her. How could she separate the church's servants from God? They were compelled to do his will, were they not?

Finally, she said, "You believe that a man, called to the throne by God himself, can be in error?"

"Och, aye," he said as though he wasn't committing blasphemy. "If I ken one thing, I ken what it is tae be a *man*. I may be created in his holy image, but my thoughts are nae often aligned as they ought tae be. A king is nae different than any other man. It's our choices that please God, less so than what our sires have done."

Edyth felt her heart quicken at his words. She wanted to believe them. "What of the church then? Do you believe the church can be in error? You...you'll remember I spoke of my mother?" She could say no more, waiting with bated breath.

"Aye, I remember," he said. "I dinnae ken the man who condemned her, and I dinnae ken yer mam, but I can see the fruits of her efforts in ye. How could a mother wi' evil in her heart raise a lass such as yerself, who I have only seen tae be kind and forthright? A man of God is just as corruptible as any. In truth, I believe that any man or woman sworn tae live God's laws will be held to a higher standard. Her condemner will be punished for his misdeeds."

Her heart warmed slightly from his words. She wanted them to be true, but her experiences were a harsh teacher.

"I've always thought God had a rather high regard for women," said Ewan. She felt him shrug and stretch his shoulder again. "Despite what men might preach otherwise, God would nae have given such deference tae Mary, aye?"

Edyth fell silent, thinking on his words. She knew all too well the cruelty—and previous kindnesses—of those who had once loved her. She'd never before considered that a man of God could be corruptible until now. Before Father Brewer's lies had spread through their village like wildfire, she'd stupidly swallowed all his words and now could find no way to sift through the tangle he'd created. Where did God's truth stand and Father Brewer's lies begin? What else had he lied about?

Maybe all men were alike, bent by the winds that blew them. But no, there was her father who did not bend easily, at least not to malfeasance, and this man, Ewan, whom she found to be decent. But how was she to know for certain? How would she ever know and recognize the difference?

"Tell me of your childhood," suggested Ewan, changing the subject. "What talents did yer parents foster in ye?"

"The usual, I expect. Except," she paused, a smile coming to her face, "my father had no sons to teach swordplay or hunting, so he did much in secret until my mother put a stop to it. She said that the baron would not want a wife who was schooled in such unladylike subjects."

"A baron?" asked Ewan. "Ye're betrothed then?"

Edyth waved a hand in a dismissive fashion. "I was. Once. He never came back from the king's campaign in France."

"Och, I'm sorry."

Edyth shook her head. "No, I didn't want to marry him. I was relieved, as shameful as that is."

"Ye didn't want tae be a baroness?" he asked, surprise coloring his voice.

"Much to my mother's dismay, no. I knew better than complain about it, but she knew. She'd lecture me often enough about me doing my duty. She used to say that marriage was the only form of business a woman could indulge in that could reap any real wealth. I was prepared to do my part, but a title such as that means little to me."

"I would think you are uncommon for an English maiden."

Edyth frowned, wondering at his meaning. "Because I do not want to marry a stranger, only for a title?"

She felt him nod. "That, and yer father's attention tae yer education. Swordplay?" he said with a laugh, and then he sobered. "Yes, I can see that now. Ye wielded that sword against the deserter in the glade."

She said nothing, listening to Harris's huffing as they climbed a steep ridge.

"Tis a compliment I give ye, Edyth." He gave her a nudge with his shoulder, pulling a reluctant smile from her. "I spar in the yard with my retainers every morning at dawn. I would see ye there," he teased. "What other unladylike subjects have ye fostered? I must know," he asked, a smile in his voice.

She smiled in turn. "I had a good friend, James, who tutored me all subjects boisterous, irreverent, and unladylike. We used to take turns spitting from the balcony of the church." Her cheeks pinkened at the admission. What a little horror she'd been. "My talent grew to the point that I could hit any target he dared me to. Once I hit the priest's biretta as he passed under the balcony into the nave."

Ewan did laugh then, a rich, throaty sound that was infectious.

She laughed herself, feeling lighter than she had in weeks.

"A moving target! Was he also your archery tutor?" he asked, a smile in his voice.

Edyth laughed despite herself and then grimaced. "Sadly, yes. Initially my father had encouraged the sport, but after my mother had put an end to it, James took up the mantle of teacher. To be fair to them both, I am simply out of practice."

"To be fair to *you*," he said, "it's one thing to practice hitting a target for amusement and quite another to use a bow in open combat."

How true that had turned out to be.

They rode on in an easy silence until Graham, who was not so far ahead as not to be seen, slowed his horse and waited for them to approach. When they reached him, Edyth gasped at the view. They stood at the edge of a tall bluff overlooking a city.

"Bothwell, Milday," said Graham.

The city below sparked gold in the late afternoon sun. A huge cylindrical donjon sat high on a steep bank, overlooking a wide river. Smaller buildings were set in neat rows along the river's edge and beyond, hugging the hills.

"We'll have a good meal tonight!" said Fingal, bringing up the rear. Iain's horse was tied to his saddle. It couldn't have come at a better time, thought Edyth at seeing Iain's pale, stricken face.

"Aye, and a proper bed," added Graham.

It didn't take long for them to descend the ridge overlooking the quaint city. Edyth wished she had two sets of eyes; there was so much to see. There seemed to be people everywhere, driving goats, sheep, and cattle. They passed wagon after wagon, full of wares, lumber, straw, and she'd even seen a man with a cart full of bolts of cloth. It appeared to be a very wealthy city, but when she'd shared her thoughts, Ewan had explained that they were most likely the taxmen, returning home after gathering their share of the quarterly rents.

They passed many shops, some of which emanated delicious smells that made her stomach growl with hunger. It had been many days since she'd had a hot meal.

They dismounted in the muddy, bustling yard of a rather squat building. Geese ran, honking noisily, trying to avoid a young boy chasing them with a stick. Several young men left the shadowy confines of a sparse, leaning outbuilding to take their horses. Ewan handed them each a coin, nodding his thanks, and then he led the way to the door of the establishment.

Edyth's legs were rather wobbly, but with the promise of food and proper rest, she forgot all about her aching joints and raw skin. Ewan spoke with a slender, hunched old woman, gesturing to the company standing near the door, and before long, she found herself in a small attic room, washing her face and hands from a clay ewer and basin. She sighed, content, and looked around the room. There was a sturdy looking bed, complete with a straw stuffed mattress, a bedside table complete with candle and flint, and a shuttered window.

She pushed aside the shutters and spied an alleyway full of crates and barrels not far below. The smells of a city met her nose, human and animal waste mingled with woodsmoke. The sun was setting, painting the opposite structure with golden brushstrokes so it seemed to glow from within. She tried to dust off the grime from so many days on the road but only succeeded in hurting her chapped hands. Giving it up, she tried to smooth her hair into some semblance of order and went down to dinner.

The men were all there, even Iain, who, she was happy to see, had an appetite. Fingal stood and moved down the bench to accommodate her so that she sat sandwiched between him and Ewan. Graham nodded to her from across the table and passed her a horn cup full of ale. Edyth grasped it and had to stop herself from gulping it down. It was golden, earthy, slightly sweet, and delicious. Even after only a few sips, she started to feel a warmth grow and spread through her body.

There were other patrons eating, talking, laughing, and Edyth watched them as they waited to be served. They didn't have to wait long. A rather buxom woman exited the kitchen carrying two large trenchers of food. One was piled high with several small loaves of brown bread. The other held three whole roasted rabbits, golden and crispy, and several lake fish.

Edyth's mouth watered. Ewan broke off a thigh of the largest rabbit and handed it to her without comment. The rest of the men tore their shares of the meal, stabbing the fish with their dirks. She thought it must be the most delicious fare she'd ever had. She even followed Fingal's example and used a bannock to sop up the drippings from the trencher. Edyth had to force herself from licking her fingers clean.

Graham burped loudly then and, remembering Edyth's presence, excused himself. "Apologies, lady," he mumbled, but Edyth merely laughed. She excused herself, feeling the need to wash her hands and relieve herself, but when she stood, she accidently ran right into a very large, very smelly man.

"Oh, my apologies," she muttered, curtseying automatically. "My fault. Please excuse me."

The man's large blue eyes narrowed in a marked manner that told Edyth he didn't like her being there.

"Watch where yer steppin, ye English bitch. I'd teach ye a lesson, but it looks as though someone has saved me the trouble."

The deafening sound of benches being shoved aside filled the room.

All four of her men—for that was how she thought of them in that instant—were standing, equal looks of derision on their faces. Ewan took her upper arm in hand and pulled her behind him. Graham then copied the move, so she was at the back of the party, trying to peer around him to see what was happening.

"Watch how ye speak tae those in my company," growled Ewan, taking a step toward the man who, Edyth thought, was twice the size of him. He was much larger about the middle than Ewan, but he *was* big and could very likely inflict a lot of damage. It didn't seem to deter Ewan, however.

The large, angry man took a menacing step toward Ewan so that they were toe to toe, looking as though he'd like to spit in his face. Edyth's heart hammered. Iain was standing, but he looked rather pale, and she knew he would not do well if a fight ensued.

"Yer English whore is in my way," said the big, red-faced man. "She is no whore," said Fingal, his voice full of gravel. "Ye'll apologize tae the lady. Now."

His lip curled; the man looked past the men to Edyth, whose very purple, swollen face was peeking around Graham's elbow.

"Aye, she's too ugly tae be a whore. Where did ye find such a creature? Ye should have put her out of her misery instead of making a pet o' her."

Edyth didn't have time to be offended. Iain was swaying on his feet, and she had to do something quickly.

Without deciding to, Edyth dipped around Graham and pushed to the front. Ewan caught a fistful of her skirts and pulled her back toward him, but she did her best to ignore him. Her heart hammered a tattoo against her ribs, but she lifted her chin and faced her foe.

"Come now," she said, her voice steady despite her fear. "Let's not spoil the evening with such hostilities." Her good eye roved around the room. She took a deep breath and tried her best to force a smile. "I am what you say, sir: English. I don't like it any more than you do, but what is to be done?" she asked. "As you say, I've plainly already been punished for it," she said, gesturing to her swollen face. "It wouldn't be sporting to punish me twice."

Some unseen person shouted, "Aye, leave off, Lach!"

"I cannot help it," continued Edyth, "that I was born on the wrong side of this island, any more than you can help being born with such an unpleasant personality."

The man's steely gaze flickered from her to those standing behind her. Not a sound was heard in the small room for several heart beats. Surely it would pound straight out her chest if the man in front of her did not first pound her into dust.

But he did not strike her or anyone else. The uncomfortable silence was broken by an inelegant snort followed by a high-pitched titter. His lip twitched as though he, himself, were trying not to smile.

The creaking of the kitchen door was overly loud to her ears as the maid entered once again, her hands full of pints. Sizing up the issue at once, she marched right over to them and pushed Lachlan aside with her hip. "We'll have none this nonsense, aye? Ye'll all sit yerselves doon and eat."

When no one moved immediately, the kitchen maid's eyes narrowed dangerously. "Ave ye got neeps in yer ears? Sit and eat or get out!"

"Pah," said Lachlan, dismissing them all with a wave of his hands. "No' worth it. My supper's getting cold anyhow." And with that, he turned his back onto them and took his place on his bench seat.

Edyth's legs felt like jelly; she took a steadying breath and turned to Ewan. His eyes held an emotion she could not begin to name.

"Iain cannot afford a fight," she whispered in explanation.

He nodded once, a bewildered look upon his face. He seemed to shrink as his shoulders lost their tension.

"I'm going to my room," she said, nodding to each of the men in turn, all wearing similar looks of bafflement. "I will be back soon. Please...please don't fight on my account."

She was halfway up the stairs before she realized that Ewan was following her. "Do ye always rush headlong into danger, Edyth?" he asked, making her jump. She clutched her hand to her heart. She could feel its wild rhythm even in her ears.

Edyth wondered how much more her heart could take. "No more than you."

"I couldn't let ye go alone," he said as explanation for his sudden appearance.

She turned and continued up the rickety flight of stairs to her door. "Thank you for taking up for me." The corridor was dark, and she couldn't see his face properly, but she thought the flash of white teeth meant a smile rather than a grimace.

"You're full of surprises, Edyth."

She didn't know what to say, so she said nothing. They both stood there, staring at each other in the dim light. The silence stretched on. Ewan's frame seemed to fill the small space, taking all the air with it.

She felt both hot and cold at the same moment, equally triumphant and alarmed at her daring nerve. A large, warm hand grasped her own. Ewan turned her palm to his view, the blistered skin winking pink in the low light. A finger, as soft as a feather, touched her palm, then just as softly, her swollen cheek. "What that man said... ye should not believe it, Edyth. Never has a lass been more beautiful than ye are at this moment."

The breath caught in her throat, her heart skittering. She thought of her shorn hair, her bruised face, her broken hands, and she could not see any beauty in them, but still, his words were a balm to her bruised pride. Lachlan's words had been hurtful, though she'd done her level best to distract herself from them. They were there, though, pinned to her mind for later reflection.

"Yes, in the dark, I'm bound to be," she said, choosing humor over truth. It was safer to tease than to expose the painful truth that her pride had been wounded.

Ewan gripped her fingers in his own and shook his head, his lips pulled into a smile. "I would still think ye bonny were I blind."

Edyth blushed hotly and felt stupid with inexperience. What could she say in return? That she thought him beautiful as well? Thank you? Instead, she stammered, "I'll be right back," as she opened the door to her room and slipped inside. Once separated from Ewan, away from his overwhelming presence, she leaned heavily against the door, feeling as though she'd run a race.

* * *

The evening turned out to be rather pleasurable, despite their earlier hang-up with the Scot, Lachlan. After seeing to Iain's injury—Edyth was happy to see the swelling greatly reduced—she'd returned to the public room for some entertainment.

Edyth had been surprised to see that the man Lachlan, along with two others from his party, was now sitting at their table, playing dice with Graham and Fingal. She sat with them, watching the game, listening quietly to their banter.

Before long, the banter slowed, and the subject turned to war. *While that English whoreson Longshanks might have the advantage of a larger cavalry, he's no match fer our brains. We are better positioned. The French will support our cause. They don't know these mountains as we do.* Of course, everyone agreed, and on and on it went.

Finally, having her fill of superior Scottish weapons, brains, allies, and everything else under the sun, Edyth stood to go to bed. Having had quite a bit of wine to drink herself, she offered a parting gift to the glassy-eyed men seated around the room.

"It seems to me," she said, thinking to offer the logic that was so obviously missing from the conversation, "that you might learn at least one thing from the English, despite all your superiority." All eyes rested on her then, and she prided herself that she didn't blush or stammer. Emboldened by the drink, she cleared her throat to be better heard. "At least English soldiers are smart enough to protect themselves with deerskin breeks. Even that bit of protection is better than bared legs."

"Och, aye," said Graham, good humor glinting in his good eye. "They might at that, but do ye think bollocks like ours would fit in wee English breeks?"

Edyth's face flushed crimson, and she closed her mouth with an audible snap. The roar of laughter that met his remark carried her all the way up to her room.

As Edyth lay in the bed, grateful for the safety and solitude of her room, she felt a lightness in her heart she never thought to be reacquainted with. She felt that, among these men, she had found a bit of herself she'd thought she'd lost, maybe a good bit of foundation to build upon.

That night, she did not dream of her parents.

Chapter Eight

It was late into the next day when they finally made it to Ruthven land. The village of Perthshire was quaint and spread with lush, rolling hills, building in height until they kissed the feet of the rugged, snowcapped mountains beyond. A wide, glassy river wound lazily through the center of the village, snaking in and out of the hills to disappear far to the north. Inviting, grassy flats swept from the hills to the river so that the banks were as a glade, verdant and rich with spring pasture. The rich browns of recently tilled earth set in neat rows surrounded huts and houses of all kinds. A large tower house set a good distance away from the river drew Edyth's eye.

Ewan and his men stopped on the peak of a hill to take in their home in the setting sun. A hawk screamed overhead, gliding across the vast expanse and into the sun, where it disappeared.

"It's beautiful," said Edyth on an exhale. Perhaps the scene was so vastly welcome simply because it meant the end of a long, arduous, and extremely dangerous week, but it was a very welcome sight. "Aye. Truly," muttered Ewan, who seemed to appreciate the view as much as she.

All that day Ewan had answered Edyth's questions about his childhood in Perthshire. She'd enjoyed hearing about his habits and pastimes. She'd learned he had an older sister, married and gone now, whom he had teased and tormented to no end. His younger sister, Cait, still lived at home with their mother, whom, in his maturity, he'd chosen to dote upon rather than torment. He'd fostered with the Caimbel clan from the age of seven to twelve, where he'd been educated in the domestic arts as well as in the skills of knighthood.

Upon returning home at the age of twelve, he'd been tutored by a monk in languages and history, which he hadn't cared for, much preferring working with his hands over memorizing scripts and phrases in Latin, to which she heartily related.

She'd been sorry to hear of his father's passing and Ewan's absence for the last two years while he fought for their allies, the French. Ewan's father, Malcolm, had cleverly played both sides of the political divide, publicly showing support of the English king by pledging his fealty and coin but privately sending his eldest son to fight for France with a handful of fighting men.

Edyth had been mostly sheltered from politics, only hearing secondhand the goings-on from servants and from listening at doors. She'd known, of course, that the two countries' long-standing friendship had come to an end when her king had cunningly subjugated himself into Scotland by demanding an oath of homage from the Scot's king, Baliol, which he'd had no choice but to do.

Ewan had explained to her, further, that King Edward had grown angry when Baliol's nobles—his own father among them—had refused to supply the English with men for his war against the French. In retaliation, he'd sacked Berwick, killing over ten thousand people. This put Ewan in a tenuous position as the new earl of Perth. Ewan would have to make some profound decisions, and soon, that could harm his people and their way of life.

"If I pledge my fealty, as many others have done," he'd said, "and Edward takes Scotland, my lands will stay intact. I may even be granted more lands, as a reward. If not"—he'd shrugged— "I could lose all. Either way, men will die. But for which cause should they fight? Land? Or for freedom?"

Edyth wasn't sure of the correct answer herself but wondered what course of action Ewan might take.

As they neared Ewan's home, he explained about its construction. The tower house was a modern, newly constructed four-story goliath. Other buildings, including the great hall and a kitchen, stood beside the house, both of similar construction: stone and mortar, tall and elegant. The thick outer wall surrounding the outbuildings could only be breached through the portcullis, which was a menacing, many-toothed thing, heavily armed with archers and pike men.

Many people, most of whom she could not see, hidden in their places of duty as they were, shouted out their welcomes at their laird's return. Somewhere a bell rang cheerily, heralding their arrival. When they entered the inner courtyard, a door set about six feet off the ground opened suddenly, revealing two women, dressed rather richly, one old and one young.

The younger raced down the stone steps to the packed earth and gravel yard, her dark hair blowing about her in the wind. Her face, which had reflected her joy at seeing her brothers come home again, faltered, changed, and slipped into a question when she noticed Edyth wrapped tightly in a plaid with Ewan. The older woman—Ewan's mother, Edyth supposed—descended the stairs much more sedately than her daughter but with much the same expression.

Ewan pulled the plaid off them and dismounted, picking up the younger woman and giving her a bone-crushing hug that made her laugh. She looked expectantly around and found Iain's ashen, weak frame.

"What's happened to you, Iain? Ye look as though ye've swallowed nettles."

Iain attempted a smile, the corner of his mouth twitching. "He's injured and been fevering for three days," said Ewan by way of explanation, greeting his mother with a hug.

"What's happened tae the gomerel?" asked the younger woman, her worried expression belying her words. Graham helped Iain to dismount and held him steady while Fingal took their horses away with a respectful nod at his lady.

Ewan reached up and helped Edyth down, who was pleased her legs did not collapse completely. They felt like water, but she only needed a brief, steadying hand from Ewan.

"Oh, I stepped in front of an arrow no' meant for me," said Iain airily, a smile in his weak voice. The two women gasped, identical expressions of shock and worry on their faces.

"What happened? Who was shooting at ye?" asked the younger woman, making Edyth's face erupt with heat. The wind whipped through the yard, disrupting their skirts. The older woman's mourning veil blew violently about in the wind.

"Please take him in, Graham," said Ewan, ignoring his sister's question. "A storm is coming, and he'll no' thank me for getting him wet again."

Graham nodded and followed Ewan's command, half dragging, half carrying the man away to the stairs. Edyth wondered how they would traverse the obstacle when Ewan spoke again, pulling her eyes away.

"We ran into some English deserters," said Ewan succinctly, dismissing the details as though they were trivial. He touched Edyth's elbow, drawing her eyes. "This is Lady Edyth DeVries. She's been tending tae Iain."

Edyth curtseyed as best she could. Her legs were so wobbly that she feared she might fall on her face, but she managed it with only a little wobbling.

"This is my mother, the dowager countess Ruthven," said Ewan, nodding in her direction. "And this is my sister, Catriona."

The two women's gazes settled on Edyth. They smiled politely and curtseyed with questions in their eyes.

"Come," said the dowager countess, looking at the darkening sky with a slight frown. "I suppose yer all hungry and eager for rest. There will be something in the kitchens to tide ye over until we sup."

Edyth had been shown to a richly appointed room on the third floor by a servant, who'd later brought her some hot water, linen for cleaning herself, and a bit of food. The servant had helped her undress and had taken her borrowed, blood-smeared gown for cleaning, leaving her in her rather smelly shift. Edyth had been too tired to care that she had nothing to change into, only having eyes for the large bed piled high with quilts. She cleaned herself gratefully, however, grimacing at the soiled condition of the cloth after she was finished. She must have been quite the sight. Edyth then gave into the temptation and fell upon the bed, oblivious to the world around her.

She didn't know how long she'd slept, but it couldn't have been long. She was awoken by a servant nudging her awake, muttering under her breath. She was a quick woman for her age. Small and shrunken, hunched and toothless though she was, she shuffled in quickstep from place to place with surprising speed. Edyth's mind struggled to awaken, and she sat up, rubbing the sleep from her eyes.

"Lady Cait's lent ye some clothes, seeing as yer's need tending to," she said as way of greeting. "Lift yer arms. That's a good lass."

Edyth obeyed, bending over to accommodate the differences in their heights, then stood to let the soft, clean chemise fall to her ankles. The bliaut presented to her was a rusted red color that she vainly worried would clash with her hair, but she pushed those thoughts aside as quickly as they surfaced. She was grateful to simply be wearing something clean for a change. It felt like ages since she'd had anything that felt so grand.

The servant then brushed Edyth's short, knotted hair with a boar's brush she pulled out of her pocket, *tsking* loudly. She pulled out several grass tassel heads and seeds from various other plants, handing them to Edyth in a marked manner as though to shame her, but Edyth only fiddled with them abstractly as the woman attempted to tame her uneven locks into a semblance of order.

In the end, the woman braided clumps of hair on each side of her head and pulled the braids to the back, effectively hiding the shorn portion of hair, while also making her out to be somewhat civilized. She made no mention of Edyth's bruised face, but Edyth caught her eye twice as the woman tried not to look.

"There noo," said the servant, grunting softly as she bent to pick up Edyth's discarded underclothes. "I'll show ye down tae the hall then."

Dinner was served on the lower level in a private rectangular room complete with a sizable hearth. Large clay pots sat in and around the fire filled with food carted in from the kitchen outside using wooden poles so that the carriers didn't burn their hands.

There was a long table set in the middle of the room, a high candelabra lighting the fare on each end. The far wall boasted a Ruthven coat of arms—two rather majestic rams battling on a shield of red and white—set prettily above an elaborate tapestry depicting a hunting scene.

There were several people already seated, only some of whom she recognized. Ewan stood when she approached, waving her over to the table, his head tilted to better hear the man on his left. He nodded to the man, speaking in a rapid, guttural language she assumed was Gaelic, but he stopped as she reached him, giving her a smile.

"Lady Edyth," he said, his white teeth flashing in the candlelight. "Ye look very bonny this e'en. Please, do ye sit, and I'll introduce ye around. This is my captain, Rory," he said, indicating the man he'd been speaking to.

Rory stood with alacrity, offering her his seat. "Pleasure," he mumbled. He was just as tall as Ewan but with shoulder-length salt-and-pepper hair. His bonnet had a handsome woodpecker's tail feather stuck in it at an angle.

"Thank you," she said, "but you needn't give up your seat, Sir Rory. I do not need special treatment."

"Yer a guest o' the Ruthven's, Me Leddy," said Rory, a heavy brogue accenting his speech. She smiled despite herself, loving the sound of it. He took her hand, bowing over it. "Ye'll be made tae feel out o' sorts fer all our doting." He kissed her hand, his whiskers prickling her skin. She liked him immensely.

Touching Edyth's elbow, Ewan drew her attention to his mother, seated behind him. "You'll remember my mother."

She was a tall woman, slightly built, but appearing strong for someone of her age. Her face was shadowed from the wimple she wore, but when she turned in greeting, Edyth saw from whom Ewan had inherited his dimple. She was a strikingly beautiful woman with dark blue eyes, long lashes, and age lines indicating a life full of laughter. She smiled kindly in greeting. "Good e'en to ye, Lady DeVries."

Edyth curtseyed, lowering herself with more confidence after her rest. "And to you, Dowager Countess."

The dowager motioned for Edyth to rise, appraising her with eyes so like Ewan's. "Ye are welcome here, lass. Please make this yer home so long as ye'd like. Come, sit by me so I might satisfy myself with endless questions."

Edyth blanched slightly at the comment but saw the smile in the woman's eyes. Ewan pushed her chair in. She felt jittery but didn't quite know if it was from lack of food or from nervousness.

"Cait is late again, I see," mumbled the dowager, her eyes drifting to the door, then back. "Ewan, do see that a servant goes and fetches that wretched girl. That's a good lad." She sighed and motioned for a servant to fill their cups. "My daughter is a lively creature, constantly flitting about in a fury of activity but is forever vexing me with her tardiness. How a lass with her brains cannae attend tae the time, I dinnae ken."

Edyth smiled, warming to Cait already, having been scolded so often by her own mother for the same reasons. She shrugged. "Tis the curse of raising a daughter, I suppose. My mother used to say that I would purposefully apply all my energy in the wrong pursuits simply to vex her."

The dowager's thin eyebrows rose in consideration. "Och, aye? Mayhap I was just as troublesome tae me own mam, but I cannae recall. That's the blessing of old age, I suppose." She chuckled and lifted her cup of cider to her lips. She paused before drinking and winked cheekily. "Ye cannae recall yer own sins or at least be troubled by them if ye do."

The table was very richly dressed, with tall pewter candelabras that held elegantly shaped tapers. The light from the narrow cross-shaped windows was weak, but Edyth could see that the sun was low in the sky. Wind whistled through the openings intermittently, sending the flames dancing atop their wicks. The wall and floor were wet where the rain had blown through, and Edyth was again reminded how blessed she was to be out of the elements and here at Ruthven keep.

"How are ye liking Perthshire so far?" the dowager countess asked.

"It's very beautiful," replied Edyth. "I've never seen such mountains."

"Aye, I suppose ye'll no' see much in the way of mountains in Carlisle."

Edyth shook her head and took a sip, glancing around the room. She saw Fingal enter, bowlegged as ever, but his long hair had been combed back, his receding hairline accentuated. She'd seen Graham when she'd entered earlier, in discussion with someone she hadn't met, but not Iain. She felt bad for not having tended to him as soon as they arrived, but she'd been so tired and perhaps they had their own physic.

"Erm," she started, replacing her goblet. "Will Iain be joining us?"

The dowager's long mouth curved into a slight frown. "He's sleeping, and I didn't wish tae wake him. When he does, he'll be fed forthwith, dinnae ye worry." She patted Edyth's hand absently. "I ken ye've a touch o' the healing arts about ye, as Ewan said, and I thank ye for your attentions tae Iain on the road. How lucky it was that my boys came tae find ye."

How lucky indeed. Without them, she would be dead...or at least wishing she were. But then again, if it hadn't been for her, Iain wouldn't have been wounded.

"How is it they came by ye?" asked the dowager, her keen eyes sweeping to her own, pinning her to the spot.

Edyth swallowed heavily, her fingers knotted in her lap. What would the woman think of her? Surely Ewan had already told her all—or at least part—of her story. She knew she was from Carlisle at the least. Edyth took a breath, careful with her words.

"Luck was on my side. Your sons followed the smoke from my campfire while looking for thieves, which was fortunate as they'd just appeared before me."

The woman nodded knowingly, her eyes penetrating. "Aye, fortunate indeed. A blessing from God, no doubt, that ye had the presence of mind tae build that fire. Otherwise, they wouldn't have known where to look."

Edyth fiddled with her cup, transported back to the wood. She hadn't considered what might have happened if she *hadn't* built that fire. She would most likely still be out there, wandering aimlessly, cold, afraid, and in considerable danger. At the time, she'd taken the time to start the fire simply out of fear and from cold and then had cursed her rotten luck—and stupidity—once the brigands had appeared. Before the dowager had mentioned it, she hadn't considered that God had any sort of hand in it at all. She didn't know and probably never would.

"How did ye come by such a mark?" asked the woman pointedly. "No need tae be embarrassed, lass," she added as Edyth's hand immediately went to the bruise on her cheek. "I wouldnae normally ask, but Ewan tells me that ye've had more than yer fair share o' trouble. Did yer man do this tae ye? Is that why ye were running awa'?"

Edyth shrugged, uncomfortable. She didn't want to speak of her reasons here, where anyone might hear. Luckily, she was saved having to answer, for Cait appeared then, as bright as the sun, drawing everyone's attention.

"Ah, here is the lass, but what of Ewan?" asked the dowager. Cait was a beauty, and Edyth was immediately envious of her. Her chestnut hair fell in a ribbon down her back, all her proportions in vogue. She filled her gown much better than Edyth did, as scrawny and knobble kneed as she was. Cait's dark hair, eyes, and ivory skin left Edyth feeling like a freckled toad. But the girl smiled warmly at Edyth, then greeted her mother with a curtsey.

"Yer late again, Caitriona," said her mother, her steely eyes boring into her.

A dainty, long fingered hand swept her silken hair over her shoulder, her cheeks turning pink at being chastised. "Aye, Mam. I'm sorry," said Cait, her eyes darting to Edyth's, then away. "I'll try tae be more mindful."

"Mmph," said the dowager, a silvery eyebrow raised in doubt. "So I've heard before."

"Mother," said Ewan from behind her, giving her a quick buss on her cheek. "Let the lass be. She was tending after Iain."

Cait smiled at her brother, an expression of thanks on her face. Ewan moved behind his seat on the other side of Edyth and raised his cup. The noise in the room fell away as all eyes turned to their laird. "No happier fortune can be found," said Ewan, his baritone easily reaching all ears, "when such hearts are knit together. And to new friends to share our table." He looked about him, his eyes resting lastly on Edyth. "We are fortunate, indeed, tae have lived another day in freedom." His eyes grew dim, looking inward, and Edyth wondered what he saw. A battlefield in France? Or one to come on his own soil? She felt a chill and shivered slightly, thinking of her own freedom, so recently won.

"The world is changing," said Ewan, looking into his cup. "May God watch over us and direct our feet. *Slàinte mhath.*"

"*Slàinte mhath,*" the room repeated.

Ewan sat down and the buzz of conversation returned to the room. Servants passed out steaming trays piled high with food gathered from the pots in and around the fire. It smelled delicious; Edyth's mouth watered as Ewan cut into a beautifully made meat pie and offered her the first taste as his guest of honor. Necks craned to watch her as she took a dainty bite; she smiled her appreciation. "It's delicious," she said to murmurs of approval around her.

Hands reached as they all filled their own trenchers, and cider was poured into pewter cups. Cait paid little attention to the passing food, her eyes, instead, intent on Edyth. "Are ye really from England, as Ewan says?"

"Yes," replied Edyth, nodding thanks to Ewan as he offered her bread. "Lately of Carlisle. Have you been there?"

Cait's eyes were wide and curious. "Oh, nay. I've ne'r been sae far south," she said, horrified. "What is England like? Is it true all ladies are presented tae the queen at court? Or that ye eat honeyed sweets at every meal?" Cait was clearly hungrier for talk than food. She leaned forward, ignoring the platters of food that passed her.

Edyth smiled despite herself and shook her head. "I've never been to court. My father was quite against such a thing. And as for sweets, I had no say in the dessert menu. If I had, I'd certainly have had the cook prepare cakes in favor to his other fare."

Cait looked disappointed in her answer, but it did not detour her from asking more questions. "Do English knights recite poetry tae their lovers as Lancelot to Guinevere?"

Edyth scoffed. "They are as any other man, self-involved and dreaming of the glories of war." The baron of Wessex hadn't sent her any such attentions, not that she'd minded, but her experience with men left them wanting in romance. She took a sip of her cider, relishing in the good food after so long eating oat cakes and stale bread.

Cait frowned and cast a fleeting glance at her mother, making sure she was preoccupied, no doubt. Edyth saw that the dowager was in conversation with a rather dour-looking man on her right "Is it true Englishmen ne'r laugh?" asked Cait in a loud whisper. "Da always said the English walk around as though they have pikes stuck up their arses." She giggled, her eyes dancing, but then sobered at Ewan's stern look.

"Eat, Cait," commanded Ewan good-naturedly. "Ye'll wag yer tongue til it falls off and die of starvation." He threw a pinched bit of bread at her, which she caught easily in her mouth, but she then blushed under the steely stare of her mother, who, Edyth suspected, didn't miss much of anything. "Sorry, Mam," she muttered.

Casting her eyes to her empty plate and discovering it empty, Cait hurriedly spooned portions of the food from the center of the table onto her trencher, studiously avoiding her mother's eyes.

"What sorts of tales are English lassies told of Scots, then?" asked Ewan, his brow raised in curiosity.

Edyth felt her face warm at the question, thinking of all the tawdry and barbaric stories she'd heard about the Northmen of Scotland, none of which were worth repeating. At least not in this company.

Cait's smile returned to her face, her long fingers pausing on the stem of her goblet. "Oh, ye've got her now, Ewan. Yes, Edyth. Ye must tell us."

"Oh, the usual," she replied with a shrug. "The men are short-tempered, bullish, prone to strong drink, and lust filled."

Cait laughed and clapped. "So no' far from the mark," she said, her eyes twinkling. "And the lassies?"

"The women have wicked tongues and strong backs." Ewan gave Edyth an appraising look.

"That's a mite better than I expected," said Cait, appreciative.

"They have to, you see," continued Edyth, hiding a smile behind her cup. "Otherwise, their drunken husbands would never make it home."

They both laughed, Cait most of all. Her laugh reminded Edyth of the chimes outside of the garden gate at home, a light and pleasant sound, easy to come by with the slightest bit of wind.

"How are Englishwomen perceived then?" Edyth took another bite of her meat pie. It was warm and velvety and danced on her tongue. She couldn't remember ever having a more pleasant supper.

"Och, yer all simpering weaklings, o' course, and all as stiff as boards in their marriage beds," said Cait, lowering her voice so as not to be heard by her mother. Her eyes darted to the dowager and back, alight with good humor. "Tis good tae hear the English think so highly of us. Ye're nay wrong! Has our estimation of the English hit its mark then?"

"I cannot say," said Edyth, shrugging. She didn't know what to make of her people. "Up until recently, I would have said the English are noble and good."

Cait's happy expression faltered at Edyth's serious reply. A knowing look appeared in her eye, one Edyth did not like to see. It robbed her of her playful youth, which she had so been enjoying. "And now what would ye say?"

Ewan reached his arm across the table between the two ladies to spear a piece of fruit with his eating knife. "I would say," he remarked offhandedly, "that Lady Edyth has made a wise choice tae leave her home and venture sae far north, where the fare is sae fine and the company sweet."

Taking the hint to move onto lighter conversation, Cait's soft smile returned, her eyes speaking a hidden language. "Let us eat," said Cait, reaching across the table to briefly squeeze Edyth's hand. "Then we will dance!"

The tables had been pushed to the sides of the room to accommodate the dancers and the shutters thrown open to combat the heat of so many frolicking bodies. A lute was produced and then, after, a drum. The dances were nothing like the solemn, courtly dances of England in which Edyth had been tutored. The quick beat of the drum and the rise and fall of the lute's melody reverberated through the company of dancers, making them spin and leap as though connected by the strings of a marionette.

Happy to watch and clap as others danced, she was shocked and nervous when Ewan suddenly appeared, taking her hand and leading her into the fray. His hand was large and rough with callouses, which swallowed her own.

Smiling, he bent his head to her ear so she would be sure to hear him. "Dinnae tell me yer afraid of a wee carole. Smile, lady. It's supposed tae be fun."

"I don't know the steps," retorted Edyth, even as she hooked her arm through his.

"I willnae let ye fall. Here, take Rab's arm too to make a chain. Good. Just move yer feet, and Rab and I will do the rest."

They moved about the room in a circular motion, feet stamping to match the rhythm of the drum. Then Rab let go of her arm to hold his partner's waist, and Ewan grasped her own. Her stomach seemed to fill with butterflies at his bold touch. He lifted her, swinging her in a circle, then swept her around, her feet moving of their own accord. His hand, so solid in her own, led her to and fro until she was dizzy with laughter. Feeling as light as a bird, she wondered if she were, indeed, flying.

The song ended, and Ewan's smiling eyes met her own. "Ye are a bonny dancer, Edie."

She smiled in return, liking the nickname he'd given her. He squeezed her hand before letting go. They walked to the side of the room where his mother stood with watchful eyes.

"Oh, to be young again," said the dowager, patting her son on the forearm. She smiled, though it didn't quite meet her eyes. "It's a pity your father isnae here. He'd be proud o' the man ye've become."

Kissing his mother's hand, Ewan's eyes softened. "Aye, Mam. Tis a pity he's no' here. Come, dance with yer son. Da willnae mind."

"Och, no, but I thank ye. I've a mind tae go and lay down. I'm suddenly weary."

Standing alone, watching Ewan guide his mother through the throng of people, her happiness deflated slightly. Ewan had spent the majority of his life away, doing his duty. He'd missed so much, fostering away and then in France fighting. It didn't seem right or fair that she, a maiden, lived a life full of memories of time well spent with her parents.

Perhaps Ewan had been right. Perhaps he was the cursed one.

She did not see at first. There was only blackness, but she knew this place. She knew even before it began what she would find. Glossy, green-black wings beat above her in the air, pulsing in rhythm to match her accelerated heart. There would be far too many to count. The rustle of their feathers sent a shiver up her spine. Cold mud seeped between her toes. The wind whipped at her chemise, tugged on her hair. It's only a dream, she lied.

Just as she knew it would, the scene around her blossomed into life with a hundred screeching cries from the crows overhead. She stood on a hill, overlooking the aftermath of a most gruesome battle scene. Just as she had seen before, men and horses lay in their gore, none moving, a feast for the birds. She hugged herself; her shivering arms did nothing to ward off the tide of cold emotion surging up her body, however. She did not want to see it, yet she could not turn away.

Somewhere, a standard snapped against its pole, waiting to be stolen by the wind. She knew this story. She knew how it ended and held her breath, afraid to once again see the dying man who would be at her feet—the man she could not save.

As she thought of him, he materialized before her in the cold dawn. She could hear his labored breathing, wet from his life's blood welling up from his lungs.

Sorrow, as heavy as a stone, weighed her to the earth so that she could not move, forced to witness the scene. Compelled, she met his direct, blue gaze, and a horrible realization juddered through her. She knew these eyes. She knew his curling brown hair, matted with sweat and blood though it was. She knew the strong line of his jaw, stubbled russet gold and red. She recognized the curve of his lips, full and wide and severe, yet beautiful. She hadn't recognized this man before because she hadn't yet met him. But now he had a name.

She felt her mouth form the word, calling to him, but it was carried away by the wind and swallowed up with the cries of the birds.

Her breath caught in her throat at the sight of her friend laying impaled and dying. Frantic, she redoubled her attempt to move her body, to kneel at his side and comfort him, but she was as a statue, condemned to only witness. What was worse, Ewan saw her. His mouth moved soundlessly, blood spilling from his lips. It trailed down the sides of his face where it melded into the muddy ground.

Tears stung her eyes and the back of her throat. The crows were dropping from the sky, eager to tear into the feast laid before them. A large corbie landed on Ewan's chest, its long tail feathers encumbered by the pike protruding up toward the sky, one beady eye registering her. Its cawing reverberated in her ears, jarring and discordant.

The bird hopped closer to his face, cocking its head to better preview the victim, its shiny black beak reflecting the dull light from the sun. It pecked furiously at Ewan's nose, once, twice, tearing tender flesh. Blood bubbled up from his mouth on a cough, spilling down his chin with a sickening gurgle.

Her lament was muted, but she could feel her throat tear with her rage as she shouted at the bird. It peered at her, curious, and spread its wings wide, crying out before it took to the sky. Edyth followed it with her eyes as it rose.

She turned, permitted to follow. The hill tapered up the wide, sweeping slope, strewn with bodies, and at the top of the hill, a magnificent brown stone castle towered over the field. It was vast, with six towers encompassed inside of its ramparts.

Edyth suddenly felt quite queer, as though giddy with illness. The edges of her vision darkened and narrowed until she was blind. And then just as quickly as it had come upon her, the darkness left her, and she was flying as the crow, seeing the landscape race past her far below. Edyth saw the Firth opening up wide, yawning like a huge beast. A flag was being lowered in the yard. She could see it clearly with the keen eyes she was seeing through: an azure shield whereupon three ripened sheafs of wheat were displayed. Gone was the yard, replaced by a gibbet and the shadow of woman, crumbling to dust to be carried off with the wind.

A heavy knock sounded on her door, startling her awake. The room was still dark, but she heard the plaintive bells calling the people to prayer. It would be close to dawn now. Edyth shivered and blinked in an attempt to erase the images from her dream. Yes, only a dream. She wiped her teary cheeks with the back of her hands and sat up.

"Who comes?" called Edyth, her voice raspy from sleep. She swung her legs over the side of her bed and caught her robe, draping it about her shoulders.

"It's Cait" came the muffled voice behind the door. "Unbar your door."

Edyth's feet shuffled into slippers and crossed the rush-strewn floor, her breathing labored. The vision was still playing in her mind, heavy and ominous. *Dream,* she reiterated.

True, as a child, she'd had such dreams from time to time, little hints from the deep recesses of her sleeping mind as to where she'd misplaced her shoe or a favored doll. Only once had a dream foretold of something more ominous, but that had been so very long ago. Besides, her mother and father had encouraged her forget the disaster she'd seen in her long-ago dream, which she'd been all too happy to do.

"Coming," she said, brushing the hair out of her eyes. Repressing a shiver that had nothing to do with the cold, she lifted the bar from the door and swung it open. Cait was fully dressed and ready for Matins, looking rather chipper for such an early hour.

Cait smiled at Edyth, a teasing glint in her eyes. "Och…I can see noo why ye didnae answer tae all my pounding. I think my hand will be bruised for certain. How much wine did ye drink last night?" she asked, snaking past Edyth and into her room.

Edyth had only had one cup, but perhaps it *had* been too much. Perhaps the wine had caused her to dream such terrible things. The thought lightened her spirits only momentarily, though, before she remembered that she'd had the same dream previously, except with the ending with the fortress.

"God's teeth! It's verra cold in here," said Cait, rubbing her hands together. "Ye should nae bar yer door. The servants cannae come in and start a fire in yer brazier, nor wake ye as they ought."

Edyth nodded, feeling foggy and sluggish.

Cait busied herself arranging Edyth's clothing, which she'd draped carelessly over the back of a chair after dinner. "Never ye mind. Here," she said, beckoning Edyth closer with her woolen kirtle stretched across the span of her hands, "I'll see ye dressed. Quickly noo, the bells are nearly finished."

The wool dyed fabric was heavy and vastly welcome in the cool of the morning. Edyth was surprised she couldn't see her breath. Cait pulled the ties to in the back and fastened them while Edyth pulled the sleeves on over her chemise. The white of her chemise spilled, bell-like, out of the bottom of the woolen sleeves and covered half of her hand. Finished, Cait helped attach the sleeves to the kirtle and buttoned up the sides along her forearms, all within record time.

"Ye've left it awfully close. We dinnae have time tae tend tae yer hair properly." Edyth ran her hands over her head and felt the snarls from her nightly movements. Cait hurried to the sideboard, her steps stirring the rushes on the floor with a pleasant, homely sound and produced a comb of bone.

Edyth sat in the chair to better help Cait, who was shorter than she was. Her new friend ran the comb through her thin hair as carefully as she could and had to tease out a rather large tangle but made very quick work of it.

"Ewan told me what happened to yer hair," she said, sounding neither pitying nor falsely cheerful about how it must look. "I think it looks like the haircut he gave himself at eleven. He looked like a dandelion clock with half its seed missing!" She giggled and set down the comb. "It's only hair, aye? It'll grow back. Besides, ye're as bonny as ever, e'en with it cut."

She patted Edyth on the shoulder comfortingly and then said, "Come. We're verra late, and I dinnae wish to say more penance prayers than I already have to." She placed a veil on the top of Edyth's head to cover her properly and led the way out the door.

The chapel was far from her room, and they ran most of the way, mostly in the stretches where no one could see them, and then they would slow to a walk once they reached open common areas, their breasts heaving for air. No one seemed to pay them any mind, however.

It had been well over a month since she'd set foot in a church— or even prayed—but due to their lateness, she didn't have the time to become anxious over the fact.

She followed Cait into the richly appointed, vaulted room, curtseying and crossing herself before taking a place at the back of the church. Ewan and his mother were at the front; she could see the backs of their heads bowed respectfully near the priest. Thankfully, no heads turned to see their late arrival.

Cait slipped into the back pew, kneeling with her hands pressed reverently, giving no outward sign that they were late or that they'd just run what felt like a league.

Edyth eyed the priest nervously, trying to slow her breathing and look as inconspicuous as possible. If she sat just so, the large man in front of her blocked her from his view.

The priest raised his voice in song, his arms outstretched toward his audience. Cait crossed herself and mimicked the priest's song, finishing with a drawn out "amen."

Seeing as how there was no Father Brewer present, whose black eyes she'd always feared, it wasn't too long before she found herself relaxing. Closing her eyes, she allowed the smell of expensive beeswax candles to waft over her, and before long, she was far away, remembering.

Each spring, she'd helped her mother and the servants boil the emptied honeycombs and sift out the debris. They'd worked in a merry companionship preparing the wax and then dipping the strings again and again to form the necessary candle supply for the year. The beeswax candles were only used for special occasions, of course, but the smell of it reminded her of happier times.

She'd had the honor of lighting the Yule torch ever since she'd been able to walk. Her father told her that he used to lift her high enough so she could see, then help her light the torch with a lit rush. She loved watching the flame dance as they ate their holiday feast. Stuffed with sweets, she'd sit in his lap as he told her stories, watching the flame dance until her eyes could stay open no longer. The strong, safe arms of her father would then carry her to her bed; she remembered well the floating, suspended feeling of being carried by him before being tucked into her bed, safe and warm. Secure.

In that moment, she felt soothed, as a balm to chafed skin, and she tried to hold the feeling for as long as she could. But just as the ebb and flow of the tide, she could not stop the feeling of loss and desolation that crept back in. Her father was dead. The good feelings she'd conjured slipped away like water through her fingers, and she was left as she had been these past weeks—hallow and scared, exhausted in mind and body.

Cait nudged her with a sharp elbow and she looked about, blinking.

Ewan and his mother were standing in the aisle, looking at her expectantly. People filed past them, out the door and into the weak light, mumbling their "good mornings."

She stood hastily, only tripping slightly on her long skirts, and lowered herself in deference. When she looked up, for only the space of a heartbeat, it was not Ewan's handsome face she saw but as she'd seen him in her vision: broken beyond saving, his life's blood weeping from him with every breath.

"Are ye well, Lady Edyth?" Ewan asked. Her heart increased its cadence and she forced a smile. He was more handsome than any one man had a right to be.

"Yes," she said, not able to meet his gaze. Somehow, looking at him felt as though she were looking into the sun. "I'm quite well. Thank you." She looked to his mother, feeling the weight of his heated gaze, and managed a real smile. "Thank you again for your hospitality."

The dowager inclined her head magnanimously. "I trust you slept comfortably," said her hostess. "If you are in need of any comforts, please let me know. I shall do all I can to accommodate you."

Edyth bobbed her thanks and stammered, "Not at all...I'm most comfortable. Thank you."

"I'm glad you could make it today, Catriona," said the woman in a marked manner.

Cait blushed at her mother's look. "I was only a very little late."

"Mmph," said her mother, struggling to contain her facial features, which wavered between long-suffering frustration and amusement. "If extra prayers are no' motivation enough tae get ye here on time, then perhaps I need to speak with the priest. Surely he can devise some other punishment as motivation. Unless yer laird has any ideas?" She turned to Ewan, tilting her head at a sharp angle to see his face.

"There is always muck to be carted from stalls," said Ewan. "Now that Iain is unable to help, I could use another set of hands."

"Or chamber pots to be scrubbed," said her mother, with a meaningful look.

Cait looked disgruntled, her lips pressed into a white line, but said nothing. Her cheeks blossomed pinkly, and Edyth's heart went out to her. How mortifying to be scolded in front of a new friend.

"Please, if you must punish Cait, you must also punish me," admitted Edyth, feeling responsible. "I'm afraid I am the reason we were late. Cait was kind enough to wake me for Matins."

A crease formed between the dowager's eyes. "Did no servant come to wake you?"

"I'm sure they had, it's just that," she paused, her face flushed with embarrassment, "I'd barred my door before bed, and I did not hear their knocking."

The old woman looked between Edyth and her daughter, her face a mask. After a long pause, she said, "I suppose your heart is in the right place, daughter." Her mouth pursed slightly, and then she sighed. "Come, let us ladies break our fasts, then retire to the solar."

"Lady Edyth," said Ewan, holding her back with a touch to her elbow. She watched as the dowager and Cait exited the church, the light of day swallowing them whole. His eyes were soft and dark, reminding her of the color of water at twilight. Fathomless. "Yer quite safe here," he said in a low whisper. As he searched her face, she wondered how the heat from his long fingers still touching her arm could feel so intimate after spending so much time pressed bodily against him on a horse. "None will harm you. Ye needn't bar yer door...ye have my word."

"I know I have protection here," Edyth assured, thinking she'd somehow insulted him. "I...it's just that so much has happened in such a short time." She shrugged, not able to articulate her feelings. The sense of security she'd unwittingly taken for granted since childhood had been stolen from her, and she felt exposed to unforeseen dangers, regardless of the strength of his fortress. Or his arm.

"I see," he said. And perhaps he did. He nodded a bit, his lips pressed together so that the dimple in his cheek appeared. "Ye'll find yerself again, Edie," he promised quietly. He squeezed her arm gently as if to punctuate his words. "You'll be changed, o'course. Ye cannae grow from the ashes of your life into the same being, but you'll find bits along the way that will remind ye of yerself."

"Do you think so?" she asked on a breath. She wanted to believe it. "I know," he said with surety.

"How?" she asked, her eyes wide with wonderment. Such a thing felt impossible. Leastways she couldn't rightly recall what she'd felt like without the constant splinter that now pierced her heart.

"Ye live, lass." said Ewan simply. "Ye pick up what's left of yer life, and ye live. It's no' easy, and it's takes practice, but the burden will become easier tae carry with time."

Edyth's heart wrenched at his words. *Time.* Time was slow and arduous. But it would pass regardless of how she lived. Could it be so simple? Edyth studied her fingers, thinking nothing felt so daunting as living and waiting, hoping that one day she would wake to find her current sorrows lifted. "What if it's too heavy for me to carry? Already I grow weary...." She trailed off, unwilling to speak further lest the emotion in her chest turn to tears.

"When it's become too much, ye put it down, lass, and let someone else bear it for a time."

Edyth licked her lips, her breath shallow, her mind a muddle, and met his direct, kind gaze. "How do I let it go?"

Ewan smiled at her and handed her his handkerchief. It was soft and smelled of leather and a general maleness that comforted her. "It's no' all that difficult. Ye must only speak your heart, Edie. Speaking—confessing—your troubles lifts them for a time."

Confession. Edyth frowned, looking toward the altar at the front of the chapel, where the priest had conducted Matins. She didn't think she could speak to any priest even though their conversations would be considered confidential. It was a nice thought, but her present feelings toward the Church made it difficult to trust any cleric.

Ewan, catching her gaze, said, "If ye can trust me, Edie, I would hear yer heart and bear yer burdens when needed. Gladly."

Edyth wiped her nose, her heart a riot of emotions. There was shock at his kindness so boldly offered and a fondness for the man she had only met a week ago, but there was also surprise. She was surprised to find that she *did* trust him.

"You are very kind." A priest reentered the room from an unseen door, his footfalls echoing in the vast space.

When Ewan's gaze rested on her again, she saw how his mouth softened, one corner twitching into humor. He gestured to the balcony above them, its heavy balusters carved with expert hands. "Now's as good a time as any. Do ye feel up to a spitting contest? Name the distance, and I will see if I can best ye."

Edyth smiled despite herself, laughing softly. She shook her head, marveling at his ability to reach her broken, hidden places and then soothe the pain away with a smile. "You could never win," she said. "It's best not to even try."

Ewan's answering laugh made the clinging whispers of her dream all but disappear.

Later that week, Edyth found herself upon a steep mountain, overlooking the wide valley that Ewan called home. The watery sun seemed to stroke the tops of the mountains, as though it couldn't help but stretch its fiery fingers from behind the clouds to touch the rocky outcrops above them. While rain was still falling across the valley, the winding river was still as smooth as silk. Even from this distance, she could see that the surface was only disrupted here and there from water birds, rings spreading outward from their feathered bodies.

"Ye seem pleased," said Ewan from beside her, his sapphire eyes resting on her instead of the remarkable view. "The view is worth the hike, I hope."

Edyth smiled at him, glancing to him only briefly before her eyes returned to the scene. "Worth it and more."

"I would apologize for the climb, but you didn't seem put out by it at all. Are you also a mountain climber as well as swordswoman?"

Edyth laughed, feeling lighter than air. She filled her lungs with the aromatic scent of coming rain, reveling in the wind rustling her skirts and hair. "The exertion required to get here is just as pleasant as the view," she said. "Thank you for bringing me here. There is something about nature that lightens my heart."

"I quite agree," mumbled Ewan, picking up a sliver of rock and throwing it. They watched it silently, arching high and far, before it fell with a clatter onto the rocks below, rolling and tumbling through bracken.

The rocky outcropping they stood on was wide and flat, speckled with lichen and broken twigs. Ewan sat in a fluid motion, his legs crossed at the ankles. He plucked a sprig of stubborn grass that had pushed triumphantly from the slightest crack in the rock. "I've always been endeared by these wee bits of grass," he said offhandedly, twirling a blade between thumb and forefinger.

Edyth spared a glance. "I suppose they are rather hearty," she agreed. "But most things in nature must be."

"Mmph," Ewan agreed, holding the plant up to view it more closely. "But the grass is singular, don't you think? There is no real soil to speak of here, just some loosened bits of rock that have eroded enough to turn to dust. It must fight the elements as other plants do not. The sun can easily scorch it here, with no protection, and the rain washes away all its seed—or most of it. And what the elements do not kill, the rabbits and deer eat. How stubborn this little plant is, to demand a life."

Edyth had never considered it but agreed with him. "All things have a place, I suppose. And all things want a life."

"Aye. They do want that."

He looked sad, she thought, or perhaps only preoccupied. "What is troubling your mind?" she asked, settling on the granite slab he was draped against. One booted foot was stretched out before him, the other leg bent to provide a resting place for his arm.

Their young companion, Tavish, could be seen farther up the trail, swinging a stick at the heads of thistles with the fierce savagery of an executioner. He'd acted as chaperone the last two days as Ewan had shown her his home.

Ewan's eyes tracked the path of a hawk high above, black against the pregnant clouds before settling on Edyth.

"I'll be leaving tomorrow, Edyth. I must attend to some matters with my own folk as well as speak to some of my neighbors to the south."

"And this troubles you?"

He shook his head, his lips pressed into a thin line. "It is what is to come that troubles me. I cannae see the future better than any man, but I can *feel* that something is coming." He took a deep breath, his thoughts as clouded as the heavens above them. "My father warned me tae never trust what a man says but tae watch and see what he chooses. I think ye'll ken something of what I speak."

At her nod, he continued, "I don't know what my neighbors will do, but I ken what they'll say. They'll say that we must unite the clans in order tae drive King Edward from our lands. They'll say they will fight and stand with me tae preserve our lands, but what will they *do*? I cannae trust them, and they willnae trust me."

"But why? Surely King Edward's invasion can unite the clans, despite any previous prejudices."

"You'd think so," he said wryly. "With no clear ruler, the clans squabble over rights tae the throne. The Comyns, the Bruces, and all their kin, however distant, are divided. While they might agree that King Edward has no place in Scotia, they will certainly disagree on who should rule once he's cast out.

A Comyn will refuse to fight alongside a Bruce, for instance, unless it's agreed and sworn upon that they will pledge their fealty to a Comyn king. And the Bruces, who feel they have as much right to the Scottish throne, will swear no such fealty."

"What will you do?"

"I am a son of Scotland and a soldier. I will do my duty, whatever the cost."

Edyth's stomach dropped at his words. She was afraid to ask what he meant because she already knew the answer. He would fight and die defending his freedom upon the lonely hill, just as she'd seen it in her dream. Just like the fire she'd seen in as a young girl, turned to reality.

She had to stop it from happening. But how could she? "Can war be avoided?" she asked, feeling suddenly cold.

Ewan ran a hand through his hair and blew out a breath like a bellows. "Will Edward be appeased with only one Scottish garrison?"

"No," she said simply. "He is not a peace-loving man."

"When I return," Ewan said, meeting her gaze briefly before looking back over the valley, "I will take ye tae the MacPhersons. Maybe there ye will be kept safe."

Edyth thanked him, but she did not feel the words. Instead she felt a familiar heaviness engulf her heart. Rain droplets spattered on the rocks around them, perfuming the air with the scents of freshly turned earth. The rain had finally reached them, as all things do with time.

The page, Tavish, appeared then, a thistle sprig jauntily stuck into his bonnet. He pulled a swath of his plaid wrapping over his head, a wide smile on his face, and handed Edyth her cloak. She'd taken it off after the steep climb, having grown too warm to wear it. "Do the English no' defend themselves against the rain?" he teased.

Edyth tried to smile and let the boy help her into the heavy woolen cloak she'd been given from the Lady Scott, but she couldn't stop seeing the bloodied Ewan from her dream, grotesquely impaled and surrounded by his dead friends and foes.

"Are ye well, lady?" asked the boy. "You'll no' be cross, aye? It was only a jape."

"I'm not cross," she assured him, "only overcome with the beauty of your home. How lucky you are to live in such splendor."

"Och, aye," said the boy earnestly. "I've no wish tae leave it till the day I die."

"Let's hope that's a very long way off," muttered Ewan, his solemn face turned away from them. "I pray for it."

Chapter Nine

Edyth's time at Ruthven keep the past fortnight had been like a dream come true, save for one thing. The visions of Ewan's death would not leave her, no matter how hard she tried to distract herself. It did not matter how many walks she took, how many hours she spent in the women's solar embroidering, nor how earnestly she studied the tomes she'd brought with her. In her waking hours, her visions waited within the shadows of her mind only to materialize, full of color, when she could hold her eyes open no longer.

The stables were cool and dark and welcoming in her current state of mind. The rhythmic *shush* of the brush on Harris's flanks lulled her comfortably, easing her troubled mind. It was early still; only a few servants bustled about, carrying fags for the kitchen fires and buckets of water past the entrance to the stables in the predawn light. She'd awoken not long ago, troubled once more by the same tortuous dream. Drenched in sweat and afraid to go back to sleep, she'd chosen instead to avoid it altogether and had found herself here, with Harris, whose silent companionship demanded nothing from her.

The dream had been slightly different this time but just as troubling. This time, she'd stood on the ramparts of the great brown stone keep overlooking the field. Pikes and halberds had winked in the distance, where row upon row of fighting men awaited battle on the foggy field. An ensign had snapped and flapped above her head in a rhythm of beating wings.

Someone had spoken. A woman. *Save him*, she'd commanded, then an arrow, swift and deadly, had flown past her eyes to embed deep in a shadow. Save who? But Edyth knew. She couldn't *stop* seeing. Ewan lay dying, his life's blood spurting from him with each breath he took. She could feel his eyes even now, silently pleading for help, for death, for her to *do* something—anything—but she was powerless. Why was she having these dreams if she had no power to change her circumstances?

Her hands dropped to her sides, the horse brush dangling from limp fingers as a new thought struck her. What if Father Brewer had been right? What if her mother *had* been a witch and Edyth had inherited the curse? Why else would she be dreaming such things? The thought was startling enough that she caught her breath, her fingers trembling. What other explanation was there for the visions she was having? They didn't feel like dreams but premonitions.

Her mother had had gifts. She'd called them talents. Edyth had helped her gather flowers, stalks, leaves, seeds, and all manner of living plants at all hours of the night and day, just when her mother had said they would be the most potent. Edyth hadn't thought anything of it, being too preoccupied with other things. Why would she have questioned this knowledge her mother had possessed? Edyth had learned from her mother, just as her mother had learned from her mother. It was passed down from woman to woman, generation to generation. If her mother was a witch, then didn't that mean she was too?

But her mother had never claimed to have dreams as Edyth was now experiencing. In fact, when Edyth had asked her mother as a young girl about the fire she'd seen in a dream, which had come true, her mother had only said it was coincidental. To not let it trouble her. To forget and move on, which she'd been happy to do at such an age. And when no other such visions had plagued her, it had been easy to dismiss it had even happened.

A dull thud sounded as the brush she loosely held fell to the earthen floor. She wiped her clammy hands on her skirt and retrieved it, feeling overwarm, her mind reeling. What could it all mean?

God did not favor witches, and being such, well, it could be the only explanation for his recent wrath. The thought burned within her, sparking her anger. *If I am a witch, then it is His doing. I had nothing whatever to do with it!*

She breathed sharply through her nose, forcing her anger down, away. So much was buried deep within her heart that if she stuffed one more sorrow, one more mite of anger, surely her heart would burst.

Trying for rational thought, she pushed thoughts of witches away with a slight shake of her head. There had to be a logical explanation for the visions she was experiencing. Perhaps her dreams were simply her secret fears manifested while she was unable to distract herself as she could in her waking hours.

She trusted Ewan after all—had chosen to simply out of necessity—but that trust had deepened and changed after so much adversity together. To have him ripped from her, in death as her parents had been, would be a nightmare realized.

Surely the dreams were a product of her overactive imagination. Ewan had left two days ago, just as he'd said. Perhaps when he returned, she would feel better. And then he would deliver her to Meg. Edyth ran a shaking hand on her skirts, clammy and cold.

An ostler entered then, yanking her from her thoughts. He stopped short at seeing her in his stable, the bones of his face outlined in the light from his lantern.

"Lady," he grunted, his voice as crusty as old bread, "are ye just getting back?" His eyes were as black orbits save for the gleam of light from the candle, and it made her shiver in the predawn cold.

Edyth replaced the brush on a stool. Feeling jumpy and nervous, she wondered at his words. From where did he think she was coming? Did he think she was sneaking about? A spy imparting gleaned secrets to some unknown benefactor in the dark of night? He certainly seemed wary of her, but it was perhaps only due to having a stranger in his place. Edyth's breath seemed to die in her lungs as her mind spun webs of possibility.

He said something else, plucking her out of her reverie. "I say, are ye wishing tae leave then?"

She shook her head, her mind too jumbled with thoughts to think clearly. "To where would I go?" she asked with a shrug. "I came only to see my friend."

She stroked Harris's warm neck as he bent to his breakfast, the sounds of his chewing loud in the awkward silence.

"And not tae Matins, I see." The man shuffled through hay and manure, the light from the lantern slinging shadows in the small space. She could see that he was old, but not as old as she'd first thought. He was taller than the weak light had first afforded. His gray eyes were clear and sharp with intelligence, but his face was carved with harsh lines as befitted a man who spent his life out of doors.

He was wearing hose and a long yellow tunic, covered with a swath of plaid the same color as Ewan's to ward off the cold. Muted greens, golds, and browns expertly weaved through the gray wool into a beautiful and precise pattern. His skullcap was a brown leather, the same dull brown as the hair hanging in strings about his ears.

He seemed to consider her for a long moment, then said, "If yer friend should care fer some winter apples, ye might find some in yon wee basket." He pointed his chin at an exceptionally large bin woven from branches attached to the side of the far wall.

Hanging his lantern, he removed the candle and set about lighting more, which hung at intervals in the dark space. The stable, in better light, was homely and well stocked. Tack hung from the rafters along one side of the room where the beams were exposed, but a loft, presumably full of hay by the looks of it, covered most of the ceiling, keeping much of the beast's heat from escaping the small, rectangular windows cut into the walls at the eves.

"Thank you," said Edyth, retrieving two of the withered fruit. Harris lipped them eagerly from her hand, the soft bristles on his lips tickling her palm.

"I'm Edyth," she said, giving the man a polite smile.

"Aye. I ken fine who ye are," he grunted, bending over to replace a lead rope that had fallen to the dirt floor. "The entire village kens all about the English lass the laird has brought home."

Edyth raised an eyebrow at his words but said nothing. While he hadn't said anything necessarily unfriendly, his tone wasn't exactly welcoming.

She only half listened as the man busied himself pitching hay into stalls, where huffing noses greeted him. Harris had been well tended. The horny patch on his elbow had been shaved off, she saw, and his shedding winter coat all but combed away. She wanted to speak to Harris as she'd grown accustomed to doing, to spill out her heart and mind but was shy of it with the man so close. She stroked him absently, thinking about her dream, wishing she had a friend to confide her worries to.

"What says the beast then, lass?" asked the man, his voice muffled amid the quiet movements of horses and falling hay.

At her confused look, he expounded, "Ye said ye came tae visit yer friend. If the beast is yer friend, what does it say?"

Edyth frowned and looked between the man and Harris. "He doesn't say anything to me," she said finally, confused.

"No?" he said, giving her a frown of his own. "That's mightly strange. Gealach here," he said, motioning with his pitchfork to the stall, holding a pink-nosed gray, "has plenty tae say, in his own way. His ladylove, Banrigh, down there," he said, gesturing with a jerk of his head to the end of the stable, "breaks his heart on the regular. We speak o' it occasionally. All out of her hearing o'course."

"Of course," replied Edyth, who could not help but be intrigued by the man's strangeness. "And what does she have to say about it?" asked Edyth, her mouth tugging into a smile.

The man shrugged, making a *tsking* sound. "Och, she's too good fer the puir lad, not that I blame 'er. Her sire was a Spanish palfrey, long and elegant and swift as the wind."

"And Gealach?" said Edyth, doing her best with the horse's name.

"This rouncey?" he scoffed.

"There are many good qualities for an ordinary horse," she argued. "Breeding cannot account for everything. What of his spirit? What of his disposition?"

The man leaned heavily on his fork, nodding his head with a look of consideration in his eyes. "Och, aye. As I've telt 'er. But Banrigh was born tae a particular life, aye? She willnae want to sully her stock with his seed. It would be shameful tae her mind. And no doubt she's right. Tis best tae keep tae yer own kind, as they say. Tis something ye should take heed of yerself, lassie, and no mistake."

She could feel the smile slide off her face at his words. "What are you suggesting?" asked Edyth, the guarded feeling planted inside of her growing rapidly.

Ceasing the practiced movements of feeding hay into stalls, he stopped to give Edyth what she thought was a rather cool gaze. "Laird Ruthven is good man. A good *Scots* man who's just lost his Da. He's got enough tae occupy his mind without some... Nay, it doesnae hold tae call ye names, lass, and I willnae. But none 'ere would like tae see him get his head turned by some English chit with naught to her name when his family has plans for him with the Stewart lass."

Edyth clenched her jaw, her mind reeling. What was he suggesting exactly? Did all the servants think she'd played the damsel in distress just to trick him into some sort of attachment to her? It was laughable! "Oh, yes," said Edyth sarcastically. "You've caught onto my game now, sir. Risking all, I wandered into Scotland on the vague hope of stumbling upon your master so I could steal his house and lands." She laughed humorlessly, her anger making her shake. She wanted to say many things, mostly about him sticking his overly large, ugly nose where it didn't belong, but she swallowed the insults away.

She turned on her heel to leave, her face hot, but thought better of it, unable to resist. She turned back in a swirl of skirts and pointed her finger at the ostler. "What would Lord Ruthven think of your estimation of him? Is he so easily manipulated, sir? Is that what you think of him? You have shamed us both."

Edyth turned and left, unseeing. She was mad with fury and splashed through several deep puddles, soaking her feet and hem. Was that what everyone thought of her? And what of the dowager and Cait? Did they think the same? She scoffed, the sound swallowed up between the outbuildings as she made her way toward the keep.

The sky was lightening, changing from inky black to woolen gray at the horizon, the few stars visibly winking out as the greater light overtook them. There was a rising wind. Low clouds fat with rain moved overhead, as menacing as a boiling cauldron. It would pour soon but would move through quickly by the looks of it. Impervious to rain, more people were about, crossing the yard with wheelbarrows, rakes, wagons, and other various assortments of tools. She didn't want to go back to the keep to be met by false solicitations from servants. Besides, she didn't want to be cooped up. She needed air. She needed to run. She wanted a *fight*.

Looking about her, she spotted a possible sanctum. Against the curtain wall was a long ladder leading up to the bulwark catwalk. Unmanned as it was—or so it appeared—she rushed to it, not caring who saw her ruck her sodden skirts so she wouldn't trip herself up. The smooth, sturdy wood was damp but not dangerous. The ladder shuttered and jumped as she climbed, swift and unafraid. It felt good to do something shocking—or at least unexpected—and she half hoped she'd be met by a surly knight at the top, just so she could shout at someone.

The view was even better from up on the wall; Edyth drank in the sights, feeling a riot of emotions. The rain was falling in the basin, streaks of water obscuring the landscape like spilled milk over a page. The rain clouds looked bruised, blue and purple and gray-green all at once, roiling and coiling upon themselves.

Scotland was wild, as wild as her heart felt at that moment, and tears filled her eyes. "You're cruel and unfair," she said, unable to contain the bitterness that had been growing in her since Thom had come to her mother with a tale about Father Brewer and his sister, Annie.

Edyth waited for an answer, nothing so obvious as a lightning bolt to her heart, but *something*, anything that would denote that God gave a damn about her. Raindrops spattered against her face, the rock wall, mingling with her tears.

"Do you not see me?" she half-shouted to the gray sky. Her chest heaved as she tried to catch her breath. "My heart still beats," she said, pounding a fist against her chest. "You would not give me death as a mercy, yet you give me no respite."

Thunder rolled in the distance, but she barely heard it for the roaring in her ears. "I have done everything you've ever asked of me," she railed. "You take all and give nothing in return. You have robbed me blind!" A sob left her as she fell to her knees, the rain clouds opening above her. Rain fell in sheets around her, unheeded. She cried into her knees, her arms wrapped tightly around her legs as her cloak grew heavy with water. "Am I also refused a friend?"

She didn't cry for long. She was too angry to wallow. As her tears dried and her breathing settled, her thoughts began to take shape once more. She didn't really understand why the ostler's words had triggered such emotions in her, but she felt that Ruthven Castle was no longer a refuge for her. All the better, then, that Ewan would be taking her away soon.

All the kindnesses from the people she'd met seemed false now, just as it had been with her own people. She could see them in her mind's eye, smiling to her face and then gossiping about her as soon as she was out of their sight. What had the ostler said? He'd accused of her having designs of subterfuge and duplicity. It sickened her to think she was viewed in such a light.

Ewan's face swam before her, and her heart softened of its own accord. Ewan, at least, didn't think such things about her, surely. He, Iain, Graham, and Fingal knew her heart. They counted her as a friend. Didn't they?

She sniffed and wiped her nose on her sleeve, her hair sticking to her face in patches. But if people were thinking and saying things that weren't true, the lies could still cause shame to come to his family, and that was the last thing she wanted.

Thinking of leaving him, never again to see his face or speak to him, caused her heart to constrict as though in a vice. And while the plan had always been to leave, something within her had changed. She felt tethered to him, the connection unwanted but there all the same. She'd bared her soul to him—scars and all—and he'd accepted her as she was, with no demands or judgments. How was she to cut the bindings of their friendship as though they meant nothing? She could more easily cut out her own heart.

There was only one solution that she could see. She would have to train her heart to feel nothing for him. She would bind her heart against him, and maybe, just maybe, it wouldn't hurt when the blade separated them.

Shivering, Edyth wiped her eyes and made her way back down into the yard. The rain cloud had moved past, drenching the grassy fields to the north of the keep. Distraught as she was, her mind a muddle and her emotions so close to the surface, she couldn't help the curse word that left her mouth as her body collided with another as she turned a corner.

"Agh!" cried the woman she'd run into, her hands flailing in an effort to stay upright. They teetered against each other for a moment before finally regaining their balance.

It was Cait. Separated, they stared at each other for a few heartbeats, and then Cait's mouth stretched into a wide grin, her teeth bright in the early light. "What did you just say?"

Edyth felt her bad mood lighten just being around the girl. "Sorry," she said, unable to help echoing Cait's smile. "You've caught me in a rare temper."

"Not at all. I'm rather impressed. Ye've been spending too much time with my brother, sounds like."

Blanching, Edyth bit her lip, the ostler's words chasing her good humor away. Perhaps the man had been right. Perhaps she had been spending too much time where she did not belong.

"Are ye well, Edyth? Have ye been crying?"

"No," Edyth lied. At Cait's raised eyebrow, she relented. "I had a bad dream, is all."

"Is that why ye were no' at Matins?" Cait searched her face, waiting for her to explain, but when Edyth said nothing, Cait took her arm, steering them in the opposite direction of where she'd been going.

"I've been ordered tae thin out the wee herbs in the kale yard," Cait explained, pulling her face into an expression of distaste. "They're all bunched up, like, and need more space. It's part of my punishment, but—" She paused here, looking shy, her cheeks tinged pink. "Will ye come along?" she asked, her eyes pleading. "It's miles better than scrubbing chamber pots, and that's the truth, but with company, the chore will nay seem so very difficult."

Barely pausing for breath, she rushed on. "I ken as how yer a guest, but Ewan's nay 'ere tae chastise me, and Mam will no' notice, seeing as how she's speaking with the staff about the hunt coming next Friday, week."

"Of course I'll help," Edyth interrupted, really meaning it. Distraction from her own thoughts was exactly what she needed.

"Och, aye? Do ye like grubbing about in the dirt then? I suppose ye would, being *bana-bhuidseach geal*."

Edyth cocked an eyebrow at her friend, taking the basket from her hands and following her. She'd heard that term used before. "What is bana voochach?" she asked, knowing she was butchering the pronunciation.

Cait led the way, carefully navigating the worst of the puddles in the muddy yard past the stable. "I suppose it translates tae *witch* in English," said Cait without looking at her. She hopped over a rather large manure pile melting in a puddle of rainwater and only looked back when she noticed Edyth hadn't followed.

"Is something wrong?" asked Cait, her fine dark brows creasing in concern. "Ye look as white as a sheet."

Edyth shook herself mentally and forced herself forward, pulling up her skirts as best she could in the deep mud. "Ewan called me that before, when I was helping Iain in the wood.

I'd forgotten. It's not...*bad* then? He made it seem like it was something good."

Cait pursed her lips in thought. "Aye, did ye think he'd call ye a nasty name?"

"No, it's just that in England, being called such would be...dangerous."

Cait made a sound in her throat that Edyth took for interest. "Ye mean they fear wise women?"

"Well, yes. In general, they look upon witches as wicked creatures. I heard that in London, a woman was once imprisoned and then later killed for conjuring a storm that sank one of His Majesty's ships."

"And do ye believe it?" asked Cait, her eyes large and limpid. Edyth shrugged. In truth, she *had* believed it, but after witnessing her own mother's witch trial, her opinions had taken a rather rapid turn.

"If I had the sort of power tae do such a thing, I wouldnae waste it on sinking ships. Why not send the bloody rain elsewhere so we could be dry for once in our lives?" said Cait, gesturing at the sky. "Nay," she said, opening the gate at the back of the kitchen, "being *bana-bhuidseach geal* is no' wrong or wicked, Edyth."

The kale yard was nestled at the back of a long, single-story, stone foundational building. Two flues poked out of the kitchen's severely pitched roof, belching smoke. Cait deposited her basket and tools on the stone wall and handed Edyth a digging fork. "You can tend tae the garlic and I'll work on these neeps here."

Edyth had only just settled to her task when Cait said, "Tell me about yer dream then, Edyth. I can see it's weighing heavily on ye. Ye'll feel better with the telling."

Edyth almost laughed. "How like your brother you are."

"Och aye? I suppose we're bound tae be. Does he also pry where he ought not?" asked Cait with an unapologetic smile.

"He most certainly does." Edyth laughed. She hesitated, thinking of what he'd said to her in the church. *When it's become too much, ye put it down, lass, and let someone else bear it for a time.*

Could she—should she—confide in Cait? If she was to purge Ewan from her heart, it might do well for her to find a friend, instead, in his sister. She was willing to try, but was careful with her words. Edyth told Cait about the dream as best she could, sharing with her friend about her growing worry. "I fear that...I fear that it's not a dream at all, but a premonition of what was to come. I've seen such things before. Long ago." Edyth's mind filled with the distant memory, no doubt muddled from time and from her own suppression, the great fire that she'd dreamt of as a young girl. And how, soon after, she had seen it come to life.

Cait was a good listener, rapt with interest. Her face was pale enough to show the light smattering of freckles across her nose. "Holy Mother of God," whispered Cait, clasping Edyth's muddied hands with her own cold, black fingers. "Ye *are* bana-bhuidseach geal."

"I don't know for certain what it means," countered Edyth, feeling both relief and panic in the same instant. "My mother couldn't even tell me what my dreams meant as a young girl. Cait," said Edyth, her heart in her throat, "what does it all mean?"

Cait swallowed and shook her head, letting out a pent breath. "Ye must tell Ewan what ye've seen and then pray tae God that he'll heed yer words."

Feeling as though she'd just run a race, Edyth's limbs shook as though with fatigue, her heart beating a tattoo against her ribs. She hadn't realized how frightened she was of putting voice to her fears. But she had. And Cait was not scowling. She wasn't calling her names, nor was she throwing stones. In fact, Cait seemed to genuinely believe her.

"Tell me again about the battle," commanded Cait, digging at the roots of plants with renewed vigor. "Any bits ye can recall. What was on the ensign ye saw?"

Edyth closed her eyes, seeing it form once more in her mind. "Three sheafs on an azure field. It...it was torn from its pike by the wind. It fell among the dead."

"That's the Comyn crest," said Cait, her eyes far away as she thought.

"Do you think it means anything?" asked Edyth, absently pulling apart a large clove of garlic.

"The house will fall, I suppose," she said, looking worried. "But when? Where will this happen?"

Edyth shrugged. "I don't know. I don't know what it means, but I see it again and again. It will not leave me, even in my waking hours. It's all I can think of."

"What does it have tae do with Ewan, I wonder?" asked Cait, a frown upon her face. "Tell it all tae me again, if ye please, Edyth. Leave nothing out."

"Quit yer twitching," grumbled Fingal good-naturedly.

That was rather like the pot calling the kettle black, Ewan thought, as Fingal was presently whittling a stick with his dirk as they waited. The shavings littered the rush-strewn floor, lost, just as his thoughts.

Graham, who was far more patient than he, sat across from them, arms folded, his good eye closed in supposed sleep. While the weather had been fine and their journey to Hay uneventful, they were, all of them, tired and hungry.

More than that, though, they were all eager to learn the reason for the summons. They'd arrived amid at least five other barons to the keep, all who had received the same message to come on this day to discuss important matters pertaining to Scotia.

Robert Dundas was there, speaking privately with John Comyn, lord of Badenoch. He recognized him by his bright red hair. John de Strathbogie, Robert Bruce, and the earl of Atholl were speaking with the earls of Menteith and Ross, all wealthy men with large numbers of fighting men at their disposal.

"They'll want tae speak about England's impossible demands," said Ewan yet again. "Perhaps now is the time to fight, d'ye think?"

"Aye, could be," grunted Fingal.

They'd been placed in the great hall, where the men mingled among each other, all of them looking grim. Finally, Sir Gilbert Hay entered the hall, walking as though on a cloud, his skeletal frame accentuated by his dark tunic. The chatter ceased as he beckoned them forward. "Thank you for coming, good sirs," said Sir Gilbert in his wispy voice. "Please follow me to a more *accommodating* apartment."

Fingal nudged Graham none too gently, motioning with a single thrust of his chin toward the high table that the meeting was about to begin. Gesturing for them to stay, Ewan stood and followed the group of men out of the large room into a much smaller chamber at the back of the dais.

The table was large and filled the majority of the windowless room. Selecting a seat between Robert Dundas and the lord of Badenoch, Ewan rolled his shoulder, his eyes roving over the men gathered there.

"As you're well aware," began Sir Gilbert, his black eyes flitting from man to man, "our king's alliance with France has brought about some unpleasant consequences. The sacking of Berwick was no doubt meant to awe us into submission, yet you and I know ourselves far better."

Several grunts of approval sounded in the small room, but some of the men, Ewan noticed, looked wary.

"We are simple men," said Sir Gilbert silkily. "We ask only to be let alone, and yet we are forced to pay for a war against France—our allies—by a king not of our making. Baliol has little choice left to him but for the sons of Scotland to rise and unite. The time has come, gentlemen, to fight."

Such a bold statement was bound to garner strong opinions, yet Sir Gilbert did not flinch at the many voices directed at him.

"Where is Baliol then? I don't see him here at this meeting discussing war," asked the earl of Atholl.

"Unite the clans, he says," said another man. "It would be easier to get water from a stone."

"So *you* say," said another. "Who made you the authority?"

Sir Gilbert stayed any irritation he may have felt and merely waited, his long fingers curled around the arms of his chair, his fingernails an even lighter shade of gray than his skin.

"Fools," hissed Robert Dundas on Ewan's left. He stood, shaking his head like a lion dislodging flies. "Ye'll squabble even now, with Edward breathing down our necks! He's taken our largest port and killed thousands of men! Do you think he'll stop there? Fools!" he repeated, jamming a blunt finger into the tabletop. "Tell them, John," he demanded.

All eyes turned to the Red Comyn, the lord of Badenoch. He cleared his throat and nodded, looking resigned. "I've just left King John at Haddington. My aunt, Marjory, holds Dunbar against her husband, the earl of March. According to Marjory, he's been commanded to return to Dunbar Castle and fortify it against Scotland. He does not suspect his wife will fight against him."

It was no secret that her husband, Patrick, the earl of March, supported England. King Edward's grasp on Scotland was tightening, and if he took another important holding in the lowlands, Ewan wondered if he'd ever stop.

"Need I remind ye fools," interjected Robert, that Dunbar Castle is a key installation along the coastal road, and if we lose the coast, we lose much."

"Thank you," intoned Gilbert, nodding once in appreciation. "Quite right. We cannot allow Edward to take Dunbar. The question remains, who will stop him?"

The silence in the small space was a thick, living thing that seemed to choke them all into silence. Ewan took several deep breaths, trying to order his thoughts. War sick and wounded, he wasn't eager to lift his sword against England again. But could he afford not to?

It was two days later when Ewan, Graham, and Fingal returned, looking weary and disheveled. Ewan was markedly distant, though Edyth knew it was best that way. Now that she knew tongues were wagging about their relationship, however innocent it might be, she should welcome his disinterest.

Still, when he only nodded briefly to her at dinner, engaged instead in conversation with Rory, she had to scold her heart into behaving. Disappointment was felt, though, despite what she told herself to think and feel.

The food was as excellent as ever, but she couldn't find her appetite. Cait gave her meaningful looks, eyes darting to Ewan and back from across the table, but Edyth did her best to ignore her. What was she to do, stand up and announce to everyone in the room that she was, as Cait had said, one of the cunning folk? She will still coming to grips with the realization herself.

And despite Cait's reassurances that being such wasn't a bad thing—perhaps awed and feared in some respects but not malicious and evil—Edyth could not fight against her own experience.

Feeling suddenly tired, she excused herself from the table and retreated to her spot on the curtain wall, away from Cait's nudging foot and the oppressive weight of Ewan's presence.

It was some time later, as Edyth sat, unseeing, at one of the tall windows that lined the women's solar, when Ewan's squire came to fetch her. The young man, Alec, he'd informed her, brought her to a spacious office on the second floor, the door hidden at the end of a dim corridor. Upon Alec opening the door, Edyth hesitated, her senses overcome with the scent of Ewan. This was his place. His office.

Many candles were lit, lending a welcoming charm to the richly appointed room that beckoned her to enter.

"I thank ye for coming so quickly, Lady DeVries," Ewan said, looking rather austere. He stood behind a ornately carved desk, neatly organized. Gone was her pet name, replaced with a title. Formality had returned, and while that should have pleased her, she felt her heart wilt despite herself. She nodded, not trusting herself to speak.

"I'm afraid I must apologize to you once more." He ran a hand through his hair. It stuck up in all directions, the curls tangling and seeming to grow before her eyes.

She shook her head. "I can recall no reason for an apology."

Moving to pull out a chair, he gestured for her to be seated. Hesitating only briefly, she obeyed but rather felt like a cornered mouse. Ewan sat across from her, sighing as he settled into the over large chair.

Upon the table sat letters stacked neatly to one side, inkwell, parchment, quills, and penknife all arranged just so. After a long pause, he opened his mouth, shut it, then opened it again as if he was nervous. Indeed, she rather thought his nerves were catching.

"I regret that I cannae bring ye tae yer cousin, the MacPherson, as I'd promised."

Traitorous relief flooded through her, even as her mind objected. How could she stay when she had sworn to cut him out of her heart? It would be a torment! But her heart...her heart seemed to swell with the prospect of more time spent with him. "Oh," was all she could manage to say. She knotted her fingers together in her lap, desperate to run, desperate to stay. "Has something happened?"

"I received some disturbing news while I was away, and I must leave again tomorrow for Dunbar." He paused here, his black eyes a weight. He cleared his throat and rolled his shoulder, seeming unsettled to her mind. "I know I told you I'd take ye myself, and I wish I could, but—" He paused, his usual calm replaced with suppressed feeling. "I am a man of my word, Lady DeVries. I dinnae take promises lightly, but I regret that I must break my promise tae ye. Yet again." He sat stiffly, his usual relaxed state abandoned.

Her mind reeled, wondering what had caused such a change in her friend, and then she remembered that she shouldn't care. "You've broken no promises to me, sir."

"I have," he said, sounding annoyed. "I told ye I'd keep ye safe, lady, but I nearly drowned ye, then left ye alone in the wood tae be murdered or stolen away by those damned Douglases." With some effort, he pushed his emotions away, his jaw clenched tightly. With a visible effort at calm, he met her gaze, his thoughts and emotions hidden once more behind a mask.

"Rory will take ye in my stead. I trust him with my life. And yours."

Edyth's mouth had gone very dry, and she had to try twice to swallow. She closed her eyes, feeling as though she were awash in a river. Suddenly she understood what was happening. Or rather, what was about to happen very soon. "You've been called to fight with the Comyns."

The room had gone very still. She could hear her own heart, steady and strong, could feel the breath he held in his lungs.

"How...who told you that Marjory Comyn has called for aid?"

She opened her eyes then, the strange feeling seeping from her as she met the blue eyes of the man who'd laid dead at her feet for so many nights. She hesitated slightly but pushed on, forcing herself to say the words. "Do you believe in fate, Sir Ruthven?"

Ewan looked taken aback. "Fate? Do no ask me trifling questions, my lady. Who told ye of the call to arms? Was it Cait? Has she been listening at doors again?"

Edyth licked dry lips and shook her head. "I didn't believe...before. Initially I thought it was only ill luck that my mother was accused, but I had hope because she was innocent. The innocent are supposed to be vindicated, aren't they? But then...then I thought that maybe it was that God was punishing me when I was made an orphan and displaced from my home." Edyth took a steading breath, holding Ewan's piercing gaze.

"But no," she continued softly, "I haven't been a victim of ill luck, and it hasn't even been God's misplaced justice. I see that now. Your mother brought it to my attention, but I couldn't see through my own suffering until I recalled a dream from my past. Cait explained what it all meant."

Ewan sat very still, his head bowed toward her as though to catch the words she was not speaking. "I don't understand."

Edyth spared him a small smile. "No, I don't imagine that you do. I don't understand it either. You called me a witch yourself, Ewan, and Cait helped me to see that I am very much like my mother after all." She paused here to draw breath—or strength.

Seeing he still did not understand, Edyth leaned forward, her voice wavering just over a whisper. "Cait says I am one of the cunning folk. A witch. Whether that is true or not, I'm not certain. Maybe it's witchcraft, or maybe it's fate or God. It doesn't matter to me. What *does* matter, what is important, is that I was brought to you for a purpose. As painful as my path has been getting here, I do not begrudge my discomfort if it means I can save you."

He opened his mouth, shut it, then opened it again. "Lady Edyth. Forgive me, but you're no' making any sense. Of what are ye speaking?"

"I've seen what is to come," she said, pressing her lips together tightly as she waited for his reaction. He only stared at her blankly. "I've seen the aftermath of this battle with the English," she added. "I've seen you dead—dying—at my feet, but I cannot help you there. I can only help you now. I must act now."

"You've *seen*?"

She nodded, terrified and anxious of what he might say, but she had to speak. Staying silent would surely be damning him to a terrible death. Doing so would be as if she, herself, drove the pike home. "I've dreamt of your death for weeks now. I cannot escape it, no matter what I do." Her voice waivered slightly and she bit her lip, remembering the pleading look in his eyes as he lay upon the field.

Ewan leaned back in his chair, his face unreadable. "I see," he said after a long pause. "Do ye also dream of your parents' deaths?"

Edyth hesitated. "Well, yes, but it's not the same." Edyth hated the pitying look that came into his eyes.

"You've seen more heartache and sorrow in the last month than any one person should experience in a lifetime. I think...I believe it's only natural to fear the loss of others you've grown to care for."

"Yes," she agreed, undeterred. "I had the same thought, but I can *feel* that there is meaning here."

Before he could speak, she rushed on. "Sir Ruthven, I was raised by a father who wanted a son. I spent countless hours with him, being tutored as a son might in my younger years. I know how to set a trap. I know the blessing you say over an animal fallen by your hands. *I know how to hide*, and yet knowing what I do, I still started that fire in the wood after I'd narrowly escaped from those women on the boarder. I lit the fire, Ewan."

Taking his raised brow as an invitation to continue, she said, "Your mother recognized it for what it was. If I hadn't built the fire, which I knew was dangerous, you would have never found me. I was led to do it, you see. It was the only way."

Inching forward in her seat, she rested her heated palms upon his desk. The wood was smooth and cool and seemed as vast as a chasm, separating them. "After you rescued me from those men in the wood, I dreamt of you. I saw you laying upon a field, dying. And not just you. Your kinsman too. At first I wasn't sure it was you, but the vision kept coming, night after night. I can't escape it, even now. I knew it would be the Comyns because I saw their crest upon a standard: three sheaves upon a field of blue. It...it was torn from its pike and lost in the wind."

Edyth watched him swallow as he considered her. He was silent for several moments, then he said, "And you make it a point to know the crests of all the clans in Scotland?"

Finding it hard to stamp down her frustration, she took a deep breath. Cait had warned it would be difficult to persuade him. "I would not have come to you with this if I was simply having nightmares. I have seen your death. Again and again, always the same. Always, you lie there, and I cannot help. I am bound in my dreams, but I am not bound here. Do not go, Ewan. Do not answer the Comyn call."

The pitying look that had so annoyed her was replaced with irritation. "You would have me play the coward then? I have spent the last two days wagging my tongue raw trying to persuade old men to take action, and you would have me hide behind my mother's skirts."

"So you will choose death to save your pride," she said in disbelief.

Ewan stood, his hands splayed on the desk. "What of my duty?" he asked incredulously. "What of honor?"

"Hollow words," retorted Edyth, standing to match him. "Duty and honor mean nothing for those left behind. What of your mother? Of Cait?" *Of me.*

Ewan's mouth pressed into a thin line, his cheeks red. "Hollow words? Are they indeed? Those words meant something to yer mother, I would think."

Edyth felt as though she'd been slapped. She reeled backward, her heart hammering in its cage, her fists clenched at her sides. "Yes," she hissed, "and if only she had chosen her family over duty and honor, then I would still have both of my parents."

She turned on her heel and wrenched the door open, half blind with rage. Ewan followed, his hand grasping her shoulder. She turned into him sharply and shoved him as hard as she could, her hands flat against his chest. "Damn you, Ewan!" she shouted. He was far too big and barely moved, even when employing all her strength. It infuriated her. "You've got rocks for brains, you know that?"

Chapter Ten

"I gather that didn't go well." Cait met her at the bottom of the stairs, pushing off from the wall and matching Edyth's angry strides.

Edyth huffed out a humorless laugh. She lifted her skirts, stomping up the steps as though she were stepping on Ewan's head instead. "Your brother is...maddening. He would die to prevent bruised pride."

"I did warn you," said Cait between breaths. "But you had to try. Can we slow down?"

"Sorry," muttered Edyth, glancing at her friend. "What now?"

"Well, we can't give up," said Cait, her brows knitted together. "Maybe you can try again tomorrow," she suggested half-heartedly.

Edyth pulled a face. "What about Iain? Can Iain persuade him?"

Cait shook her head. "Iain would be going with him, if it weren't for his leg."

"Thank the heavens for small favors," muttered Edyth. Perhaps fate had guided her arrow as well. "Maybe someone should shoot Ewan in the leg."

They reached Cait's room and fell upon the bed, silent, each lost in their own thoughts.

"What if your mother spoke to him?" suggested Edyth.

Cait shrugged. "Ewan is laird. She would not command him or try to persuade him, even if she could. Besides, I would rather spare her yer visions of his death, if we can." She shuddered, rubbing her arms to ward of the chill.

"So he is lost to us," said Edyth mournfully.

"Do not give up," said Cait, terror in her voice. "Follow him into battle if you must, but do not give up."

Edyth sat up, her mind latching onto sudden inspiration. Sitting up beside Edyth, Cait asked, "What is it?"

Edyth turned eagerly to her friend. "You're right. I *could* follow him to battle. He said he was going to Dunbar. Do you know it?"

Cait nodded, her eyes wide. "It's on the coastal road, north of Berwick."

Edyth bit her lip, thinking fast. "If I cannot stop the battle, perhaps I can stop *him. Somehow.* But even if I could save him, how will I get there? He will not allow such a thing, and as soon as he sees me, he will send me back. Rory is to take me away soon."

Cait stood and started pacing, knotting her fingers. "What if... what if Rory is commanded to bring ye tae Dunbar? On account of your healing abilities."

"But Ewan is to command him to bring me to my cousin, Meg, if he hasn't already. Do you think he would disobey his laird?"

"No," Cait said vehemently. "Never. Which is why it must be Ewan who calls for ye."

Edyth's hopes fell. "But your brother would never do such a thing."

"Leave that to me," said Cait, batting Edyth's worries away as though they were as easily dismissed as midges.

"Ewan will send for ye in a letter. Ye can write, can ye no', Edyth?"

"Stop avoiding me, Edyth," said Ewan, though no irritation colored his words.

It was true. She had avoided him at Mass and sat clear away from him at breakfast, keeping up a very uninteresting conversation with a mostly deaf, elderly man, who kept coughing his food into her face, all to avoid facing him.

She'd made it most of the day, but he'd found her here, in her spot on the curtain wall where she'd shouted at God. She shouldn't have come here, where she'd been seen before. Next time, she'd have to be cleverer, but she much preferred this view over needlework in the solar. She loved the untamed wind that pushed and pulled from this height. At times, it blew so fiercely that she thought she might be carried off altogether.

Ewan rested his elbows on the parapet, glancing briefly at her, then out upon his lands. He was just as much a part of the landscape as the wild scene on display; his hair whipped madly this way and that, like a murmuration of starlings.

"I wouldnae wish tae take my leave with ugly words between us. Will ye no' speak with me?"

His jaw appeared freshly scraped, pink and raw. He looked young and strong and so vibrantly alive. She couldn't bear to think of him going off to battle. How could he go, knowing he would fall? "Are you scared?" she asked pointedly, searching his beautiful face.

Ewan shrugged, pulling his eyes away. Petals from spring blossoms fell in a shower of white and pink with the slightest breeze, making the ground look as though it were covered in snow. "Any soldier who doesnae feel fear is already dead."

She held her tongue, thinking that he was just that: a dead man walking. Reading her thoughts, he shot her a weak, apologetic smile. "I leave tomorrow, Edyth. I wanted tae say—" He paused, looking uncertain, as though he was searching for words. "I wanted tae say that it has been a great honor tae have met ye."

"So you will really go, even knowing you will die?"

He sighed, looking weary, and she felt the weight he bore, the weight of honor and duty. "I *must* go. And if I am tae die as ye say, Lady Edyth, I would leave with good feelings between us. Can ye forgive me for my angry words?"

Swallowing hard, she searched his face, full of stoic determination. "If I cannot win your confidence, then you will have my pardon," she said simply.

"Dinnae look at me that way, Edyth. I cannae bear it." He pulled her to him, perhaps for comfort, or maybe so he wouldn't have to see her discontentment.

They fit well together. Her head rested neatly under his chin. She breathed in the scent of him: leather and sweat and a general maleness that comforted her. She wanted to say, "Be careful" or "Goodbye," but she could not. The words were stuck in her throat. Instead, she tried to remember him as he was, the rise and fall of his chest, the thrum of his voice that seemed to make the blood sing in her veins, and the reassuring beat of his heart under her ear. Before long, it would all be gone.

His arms tightened around her. "Be still, Edyth. Ye asked if I believed in fate, and I do. I believe that fate is God's will. Nothing more. If I am fated tae die in defense of my lands, then it is God's will. Ye cannae stop it." He took a deep breath; a large hand stroked her hair. "And I wouldnae wish tae try. We cannae stop fate."

She pulled away, ready to argue, but he forestalled her with a sharp shake of his head. "No, Edyth. Dinnae sully our goodbye with disagreement. Let us part as friends."

Her heart shriveled. Suddenly cold, she wrapped her arms around herself, hugging her elbows. Her hair whipped against her face, and she bit her lip to stop her words. She would not make his parting any more painful that it already was. "Be well, Ewan," she said, her lips numb.

"And you, Edie. I...I shall miss you." He kissed her hand, his warm, soft mouth pressing against her skin for the briefest of moments, and then he was gone.

It was a long time that she sat upon the parapet alone, watching the birds sail high against the mountain, riding the wind in an effortless drift.

The sun always rises quickly when you dread its coming, but before she knew it, the day had begun. Ewan was gone, his seat at the breakfast table a glaring error. Cait gave her hand a squeeze under the table.

Iain was well enough to sit with them for a time but needed help walking up and down the stairs. He'd wanted to go with Ewan, of course, and spent many minutes complaining at being left behind but had softened his statements at a word from his mother, who remarked that she would sleep better knowing at least one of her sons was safe home.

"Will you come to the chapel to pray with me, children?" asked the countess. She hadn't even touched her porridge.

Edyth ached for the woman who had lost her husband such a short time ago and who would soon lose a son. *Did she know*, Edyth wondered. Was there some sort of motherly instinct that told her she'd kissed her eldest son goodbye for the last time?

"Of course," both Cait and Iain responded, pressing her hands and offering other words of encouragement.

Ewan is no stranger to battle. He will be home soon.
God will be with him, Mother.

"And you as well, Edyth?" asked the countess, her blue eyes, so much like Ewan's, resting on her. "It never hurts to pray for those that venture off into paths unknown. Our prayers may be all that keeps Ewan and our men out of harm's way."

"I...yes. If you wish it," she said, worried she might be intruding on a very private affair.

The doors opened, and Rory entered, his long strides eating up the distance in no time at all. Bowing slightly as he approached the table, Rory removed his bonnet before he addressed his mistress.

"Begging yer pardon, mistress," he said, straightening. "I've orders that involve the lassie," he said, motioning in Edyth's direction with a hand. "I'd like yer permission tae leave on the morrow. I'll leave Hamish here tae manage my duties until I return."

"So soon?" interjected Cait, frowning first at Rory, then at her mother. "Can't it wait, Mam?"

"I'm sure Edyth is eager to see her family," said the countess, "but I do not wish to rush you," she added. "I will leave it up to you, Edyth."

Edyth's mind raced. Suddenly the illusory plans she and Cait had whispered about were becoming a reality. Butterflies erupted in her belly at the thought of going through with their scheme, but she could not falter.

"Thank you for your hospitality, Countess," said Edyth, trying not to squirm in her seat. "I am eager to see my cousin and am grateful for Rory's escort. I...I will leave tomorrow."

The countess nodded once, bowing her head benevolently. "You have my blessing, Lady Edyth. We are indebted to you and gratified to have had you as a guest. Rory," she said, turning to him with a graceful twist of her waist, "you will take Edyth to the MacPhersons tomorrow, as requested."

"Yes, Mum," said the steward, his salt-and-pepper beard touching his chest as he bowed in parting. "Lady Edyth," he mumbled, "I'll see ye in the stable yard at first light tomorrow morning." His boots reverberated loudly, mimicking the pounding in her chest as he exited the room.

Cait was gripping Edyth's hand under the table so hard her fingers ached.

It had begun. Now was the time to set their daring rescue into action. She and Cait had stayed up late, discussing the particulars of their plans the previous night, each of them nervous, excited, and unsure, yet determined.

Ewan, traveling more slowly to Dunbar on account of the number of men he had with him, would not arrive at his destination for at least two days. Because traveling to MacPherson was a relatively simple task and would not require a great contingent of men to attend them, it was best if Rory received the fake missive from Ewan once she and the steward had already left the holding.

It must state that Ewan will send a portion of his men to meet you on your way to Dunbar, Cait had said. *Otherwise, Rory will return home and gather more men as escort. He would not risk taking you toward a battle without a host of men at your side. I don't like deceiving him, but I fear it's the only way.*

Once they had traveled a full day, Edyth was to inconvenience Rory by steeping a bit of broom into his tea. Guts griping, Edyth could steal away from him and arrive at Dunbar alone. From that point, plans became less detailed, but she had to get to Dunbar first. Saving Ewan depended on it.

"Up you get," said the ostler, motioning to Edyth to climb onto the mounting block. Her skirts barely blew in the breeze, heavy and cumbersome. Wishing for her father's hose and mended tunic that were currently rolled up into her satchel, she nevertheless scrambled atop Harris and reached for the reins.

The ostler did not meet her eyes directly, though she was sure he felt her stare burning into him. She wondered if he was sorry for his words to her in the stable. But perhaps he kept his eyes hidden so as not to betray how relieved he felt that she was finally leaving. Regardless, she could not help the rude stare she was now giving him.

Rory's mount danced as the man's considerable weight fell upon its back. The torchlight from the yard reflected in his studded jerkin. Edyth looked to the edge of the yard where the shadows deepened. There stood Cait, wrapped in her plaid, the reassuring smile she hoped to see nonexistent. Instead, her friend's pale, worried face loomed in the darkness. Cait's hand raised in a goodbye salute, her eyes full of unspoken caution and well wishes.

"Tch," said Rory, nudging his great steed forward. "We'll see how far we make today, lady. If ye need tae stop, just say the word."

"How far away are MacPherson clan lands?" Edyth asked, pulling her eyes away from Cait. Harris followed closely behind, his gentle nicker like a greeting from a friend.

"Och, a fair ways. Two days if we push the horses. Three if we go gentle. We'll have tae travel through Stewart and Donnachaidh clans afore we reach MacPherson—friendly tae us both, have nae fear, lassie—and all on good roads. Ye aren't worrit, are ye?"

"Not worried. Only curious," said Edyth, thinking of ways she could stall their progress. She didn't want to go too far north—in the wrong direction—only to have to backtrack and waste valuable time getting to Dunbar.

They rode in companionable silence for most of the morning. Rory's whistling kept them both entertained. Some of the songs she knew, and she sang along with him, feeling at ease in his company. The landscape was beautiful; spring was in full bloom, so the slopes of the mountains and the meadows were filled to bursting with bright colors.

When they stopped for lunch, Rory regaled her with stories from Cait's, Iain's, and Ewan's childhood, full of mischief and laughter. Her favorite story by far was when Cait, in retaliation for her brothers locking her in the root cellar under the old kitchen, had taken great care to empty their pillows of wool and replace it with dried manure from the stable yard. "Her faither," said Rory, through laughter, "the puir soul couldnae keep a straight face long enough tae scold 'er properly—never could. That lassie was trouble from dawn tae dusk, but Malcolm could never stay angry long when it came tae his Cait. And well she knew it!"

Fate proved to be on her side. Not long after lunch, on their second day, they'd come across a drover desperately trying to unstick a sizable cow from a mire near the road. Sweaty and exhausted, he was happy for Rory's help, who was able to use his horse to pull the animal free.

"Sorry about the delay," said Rory, wiping his forehead with a handkerchief. He'd removed some of his armor during the labor, and forgetting it, they'd had to backtrack to retrieve it.

"No complaint from me. I was able to pick these," Edyth answered, showing him a fistful of reseda leaves she'd gathered. "These will make us a lovely tea to go with our supper tonight."

"Mmph," grunted Rory in response. "I'm pleased ye were able to pick yer weeds, lass. Let's be off the noo, aye?"

As the hours passed, Edyth's thoughts turned inward as she reviewed their plan. Tonight—or early tomorrow—the messenger would be sent to them, and they would turn south to be met by an imaginary portion of Ewan's contingent of men. It was then that she would give Rory her special tea and, if it worked, steal away.

Once in Dunbar, she would announce her abilities as a physic and offer her skills. Cait had suggested using the same tactic on Ewan as she had planned for Rory. "You must prevent him from taking the field, even by poisoning him with broom if you must." But Edyth rather thought not even loose bowels would stop him from battle. He'd probably just soil himself and keep fighting, the great fool.

By the time the shadows shifted, making everything appear strangely elongated, Rory told her that they would make camp at his favorite spot along the western road.

It was beautiful. The mallow grass was tall, swaying in the breeze with a pleasant rustle. Beech trees dotted the open space, the gilded rays of the setting sun cutting through the outstretched branches, painting the landscape with dazzling, dancing shapes.

Rory left her to hobble the horses while he gathered fallen branches for a fire. The air even smelled different here: damp and earthy but sweet with spring flowers.

The horses were happily eating and the fire starting to catch when he came. First they heard the pounding hoof beats from the unseen road, then the cloud of dust rising above the line of trees stretching along the path they had just left not a half hour before. Rory stood, his hand on the hilt of his short sword, his eyes squinting in an effort to see the rider.

Spotting them and their fire in the glade, the rider pulled up sharply on the reins, his horse screaming at the abrupt command.

"It's Arthur," said Rory, running to meet the rider halfway.

Edyth watched as they spoke out of reach of her hearing, but she didn't need to hear them. She knew what was in the missive the rider was now handing to her escort. She'd penned it herself, copying Ewan's handwriting as best she could from the letters Cait had provided for her.

Rory and the rider were looking at her now, the cloud of dust settling around them.

"Here we go," said Edyth to herself, swallowing her nervousness.

Two days later and dozens of miles closer to Dunbar, the tea, true to her expectations, inconvenienced—and no doubt embarrassed—Rory. Soon after ingesting it, which Edyth was careful to only pretend to drink, Rory's bowels gurgled so loudly, and he excused himself so hastily that she felt a little sorry for the unavoidable act.

Taking advantage of his absence, she changed out of her skirts and into her father's clothes, careful to stuff her fur with her discarded clothing to make it look as though a person was lying within. She had to add some sticks and ferns to add to the bulk to make it more realistic and then climbed into her bed, waiting for Rory's return from his latest episode.

Edyth did feel guilty every time he excused himself, clenching his buttocks and quick-stepping out of her general vicinity, but she easily steeled her resolve by thinking of Ewan's broken body.

When Rory returned, she feigned sleep, feeling his eyes on her. She lay still, waiting for him to fall asleep or to excuse himself again before slipping away.

It had been her job to hobble the horses while on their journey, and every other night, she had done just that. This night, however, so close to Dunbar, she had only hobbled one horse and left Harris simply tied to a tree branch, out of sight.

Edyth had known it was time to part ways with Rory once he started remarking at how they should have been met by Ewan's escort by now.

Full of nervous energy, it seemed like a long time before Rory settled into sleep, but after the moon had risen, she finally heard Rory's restless movements cease and his now-familiar soft snores begin. Steeling herself, she carefully and quietly slipped away.

Without Rory, her anxiousness increased tenfold. Tucking and retucking her hair under her cap, she tugged Harris forward, eager to get to the village before dark. He'd gotten a stone in his shoe, and finding it too late, she now had to walk him.

Her nervous condition was not solely due to being alone on the road, however. Rory could recover long enough to come after her— on a hale horse—and snatch her up at any moment. He wouldn't likely let her out of his sight again, nor did she want to explain her escape from him.

Going slower had some advantages, though. She'd picked handfuls of tormentil and bog myrtle that she'd spotted on the side of the road, each useful in their own ways. If she couldn't stop the battle from happening, maybe she could use her knowledge of healing herbs to help in some way, however small.

It was a good time to practice what she would say when she got there, in any case. Cait had explained the strange circumstances taking place at Castle Dunbar, which she'd gleaned from her talent of listening at doors.

Cait had explained that Edyth would not find the lord of the castle but his lady wife instead, who held the castle against him.

Marjory, a Comyn by blood, did not follow her husband's political leanings. Her husband, Patrick Dunbar, earl of March, preferred to align himself with England and demonstrated his fealty by joining his forces with the might of Robert de Clifford, King Edward's sheriff of the north.

Having left his castle in this pursuit, his loyalist wife called upon like-minded loyalist clans, raising a call to arms. Patrick Dunbar was on his way, presumably still joined with de Clifford, to take back his own home and fortify it against the Scots. Little did he know that his wife had petitioned King Baliol for help, and that he'd answered.

It was nearing daybreak when she spotted the sleeping village of Spott, nestled serenely at the base of a sloping hill. Her breath caught in her throat at the sight, so familiar to her, though she'd never seen it with her waking eyes. The keep, now looking black in the darkness, loomed over the field of battle, cut down the center by a fast-flowing stream.

Empty now, the open field was inviting, but Edyth took no liking to the beautiful scene laid so quaintly before her. Feeling a cold that had nothing to do with the predawn chill, she pulled her hat more securely over her ears and urged Harris forward. The little village boasted no more than a few dozen buildings, but as she entered the gate, which squeaked loudly in protest at her disruption, she was surprised to find no one about. Yes, it was early yet, the light of the sun not yet over the horizon, but animals must be seen to, crops planted and tended to. The work of living began at such an hour, and yet here, now, there was no life.

Pausing at the corner of one hut, she looked around her. There was no smoke from homely hearth fires or any sounds, save for her own breathing. She looked into a pen, full of signs of hogs, yet saw none.

She frowned, worry rising within her. No birds. No crickets. No people or animals. Thinking better of it, she thought to retreat into the woods and avoid the road to the keep. Perhaps she should follow the curtain wall to the gate.

"Dinnae move, or I'll split yer skull like a wee walnut," warned a steely voice directly behind her.

Edyth doubted if she could have moved had she wanted to. Her heart in her throat, her blood running cold, Edyth felt frozen in place, barely breathing.

There were two of them. She felt the point of something sharp push against her spine between her shoulder blades at the same time that she saw a man step from the shadow of the building in front of her.

"What business do ye have skulking around my village, laddie?" asked the man in front of her. He was in full armor, his studded hauberk hanging low over his hips, making him seem as thick and as straight as a tree trunk. His hand rested on the hilt of his sword, his gauntlets clicking with the smallest movement.

"Did ye see his clothes, Den?" asked the man behind her. "Best check his bag...mayhap 'es a messenger, aye?"

She stared, her mind racing, afraid to move.

"I asked ye a question, and I expect an answer." The man in front of her stepped closer, his black eyes shining within his steel-nosed helmet. "This village was emptied two days past and the English marching closer by the hour. I'll ask ye once more. What are ye doing here, in my village, laddie?"

Edyth was, quite simply, afraid to speak and give herself away, but she couldn't very well remain as she was. They didn't seem the kind to waste their time with diplomacy.

She took a breath in an effort to force her heart back to its rightful place and said a prayer. It was her first honest prayer in quite a long time and remarkably straightforward. She simply said, *Help.*

"I've come to assist," she said.

The point of whatever was in her back increased its pressure. Den's eyes narrowed dangerously, his mouth pressing into a grim line. Edyth saw him nod once, and then she was on the ground, a knee in her back, her hat ripped from her head.

"You sound English." The man breathed to her back. His breath stirred her hair, tickling her ear.

Her satchel was wrested from her, the strap pulling her hair as it was ripped from her body.

"I'm a physic," she wheezed, trying to draw breath.

Hands patted down her body, searching, and pulled the dirk from her waist. She heard more than saw the contents of her satchel fall to the ground as it was upended, bits of herbs, ribbon, and her mother's herbal book thumping and bouncing onto the soft earth.

"Is that all ye've got for us?" asked the man on her back. He flipped her over and searched her again, this time pulling his hand away in shock as he brushed his hand across her chest.

"*Is e nighean a th ann!*" he shouted, his shocked face staring at her dirtied face.

"A lass?" asked Den, looming over her. Their faces were in shadow, the sun's first rays turning the sky purple. They both stared at her as though she were a bug they'd never seen before.

After a long pause, Den rubbed the back of his neck and said, "We'd best take 'er up tae the mistress then, aye?"

Chapter Eleven

Men filled the hot room, hunched around a small table so that they looked like a large lumpy mass, all connected bodily. Upon their entrance, the room, which had been filled with the low, murmuring buzz of coconspirators, had ceased, replaced with a silence so thick Edyth could feel it pressing in on her eardrums. Her heartbeat quickened, and she licked her lips in nervousness.

The room smelled of woodsmoke, sweat, and whiskey. The central figure of interest appeared to be an intricately drawn map littered with an odd assortment of objects—an inkwell, a smattering of what looked like walnuts, coins, and a wax seal brick strategically placed around its weblike contours.

All lost interest in the map, however, when Edyth was unceremoniously thrust through the door. Though all the faces were shrouded in dancing shadows, she could feel the weight of their stares like a heavy cloak. The unnatural quiet her presence had generated made the hairs on the back of her neck stand to attention.

Edyth swallowed with effort and tugged on her pinioned arm weakly. She knew it was pointless to fight. Where could she run that they would not find her?

There was a grunt on the right of the crowded room, a bustling of movement, and then a woman emerged, rather short and sturdy with silver-gray, cold eyes and hair as black as ink. Her skin was flushed, her cheeks ruddy with either the exhilaration of war making or in anger at being interrupted. Maybe both, thought Edyth.

"Who are you?" demanded the woman. Her voice cracked like thunder in the intense quiet of the room. She was standing far too close for Edyth's comfort. She could feel her breath on her chin, feel the rise and fall of her breasts—though she wasn't quite touching her—and could see each crease of her skin around her eyes as she glared up at Edyth.

Edyth took an involuntary step backward from the woman and bumped directly into the guard, whom, at this exact moment, she was grateful for. If he hadn't been physically holding her, she didn't think she'd have the nerve to stand against the fierceness of the lady or the room's other surly occupants.

"Does she have a tongue?" demanded the woman, her eyes flicking to the guard standing behind Edyth and then back. Edyth would have thought her eyes beautiful, if not so menacing.

"Dunno her name, Countess. She hasn't said naught but two words o' sense since we found her, but she's said enough fer us tae ken she's English."

One black brow arched in reply, her eyes dilating like a cat about to pounce on its prey. Edyth fumbled into a half-curtsey, the best she could do with the guard holding her arm as he was, and then stood on shaky legs.

The mouth of Marjory Comyn, the eighth countess of Dunbar, curved into a smile so sweet that it confused Edyth. "What do ye mean by bringing this.. *guest* here, Dennis?" she asked, her voice thrumming through the room as though she'd shouted.

"I...the lady," stuttered the guard, "she was caught skulking around the village. I thought that ye'd like to see to her yourself, seeing as how she's English."

Her penetrating stare bore into Edyth for a breath, and then her eyes narrowed onto that of her guardsman. The countess pursed her thin lips briefly in contemplation, then nodded to herself as though coming to a decision.

"Indeed," said the countess, and even Edyth could see the restraint of the woman as she took a restorative breath and blew it out, her hand resting against her ribs. "Ye've got the brains o' a *sheep*," she spat at the guard, and Edyth saw the flash of metal glint across the sgian-dubh she'd produced from, seemingly, thin air.

"Only a complete fool would bring the asp straight to our breast as ye have so skillfully done. I should lock the likes of ye up together!" The woman thrust the blade of her dagger under Edyth's nose and smiled at her quick intake of breath. Edyth would have recoiled from the danger if not for the wall of bone and muscle pressed against her back.

All was quiet save for Edyth's heart, which was beating so furiously in her ears that she was sure the woman could hear it.

"Countess, I know the lady," said a calm, familiar voice. She hadn't noticed him before in the huddle of men, but the smooth thrum of his baritone was unmistakable. Relief surged through Edyth like a wave rushing the shore, so much so that she felt her knees turn to water.

He came forward, jostling those around him to stand in what open space was afforded him nearest the door. Edyth annoyed herself by noticing that he was even more handsome than she'd remembered. With his chiseled, unshaven jaw limned with golden candlelight and his midnight-blue eyes alive with danger, why she would challenge even Sister

Mary Agnes from the rectory in Carlisle to not stand, open mouthed in awe at this, God's creation. Never mind that he was more graceful in movement than she could ever hope to be.

He inclined his head politely to the countess and then to Edyth, the perfect appearance of control and dignity. And anger. Yes, there was a flash of anger that he spared just for her. Damn. There was no use fretting over it. Cait *had* warned her, after all.

"Laird Ruthven, is it?" the countess asked, lowering her dirk to her waist but not sheathing it. "How do ye ken this prowling Englishwoman?" Her fine, dark brow was arched in wait as she surveyed him. Edyth wondered if her acerbic look was sharp enough to cut through flesh.

He bowed slightly and quickly, his face a mask. "She is a skilled physic, Countess. My brother has lately been injured. She has been tending to his health."

An expressionless stare moved from Ewan to Edyth. She looked Edyth up and down, took in her rumpled appearance, and said, "And yet she left her charge's sickbed tae be found sneaking around a Scottish holding? I've let you into my home for the trust my advisors had for your father. You are his son in body, yes, but what of character? Could this *lady*," she said the word in a way that conveyed deep skepticism, "be guiding ye along by yer bollocks?"

Ewan did not appreciate either insinuation, if the cool look he cast the countess was any indication. "My presence here is evidence enough of my honor as a soldier and son of Scotland." Edyth was grateful that his anger was not directed at her. She wanted to shrink from the fire she saw within him.

"A word of caution," he continued, "in the future, when friends come to your aid, it would behoove you to nae insult them. When the battle is done, we will be in need of her talents."

"A strange way to offer me your skill, lurking where you ought not."

"I wasn't lurking," blurted Edyth. "I was gathering herbs. That is all."

The countess made a noncommittal noise in her throat, her eyes narrowing with suspicion. It made Edyth want to squirm, but she held herself steady, thrusting out her chin determinately. The countess looked to the guard, who let go of Edyth's arm to fumble in his sporran. He produced Edyth's meager pickings, now wilted, so the ends that were not supported by his hand laid limp, trailing downward toward the floor.

The countess looked angrier than ever. Her thin lips disappeared entirely as she glared at the contents in the guard's gloved hand. "Take her to the tower, Dennis. I will deal with her later."

The guard immediately seized Edyth's arms, pinning them to her sides. Edyth, taken aback by the heaviness of his hand, stiffened but did not struggle. She would never forget the look on Ewan's face as she was pulled from the room. He would never forgive her.

∞

The door opened with such force that it bounced against the stone wall opposite. Edyth scrambled to her feet to meet Ewan's tall frame as it filled the darkened doorway; she didn't need to see his face to guess his feelings. The very air was charged with his anger.

Edyth spied a guard in the hallway, a torch just out of sight illuminating the side of his face. Ewan shut the door, and it took a moment for her eyes to readjust to the dim.

Ewan walked before her, his hands folded behind his back, pacing for several steps, saying nothing. A muscle in his jaw jumped, and Edyth waited, holding her tongue. Somehow, she knew speaking just now would loosen the tight rein he held on his temper.

After several rounds about the room and after punching the toe of his boot into a chipped stone wall several times, he turned to her in a semblance of control.

"I cannot believe I've need to ask ye this question," said Ewan, pausing to take a stilling breath," after all ye've been through, and all I've done to aid ye, but what in the name of God are ye doing here?" He didn't give her a chance to answer. "I gave ye explicit instructions, yet ye just wander as ye please, paying no mind to what trouble ye cause yerself or *me*."

Edyth crossed her arms over her chest, hiding her shaking hands. "Yes, that's right," she said, nodding in earnest. "I do as I please, though why you feel you have a say in my choices, I'll never know."

Ewan stared at her as though he'd never seen her like. "Why I feel I have a say?" he repeated, incredulous. "Do ye recall how it was when I found ye, Edyth?"

Edyth waved a hand as though to dismiss the dire situation he'd saved her from, though her cheeks warmed uncomfortably. "Yes, yes, we both know what a bloody hero you are. You're also as stubborn as a bull! You know why I'm here!"

His brows rose to new heights. "More dreams, Edyth? We've spoken of this! Ye think I can dismiss a call to arms? What of my duty? My name—my father's name—means something, Edyth! I cannae turn my back on my responsibility."

"What of my vision? What of your death?"

He shook his head, exasperated, but held his anger in check. She could see it—feel it—bubbling beneath the surface. "I am prepared to die, Edyth, but are you? They're dreams, woman. Nothing more."

Edyth shook her head and clenched her teeth against her mounting anger "No. You're wrong. I saw you... I saw it all. It's terrible, Ewan! You wouldn't be so quick to discount it if you'd seen what I have."

He glowered at her, refusing to budge even an inch. "Ye don't need to tell me how terrible it is. I've lived it, remember?"

"It will be a pike...buried in your chest, but you'll not die quickly. No, you'll suffer and struggle while you wait for a slow death." Edyth pointed an accusatory finger at his chest, her face pale. "If *you* will do nothing to change it, then *I* must."

Ewan seemed to grow angrier at her words. "And what if it is true? Would ye have me run like a dog and cower? Do ye wish me to throw myself at English feet all to live another day? I will not!" His eyes seemed to glow, wide and wild, his face ruddy with anger.

Edyth scoffed. "Stupid man! Of course, you think I mean to insult your honor. Nothing could be worse, could it? You will die for pride's sake?"

"What else do I have of worth, if not honor?" Ewan demanded.

She ran both of her hands through her hair, at a loss. She took several deep breaths, striving for calm. It was with a great effort that she lowered her voice. "Please," she tried again, "can you just listen." She reached for his hand. It was large and warm and calloused.

"I cannot change my parents' deaths, and I wasn't meant to. If I had been meant to change their fates, then I would have seen it as I see your death. Don't you understand?" She searched his face, but it was hardened and angry. "Why will it not leave me?" she asked, anguished. "I see that you will not run. You cannot. What I ask of you now is to change the countess. Change her mind. Change the battle."

Ewan pulled his hand free and pierced her with his blue-black gaze, pinning her to the spot.

"Change something that hasn't even happened yet? Edyth," he said, his irritation loosed, "this is no place for ye! You're speaking about things ye know nothing about! You're a damned fool to take such risks. Do ye ken what could have happened to ye?" he asked, his brow wrinkled in accusation. He ran both hands into his hair, making it stand up on end in odd angles. "Oh, but ye *do* ken!" It was his turn to shout now, one long finger pointed at her chest. "That's the trouble o' it. Ye havenae learned a damned thing.

"Why couldn't ye at least wear a gown? Yer da's English clothes on an English lass, found in the dark o' a village that's already been emptied o' its inhabitants doesnae smell afoul to ye? Because it does to every person who was in that room below. Aye, if I didnae ken better, I'd wonder myself." He looked sharply at her, then his eyes narrowed in sudden accusation.

"You insolent, pig-headed...Scot!" shouted Edyth, matching Ewan's anger. "What of *my* duty? I cannot simply ignore what my heart demands. If you had seen—" her voice waivered, remembering, but she swallowed her words. It did no good to try and scare him from battle with the promise of pain. "You speak of duty and honor, but you will not give me the same courtesy. I will not sit idle and rob you of a life when it is avoidable."

"You don't have a say in this, Edyth. I gave ye my word I'd keep ye safe, and then ye ridicule me for seeing it done! I left ye in Perth for a purpose!" He, clearly at a loss, paced before her like a great, stalking cat. "I cannae even imagine the hell ye put your poor father through!"

"You dare!" Edyth pushed against him, flat palms upon his jerkined chest. He barely moved. "I came to be of *use*. I came to save lives...yours included, you dimwitted ass!"

"I'm an arse now, am I?" Ewan demanded, taking a menacing step forward. They were toe-to-toe now, only a few inches apart. She could smell him, feel the hot gusts of his breath on her forehead. "I try to keep ye from getting killed—raped on the road—and ye defy me the first chance ye get."

Edyth felt herself bristle. "*Defy* you?"

"Aye, *defy!*" he railed, any semblance of control gone. "Ye plunge yerself back into danger when I finally have ye safe!" His voice broke on the last word, and he turned away from her. She watched him wrestle with his anger. After a long moment, his breathing returned to something like normal, and he turned to her again, his eyes filled with something she could not define.

"Aye, I am an arse," he said quietly.

His demeanor frightened her.

He stared down into her eyes, searching. For what, she didn't know. He took hold of her upper arms, his hot hands branding her through the fabric of her shirt sleeves. Edyth flinched in reflex, her body responding to the heat of their exchange. He tightened his hands reflexively, holding her steady. He swallowed. Edyth followed the path of his throat as it worked. He hadn't shaved in several days. Little coppery spikes of hair stuck out at every angle along his neck and jawline.

Finally, softly, he said, "I need ye kept safe, Edyth. I need ye whole and well." He shook her softly then as though he could compel her to understand through sheer will of force. "I've made ye a promise that I intend tae keep, Edie. I willnae fail ye again."

With a sigh, he let go to stroke her hair, placing a lock behind her ear. Her skin tingled in a trail where he'd touched her. "I did send ye away, aye. But if I'm tae die, as ye claim, then I will have ye be as far from the danger as possible. I wanted ye with yer kin, protected and safe."

"Yes, you did promise me," she reminded him. "You promised you would keep me from harm, so long as it was in your power to do so. But what of my heart? What of my torment? You would make me live with the blood of your people on my hands? You make promises, then forswear yourself in the same breath, Ewan. How could I live with myself if I ignore *my* duty? Saving you *is* saving myself."

Ewan studied her face, the stony mask of anger melting away to one of resigned acquiescence.

They stared at each other for a long moment, sharing breath. "My, ye are a brave wee thing, Edie," he whispered.

"How is it," Edyth asked, pausing to lick the dryness from her lips, "that you can worry for my welfare, but I am not given the same courtesy?"

The barest of smiles touched the corner of his mouth, and he looked at her briefly before turning his attention to his hands. The palms of them were upturned so that Edyth could see the hardened calluses from blisters past, yellowed and slightly transparent. The palm of his right hand was rather pink...a new blister forming, no doubt from the hilt of a foreign blade. "These hands have known little else, save violence. Least ways I can't rightly recall what they looked like before I fostered with my uncle so many years ago."

He closed his fingers into fists and exhaled, his eyes returning to hers. "Worry for those I care for has been my life's work. It is all I've known and has usually required a sharp blade if not a sharper tongue. Sometimes I dinnae ken which is more cutting. Please," he said, "forgive me for my harsh words. Ye dinnae deserve them."

Edyth's heart seemed to stop altogether and then restart with force at his words. He said he cared for her.

"Why can't ye have visions o' me growing fat and old, sittin' on piles of gold?" asked Ewan.

The tension left Edyth all at once, and she laughed breathlessly. She shrugged and said, "For the same reason you can't listen to reason the first time it knocks you up side the head."

Ewan didn't exactly smile, but his lips twitched as though itching for one. He shook his head, eyes intent on her. "I'm not sure there's anything I can do to persuade her. She's a damned obstinate woman, not unlike someone else I know."

Edyth smiled up at him and shrugged once more. "Stubborn women can be moved. You just have to apply the right force."

"Yes, well, since I've never mastered the technique required, maybe it's you that should be doing the persuading. Speaking of," he said, swiveling his head to look at her, "what have ye done with poor Rory? How did ye persuade *him* to let ye come? It's not like him to disobey orders."

Edyth had forgotten all about Rory; the mention of him made the guilt she'd pushed and hidden away awaken suddenly and shake the bars of its prison. "He was told you'd sent word that I was needed as a physic," she said, careful to keep Cait out of it, her face flushing. "He brought me as far as East Linton and...and I poisoned him so I could slip away."

"Poison!" he said, stunned, his eyes wide in shock. "Poison?" he hissed, quieter this time, shooting a glance at the guarded door.

"Twas only a bit of broom steeped in his tea," said Edyth with a dismissing wave of her hand. "He'll be put to rights after it passes through him. I do regret the discomfort it will cause him, but I knew if he brought me all the way to Castle Dunbar, you'd have him take me right back, and—"

"Damn right I would have!" he interjected emphatically.

"I couldn't chance it," she said. "And once I got into the village and saw it emptied, I thought something had gone terribly wrong. But I hadn't seen any signs of battle."

"There has already been blood spilt," said Ewan, taking her satchel from his shoulder at last. He tossed it to her, and she caught it against her chest, openmouthed in surprise.

"Whose? When?"

"In the night," answered Ewan. "The Black Comyn's son, the lord of Badenoch, was injured while scouting. Some of his men died, and he is sorely wounded. He's got arrows sticking out o' him. That's the reason I've come," he said, motioning toward her satchel.

"Marjory's willing to let ye out of here, so long as ye can save her cousin's life."

Dread filled Edyth from her toes to her heart, weighing it down uncomfortably. "What if I can't save him?"

Ewan gave her a look of regret when he said, "You must."

The enormity of the task that lay before her filled her with dread. She was lying to herself, thinking herself equal to this task. Cait had explained that the cunning folk could cast spells, command the elements to work in their favor, and heal the sick, among other talents. She could do none of those things. All she could do was bind a wound, make a poultice, and hope the ague didn't take them.

Not for the first time, she wished for her skillful, graceful mother. She would have known exactly what to do for the dying man. In her mind's eye, Edyth saw her mother going boldly to her death, the early morning sun seeming to light her from within, a hundred miles and a lifetime away. Skirts astir in the ever-present wind; wisps of her coppery hair, now severely streaked with white, escaped the strict hold of her plait to float and dance like so many leaves.

Edyth could see her now, her long fingered hands bound yet clasped calmly as though merely waiting for her tea rather than the gallows. She'd stood as tall and as straight as an arrow and had looked down upon Father Brewer with such distain that he'd demanded she be turned away from him.

Her mother had been as confident in death as she had been in life, always knowing who she'd been, as still as a stone, and just as unmovable, even as the noose was tightened around her elegant neck. Thinking of it, Edyth felt the weight of shame at her own fear and uncertainty.

Not skilled enough for this task, the Comyn would die, and she would soon follow. That she knew in the very marrow of her bones. It rankled, unsettling her further, that she would die having never learned who she was. Yes, she knew things *about* herself. She was proud and short-tempered, neither profoundly intelligent nor markedly stupid. She was mediocre in every sense of the word. She was impulsive and prone to fidgeting. She was too thin, too tall, too freckled. Too unsure. Too cowardly. Too little like her mother. But given a life, who would she have grown to be?

Who was she indeed? She had literally dressed as her father and had regurgitated medicines from her mother's book of herbs as though she knew what she was doing. She was a pretender, an imitator, and nothing more. She had merely tried on others' lives when she didn't know what to do with her own. It was only now that she realized how poorly they fit, like too-large shoes that made her stumble and fall when not careful.

Suddenly very weary, Edyth slowed her steps behind the guard escorting her.

"Keep up," he barked, gesturing impatiently with a shake of his head. The halls were dark, as all keeps were, wet and musty and riddled with rats. The castle was a labyrinth of stairs and hallways, the walls several feet thick. Escape was impossible. She had no idea where she was, so she turned her mind away from daring escapes with Ewan and onto the task at hand.

The only problem was that instead of discovering in her mind some solution, she only saw Ewan, skin stretched tightly, burned from the relentless sun, pecked to pieces by the corbies.

A shiver raced down her spine. He, like her mother, was ready to die, with the knowledge of truth and duty written upon his heart. But still—even as every step took her to her doom—she knew that she had done right. She would rather die here, in the pursuit of saving her friend, than to live a life full of regret because she'd been too afraid to try.

And you think you're so different from your mother, a voice seemed to say. She looked about her, feeling as though someone or something was near…some force of nature, felt but not seen, walk in step with her.

With the shutters drawn and only a few long tapers illuminating the head of the bedstead, she wasn't sure how many people were in the room. An injured man—the Black Comyn's son—lay on the stately bed; she could see his feet splayed out, toes pointing east and west. The white of the linen bedsheet covering him glowed like the moon in a starless heaven. Someone was praying; she could hear their plea to St. Michael, "Divina virtute in infernum detrude."

Darkened, shapeless forms were perched on either side of the bed like gargoyles, the light illuminating bits of their person here and there as they moved—a nose, straight and long, as its owner bent to whisper into the injured man's ear, a hand, fluttering spiderlike to smooth the hair back from a broad forehead, then retreating once more like a snake into its hole.

The air was thick with the metallic scent of spilled blood and bitter sweat. Edyth could taste it on her tongue, and she swallowed compulsorily.

A hand at Edyth's elbow made her jump slightly. It urged her forward, and as she came closer, she saw what the dark had concealed. Marjory Comyn's wan face stared at her from where she sat at the head of the bed, the candlelight making her eye sockets appear empty, save for the steely glint of light on a glassy orb.

A bloodstained handkerchief dangled from her hand. Edyth recognized Marjory's uncle standing on the other side of the bed, surly and huge. John Comyn, lord of Badenoch, sent by King John to defend Dunbar Castle, was massive and as dark as his name implied. His enormous hands opened and closed repeatedly, craving action, Edyth supposed. "My husband took our *bana-bhuidseach geal* with him when he left," Marjory said in way of greeting. "Work your magic, Lady Edyth, and your life will be spared."

The words echoed in her skull, reverberating outward like ripples in a pond. *Save him. You must.* Edyth had heard those words spoken before; she recognized the voice from her dreams, but instead of them being spoken on the ramparts, it was here, in the quiet of this chamber that dream met reality. And it wasn't Ewan whom the voice had demanded she save but this stranger.

Edyth's mouth was very dry, and she had to try twice to swallow. "What's happened to him?" Edyth asked, feeling detached from her own body. The question was pointless. She knew what had happened because Ewan had told her, but she didn't know what to say, so she filled the empty space with words.

"I sent him to scout for the English, but the great smout got ambushed close to Bransly Hill. Dennis and Robert are dead," John Comyn said, reaching to wipe more blood from the man's pallid face.

The injured man had a large cut that ran from his left nostril to his left eyebrow, just missing, thankfully, his eye. "The blood is running freely. That's good," she heard herself say.

His nose was slightly deflated on one side, the cartilage of his nose hanging free from his face. She'd need comfrey leaves and her mother's gut suture thread. That was the extent of her knowledge for this man's grievous wounds.

"Make haste, witch," said Marjory, gesturing to the satchel hanging from Edyth's body. "Come, he has other wounds that you will tend to." With that, she carefully pulled the coverlet back to reveal the depth of his injuries.

Arrow shafts protruded from his abdomen, broken off close to his body. Blood trickled freely, pooling around him into the straw mattress.

"Did you break these shafts?" Edyth asked his father. He was nearly as pale as his son, his eyes sparking black in a bone-white skull. "No," he rasped. He cleared his throat and tried again. "The lads who saw him fall did it before they brought him back. He couldnae ride astride, so they had tae lay him over the beast's back. They cut the arrows short so they wouldnae pain him further."

He shifted on his heavily booted feet and leaned over the bed to better see the extent of the damage. "Shall I hold him for ye, then, so ye can cut 'em out?" His voice was forcibly gruff, as though he could simply scare the affection and worry he felt for his son away.

"Surely there is a tonic or a wee charm ye can give him?" said the countess, her eyes wide, her voice aghast.

Edyth felt her heart thaw ever so slightly toward the woman. While she had treated Edyth with no ounce of courtesy, she could respect and understand the desperate feelings she must now be having.

"Here," said the father, digging in his sporran and producing a flask of some strong spirit. He put one hairy, thick arm under his son's shoulders to lift him and pressed it to his lips. The patient groaned at the movement but swallowed several hearty mouthfuls before coughing and sputtering. This dosage was prescribed several more times while Edyth's mind raced.

What should I do? thought Edyth, casting out for what, she didn't know. Her mother? God? Something, anything, that could aid her, still her racing mind and replace the hollow terror she felt with confident action.

Not knowing what to do but feeling that she ought to do *something*, she moved closer to the bed. Although there was quite a lot of blood, it was not spurting out around the shafts. That seemed good. "Cut the sark from him," she commanded. Her voice was strong and did not waiver. A knife was produced, from where she did not notice, and the pieces of the sodden shirt were folded back as the petals of a blooming flower.

His muscled chest, white and gleaming with blood and sweat, raised and lowered with each breath, the cage of his ribs expanding and contracting, the shaft of the arrow mimicking his movements.

Edyth's mind cleared as an image formed in her mind, sure and distinct. There, just under the last of his ribs, the arrow had notched itself. She imagined that the bone was cracked, nicked, from the force of the blow, and as painful as it surely was, Edyth knew it had not harmed him further.

The other arrow, however, was more difficult to judge. Low upon his abdomen, just above his right hip, the dark spot of blood revealed the location of the wound, but she could not see a shaft.

"The pressure of his body against the saddle pushed the arrow in deeper," she heard herself say. "This...this is a grievous wound."

"You mean to cut him open?" asked the countess, stricken. "Surely ye can pull it free."

Edyth met the woman's fearful eyes. "If the sinew holding the arrowheads to the shafts has softened and loosened their hold, I will have no choice but to cut them out."

Marjory's already white lips drained of what color they had as she pressed them together unhappily.

"Do it then. Pull them out and be done with it," growled the patient, his breathing fast and shallow, his eyes dulled with pain.

"Of course." Edyth did not need to open her satchel to know she was woefully short of any useful implements for removing arrowheads. "I don't have any grasping tools." *Only weeds.*

The countess snapped her fingers and someone bustled out of the room hurriedly. "You will have what you need. Tell me what else you require."

"A kettle with hot water. For my herbs," said Edyth, removing the satchel slung across her chest. "I will need a knife. Your guard took mine."

The Black Comyn quickly withdrew a long dirk and offered it to her, but Edyth shook her head. "I will need something smaller, and very sharp."

An array of proffered implements were immediately laid before her from the occupants in the room. Edyth selected a short sock knife, her hand trembling ever so slightly.

"You will hold him," she commanded, her eyes resting on the patient's father.

"I will need these steeped in a kettle." Rummaging through her satchel, Edyth filled her hands with both dried and fresh, albeit wilted, herbs.

Jumping from her seat, Marjory used her skirt to pull the iron kettle from the hearth fire and brought it to the bed. "It's just water for washing."

Edyth quickly deposited the ingredients into the steaming mouth of the pot and wiped her shaking hands on her skirts. "I will need cloth for binding the wounds."

Hastening to the chest at the end of the bed, Marjory pulled out a neatly folded linen and set to work ripping it into manageable strips.

Edyth looked down on her patient and inhaled the scent of his sweaty, blood-soaked body, a strange calm settling over her. *Help*, she prayed again, *I don't know what to do.*

Odder yet, an answer came to her mind, formed as a thought. It could have been her own, yet it was separate and distinct, and quite familiar indeed. She closed her eyes briefly, welcoming the humming, living chord that was strung from her soul to that God in heaven she had thought had abandoned her.

"Hello," the voice seemed to say. "I've been waiting for you."

Tears prickled the backs of her eyes then. Was it relief she was feeling now or something more? Regardless, when the servant returned with a variety of the blacksmith's tongs, it was with steady hands that Edyth set to work.

"Put the iron in the fire," she said, her voice full of authority.

She nodded to the Black Comyn, and he took his place at her side, bracing his hands on his son's shoulders.

"Bite on this," she said, placing the leather strap of her satchel into the man's mouth. His breathing increased, whistling through his nose. She felt his fear and his determination; she placed a hand on his shoulder and spoke softly to him.

"I will work as quickly as I can. Try and hold still. Scream if you must, but do not move."

He nodded once and set his jaw, his eyes screwed tightly shut.

Chapter Twelve

A line of mounted English cavalry stretched along the tree line— hundreds of helms, spears, and tips of bows—winking in and out of sight as they disappeared into the fringes of the forest. The small village Spott was still and quiet, save for the guards at the village gate. Some of its inhabitants had come into the protection of the castle walls, others had fled to their respective sides to fight, and a few had fled in wagons heavy-laden with their prized possessions to places unknown.

The sun was rising too quickly as it wanted to do whenever people needed more time, its light glinting off armor as though winking in shared confidence of what was to come. Edyth's mouth was dry, and she had to force a swallow, mentally reviewing her list of tasks still to be completed.

Checking her patient once more for signs of fever, she tucked the blanket carefully about his shoulders and, grabbing a discarded plaid, wrapped it around her shoulders. The balcony off the room was small but well protected, its wall rising to Edyth's chest. Majory's smaller frame was nearly swallowed up by the rampart, but she could still see. Her eyes were distant, far out into the forest where the host of unseen English awaited them.

"We've taken possession of the western slope—the high ground," said Marjory, her voice as far away as her thoughts. After a pause, she took a deep breath and turned to Edyth, her silver-gray eyes solemn. Pointing with her lily-white hand toward the ridge where the tops of tents were just visible, the smoke of struggling fires snaking slowly up and away, Marjory's face betrayed her worry.

Gone was the woman in the war room, whose steely resolve had frightened Edyth. Now seeing the fear in her eyes, Edyth was frightened for an altogether different reason.

"Will he live?" she asked, not meeting Edyth's gaze. She was looking over the western slope again, at the loyalist Scots arranging themselves, commanded by their lairds. Closer to the keep, there were a number of men still dressing, sharpening weapons, and awaiting their steeds.

The countess had stayed all night by her cousin's side, despite there being little to nothing she could do for the man. She was stubborn. Maybe just as stubborn as herself, Edyth thought.

Draping the borrowed plaid onto Marjory's shoulders, Edyth answered her as truthfully as possible. "If the ague does not take him, he will live."

Marjory nodded ever so slightly; her lips pressed into a thin white line, but she said nothing.

The host of Scots that had formed lines upon the high ground were an impressive sight. Mostly made up of calvary, their breath mingled with that of their beasts, snaking up like so many tiny fires in the dewy spring air. The Black Comyn was already afield, shouting commands to his men, who stood in ranks. The Comyn flag, dutifully held by his page, fluttered weakly.

Edyth knew that flag, had seen it so many times. She could recite its appellation even at this distance. *I exist.*

Edyth shivered, but not with the cold.

As though Marjory had read her thoughts, she said, "I fear that I have signed my death warrant. You should flee, *bana-bhuidseach geal*. I have no quarrel with you, and it would be a sin for me to promise you your life, then bid ye stay to die by another's sword." Her heavy-lidded eyes were ringed with sleepless shadows. Perhaps now was the time to persuade her of her folly.

"I have seen this day," said Edyth softly, meeting Marjory's hollow expression. The woman's eyes searched her own, trying to see what she, herself, had seen.

"Tell me," Majory commanded, breathless.

"This sweeping hill down to the vacant village is empty now, but soon it will be filled with gore." Edyth looked away from her unlikely confidant and saw, in her mind's eye, the fallen, broken men. The gutted horses. The black earth hungrily drinking their life's blood.

"Whose?" she asked. "Ours or the English?"

Edyth swallowed and shook her head to rid her mind of the gory images. "Your house and all these that stand with you" she said, opening her eyes to behold the ashen face of the woman sharing her blanket, "will fall."

Marjory inhaled sharply through her nose, her eyes tearing from Edyth's to the field. "And what of me? Have ye seen my fall as well?"

"I cannot say. I did not see your death, but…" Edyth faltered, unwilling to guess at the gibbet and the shadows she saw in her dream. "Just shadows," she whispered, not meeting Marjory's eyes. "I cannot say what becomes of us women."

"What have I done?" Marjory asked. Her hands were trembling.

Edyth caught one and held it between both of her own. "You have done your duty," said Edyth. "And now I must do mine. You must call off the battle, Countess. You must concede."

Marjory's eyes, full of fear, narrowed in anger as they pinned Edyth to the spot. "You think I am afraid to die?"

Shaking her head, Edyth put a calming hand onto Marjory's shoulder. Bristled as she was in anger, she was halfway surprised when Marjory did not shake her loose. "You are no coward, Countess. Indeed, what I ask of you now will take more courage than facing death. You must risk your position of influence and the regard of your people. You must accept defeat today, and in so doing, your people will live to fight another day."

Marjory's anger changed shape; Edyth could see the thoughts skittering about behind her frightened eyes. "You do not know what you ask of me."

That was true, Edyth thought. Perhaps giving her castle to King Edward would take more courage than she had, but what would be the cost otherwise? Edyth recalled Ewan's words to her atop Harris as they were nestled together, sharing their stories.

Love for your home and love for a way of life are rooted within a man's breast; to tear it out would wound enough to kill. Not your body, aye. Not your soul, for that belongs to God alone. But the wound, once made, cannae be staunched. Slowly, your life—and your way of living it—will wither away to be forgotten. In time enough, the home ye loved will be gone. Replaced. Forgotten. And that is why we fight. We fight to remember our ways. We fight tae no' forget who we are.

To ask the strong woman in front of her to concede her home to an English king seemed impossible. And while Edyth did not know what was to come after, she did know that this battle had to be stopped.

"King Baliol was chosen by King Edward because of his weakness," Edyth continued. "You cannot fight against Edward with such a king. You must let these men live to fight under a united Scotland, on a different day."

"You have seen this?" asked Marjory, her silver eyes searching her own, begging for assurance.

Edyth steeled herself as she lied. "Yes. I have seen it." She'd always been a terrible liar. Even now, she felt her cheeks heat.

"What will happen?" Marjory asked, her fingers biting into Edyth's forearm.

She hesitated and looked out onto the field, where the remaining men from the yard had joined the main force, little bodies pressed together in neat rows.

"We're running out of time, Marjory. Say the word, and I will bring it to the front."

The strength seemed to leave Marjory as she fell against the ramparts, her hair tugged free from her braid. It floated above her in the wind, her face gone white.

The countess Marjory Comyn of Dunbar nodded her concession.

Edyth stole away, only pausing long enough to grab a scrap of linen besmirched with Comyn blood.

Ewan had positioned his men on the farthest edge of the western slope, hoping to flank the English once they attempted to cross the river cutting through the field. The wind was low, but the cold was cutting in the early light of the new day.

He stamped his feet, trying not to think about Edyth's predictions. She'd scared him, made him second-guess himself, and he couldn't afford to have a scattered mind, no more so than torn convictions. He crossed himself and said a quick prayer. *If I am to die today, Lord, let me do it well. I would have my father be proud to see me when I meet him.*

His horse was nervous, pawing the soft earth and pulling at his reins. "*Bi sàmhach. Ma tha i ceart, bidh sinn ann am pàrras a dh' aithghearr.*" *Be still. If she's right, we'll be in paradise soon.*

Someone shouted, and a flurry of activity erupted on the far side of the hill, closer to the keep. His eyes followed the pointed fingers of some of the men to the base of the hill, where a lone rider, bent low over his horse's neck, was riding hell-bent for the opposite side of the hill.

He watched, confused, as the boy rose upon the stirrups, his rear end held high in the air; it appeared as though he were struggling with something in his sark. The rider braced himself as the horse took the river in a great, bounding leap. It landed with its back feet in the water and, spurred on by its rider, jumped and struggled up the steep embankment onto the opposite side. He could hear the beast's protests even from so far away.

As the horse took off again, and the rider with it—struggling still with one arm tucked into his shirt, the other held fast to the horse—the rider's hat blew off with the force of the speed at which he rode.

The shout in Ewan's throat stuck, ineffectual, as he watched in horror. He knew that rider. He knew the flaming trail of red hair that streamed behind her. And he knew, as soon as she pulled her hand free of her sark, what she would hold.

The pale streamer unfurled, held fast in her fist. She held it aloft even as the horse beneath her ran at a full gallop, leaping over obstacles he could not see.

The Scottish line stared, entranced, as the white flag of truce was carried straight to the waiting English lords now riding out to meet it.

Edyth followed the retainer through dark passageways, down steep, winding stairs, and through the grand hall and out the other side, before coming to a wide, heavy oaken door set with fat hinges. It was so dark in the corridor that, until her escort rapped on the door, she didn't know it was there.

"Come," said a deep voice from behind the door. The retainer turned the stout door ring with a scraping of wood on stone and pushed her forward, causing her to stumble to catch herself. Everything about the room seemed to denote that a woman had no influence there. Heavy oaken furnishings surrounded the room with little to no furs or linens to soften them. Tall iron floor candelabras dripped aged wax down their spiked bodies to pool on the floor. Weapons covered the walls: several ugly maces, swords of all sizes, shields, axes, and pikes. There was little space for anything else, save for a suit of armor polished to a bright sheen, which stood in the far corner behind an enormous desk.

The desk itself was covered in dozens of sheets of paper, scattered haphazardly, with a variety of writing implements thereon. The most compelling subject in the room, however, was the man seated behind the desk. He had thinning, snowy white hair, a thick growth of whiskers to match, and such severe lines around his mouth that Edyth doubted if he'd ever smiled a day in his life. Indeed, he seemed to glower at her from behind heavy-lidded eyes even now. The portion of his body on display to her appeared to be rather strong and spry, from what she could tell. He was oozing with arrogance, and it was not difficult to dislike him.

He looked her up and down openly, his mouth set stubbornly. "Yer much prettier than I expected. They told me ye'd chopped off yer hair to disguise yerself, but no man would mistake those curves, never mind you dressing as a man. Sit," he commanded, indicating a chair in front of her.

Edyth moved to the chair, not bothering to correct him, choosing, instead, to save her breath. She knew she must keep a cool head above all else, but it was rather like trying to catch a fish with her hands. Already overly tired in every way possible, she couldn't get ahold on her jumping, tripping nerves. She swallowed and hid her hands in her tunic, afraid he would see them shaking, thankful for the desk separating them. She was so tired of other people dictating her life and, more tired still, of condescending men.

"Edyth DeVries," he said, cocking his head to the side to examine her. "I see yer surprised at my knowing yer name. Did ye ken that yer quite infamous? No, that's no' quite accurate. I most likely would have never heard of you except that my captain is quite familiar with you and your deeds. Do ye mind him? Robert de Clifford?"

Edyth's heart tripped over itself. She had heard, of course, that he was the new lord of Carlisle. Father Brewer would have informed him of recent events, all colored to his benefit, no doubt. A guilty man cannot rest until all loose ends are tied up nicely in his favor. He, apparently, had not forgotten about her.

"I have not had the pleasure of being introduced to Sir de Clifford," said Edyth, relieved she sounded almost pleasant. Inside, however, the burning rage she'd quashed for so many weeks erupted to life.

"Indeed. No doubt you thought you had outrun him," said the Earl of March, passing a long-fingered hand across his knee as though to brush away a spot. "But," he continued conversationally, "his reach is not so small as to let a wee English chit escape justice."

Edyth pursed her lips, not understanding of whom they were speaking. "I cannot discern your meaning, sir. By what account could such a man have interest in me?"

The earl merely shook his head and cast her a disparaging look. "Let us no' play these childish games, lady. We both know yer wickedness. While others might be bewitched by yer silver tongue, I am no' so easily ensorcelled."

He cleared his throat and leaned more heavily into the high back of his chair. "Robert was certainly surprised to hear your name mentioned today," he said again as though they were friends, chatting about their latest hunt. "He's heard your name repeated many times, now that he has taken the place of your father in Carlisle." He paused, considering her with shining eyes. He waited, no doubt hoping she was squirming inside with fear, and perhaps she would have been if she wasn't so full of disgust.

Finally he spoke again. "People within Dunbar naturally assumed you were working with us, which does make some sense, I suppose, with ye being English. Perhaps that's no' such a bad idea for future campaigns: hiring a witch as a spy has some merit."

Edyth said nothing. She stared at the man, her fingernails biting into the flesh of her palms. It was all that was keeping her from flying at him from across the desk.

"But," he said, in a commiserating tone, "we both know that to be a falsehood. *We* know why you are here. Upon hearing your name, Robert immediately informed me of recent events. Do ye wish to hear them?"

He didn't want an answer from her, and she didn't give one. He leaned forward slightly as though to force her to hear him. "Robert told me how you narrowly escaped the church's justice...on the wings of a conjured serpent, no doubt. And now you are here, practicing your maleficarum against His Majesty's campaigns. Do you dare deny it?"

"I do," said Edyth automatically. "What magic is it I'm supposed to have done against King Edward?"

"Ye've bewitched my wife tae fight against me, her husband," he hissed.

"And yet I surrendered the keep, against her request or knowledge. Your accusations are unfounded and ridiculous."

What she said wasn't exactly true. She'd scared Marjory into taking action, but her husband needn't know that.

"I cannae pretend to ken what maliciousness ye've spread amongst these walls and beyond, but yer reputation precedes ye, witch."

Edyth could picture it all: Father Brewer, unable to let her live peaceably for fear of his secret coming back to haunt him, used de Clifford's military power and position with the king to defame and, ultimately, kill her. Just as he had her mother. Her father, who had not cowed to the wicked priest, also had to fall. Now it was her turn. The trouble was, she was too much like her parents. She would not cower to Father Brewer, to this man, or any other as long as she lived. Feeling a current of angry energy course through her body, she took a deep breath, trying to control herself. She bit her lip, and when she felt she could speak, she said, "You have nothing to charge against me, save rumor. Condemn yourself, sir, with lies from a wicked man. It doesn't matter to me."

The earl threw his head back, exposing his whiskered throat and laughed. "You would speak heresy against a man of God even now," he chortled, his amusement bright in his eyes. "My God, ye've got ballocks bigger than any man in my charge."

She pressed her lips into a thin line, waiting for him to finish chuckling.

"You have laid no charge against me," said Edyth, annoyed. She made to stand, but the earl, all signs of amusement now gone, surged forward in his seat, hissing at her.

"You will stay where ye are, until I've dismissed ye!"

She glared at him, considering her options, which were few, and settled into her seat once more, sick at heart and so full of disgust it was all she could do to keep her head.

"You will hear what charges are laid against ye," he said, his violent temper hidden once again. "The charges are many, but I will do my best to recall them as I heard them." While Edyth didn't think he looked exactly gleeful, he certainly looked to be enjoying himself. Settling himself so his forearms rested on the tabletop, the earl leveled her with a menacing stare that reminded her of a cat playing with a mouse.

"It's known to all of Carlisle and beyond," he began, his eyes alight, "that ye conspired with yer whore of a mother tae bring the pain of disparagement to a man of the cloth. Once he learned what ye were, the twa of ye wove wicked spells of dark magic tae bring sickness upon him.

"And when his faithfulness saved him, ye defamed him further still with lies born from the devil's own lips. When the villagers tried to confront ye, ye ran for it, like the coward ye are. But the devil doesnae take care of 'is own. Ye should 'ave kent that. What's more," he said, his lip curling with disgust, "ye've secreted away another of your wicked sisters in the hope that she would evade justice. Where have ye hidden that wee wretch?" he growled. The spittle that had gathered at the corners of his mouth during his speech fell at last, punctuating the oaken table like so many tears.

Of that crime, she *was* guilty. She had, indeed, helped her mother hide poor Annie away, where Father Brewer could not hurt her. "She's dead," said Edyth flatly.

The earl sneered and shook his head. "I think not. You, neither of ye, will evade justice if I have anything tae do with it!"

Justice? It was her turn to laugh. Edyth tried to keep a tight rein on her anger, but it was proving impossible. She had a thing or two to say about *justice*. She couldn't settle on one thought, her mind jumping from her mother to Annie to Thom to her father to the priest who had stolen her life away from her.

"I see ye want tae play the innocent," continued the earl, "but I am no fool, lassie. I ken what evil deeds you've done, and I will not let you slip away to befoul a man of God. Your sinful mother met a rightful end, I'm told. Does it comfort ye to ken ye'll soon join her in hell?"

She *hated* him. She wished she were a witch in truth, one like from the stories she'd heard; she'd conjure some winged beast to devour him where he sat. "You want to know my true crimes?" she blazed, pounding her fist on the heavy desk. "I am guilty of being a woman! I am guilty of independent thought! Of having no natural-born, God-given rights! What can I do against the words of a wicked man? What recourse do I have against deceit such as this? Do you want to know what *that man of God* did to poor Annie?" she railed, her voice cracking on the girl's name.

"Enough! I will not hear you weave a spell of lies!" he cried; his voice was raised as high as her own, his eyes bright with anger. Or was it victory at unsettling her? She didn't care. She was so tired—so, so tired of being afraid.

She brought her fists down on the desk once more, making the ink pot jump, her eyes afire. "He took her into the confessional, and he raped her is what he did! In the *church* and God did nothing to stop it! *Nothing!* And when my mother learned of it, she could not turn a blind eye. That wicked, foul, disgusting man murdered my mother in the street!" She bit back a sob, heaving for air. She stood erect and leveled a caustic look at Patrick Dunbar, the Earl of March, a finger pointed at his black heart.

"If you do me harm, you *will* answer to God for your crime. I swear by the only thing I have—my soul—you will suffer for your misplaced *justice!*"

Edyth was proud to see that she had affected him. The hairs on the backs of his hands and wrists stood on end like a bristling dog. She saw the fear in his eyes as he stood and shouted for the guard to save him.

"Ye'll no' threaten me! Guard! Cease yer wicked tongue before I have it cut out! Come, guard!" he called, and when the man entered, he said, "Bring her back to her room and do not let her out. She'll be on the road to Yorkshire at first light."

Hours later, her anger spent and her body too exhausted to move, her door opened. At first she thought that she'd somehow spent the hours remaining to her in a stupor, without sleep, but when she looked out the window and saw that night hadn't come after all, she realized her mistake.

"Come, lady," said the servant woman, motioning toward the ewer and basin near the fire. "Her Ladyship has sommat for ye."

She *tsked* over Edyth's bruised and muddied face but was kind enough when she wiped the dirt away to not hurt her. Edyth washed the rest of her body as well as she could, grateful for the sympathy Marjory was showing her.

"Let's get ye changed, aye?" said the kindly woman. She had mouse-brown hair, knotted neatly at the nape of her neck, and soft hazel eyes that, when she looked upon Edyth with such kindness, she wanted to hug her.

She'd brought a beautiful gown. Deep green wool the color of the black pines fell in folds from her waist, the creamy chemise underneath showing through at the wrists, elbows, and along her shoulders and neckline. It was an elaborate article of clothing to go to one's death in.

Last, the woman brushed Edyth's hair and styled it, but Edyth took no notice of it. Her mind, preoccupied as it was, did not have room to care about her appearance.

"The guards have been changed. It's time tae go. Quickly noo. We dinnae have much time afore the king arrives."

Shock and fear lanced through Edyth. "Which king?"

The woman's mouth pressed into a thin line before answering. "The wrong one," she said before opening the door and leading Edyth down the corridor.

"I must thank ye for yer service tae my cousin," said Marjory, not looking away from the narrow window. She was watching her husband's retainers sawing planks from fallen trees in the yard. They had started industriously felling trees that morning for a purpose unspoken. Whatever it was, the sight and sounds produced by their labors sent a chill through her.

Marjory, already a head shorter than Edyth, had seemed to shrink further still since their last meeting. Worry for her cousin had dulled the sharp edge of her antagonism, but now the woman looked altogether defeated. Beautiful as she was, with her ivory skin and alabaster hair, without the fire of a fight in her silver-gray eyes, she looked nothing like the woman she had first met only one day ago.

"I'm sure you've noticed that my husband and I have differing views. A son of Scotland—one of the seven earls," she said bitterly. She heaved a sigh and shook her head, turning to meet Edyth's eyes. "King Edward needs Patrick. He will vote to elect a king in case of dispute. Scotland is lost to your king, I fear."

"He is not my king," said Edyth automatically, and not without some bitterness.

Marjory gave her a curious look and moved from the window. "Please, sit," she said, indicating a chair opposite her own. "I regret that I have no refreshment to offer. My rights as lady of this castle have been excised, but I have a few friends still."

Marjory settled herself on her seat and smoothed the fine, silken fabric of her overskirt with a petite hand. "Which is how you've come to be here. We don't have much time. I called ye here to repay your kindness, while it is still mine to give. I am a traitor now, ye see. Edward has taken this castle, and I am caught like a fly in a web. I'm told he will be here, himself, this very night."

"Yes, that's what your servant said." Edyth, feeling rather faint, shook her head to clear it. "But what...surely your husband will not punish you as a traitor," said Edyth, but she did not believe her own words, having met him only a few hours previously.

A brief, sardonic smile lit her face, but her eyes were sorrowful. "We both know differently, Edyth. Men, with even a little power, will do much to keep it. Do ye ken what my husband has commanded to be built in the yard of my home?"

Edyth did not want to guess but was saved answering as Marjory continued, her eyes sharp with pain. Or revenge. "Patrick's blood makes him a contender for the throne. When the counsel petitioned your king for the favor of his opinion and Baliol was chosen, Patrick was disappointed, of course, but knew better than to show his hand. He, like all greedy, betting men, will foreswear their oaths for little more than flattering words.

"If ever you question your king's honor, remember this: he first won my husband's loyalty with the promise of power, then sent him to slaughter his own countrymen. And now his wife."

Edyth felt sick. But the countess did not need to regale her with tales of her immoral king. Not only was he war-loving, but his was a court where she would find no justice, despite the evils that had befallen her and her parents. She had considered petitioning him briefly, after she'd buried them and had a moment to consider her next move. It hadn't taken long, however, for her to consider and then disregard going to her king for recompense, or even sanctuary.

"What will happen?" asked Edyth, her voice sounding far away to her own ears.

Marjory's lips thinned, bloodless. "It's quite simple. He will kill me as proof of his power and loyalty to his new king. By dispensing justice to me—a traitor—he seals his efficacy."

Edyth couldn't sit still. She stood abruptly and walked to the window. The yard was full of carpenters, sawing and hammering. Swallowing the bile in her throat, she blinked away the image of her own mother's death, her neck broken, body twitching, feet swinging. "What will you do?" she asked, holding her knotted hands to her queasy stomach in an effort to still it. She imagined the scratch of the rope on her neck and rubbed the feeling away with cold, clammy hands.

"I will die," said Marjory, without emotion.

Edyth paced back to her vacated chair and sat on the edge, leaning forward so that she could see Marjory's short, blunt fingers tremble. Despite her cool words, she *was* scared.

"What can I do? Surely there is a way to save you."

Marjory smiled grimly. "That is not for you to worry over, witch. There are plans in motion, but I willane speak of them with what little time we have together."

Marjory stood and walked to the mantle, the long red train of her robe dragging rushes with her. She opened a wooden box and pulled out a roll of parchment. "You are here for two reasons. First, as I told you, I want to return the favor of your skill as a physic to my cousin. I do not forget easily, Edyth, the kindness of others to my own blood." She leveled her pale eyes on Edyth, some of their fire returning. "Second, I would like nothing more than to disrupt my husband's plans."

Edyth held her breath, remembering well the effect her husband had on her. "What would you have me do?" she whispered.

"Do you know my husband's companion, the Marshall of England?"

Edyth nodded, barely breathing. Robert de Clifford, the new steward of Carlisle.

Marjory held the parchment aloft, her brow lifted in a question. "This missive was intercepted by a loyal retainer, though I'm sorry to say that this message most likely has a sister. It would be unlike my husband to send only one missive. It mentions you. Do ye ken what it says?"

Edyth swallowed, feeling oddly numb. She started to shake her head but then thought better of it and nodded weakly, trying to swallow her fears. "I am in possession of a secret a wicked man would like to hide. For this, I'm hunted."

Marjory's eyes seemed to sparkle with an intensity. "Our fates seem entwined, do they no'? I defend my castle against a foreign king, and I am called traitor. You," she said, the intensity of her gaze a weight, "a lady, daughter of England, called a traitor to God himself. Both of our lives in peril. We are strange sisters."

Edyth closed her eyes, the words as painful as dart to her heart.

"Women have only to use the brains they've been blessed with tae kindle the wrath o' weak and wicked men. As one who's married tae such a man, I would save a friend, even if I cannae guarantee my own safety."

Edyth's heart beat a tattoo against her ribs, so loud in her ears that she hardly heard Marjory. "I...let's think together. We can find a way to save us both." Marjory shushed her and took her hands in her own once more. They were cold but vastly welcome.

"We waste valuable time. Listen well. The missive says many things I do not believe, but it does say something that I have no doubt believing. It states that my husband and the new governor of Carlisle intend to send ye back to England for a trial."

She knew as much. The Earl of March had told her so himself. "If I go, it will be to my death," said Edyth, feeling as though she had somehow separated from her body. How could she speak of such things so calmly as though discussing the weather?

"Yes," said Marjory, her silver eyes sharp. "You will either be condemned and executed, or you will be exonerated but dead."

Edyth knew it to be true. The trials one had to endure to prove one was not a witch always ended in death. Witches floated on water, for instance, and innocents sank. And a heretic...they were often tortured until a confession was given, regardless of guilt.

"What must I do? To where can I run?"

"You must marry," Marjory said slowly and deliberately, squeezing Edyth's hands as though the force of her strength could compel her. Her words were met with silence.

Marriage? Did she mean for a man to protect her? "I would not bring harm to an innocent man. De Clifford is a powerful man and the church more powerful still."

Marjory shook her head. "Ye must marry. The more powerful a husband, the better. A husband can prevent your arrest this night. It doesnae matter who, but choose ye must, or ye'll be back in England to face the church alone come dawn."

Edyth's mind reeled. It couldn't be as simple as just choosing, surely? She could choose to be a bird and fly away, but wishing would not make it so. "But the church is bigger than England, Scotland, and France together. They will seek me out, no matter where I live."

Marjory nodded. "Yes, if my husband and de Clifford have their way, you are right. But as ye are now, with no one tae speak for ye, ye are defenseless against de Clifford and the man who drives him."

"Father Brewer." Edyth felt bile rise in the back of her throat.

"This priest is a wicked man?"

At Edyth's nod, Marjory said, "We must act quickly. Even as we speak, a messenger has been dispatched to the Abbey at Yorkshire, listing your crimes against a man of the cloth in Carlisle as well as your intent to meddle in the affairs of your king through witchcraft."

Panic rose within Edyth. Her mind reeled, snagging here and there on imagined scenes. She, being dragged to stand before Father Brewer's fallacious hearing. Of being condemned by him and those he'd poisoned against her. Of the abrasive touch of the noose as it was tightened on her neck. She shook her head, thinking instead of an unknown land and husband, burdened with her fight against the church. Surely he, whomever he was, would balk at such a duty. At such a wife.

Edyth shook her head, solemn. "I cannot marry. Who would agree to such a scheme? I, with nothing to my name, no dowry, no family, with the church after me—"

"I still draw breath. There are men in my service who would obey me."

The thought of being bound to a man because he had been commanded to did not appeal, but what choice did she have? Could she live such a life? She might be safe from de Clifford or Patrick Dunbar, but would she ever see Meg again?

She stood once more, unable to stay still. She paced in front of the hearth, considering. In retrospect, it wasn't difficult for her to imagine what her life might be like. An arranged marriage had been her parents' intent for the whole of her life. Until recently, she had never imagined a life otherwise. Only by chance had she escaped a life with the baron of Wessex. But since escaping that fate and nurturing the childish thoughts that she might yet find something more, she could not easily return to her previous way of thinking about marriage. Her heart would not easily accept it.

"Maybe if I can get to my cousin, a MacPherson, I can be matched with someone..." but she trailed off, seeing Marjory's negation.

"You cannae wait. It must be now, in secret. I have a legist here who will see it done. Ye must only choose."

She could run and hide, of course. She could ask Ewan or Meg to risk their lives for her, to secret her away. She could carve out half a life, living a lie; she might even find peace for a time, until she was discovered.

Or she could do as Marjory suggested and face her foe with lesser risk involved.

"Who?" she asked, her voice barely audible. "Who must I marry?"

"It cannot be anyone my husband has control over, which leaves only a few options here at the castle. There is my uncle's retainer, Rupert. He is a skilled swordsman and is employed as a smith on Moray, but he is a Lindsay and could bring ye there. He is a good deal older than ye, but he's a good man."

Edyth felt numb, her head floating in a fog. Marjory's voice seemed to be coming from far off. Ewan's face swam into view, and her heart constricted as though pricked.

"And then there's a Frenchman here, Alexandre, who my uncle also kens," said Marjory, watching Edyth carefully. "He can take ye back tae the continent. He is a shipwane near the coast. He is younger and a little wild yet, but he would be gone from home much of the time, leaving ye alone. A good match, both. What is your mind?"

Her mind? Her mind was filled with silly thoughts and childish wishes that could never come to pass. She hadn't known her own heart until Marjory had suggested she marry, but she knew it now. Mentally shying away from thoughts of Ewan, she slumped into her chair and looked at her lap. "How much time do I have?"

"It must be done tonight, and no later."

"They will agree to it?"

"They will do as they're bid," said Marjory, her voice icy and sure.

Edyth closed her eyes, feeling defeated. Later, she would have time to school her heart into forgetting Ewan. Now she must save herself. "It doesn't matter which then," she said, her voice wooden. "You choose for me."

Dinner was sure to be a subdued affair. King Edward had arrived and would demand oaths of fealty from all the nobles present. There was to be a celebration of his victory after the oath taking...toasts to the victors of war.

As it was, Edyth had been allowed from her room under the watchful gaze of Marjory's faithful guard, Gamelin, whom her husband—so far as yet—did not suspect. Edyth's presence here, she assumed, could only be to condemn her in the presence of so many people, including the king. She shuddered anew, urgency growing within her.

There was no king, no Earl of March, or Marshal of England seated in the place of honor, but it couldn't be long. With only a little time to locate the barrister in as casual a way as possible, she gazed about the room, doing her best to hide her anxiousness. Each face seemed as unremarkable as the next. Any one of the men could be Marjory's legist. Or her future husband.

The atmosphere in the hall was oppressive at best, the murmurs of conversation hushed and apprehensive. There were a few merrymakers, all Dunbar's and de Clifford's men, but they were met with barely repressed hostility, each group of people keeping to their own. Serving girls, laden down with drinks, laced through the milling throng of restless men and women.

"Will ye take ale, lady?" asked a flaxen-haired girl of about eleven. Edyth nodded and took the cup, simply for something for her to do as she waited impatiently for the legist to find her. As her eyes scanned the crowd yet again, she caught sight of Ewan as he entered the room, and her heart lurched. He must have felt her gaze, for their eyes met from across the sea of people and he moved toward her, squeezing through elbows and around benches.

"Edyth," he murmured, looking relieved to see her. He took his place beside her against the wall, his shoulder pressing against hers in the tight quarters. Closing her eyes at the sensations his nearness caused within her, Edyth tried to move away from him, but the stout woman standing on her other side was in her way. She hadn't intended to see Ewan, let alone speak with him, but there were *many* things she hadn't intended that were now coming to pass. At least she now had the chance to say goodbye.

"What will you do?" she whispered to him, glancing briefly at his face before looking away. His eyes were beautiful but painful for her to look upon, like looking into the sun.

His long mouth formed a thin line at her pointed question, but he met her eyes briefly before looking away. "You're being watched," he said under his breath, and she wanted to laugh. There was much he did not know and much she ached to tell him.

"Yes," she answered. "His name is Gamelin. What do you intend to do?" she asked again.

He shrugged and rotated his bad shoulder. "I'll do what I must," he said cryptically. "But I don't want tae speak o' me. I want tae ken what's happened since I saw ye last, ridin' hell-bent for the English line."

She did look at him then and saw censure, exasperation, and perhaps a little pride there.

"I did what I came to do," she said. That was true, but why, then, did she feel like weeping?

"Are ye well, Edyth?" he asked, turning concerned eyes on her. The intensity of his gaze sent her heart into a gallop.

She breathed in his scent, so familiar to her after so long in the saddle together. She wanted to touch his wavy, unruly mass of hair but clenched her hands into fists instead.

She was being silly. She was woman grown, prepared her whole life for a marriage of fortunes, not affections. She swallowed words she could not say and replaced them with, "I'm glad you're here. I want to thank you for all you've done for me."

"Why these tears?" he asked, catching one with his thumb. She hadn't known she was even crying. "Do not fear for me. My father has already publicly aligned with England. I will...think of something."

"I *do* fear for you," she muttered. "And I fear for myself. Ewan..." she broke off and wiped at her face, irritated with her mourning heart. She looked around herself, catching sight of her guard, a reminder that there was more than one life at risk here. She leaned into him, an inch from his ear, and whispered, "I cannot speak here where ears might hear, but I must say goodbye. I cannot do so without first telling you how much I...how grateful I am for your companionship."

Ewan turned his head sharply to meet her gaze, a question written there. His hand reached to her face, his fingers tucking a stray hair behind her ear on the pretense to whisper back. It felt like a caress. His breath tickled her ear. "Tell your guard you need the garderobe, then meet me in the alcove under the stairs. You know it?" At her nod, he said, "Wait for me."

Taking her cup, he emptied it in three long gulps and then, spotting a serving girl near an exit, sought her out. Edyth hesitated, thinking of the legist she was supposed to be meeting, but then pushed him out of mind as she watched Ewan's retreating form.

Gamelin was, as ever, hot on her heels. Accepting her excuse for leaving the hall, he escorted her neatly past several posted guards along the way, saving her considerable trouble, she was sure.

Doubtless all the exits were being guarded, and she would not be permitted to actually leave the keep, but inside—with Gamelin— she had a little freedom. A very little. According to Marjory, the only safe way of escape was on the arm of a man, marriage contract in hand. Somehow, Edyth doubted it would be that simple, but it was her only hope. The alternative was unthinkable.

Once they arrived at the garderobe, and after Edyth ensured that they were, indeed, alone, she explained in quiet tones her actual goal. Her guard dutifully escorted her the remainder of the way, allowing her a small bit of privacy as he waited in the shadows outside of the alcove.

The space was small and dim but private enough. It held a large wooden carving of some saint she could not name and a tapestry in deep greens and golds. She leaned against the wall as far as she could into the welcoming shadow of the saint and waited, trying not to think of her new life.

She would have to start all over again to carve out an existence with strangers. There would be no Meg. No Ewan, Cait, or Iain. She wondered about Meg, imagining how she might have changed. How different would she be from the young girl she'd once known and loved? Would she never find out? And what of herself? She wasn't the same girl she'd once been. Starting over, yet again, was frightening in and of itself, but now there was no promise of Meg to soften her way. Such were her thoughts until she was startled out of them by Ewan's sudden appearance. He seemed slightly out of breath.

"Edyth?" he whispered into the shadow behind the statue. While it wasn't completely dark, her eyes had had time to adjust to the dim recess.

"I'm here," she said, moving away from the wall.

His eyes were intent upon her, his face grim. He squeezed into the small space as well as he could, but he was a large man, and so half of his body was illuminated by the flickering torchlight, while the other half was pressed against the wall, in shadow. "There's a guard nearby."

"Yes," she whispered into his chest. "He is Marjory's man."

She felt him nod, his chin brushing against the side of her head. "We have only a little time, Edyth. Tell me what's happened."

She took a deep breath, trying to order her thoughts, but they were slippery. "I...Father Brewer has told the lord of Carlisle that I am a wanted woman for crimes against the church. I...I'm to be carted off to England and hung just as my mother unless I follow Marjory's scheme. She said de Clifford has sent word to the Abbey that I've been found. Oh, Father, God!" She clutched her hands to her belly, feeling sick. "I don't know if I can do it, but I must! I must," she hissed.

Warm hands settled on her shoulders, as though to restrain her from flight. "Wheesht!" hissed Ewan, squeezing her slightly. "What scheme have ye agreed to?"

"Marjory has a plan to marry me to a Frenchman. It must happen tonight. I don't know how it will work. Surely marriage will not stop them from taking me, but she says I cannot face a trial without a man to speak for me. Without a husband, I will be arrested and taken to Yorkshire."

She took a steading breath. "I know a husband cannot save me from the church, but Marjory says he can offer protection that I currently do not have."

Ewan's eyes widened in shock, then narrowed dangerously. "Explain from the beginning. Leave nothing out."

Taking a deep breath, she tried again and told him about her meeting with Patrick Dunbar and then her secret meeting with Marjory. "I'm supposed to be meeting with the barrister this minute," she finished. "Oh, Ewan," she whispered, her voice betraying her. He had gone very still. "I don't mean to burden you with this. It's my own fault. If I'd only listened to you."

"If you had listened to me, we'd all be dead," he said softly. The simple validation of his belief in her sent a wave of sensation through her. A sound, not unlike a sob, left her, and Ewan clutched her hands, hard.

She thought her heart might break, looking at him. He'd seen her at her worst and had helped her to pick up the pieces of her life. He'd accepted her, befriended her, when others would have not. He'd believed and trusted in her goodness, even knowing her as he did. He knew *all*, and still had handled her gently. With respect. He'd shown her how to trust once more, and that, in itself, had been the mortar that had held her heart together these past weeks. And she would never see him again. How was she to live without him? She felt as though all the strength she'd gained since leaving England was draining from her.

"I don't know how to leave you." The confession tumbled out of her mouth before she could stop them. She clutched her hand to her heart as though to keep it from bursting free of her chest. She took a deep breath, trying to hold back the tide of emotions, but she could feel it pushing, rising against her will.

"You've been a true friend...in all of this, you've been my shelter," she said, her voice wavering. Tears filled her eyes, gathered there, and rolled down her face. She didn't bother to wipe them away. "I do not know how I can repay your kindness to me. I don't even know where I'm going," she whispered, both shocked and afraid at her boldness. "I only...I just wanted to say goodbye."

Ewan brushed the back of his strong, capable fingers against her wet cheek. Softly, so softly, he traced his thumb over her bottom lip, barely touching her. It tingled; indeed, her body seemed to thrum like a tightly wound cord. It had come alive suddenly, and she was acutely aware of the smallest things: the sound of the sputtering pitch in the torch in the hall, of the heat in her cheeks and ears, and the strange way her belly stirred at his touch.

"My lady," he whispered. How was it he could make the words feel like a caress? He drew her near, pulling her hands against his jerkined chest. His fingers were at her chin, lifting, branding her, sending a ripple of sensation down her neck, through her middle, and before she knew it, he was kissing her. His lips were soft and careful, tender and undemanding, so different from the riot of feelings inside of her. She leaned into him, unsure of the mechanics but very sure of one thing: it was not enough.

She felt as though she were floating in water and on fire all at once. He pulled away slightly, a finger on her chin. "When first I saw ye," he said, "pale with fright but burning with rage"—he kissed her once more—"ye fought so fiercely." His lips moved to her neck, and she trembled. "I knew I wanted ye, but when ye cried in my arms"—he gave her a squeeze, his hands running up the length of her arms—"I thought my own heart might break with loving you."

Her body was foreign to her, her blood racing through her at a frantic speed. His mouth touched hers once more, and she matched him, returning his kiss to pour out all the love she held for him. It felt like a dizzying dream. He pulled away much too soon, his nose touching hers, their breath mingling.

"Edyth, ye brave, sweet lass. If it were me tae choose, I would claim ye as my verra own, *m'eud*ail. I would bring ye home and worship ye, all your life, for I owe ye that. Ye have awakened my soul, challenged my mind, and stolen my heart. It is yours, *mo laochain,* whether I will it or no."

A tremor ran down his throat as he swallowed. "I want ye for my own so badly it hurts, but..." he sighed then, his eyes betraying the storm within him. "Edyth, my life is no' my own. I walk on the edge of a blade between two kings. Should I fall, I would take ye with me. I would keep ye safe, always."

Strong arms enfolded her; her cheek pressed against leather so thick she could not hear his heart beating. The soaring sensation she had just experienced ended abruptly, crashing mightily at her feet; the mortar so carefully and so recently placed around her heart crumbled to dust. She felt stupid with shock. Numb, she blinked against his chest. He loved her but would not have her?

"Then I am at the mercy of a stranger, fleeing to yet another unknown land." Her voice sounded hollow, even to her own ears.

He pushed her away and grasped her hands so tightly it hurt. "No," he growled. He swore softly and shook his head as though to dislodge a pesky fly. "If ye are tae marry this night, it will be to *me*." Ewan's eyes burned into her, hungry. "I'm trying to say that if I take yer hand, it will no' be easy, for I fear there will be retribution for my aid to the countess. They would have me swear fealty to King Edward, but I cannae say if that will be the end of it. I will not raise arms against my own people as I fear he would have me do. And if that day comes, and I refuse, my life is forfeit. It's *you* that must choose, Edyth, not I. It's you who must make the choice if ye wish tae live with such a risk."

Her heart in her throat, Edyth touched Ewan's cheek, raspy with stubble. "How could I ignore my heart and marry another now that I know yours? I would have you as my husband, whatever the risk."

His lips were as a brand, claiming her own. He pressed into her, the cool wall against her back, and she wondered at the newly erupted feelings coursing through her trembling body. He kissed her hungrily and quickly, then pulled abruptly away, his eyes black with desire.

"I wish," he started, but then he cut himself off. He shook his head. "We cannae tarry here, lass. We must play our parts well, each of us, until it is done. I will find the barrister. Go, now, tae the hall. I will follow soon after."

Edyth touched her fingers to her lips, still feeling Ewan's kisses as she sat in the hall. Patrick Dunbar and Robert de Clifford sat upon the dais amid their favored soldiers, feasting as though they themselves were kings. And there, in the center, sat Edward, King of England. Perhaps it was her imagination coloring the scene, but to her, he seemed to smirk down upon the crowd.

The king stood, his crown glinting brightly in the torchlight. First praising the crowd's desire for loyalty, he then chastised the for choosing the weaker of the two sides, claiming that there was no shame in joining together under one banner—the superior banner of England. She only listened with half an ear, her mind touching and touching again on the miracle of Ewan's feelings for her.

She felt exposed to de Clifford, who sat at the king's right side, half afraid that he would single her out and brand her as a witch, but the marshal's eyes hadn't yet rested on her. The countess was blaringly absent, but no one spoke of it.

Ewan had entered the hall not long after she had, choosing a seat well away from her, but she could sense his nearness, like a flower does the sun, turning its petals unerringly toward its warmth. It had taken all her strength to hold still and not look at him, but she could see him now, standing tall and proud, long boned and well-muscled, as he waited for his turn to swear his pledge and sign his name to England. To King Edward, the hammer of the Scots.

His hair was like the ripples on a stream, dark underneath in the cool deep and kissed with the sun on the surface, burnished with gold-and-silver flecks in the torchlight. He held himself with pride, seemingly unburdened with the impossible choice, but she knew what it was costing him to pledge his lands, his men, and his life to England.

"You are Edyth?" asked a small man who had just materialized beside her. The crowd had been commanded to stand as the oaths were taken; he must have wound his way unnoticed, as short as he was—a head shorter than she herself—through the crowd to get to her. His drink was held to his mouth to cover his words. He was dressed richly in velvet lined with furs—a man of station—and she had a fleeting fear that he was to take her away for de Clifford and Dunbar's purposes but pushed the thought aside. Why let her out of her room to witness the oath taking just to drag her away before it was finished? Why the pretense of secrecy?

Edyth nodded ever so slightly, her eyes searching for Ewan once more. He was next to kneel before the king and make his mark upon the lengthy scroll at the foot of the dais. With her heart in her throat, she watched as the man in front of him replaced the quill and straightened, his face a stony mask as he turned to take his place in the crowd.

"Ye are tae meet me in the lower hall when it happens. Quickly. Out that door." He pointed with his bearded chin to the exit to their right.

Edyth looked at him and opened her mouth to ask, "When what happens—" but she stopped herself, looking away, afraid to be noticed speaking to the stranger.

"It will happen soon," he hissed. "Be wary and move quickly." He was right. It did happen quickly. One of the large men-at-arms, standing to the side of Dunbar and de Clifford, fell with an almighty clatter of armor and weapons, upon the steps of the dais, an arrow pierced through his eye. A woman screamed; swords were drawn. More arrows whizzed overhead. The room erupted into chaos. Edyth looked for Ewan but could not see him among the surging crowd.

Bodies pressed against her as she fought for the door. Tripping over feet and avoiding elbows as best she could, she was startled when a strong arm grasped her elbow and pulled her along.

It was Ewan, pushing against people with one arm while pulling her along in his wake toward the door.

"Who else fell?" asked Edyth, panting for breath.

"No idea," he said gruffly, not looking at her. He paused long enough to let a weeping woman race past him. "I dinnae think it prudent tae wait and find out, aye?"

The hallway was dark, echoing with retreating footsteps and cries of alarm. Ewan pulled his dirk and slowed, letting go of her arm. "Follow me. Close now."

He led her through darkened halls, empty of passerby save for a few errant servants, scurrying like rats to the hidden places in the keep. Edyth thought it impossible that they were not stopped by guards, but they saw none. Apparently, Lady Marjory did have a few friends left.

Finally, she could see the little man waiting against a wall ahead, pressed to it in wait. Upon seeing them, he turned to the right without comment to disappear into a room as though he were a ghost.

Ewan ushered them forward and pushed her through the same door, glancing over his shoulder before shutting them in with an uncertain future.

"Bar it," said the little man, adjusting his jerkin as he sat at a wooden table. The room was well lit, prepared for them with care. There were two others there—witnesses, she presumed—along with a comfortable settle in front of a smoored fire.

"We don't have much time, Sir Ruthven. If you please," said the man, the legist, she assumed, and waved them forward. The contract of marriage seemed to glow on the dark surface, pulling all eyes in the room. On the wide sheet of vellum, the date, twenty-eight of April 1296, was written in a large, scrolling hand.

"Peruse the title and lands listed hereon, if you please. While the abrupt change of groom has pushed even me to the limit of lawful ability, the alteration isn't an impossible one. I'd hate to be wrong, however, so please review carefully." The legist pushed the contract toward Ewan and then turned his sharp, brown eyes on her.

"I trust," he said, pinning her to the spot with a look, "that there is no other contract of marriage in existence for you?"

Edyth swallowed, thinking of the baron of Wessex, and nodded reluctantly. "I was betrothed at the age of twelve, but the gentleman died in battle a year ago."

"I see. And I'm to understand that you've no dowry, lands, or titles to your name?" he asked, his eyebrows raised gracefully in question.

"None, sir," she answered, feeling unsuitable as a match for anyone, let alone the man standing beside her. Years before, she'd been a very competitive choice for bride with a rather large dowry and a reputation as an educated and well-prepared chatelaine. Now she was no better than a pauper, receiving charity from a generous lord.

"She will share my lands and take the title of Lady Ruthven presently," said Ewan, reaching to take her hand. She hesitated, clutching his fingers. "Are you sure, Ewan?" she asked.

"Quite," he said simply, squeezing her fingers.

"Sign, lady," said the legist, his ink-blotched hand outstretched as he offered her salvation.

Chapter Thirteen

They'd made their escape among a handful of others, helped out of the castle walls by means of a low-ceilinged tunnel, black as pitch, shown to them by one of the men who'd witnessed their marriage. Stumbling out into the Ettrick Forest, she'd gulped in the crisp, spring air as though she'd had to swim the length of the tunnel instead of walk it.

Well past dark, the torches set along the curtain wall burned brightly and dazzled her eyes. Moving swiftly and stealthily, Edyth did not dare ask where they were headed; she only followed, ignoring the stitch in her side.

Members of their party fell away here and there, sometimes as pairs or as threesomes, branching out to destinations unknown, until it was only she and Ewan left, the sound of their quickened breath and the shuffling of leaf mold filling her ears.

They'd only traveled a short distance farther, perhaps half a mile, when Ewan slowed. He grasped her wrist in a silent command to be still. She watched, curious as he brought his cupped hands to his mouth and blew into them, mimicking the sound of an owl.

Seconds later, the call was returned, and Ewan smiled, his teeth flashing in the moonlight. "We've found him," was all he said before taking her hand and moving them forward.

It was Rory with horses. A pang of guilt pierced through her. She'd forgotten all about Rory! "How?" she asked, looking between the two men.

"Leddy," said Rory, greeting her with a brisk nod.

"I rode out to find him while ye were mending the Comyn's son." Ewan helped her into her saddle and, handing her the reins, said, "You can be very persuasive, my lady."

After their heated argument, coupled with Edyth's determination to get to Dunbar by whatever means necessary, Ewan had decided to at least create a contingency plan. A heavy hand rested on her knee, keeping her attention. "You've saved us all, Edyth. The rest of my men left by twos and threes after your surrender."

She took his hand and squeezed it. "Thank you for trusting me."

"I'll never doubt again," he whispered, kissing her hand.

Rory took to his horse, reminding them to move.

As Ewan took to his horse, Edyth nudged Harris forward. "Sir Rory," she said, feeling abashed, "How are you feeling?"

She couldn't see Rory's face through his helm in this light, but she could feel his eyes resting on her. She did see him shrug a bit, though. "Dinnae be offended, leddy," he said, his voice sounding tinny in his helm, "if I dinnae seek ye oot when I'm ailing. Or drink anything ye offer me in the future."

Edyth hid her smile and followed Ewan north. To home.

The women left in a fit of stifled giggles and a rustling of skirts after preparing Edyth. She'd been scrubbed down with linen cloths and bathed in rosemary-scented water; her hair had been brushed and teased and tugged until her scalp tingled. *Like liquid fire*, someone had commented as they'd arranged her hair. A long, soft-as-silk chemise had been carefully arranged, tied with little yellow ribbons at her shoulders. She was grateful for that, at least. She'd heard stories of brides being presented to their new husbands in naught but their skin. She was covered. At least for now.

There was no looking glass, but one servant had called her a beauty. She didn't feel beautiful, only awkward. The chemise was low-necked and showed too much of her small, pert breasts. Her nipples pushed against the light fabric, and she tried to rearrange the cloth to better hide herself without success.

Their unexpected news upon arrival at Ruthven Tower had been met with joy from those that mattered. Iain had kissed her and called her sister. Cait cried happy tears, vibrating with excitement. Edyth tried not to think about what other people thought. If catching a few glares from some servants was the worst that would happen, then so be it. She hoped to win them over with time.

There was a knock, making her jump.

"C-come," she said, her voice stuck in her throat.

The door opened, revealing Ewan. Behind him stood several men, all of which Edyth refused to acknowledge, her eyes dancing past them as though they were mere ghosts. They didn't jeer or laugh, though, for which she was grateful. Ewan shut the door on them with a thud and threw the bolt, his movements seeming overly loud to her ears.

"Good e'en to ye, Edyth," said Ewan as he turned to her. He seemed subdued, but perhaps it was only a projection of her own feelings.

"Good e'en," she parroted, staring. She had to try twice to swallow, her mouth was so dry.

Ewan walked to the sideboard near her, his boots thumping loudly on the wooden floor, to pour the wine that had been placed there for them. She had to force herself not to back farther away from him, his nearness sending waves of nervous energy through her limbs. He seemed suddenly a great deal larger than he ever had.

His eyes were dark, so dark as to look black in the low light. He'd shaved since she'd been carried off for wedding night preparations. His hair was damp, the curls seeming alive as he moved to hand her a cup.

"To the Lady Ruthven, my wife," he said, raising his own cup.

Mouth dry, Edyth gulped down the wine, barely keeping it from spilling.

Ewan raised a questioning brow but said nothing. He poured her another cupful, his eyes intent upon her. "Ye look verra bonny, Edyth," he said, his eyes sweeping over her from head to foot.

And then he was moving away from her, toward the hearth, her eyes unable to move from him. He set his cup down on the mantle and pulled the weapons from his body, laying them carefully on a small table. He studied the knives for a long moment before finally turning to appraise her.

"Ye look as scairt as a cornered rabbit." A long-fingered hand swept through his hair, making the curls bounce with life. "I don't want ye tae feel...I willnae force ye, Edyth, if that's yer worry."

Some of the tension left her body at his words, though that hadn't been her worry. She shook her head and bit her lip, looking into her cup of wine. "I didn't think.... Forgive me. I'm just nervous."

Ewan nodded and rotated his shoulder uncomfortably. "That's understandable. I'm nervous too."

"You are?" she asked, surprised.

Ewan shrugged and smirked, good humor coloring his features. "Och, well, I havenae been married before, have I?"

Edyth's mouth curved into a smile, his own nervousness a comfort to her.

"It wouldn't be so awkward were we no' put on display like geese in a poulter's stand."

She laughed and agreed. It had been easier before, when left to their own devices. But now they were in his home, and customs had to be seen to. Now it was time to make the contract complete.

Ewan sat on the end of the bed to unlatch his high boots while Edyth stared at the play of his muscles under his sark. He was beautiful in all the ways a man could be, and Edyth wanted to touch him very badly.

Her fingers curled of their own accord, holding air. How were they to start? Ewan met her gaze, a small smile playing on his beautiful mouth. "Come to me," he said, standing, his voice a mere whisper. She did as he asked, her heartbeat increasing the closer she came to him.

"That's better," he said, the fingertips of one hand brushing up her arm, to her neck, to rest on her jaw. He pulled her closer with his free hand, their bodies pressed tightly together. She could feel all of him, his muscled strength held in check, against her own softness, and it made her breath quicken.

"Wife," Ewan whispered, tasting her lips. Edyth melted into him, pulling him nearer, her hands on his neck, in his hair. "I've wanted tae touch ye all the day," he said, his lips moving down her jaw to her neck. "It's a torment to be so near ye and unable to touch ye." His fingers played the vertebrae along her spine, his eyes gone dark. "Are ye scairt of me now, Edyth?" he asked, pushing away slightly to search her face.

She shook her head, mute, a riot of feelings clashing within her. Running a shaking finger from his temple to his cheek, down to his jaw, she contemplated their new relationship.

She'd touched him before, but the touches had never held promise. Even with this small contact, she felt as though she had crossed the imaginary line of intimacy.

His jaw was smooth and pinkly raw from his recent shave. His neck, corded with muscle, flexed as he swallowed. Growing bolder, her hands, flat palmed, mapped his body: muscled shoulders, broad chest, sculpted stomach, down to narrow hips. They settled there, her hands stalling. Faltering. She didn't know what to do. She'd never touched a man like this. Never thought she'd have the nerve—let alone the desire—to do so.

He kissed her again. Softly at first, pulling her in, his hands erupting small fires wherever they trailed. An altogether new and intoxicating sensation fogged her brain. Heat pooled in her belly, only to spread and grow in intensity. Was this what the poets wrote about?

Ewan pulled away, panting slightly, his blue eyes turned black with desire. "I want ye, *a chuisle, a chroí*. Will ye have me?"

Edyth nodded once, unable to find her voice, and pulled his head down to hers once more, wondering at what he'd awoken within her.

Edyth's fingers inched up the course hair on Ewan's forearm, traversed the smooth hills and valleys of his muscled upper arm, to come to rest on the runneled scar, the thick, puckered flesh gleaming silver in the dim light. She'd seen him shrug and rotate his shoulder uncomfortably, usually in times of stress, but she couldn't have ever imagined the extent of the wound. Where the rounded muscle of a shoulder should be, in its place was a tight, twisted valley of scars, webbed and silver-white, spreading like fingers toward his neck and chest.

"Blade or pike?" she asked, her voice barely audible.

She felt the rise and fall of his chest twice before he answered. "Halberd," he muttered, shifting his body toward her.

"How did it happen?"

Ewan finger-combed her hair, then kissed her forehead. "It happened in Blave, two years ago. It's of no consequence. Does it trouble ye?"

Edyth frowned, her fingers stroking his tender flesh. "Your scar? No. Only to know that you were in pain." She laid her hand over his shoulder as though to shield it from future hurt. "Tell me."

Ewan sighed, reluctant, but began to speak. "The English raided and took towns all up the Garrone River. They'd taken Castillion first, then Macau, then Bourg. That didn't sit well with King Phillipe or his commanders, as you might imagine, so we were commanded to meet them—to thwart further losses in the town of Blave. The English ships were spotted coming up the estuary the day before, and so we prepared as best we could. We took to digging and driving pikes into the riverbank, hoping our good position would give us the needed advantage. I was commanded to take the men into the woods beyond our fortifications, hide in wait, until the English landed, advanced, then come at them from behind." He paused, and Edyth nestled closer, feeling cold despite the fire.

"It was a good plan," he said finally, taking a restorative breath, "or it would have been, if the English had landed at the fort. Instead they landed farther south and had ravished everything on their way north."

Ewan's soldiers were tested, battle-worn men, but even the best of men will falter when plans fail and enemies abound. The English had left their ships like ants swarming on a hill. They'd cut down everyone in sight—man, woman, and child—burning, looting, and raping. "That was the first time I'd seen a woman taken in such a way," he said, his voice so soft she had to strain to hear it. "Her screams made the hairs on my arms stand stiff and my wame curdle. Even now thinking of it makes me sick."

He pulled Edyth closer as though he wanted to pull her inside of him, where he could shield her from all future violence, his skin gone clammy.

He spoke without emotion, his mind taken to a place far away. "We were hit hard, and we scattered. If it hadn't been for the trees, we'd have all been slaughtered.

Overcome, he commanded his men to fall away and retreat to the main body of the French army. There was confusion, as there is in all battles, and he'd tried to call his men to him. His squire, Alec, afraid of being trampled or run through, had scurried up a tree, but the error had separated him from Ewan, and the boy had found himself adrift in a sea of bloodshed, surrounded by a surging mass of many-toothed weapons wielded by undiscerning beasts.

"His eyes met mine across the bloodied clearing. Terror turned to relief at seeing me, for he knew his master would come for him, and I did. I could not turn away even had I wanted to."

Dodging, fighting, Ewan had picked his course through the mess of men, killing many, nearly being killed twice himself, but miraculously, he'd pulled his squire from the tree, only to be run down by an unmanned horse.

"It didn't hurt at first, seeing as how I was more preoccupied with getting my heavy, armor-clad arse out of the mud before someone else fell upon us. But no sooner had I gained my feet and attempted to parry a blow meant to take my head than I noticed some trouble with my arm. It didnae want to obey me properly, and using my sword was costing me greatly. The horse's blow had hurt it somehow. It was numb and clumsy, and that's when the halberd pierced my armor. I couldnae lift my sword tae stop it."

Edyth traced the webbed scar with a fingertip, wishing she could have been there to help him. "How did you survive?" she asked, breathless.

"Alec saved me. He knew the strengths and weaknesses in armor. He came from behind and killed the man with one stab to his kidney. Alec pulled the halberd from my shoulder and forced me to run. I didn't fight—couldn't—and didn't see why I should lie there to let the English finish me off. We hid behind trees and ran when we could, and before too long, the French had sent reinforcements, and I was taken into a stable for mending. They put my shoulder back into place and cauterized the wound that night."

Edyth must have made some sort of sound of distress, for Ewan pulled her closer, rubbing a strong hand over her exposed arm. "Dinnae fash, my Edie," he said, kissing her. "It's just a memory is all. It cannae hurt me."

"But it does," retorted Edyth. "I've seen how it affects you still." He dismissed her worry with a wave of a hand. "It catches sometimes and feels tight, but it doesn't pain me greatly. Truly. I am blessed that I still have use of my arm, for it could have been much worse."

That was true, but still...she felt hollow inside, thinking of all he'd endured. "I wish I could have been there to help you. I wish I could have saved you the pain of the hot iron, at least."

Ewan shook his head and kissed her once, twice, then once more as though he could not help himself, lingering. "You are here now," he whispered. "If you want to comfort me for past hurts, I'll surely nae stop ye. I've plenty more scars, and I like yer manner of healing." Edyth smiled and boldly pressed her herself against him, but Ewan did not respond in kind.

His hands wound through her hair and found the scar that ran from the base of her skull toward her left ear. The wound had healed nicely, but it was still tender to the touch. Ewan traced the sensitive flesh with a finger, his eyes solemn.

"When I saw ye fall in the glade, I feared you'd never wake." He swallowed the emotion evident in his voice. "And I didnae care for ye then as I do now, Edie, for ye've stolen bits and pieces awa' from me day by day so that I fear that I will no longer be whole without ye beside me. What would happen tae my heart if something was to happen to ye now? I am strong and accustomed to brutality, but I cannae live with half a heart, and I cannae abide your suffering." He took a deep breath, his eyes black in the low light.

"Here," he said, touching her scar, "or here," he added, placing his palm over her heart. "I would shield ye from further hurt if I can." Edyth had to swallow her own emotions, so close to the surface as they were; her throat burned with unshed tears, her heart soaring to precarious heights. Fingers and legs entwined, she pressed her lips to his, breathing in the musky scent of him, of their marriage bed.

"I thought that God was cruel to take my parents from me, my home. And perhaps it was cruel, but he has also given me you. I would not change the past if it meant never meeting you. And now you are mine."

Ewan kissed her again, turning her body effortlessly to fit just so against his own. "Heal me some more, wife," he whispered. His breath on her skin made it erupt into gooseflesh, every touch intensified to near torment.

Edyth didn't think she had room enough in her frame to contain all the joy she felt at that moment. "Yes," she replied, arching her neck as his mouth moved to her pulse point, "we can take it in turns."

"That didn't take long," said Iain, looking out in the yard at the new arrivals. Ewan frowned, already discerning the purpose of their coming.

They'd only been home a fortnight. Marjory's attempts to stop her husband and de Clifford had failed. He crossed himself, thinking of the formidable woman. Rumor said that she'd hung in the yard of her home by her own husband's hand the morning after they'd escaped.

Ewan wondered idly if Marjory hadn't attempted to have her husband shot through with arrows at the pledging ceremony, if King Edward would have ordered Dunbar to stay his hand. They would never know. And now his yard was full of unwelcome visitors.

"There are only six," said Iain, divining Ewan's thoughts.

"It's the priest I'm concerned about," Ewan replied sourly.

Ewan took the scroll from the monk, dirtied from the road. From the looks of him, he could use a good meal. And a bath. "Please, take some refreshment, Brother Bartholomew," Ewan said, indicating the ewer of cider and decanter of spirits on the sideboard in his study.

Ewan seated himself behind his desk and templed his fingers, forcing calm. He had known the earl of Dunbar had threatened Edyth with church interference, but the speed at which the church had moved left him unprepared. "From where have ye traveled? It looks that ye've come far," asked Ewan, watching as the small man sipped from his cup with watery eyes.

He sat with a sigh and rubbed the back of his dirty neck. "It's been a long road, at that," said the messenger. His brown robes were dusty from the road, a darkened ring of dried sweat circled his neck and armpits. "I was dispatched from Rievalux Abbey in North Yorkshire. His eminence, the Archbishop Evesham, demands immediate attention to the matter presented in the letter." The watery blue eyes settled on the missive Ewan had placed on his desk for a moment, his face blank, before taking another drink from his cup.

Ewan's fear increased with that bit of news. He regained focus with great effort, shaking his head to rid himself of the imaginary images flitting through his troubled mind. "Forgive me. You must also be hungry. Let me call for some refreshment."

"Quite kind of you," said the monk, bowing his head graciously." Rotating his bad shoulder, Ewan stood and opened the door, trying to order his mind. He dispatched the guard quickly for food with a whispered command. "And move the priest's companions where they will no' be seen by my sister or lady wife," he added hastily.

Regaining his seat, Ewan looked over the monk once more. He was small and wiry. His beard, cut short, was peppered with gray. "Rievalux is quite a distance. I trust your journey was not too difficult with all that's transpired in the lowlands."

The little man nodded, swallowing. "I'm not one to complain, but we did see some trouble. The rain washed out the paths many a time, and people were not so friendly, even to a man of the cloth." The priest waved a hand as though to erase what he'd just said. "I mean no slight, of course. I know we are all agitated with the state of the world at present."

"Quite so," Ewan agreed. "Are the roads so terrible that you need six men in arms for your protection?"

The man's lips pursed slightly. He shook his head. "My companions come with some assurances, yes, safety being only one."

"And what other assurances are they offering you?"

The small man shifted in his seat, regarding Ewan with gray eyes. "I am here to deliver that message, my lord." He nodded at the desk separating them. "My companions assure escort of that letter and to see that it is heeded."

Ewan took a long breath in through his nose. It would take more than six hired swords to wrest his wife from him. He could order them killed, he supposed, but to what end? "Whose men are they?"

The priest paused in lifting his cup to his mouth, his face blank. "I'm not told to whom they are aligned. I am but a humble messenger, my lord. I am burdened with no such knowledge."

"Mmph," said Ewan, not believing a word. Grasping the scroll, he broke the seal with a cold snap.

It wasn't lengthy. He read it in a matter of seconds, then more slowly. Twice.

While the language was formal, the meaning was quite clear: he must produce his wife by the end of the month. If he refused, she would be seized and brought to trial. No doubt the priest's men were there to add weight to this charge—and to ensure that the abbey did not lose their messenger. In addition, if *he* refused to give up his wife, he himself would be held in contempt of the law and be punished.

His teeth set on edge, Ewan lowered the message, leveling his cool gaze onto the monk. He would gladly take the punishment—most likely coin to be paid, lands held, or even imprisonment—if it would secure Edyth's freedom, but he knew it would only delay the inevitable. Ignoring the church or angering the archbishop would not save his wife. She would ultimately be stripped from him.

Ewan knew what happened to people accused of heresy. A trial often involved torture to gain a confession. He would need to assure she underwent no such treatment. His anger threatened to overtake him. Unclenching his fists, he took a deep breath through his nose. "My wife has done nothing wrong."

The monk opened his mouth to speak, but the door opened, banging loudly as it hit the bookcase against the wall.

Iain had healed well; he stalked into the small room, dropping a tray of cheeses and cold meats onto the tabletop with a loud *thunk*. Some of the sliced ham jumped off the platter onto the desk, ignored. Taking the remaining chair left in the room, Iain moved it directly in front of their guest. He straddled it backward, leaning forward into the man's face. Ewan had never been happier to see his brother.

"Go back tae England, Priest. We already have religion."

To his credit, the monk did not show fear. Moving his chair slightly away, he turned bodily from Iain and selected some food from the proffered fair. He brought a fat piece of cheese to his nose and sniffed it before taking a bite. "Mmph. I thank you."

Ewan handed his brother the message, which he eagerly took, his eyes darting across the page. Tossing the letter onto the desk, Iain shook his head in refusal. "Lady Ruthven is no longer English, Priest. She will no' be taken out o' Scotland."

The priest spoke around the partially chewed food in his mouth. "The church sees no distinction between earthly boundaries. She is a member of the fold of God and, therefore, subject to canon law. It does not matter where she lives."

The man swallowed and leveled his eyes on Ewan. "She is permitted two witnesses at the trial. I suggest that if you want to save your wife undue suffering, you will bring her to Yorkshire, and with her, people to speak in her behalf."

Ewan sat up straighter in his chair. With his mind muddled with the problem at hand, he'd missed an important piece of information the first time the monk had mentioned it. He'd caught it this time, however. "Ye said the trial will be in Yorkshire, but her accuser is in Carlisle, aye?"

The priest paused in selecting another piece of cheese. "My knowledge of her accuser is limited," he said, the crease between his brows deepening in thought, "but now that the archbishop is involved, he will be conducting the trial. The abbot has been commanded to see the trial take place by the end of the month."

The sinking feeling that had settled in Ewan's wame changed shape. He looked at Iain, his eyes shining. If Father Brewer would not be the one conducting the trial, perhaps there was still hope to be had. "My wife's accuser will be present, surely? The abbot will insist that Lady Ruthven's petitioner state his claims before the church court."

The monk's face turned a slight pinkish hue, his eyes darting from Ewan to the cheese to Iain and back. "I cannot say, milord."

Ewan almost smiled. The monk knew more than he was letting on. Iain could help with that. "Brother Bartholomew," said Ewan politely, "I dinnae care for secrets when it involves my family. I'd advise ye tae tell me what ye ken."

Face changing from pink to green in an instant, he said, "I hold no secrets, milord!"

He made a motion for Iain to remove the man, a task his brother enthusiastically performed. Grabbing the monk by the cowl of his robe, Iain wrenched him from his chair and dragged him through the door. Ewan could hear the grunts and shuffling all the way down the hall as he sat at his desk, staring at the wrinkled parchment demanding his wife.

Iain would not really hurt the monk, he knew. But he would get answers. He didn't have much time to think; shortly after Iain's departure, Ewan gained another visitor.

"Mam," said Ewan, turning his head at her soft knock upon the open door. He ran a hand over his weary face. Standing in respect and offering her a chair, he closed the door behind them.

Her gown rustled in the quiet space as she took her seat. "You'll not hurt the poor man, Ewan," she demanded.

Ewan opened his mouth to speak, but his mother raised a long-fingered hand, forestalling him. "Never mind. I want to get to the point. Your lady wife is in considerable danger, it would seem."

"She has done nothing wrong."

"You've no need to defend her to me."

It wasn't often that Ewan saw his mother as she actually was, changed through time with the evidence of a life well lived carved into her bones. Instead, he saw her as he had in his youth, with a grace and strength that made her seem much larger than she was. Looking at her now, she seemed far too delicate. As small as a bird and just as fragile.

"I've just left Edyth," she said as way of explanation. "She has gone to the chapel to pray."

"That bad, is it?" joked Ewan, trying to force a smile, but he gave it up with an apologetic shrug. "How did she know the message was about her?"

The dowager leveled him with a caustic look. "If you wanted wife ye could keep secrets from, you should have married a far stupider person. Tell me the message."

"Ye'll remember I told ye about her escape from Carlisle? Well, it seems to me that the wicked Father Brewer has befriended the wrong man. In his haste to rid the world of witnesses to his crimes, the priest's lies have spurred de Clifford, and now Dunbar, to act. They have circumvented Brewer and have taken his claim to the abbey in Yorkshire."

His mother smiled softly and leaned back in her chair. "Brewer has set a trap and caught himself in it. What will you do?"

Ewan rubbed the back of his neck, thinking of what Edyth had told him. His mind searched, landing on the name he sought. "I must find Annie."

The room was quiet, the rows of wood-hewn pews empty. Prayer candles remained lit in behalf of family members who had passed, supplications for deliverance from purgatory. Their pulsating light lit the aisle to the front of the room, where, upon the altar, lay the symbols of the sacrament.

A priest was kneeling in the front pew, seemingly unperturbed by her invasion into the sanctuary. A soft murmuring as he prayed over his rosary was the only sound in the room. She hadn't intended to come to the chapel, but her restless, troubled mind had little room for anything other than the messenger.

She sank onto a pew away from the room's other occupant, her hands trembling, feeling as though she'd run a league. What was she to do?

She closed her eyes, thinking of Father Brewer. Fear nearly overcame her. *Holy Mother, beneath your compassion, I take refuge.* She swallowed and took a deep breath, searching her feelings.

Options were few, indeed, for one accused of heresy, let alone witchcraft. Magic was done with the aid of demons and thus was open to prosecution for heresy. That coupled with those nasty-yet- true names she'd called the priest and her knowledge of his crimes, she had no hope of exoneration.

She could hide behind her husband's walls and bring the wrath of the church upon him and his people, or she could willingly submit herself before the church court and save his clan unwanted and unwarranted turmoil. The choice was clear, yet the thought of going made her knees wobble and her heart stutter. She simply did not have the courage it took to face Father Brewer again. Running away seemed the better option, but what of Ewan? Leaving him would be a torment unto itself.

Lost in prayer and her own cyclical thoughts, it was with some surprise that she realized she was no longer alone.

"How long have you been here?" she asked, her whisper carrying in the cavernous chapel.

"Not long," Ewan answered, grasping her elbow to help her from her kneeling position.

He pulled her to his side and kissed the top of her head. "Dinnae fash, Edie," he whispered. "I will no' leave ye again. I swore tae ye in the Douglass Forest. Do ye recall?"

Suppressing tears, she nodded against his chest. "I remember."

"I also promised tae see ye safe. Do ye remember that?" At her nod, he moved away slightly to look into her anxious face. Her hands were trembling with cold. "I intend tae keep that promise, Edie. I will see ye safe home."

Edyth wanted to believe it but couldn't see how.

Chapter Fourteen

Newcastle, England

One large, limpid blue eye peeked through the slight crack between the door and its jamb. The river of rainwater that had carved a gully in front of the home's threshold soaked into Edyth's boots and weighed down the hem of her cloak. Ewan's towering presence could easily be the reason for the man's hesitancy, but Edyth doubted it.

While it had only been a few months since she and her mother had deposited Annie here, Edyth's stay had been brief, and while she might not look much different, she felt wholly changed. "Ye'll recall my father, perhaps, the former lord of Carlisle. I believe ye had some business with him in the past." Edyth was vibrating with both cold and nerves, but she stood her ground, daring the man to deny her.

After a brief pause, which Edyth took to be a battle of conscience, the space widened to reveal the shared acquaintance of one of her father's crofters and a favored shepherd. The man's pale eyes were framed by eyebrows so blonde as to appear white.

Stepping away and opening the door wide, the man's gimlet eye did not stray from them.

"I thought the plan was ne'er to return. That's what your mother said. That's what *you* said."

He wiped his bulbous nose with a handkerchief, his invisible brows knit together.

"Where is she?" asked Ewan, looking around the sparse room as though he might spot her hiding behind the broom handle or the washing pot.

The crofter's wife peered at them questioningly from the hearth table, wiping a bowl clean with a cloth.

"Away. Out," said the man.

Edyth put a restraining hand upon her husband's arm to quell the impatient demands she knew were coming.

"It's Benjamin, isn't it?" His head bobbed on his spindly neck. "I'm glad to see you've taken my mother's warnings to heart."

"Mmph. I've got enough troubles as is, with the king marching 'is men up and down through my fields and taking my livestock without a word and no payment of any kind. I've had to trade off most of our things just to replace a fraction of what the soldiers took." He shook his head in disgust. "I don't need any additional trouble...especially from the church, and that's the truth."

Edyth privately agreed. She took a deep breath and looked him in the eye, a brow raised in emphasis. "Then you'll understand with what urgency I have returned. I wouldn't have come if I had any other choice."

Benjamin's mouth compressed tightly, his face losing the little color it had.

"We must speak with the lassie," said Ewan. "We've traveled far and have little time."

Benjamin rubbed a long finger under his nose, eyeing Ewan with distaste.

"What's that got to do with me? Or the girl?" he asked stubbornly. "If yer in that big o' a hurry, why bother stopping here at all?"

Ewan let out a long breath through his nose, clearly striving for calm. "As the lady said," he replied, indicating Edyth with a nod, "we wouldnae be here had we any other choice. It's a matter o' life and death. We must speak with the lass."

"Is that so?" said the crofter gruffly. "Whose life?"

"Mine," Edyth said simply. She removed her hood, sodden with rain. Droplets fell from her sodden cloak, filling the silent space.

***

As it turned out, Annie had only been collecting eggs from the coop behind the small stable, a three-sided structure with an open face where the animals had huddled close together to get out of the rain.

Annie, fair and small to start with, seemed to shrink further still upon seeing Edyth. A light smattering of freckles stood out starkly along the fine bridge of her pert nose as her face lost all color, her eyes full of wariness.

Benjamin hastily snatched the basket of eggs from her hands, lest she drop them.

"You'll recall this lady," said Benjamin gruffly. It wasn't a question.

Annie nodded imperceptibly; her pink mouth pressed into a frown. Annie had always been beautiful. In the past, she had reminded Edyth of the tender apple blossom she so resembled: pink and fair and so very delicate. But seeing her now, with her blue eyes darting between all the faces looming over her, she reminded Edyth of a hunted rabbit, whose heart would surely fail her if given too big of a fright.

"Hello, Annie," said Edyth, her heart tugging at the fright she saw in the girl's eyes.

"I'm called Elizabeth now," she said softly in way of greeting, her eyes darting between Edyth and Ewan and back again. She interlaced her fingers tightly. Edyth could see the white of her knuckle bones glow starkly against her brown homespun. "How is Thom? I haven't had word of him since I...since I left."

Edyth's mouth tightened as her heart quickened. She knew Annie would ask about her brother, but no matter how many times she'd thought of what she might say, Edyth had found no words to convey the weight of her grief. Thom had died for *her*; his blood had been spilled so she, Edyth, could live.

An image of Thom's crumpled body filled her mind's eye, her throat tightening of its own accord. He'd died saving her, and she hadn't even been able to see him buried. The lines of Annie's person shimmered as Edyth's eyes misted with tears. "Oh, Annie. I'm sorry to be the bearer of bad news. He...he died bravely. You would be proud of him. He fell...." she sniffed and wiped her eyes quickly. "He fell defending me. I'm so sorry."

Annie's face, pale with fright or nerves, grew red as her eyes filled with tears. Benjamin took the few steps necessary to reach her side and wrapped an arm around her shoulders, glaring at them over her head, intruders into their quiet, secret lives.

Not having been invited to sit, Edyth had no chair to offer her. Edyth barely registered her husband leaving her side, her heart constricting in grief. She knew quite well the gripping sorrow Annie felt at losing her brother. She'd felt it keenly and had carried her own loss for so long she hardly noticed its weight any longer. It had simply become a part of her.

Ewan returned promptly with a chair, which the girl sank into with the aid of her guardian. The golden ribbon of her hair fell over her face as she cried, her arms wrapped around her middle as though trying to contain the anguish inside of her.

The crofter's wife—Farrah, Edyth recalled—appeared at Annie's shoulder, whispering soothing words into her ear, hugging her fiercely.

Edyth knelt at the girl's knees. "Oh, Annie," she said, her voice breaking. "I'm sorry for it. For it all. If Thom hadn't helped me escape from Carlisle, he would still be there."

Annie lifted her head, her wide, red-rimmed eyes searching Edyth's concerned face. "*You* had to escape Carlisle?" She hiccuped, her face blotchy.

Edyth nodded. "The damage *that man* has caused is—" Edyth didn't want to say Father Brewer's name. It felt like a sacrilege in this small space of mourning. She swallowed and stood, looking down on Annie's tear-streaked face. "He is not finished, Annie. He has not stopped disrupting and destroying lives."

Annie looked away, her worried eyes falling to the hands in her lap.

"The service your brother rendered tae his mistress is nae forgotten, Annie," said Ewan. Edyth thought he rather looked as though he were prepared for a battle of arms instead of a battle of words, but his shoulders lost some of their rigidity as he spoke to the girl. He moved to Edyth's side, solid and warm. "But your tormenter is free, aye? Thom's sacrifice will be all for naught if he has his way. A man like that...he cannae allow those who know o' his evil deeds tae live."

Annie sniffed and looked at Ewan, considering him with troubled eyes.

"His grip tightens around me even now, Annie," Edyth all but whispered. "I fear he will not rest until we are, all of us, dead."

Annie's eyes widened, her mouth slightly agape in shock and horror. She looked to Benjamin, her fears palpable. "He knows where I am?"

"No," said Benjamin emphatically. "And even if he did, I would secret you away, Lizzy. I'll not let that happen."

"We've come tae assure your brother's death was no' in vain," said Ewan. "We are here to call upon *your* bravery."

Annie's eyes clouded with confusion, and she looked to Benjamin for answers, but Benjamin did not register his charge's unspoken question. "No," said Benjamin flatly.

"She must," Ewan said. He looked at Annie, his voice full of regret. "Edyth's life hangs in the balance, and you, Annie, are the only one who can save her."

"No," said Benjamin vehemently, emphasizing his words with a sharp gesture. He turned on Edyth, hissing. "You said she'd not be bothered. You promised that she would be safe here...that you'd never return, to keep her hidden...to not draw attention—"

"What is it?" asked Annie, looking to Farrah now. "What is happening? I don't understand."

"Edyth has been charged by Father Brewer with heresy and witchcraft," explained Ewan, his gaze intense as though he could compel the girl to action by sheer will of force. "The trial is soon upon us. You must come and speak for her."

Annie's mouth fell open in disbelief. "Me? I...surely there is nothing I can do."

"But there is," replied Edyth, too desperate to lose hope. "I've come to ask that you to speak for me. In Yorkshire."

Annie recoiled, turning her face to Farrah, a silent plea written on her face.

"There is no one else who can, Annie," coaxed Edyth. "You and I alone know what kind of man Father Brewer is. Together we must stand against him."

Annie visibly trembled, silent tears streaming down her blotchy cheeks. "I cannot speak out against Father Brewer.

I...he told me I would be excommunicated if I said anything against a man of the cloth. He said it was a sin." She took a shuddering breath and closed her eyes tightly. "My soul will be lost if I do such a thing. I cannot lose my soul. I will not!"

"Do not believe an evil man who would win your silence with lies," insisted Edyth. "He is a *liar*."

Seeing Annie's discomfort at her blasphemous name calling frustrated Edyth. Even now, after everything Father Brewer had done to ruin their lives, Annie was still unable to name him for what he was.

Feeling suddenly weary, Edyth ran a hand over her face. She'd known it would be difficult for Annie. But as terrified as she knew the girl would be, Edyth hadn't been fully prepared for a refusal. Hesitancy, yes. Edyth hadn't prepared herself mentally for Annie's crippling inability to see through Father Brewer's lies.

"I understand your hesitancy," Edyth tried. "I know how difficult it is to sort through a distortion of truth, especially from someone you should have been able to trust." Edyth took a step toward her, her eyes begging her to hear. "Annie, picking out the bits of truth and discarding the lies feels impossible. I'm still learning how, and we were not damaged in the same way. I cannot know all of what you're feeling, but I do know this..." Edyth took Annie's cold hands into her own, helping her to stand. She searched the girl's frightened face, her streaming eyes. "I know that he will not stop. Not for gold, not for God, not for anything. He will do to others what he has done to you. To my mother. To me."

Annie's eyes dimmed as she retreated into herself. Edyth wondered what she saw—a shadow from the past or the looming mountain she had yet to climb. After some hesitation, Annie's forlorn eyes met Edyth's. "I believe you," she all but whispered, "but I cannot." Taking her hands from Edyth's, she said, "I am not brave like you. Or like Thom. I cannot face him."

"You will," said Ewan, his voice calm but certain.

"I cannot!" she screeched. She ran into Farrah, nearly knocking her down in a desperate attempt to escape. They collided, holding each other up. Annie's sobs filled the room. She shook her head frantically against Farrah's shoulder, mumbling, "I cannot face him. He cannot know I'm alive. I cannot."

Benjamin was shouting now, standing toe-to-toe with Ewan. Farrah, holding tightly to Annie's wracking shoulders, removed her from the room. Edyth watched, defeated, as the door to the bedroom shut, cutting off her only link to salvation.

"Look at what ye've done!" shouted Benjamin, his eyes alight with anger. "Get yourself gone, the both of you!"

"We willnae leave without the lass," Ewan growled. "She's coming with us."

Ewan would force Annie, she knew; he would not let Benjamin stop him from taking the girl.

Edyth barely heard them, imagining instead meeting Father Brewer in Yorkshire in a few days with no defense. She had her word only. Yes, there was Ewan—a man now to speak for her—as Marjory had intended, but Edyth couldn't see how it mattered. Even with Ewan, she would still be sentenced. He had saved her from arrest, yes, from de Clifford and Dunbar as well, but not from Father Brewer's lies. Without Annie, Ewan could not save her.

Edyth walked to the door Annie had disappeared behind, the shouting match behind her ignored. The wood was rough but cool on her heated hands. Annie was still sobbing. She heard the soft murmurs of Farrah as she tried to comfort the girl through the barrier. Hearing her cries burdened Edyth's heart and confused her thoughts. Having only considered her own plight, she hadn't spent much time thinking of Annie.

Forced to face her abuser again so abruptly, Annie was wholly unprepared for their request. And not only that, but the wrenching grief of learning about her brother's death, mere minutes ago, was an unbearable burden to have thrust upon her. And Edyth could not force her. She wanted to. Desperately. But she could not bring herself to drag her from her new place. The roots of her life had barely been replanted. To pluck her from the safety of anonymity would surely cause her to wither and, if Father Brewer had his way, die.

She pushed the barrier open and joined the women on the cot silently. She felt as a ghost, a whisp of intangible soul adrift and lost. Reaching for Annie's hand, Edyth looked at the small, calloused fingers from her many labors. Hers had been a difficult life, even as short as it had been thus far. "How old are you, Annie?" asked Edyth softly.

Annie's sobs had lessened, her body still hiccupping, but she saw the girl stir in an effort to sit up. "I-I'm not yet thirteen."

Edyth smiled. So young and yet, at twelve, she herself had been thrust into the terrifying future of a marriage of fortunes. Now at eighteen, and only just married, Edyth wondered at what she'd been like as a new maiden. Had she been as vulnerable? She couldn't recall. She sighed and patted Annie's hand before returning it to her lap.

"I'm sorry for surprising you as I have today, Annie. I know it hasn't been easy for you. Not for a long time." She hesitated, searching for the right words. "But you're wrong. You *are* brave," Edyth said. "You've spoken out against Father Brewer already. Thom told my mother so. You went to Thom because you knew he would help you. You knew he would try to protect you, and you were right. He did. He did the only thing he could think of. He went to my parents."

"Y-yes." Annie sniffed mightily, wiping her nose on her apron. Farrah still held one of her hands. "And look what it did. Farrah told me what...what happened to your mother."

Edyth picked at a bit of the quilt on the bed that had come apart at a seam. "What happened to my mother isn't your fault." She paused, looking at Annie from the shade of her lashes. "Do you know what Father Brewer said of her?"

Annie shook her head, her lips nearly colorless.

"He called her heretic and a witch. People who my mother had loved and helped, who knew her well enough to know her heart, did nothing. They...watched."

Even now, Edyth could see the crowd gathered in the square. She could see her mother, tall and as straight as an arrow, standing on the pillory platform while Father Brewer's lies wormed into the people's ears. Most stood, uneasy at first, looking around them as though to gauge their neighbor's responses. Did they believe? Would *they* speak for Lady De-Vries?

The crowd, which had started rather small, grew in proportion to Father Brewer's lies. Voice booming, people were pulled to the scene. Their hearts turned, stirred by anger. It began with just one. Someone threw something at her—she couldn't have said what it was. It sailed past her mother's head, just missing her by inches. Then someone spat.

"He'd said she had consorted with demons and cast a spell to make him ill," said Edyth, far away. "He had been ill the week prior. She'd brought him a tonic for his cough. His words twisted her kindnesses into something evil." He'd asked them, people her mother had healed, to come forward, but he'd twisted their words, too, so by the end of it, no one was sure what to believe.

"Maybe some didn't believe Father Brewer's lies, but they did nothing to stop him from murdering my mother in the name of God." Edyth looked at Annie, still, mouth slightly agape. "I will leave you, Annie." She kissed the girl's cheeks and stood. "Do not think any of this is your fault."

Ewan was waiting for her outside, leaning against the side of their carriage looking grim. Upon seeing her, he stood straight, a question in his eyes. When Edyth shook her head, he seemed to swell in preparation for battle. He took a step toward the house, his face a mask of dark determination, but she stopped him with a hand on his chest.

"No, Ewan," she said softly, looking into his stern face. "Not like this. I will not force her to face her abuser. I...I will not force anything upon her."

His eyebrows drew together angrily. "We are mere days away from the church court, Edie. No. No, if you will not force her, then *I* will."

"She has been *forced* for the entirety of her life, Ewan. We would be no better than Father Brewer!"

He looked at her as though he'd never seen her before, a startling creature. "How can you say such a thing?"

Edyth put another hand on his chest. It rose and fell in quick succession with his anger. She looked into his angry face, willing him to understand. "Imagine if Annie were Cait, or me. A child, terrified and tormented, and now mourning for a lost brother. Imagine, Ewan, being ripped from the only safety she's ever known, to be thrust back into the waiting arms of her tormenter. I cannot do it to her. I will not."

Ewan's brow contracted, his eyes resting on the closed door of the hut.

"I have you, Ewan, to speak for me. And fate. Remember," she hesitated, licking the dryness from her lips. "Remember you told me that God values our choices above all else?" At his nod, she continued, "You said that God would not stop cruelty and pain at the hands of others because it is our choices that will determine our destiny. Wicked people and good, both, will reap their reward. I want it to be true. Do you believe it?"

"I...yes," he said, the frown on his face lessening slightly. "But I also believe we must fight. I do not think God would want you to go unprotected."

"But I am not unprotected," said Edyth, tugging on his sleeve. "I have truth on my side. And you. I choose to stand before the church and declare it. Let the consequences follow."

Ewan hesitated. Edyth watched the carefully controlled emotion play over his features. Determination, fear, anger, disappointment, and finally, acquiesce.

Rievaulx was a sprawling, towering structure decorated with countless pointed arches atop expertly crafted stone pillars at each level. Nestled against rolling hills dotted with oaks, the scene would have been beautiful had it not been for the terror coursing through her frame.

Upon their arrival, they'd been asked to wait in an office near the front of the great cloister. Edyth kept wiping her sweaty palms on her skirts, her eyes searching the faces that passed the open door. She wasn't exactly sure what she was looking for. Perhaps a hint of recognition from the strangers milling about? Did they know why she was here?

On their way to fetch Annie, Ewan had told her what Iain had gotten from the messenger monk. And while she didn't approve of Iain intentionally intimidating the man, it had resulted in some useful information. The monk had reluctantly admitted that there would be no question of Father Brewer's presence. Not only that, but it was hinted at that both the abbot and the archbishop would be involved, two very different governing powers. She didn't know what to make of it.

The weighty pit that had taken up residence in her stomach moved to her throat; she couldn't get enough air.

"Be still, Edie," whispered Ewan, taking her hand. He kissed it, his thumb rubbing circles on her wrist. His touch calmed her until she saw the worry behind his eyes and his valiant effort to hide it.

Giving him a weak smile, she opened her mouth to speak but stopped short at the arrival of the abbot. He might have been tall once, but now he was stooped with age, his beard as white as snow. Shuffling into the office, with a monk close behind, the abbot moved surprisingly quickly under his own power. The glossy planes of his bald head were interrupted by a black bowl-shaped zucchetto. Coming to a stop before them, his hazel eyes studied them each in turn.

"Welcome to Rievaulx," said the abbot in a voice like the wind. "Please be seated."

They sat on the bench against the wall while the monk helped the old man into his chair. Excused, the monk left the abbot's side to stand at the ready by the closed door, his eyes diverted to the floor.

"You must be Edyth DeVries," said the abbot. Edyth felt as though he was looking into her soul with the way he studied her.

"Y-yes, though now I am Lady Ruthven of Perthshire."

He might have smiled, but Edyth couldn't tell with the way his long mouth was turned up at the corners as though in a perpetual grin. His eyes swiveled to Ewan, whom he considered for only a moment. "I have been waiting for you. I am the Right Reverend Henry the Second," said the abbot, bobbing his head like a turtle come from its shell. "I heard tell of you and your alleged crimes through the Earl of March. Do you know this man?"

Edyth's mouth pressed into a thin line. "I have met him, Father. Once."

The abbot regarded them both, his hands folded neatly against his belly. Edyth did her best not to squirm. She could feel Ewan's desire to speak—for action.

"It is my understanding that he is not a direct witness to these allegations. Is this correct?"

Edyth swallowed, her heart fluttering wildly. "No, Father. In fact, there are no witnesses—"

He held up a hand, forestalling her. "You may speak for yourself tomorrow, when the archbishop and Father Brewer arrive with his chosen witnesses. We will do this properly, my child. For now, I only need to ascertain that you understand the severity of the situation and what claims are laid against you."

Edyth blanched. Of course there would be witnesses against her, false of course, but witnesses nonetheless. She wondered who they might be, her mind swirling with faces from her past.

"This man is here to speak for you, I presume?"

Ewan cleared his throat. "Yes, Father," he said respectfully, his voice soft, but his eyes...his eyes were nearly black with emotion held in check. "I am her husband, but even if I were not, nothing could stop me from coming to her aid. Lady Edyth is..." he paused and clenched his jaw. A muscle jumped in his cheek, and he looked away from her, leveling the abbot with a steely stare. "To not speak for such a lady would be shameful."

Edyth let out a shaky breath, her heart stuttering at her husband's words. She'd tried not to think of their parting, so soon at hand. She'd tried to remain stoic, but she could feel her throat tighten with suppressed tears.

At some point tomorrow, she would be torn from him. Father Brewer would come with his lies and false witnesses, and together, they would steal her life away from her once more.

"Do you know with what crimes you are charged, my child?"

Swallowing, Edyth took a shaky breath, clenching her fists in the folds of her skirts. "I am accused of heresy, Father. And witchcraft," she said, quietly.

The abbot's glassy stare did not waiver as he nodded. "These are serious charges and, therefore, must be investigated properly and with the right authority. We will begin the inquisition tomorrow morning."

Motioning for the monk by the door, the abbot said, "With the end of the month soon upon us, the concerned parties arrived in Yorkshire only a few days ago."

The monk leaned his ear close to the old man's mouth, the shaved round of his skull fuzzy with new growth. The abbot spoke so softly Edyth couldn't hear what was said; she watched his mouth as he spoke, trying to glean any information she could, but it was in vain.

The monk nodded and left without a word, the soft *thunk* of the door closing the only indication that he had been there at all. "You are not permitted to leave the Abbey," he said, breathlessly. "You will stay here and prepare yourself for your adjuration on the morrow."

Edyth could only nod. She looked to her husband and saw her own fears reflected in his eyes.

A stout lay brother showed them to simple chambers in the western wing of the sprawling structure where they would sleep. While they were each meant to be given their own room—comprised of only one small cot and a nightstand—Ewan refused to be separated. Glad of his insistence, Edyth was relieved when the lay brother did not argue and shut the door behind him.

Exhausted from travel, little sleep, and far too much anguish, Edyth sat heavily upon the cot. She hung her head in her hands, fighting tears. She felt as though she were coming unraveled at the seams.

Ewan sat down beside her on the narrow bed and gathered her into his arms. "Ye can cry if ye need to, Edie," he whispered. "There's no shame in it."

She did cry. With the first fat tears that fell, round and heavy down her cheeks, she stayed quiet, shivering with the effort it took to contain her weeping. But as Ewan stroked her hair and kissed her forehead, whispering words she did not hear, the agony of the last several weeks broke from her in great, wracking sobs.

Disappointment, anger, and fear warred within her. There was no course she could take that would not end in added sorrow. "I'm sorry," she cried against his chest, holding fistfuls of his shirt. "I'm...I'm trying to be b-brave. Look at what I've done to you," she apologized. "I regret.... If hadn't met you, then you'd not have to endure such things."

"Wheesht," chided Ewan. "Away with those thoughts." He removed her from his lap onto the bed and, holding her upper arms tightly, stared into her tear-streaked face. "Ye may rail and cry and rage all ye want or need, Edie, but I willnae hear your regrets." He shook her slightly, forcing her attention. "Do ye hear me, lass? We chose each other, knowing full well what was to come, and come it has. I will not hear about regrets now."

He put a large hand over her heart, his voice urgent, his eyes dark with emotion. "Do no' forget it's half my heart ye hold in yer breast. Do no' let it fail so easily."

She sniffed, feeling utterly broken. "Yes," she replied, fresh tears filling her eyes. She placed her hand atop his, feeling the rapid rise and fall of her chest as she breathed. "And when I am sentenced and ripped from you, how are you to live without it?"

"You forget yourself," he chided. He lifted her chin with a finger as she looked away. "You forget who you are and that fate has placed you on this very path."

"And what if it's my fate to die?"

Ewan took her face between his two hands, his eyes shining with determination. "So says the woman who would no' let me go peacefully tae my own death. What makes ye think I'd no' return the favor?" He scoffed and fought a wry smile. "I cannae imagine fate letting go of such a willing servant, but if so, then we'll do so together. I promised ye, Edie—" His voice broke on her name, his eyes searching her own. "I promised I wouldnae leave ye again, and I meant it."

He pulled her to him, overcome, and held her fiercely. She cried softly against his chest, putting to memory the feel of him. After a time, they lay down, nestled against each other in silence, listening to each other's breathing. She didn't want to sleep; she didn't want to waste any of the time left to her, but before long, exhaustion took hold.

She awoke sometime in the night, and they tenderly and tearfully came together. There were no words between them, only feelings, and when they were exhausted, she fell asleep in his arms for the last time.

Light from the afternoon sun shone brightly into the hall of her childhood home, glittering and warm. It drew her in, filling her with a longing so intense that, had the wound been physical, she was sure it would have been fatal.

It was just as she remembered it: the cheery fire, the cat asleep in the pool of sunlight on the floor, her mother's favored chair, and the little table where she and her father had spent countless hours in the pursuit of knowledge and entertainment.

He was there now, studying the chess board, his thinning, russet hair falling around his ears as he leaned in close to the polished rock pieces scattered over the checkered board.

"Come, Bean. It's your turn." She couldn't see his face yet; so focused on the game, he hadn't looked up when he'd spoken to her. Tears pricked her eyes at the sound of his voice, at the

term of endearment he'd used for her. Teasing her for her long body that so resembled a string bean, he'd called her that for as long as she could remember. She'd loved it and hated it at the same time.

Filled with longing, she took a cautious step toward him, afraid she would somehow disturb the delicate spell she was under and wake. She drank in the sight of him, his large hands sprinkled with fine hairs, his wrinkled brow, intense with concentration, the very smell of him. He was so real. So immediate. She wondered if she could touch him.

"I'm about to take your bishop," he warned, looking up from the board at last to meet her eye. She took a shuddering breath, the lines of his body dissolving as her eyes misted with tears. "You always neglect your bishops, Edyth. Come, sit." He smiled at her, his eyes crinkling at the corners. "It's time we finish this game."

The heavily embroidered chair felt just as she remembered it— overstuffed and lumpy on one side, the threads on the armrest thinning and soiled with oil from their hands. It felt like an old friend, and she sank into it slowly, unable to take her eyes from her father's familiar face. "The bishop's path is always obstructed by friendly pawns," she replied, blinking rapidly. Her heart was starting to slow now. The initial shock of seeing her father so alive and well was wearing away, replaced instead with grateful elation.

"You must carve a path for the bishop, Edyth. It must be deliberate. Only then can he exert significant influence upon your opponent." Edyth could only stare, a smile tugging on the corners of her mouth.

"As you say," she said. She barely registered the board, moving the bishop at random. Her father tsked disapprovingly and moved a knight to take it.

"Your head is not in it, I see. What has your attention then? I'd hear it now so I can sooner have my proper opponent back."

Edyth wanted to touch him, to hug him, to feel his fatherly arms around her again, but she restrained herself. "I...I don't want to play. I would rather just hear your voice and look upon you."

He raised a suspicious brow, leaning back in his chair to survey her. "What will it be then? Shall you hear, once again, my opinions on using grubs for fish bait over worms? Or would you rather me complain about your appalling defensive techniques. You've been neglecting the riposte for far too long."

Edyth gave a watery laugh, feeling a tangle of emotions. "It doesn't matter. Lecture me on any of my faults. I promise to listen this time."

He rubbed a long finger across his bearded chin, surveying her kindly. "My daughter, asking to be lectured. It must be serious. Come, tell me what is amiss so that I may remedy it."

"Will I...will I be joining you soon?" she asked. "You and Mother? Is that why you've come?"

The teasing glint left his eye at her words. He leaned forward, his arms resting on the polished table between them. The intensity of his gaze was a weight. Her heart increased its cadence, and she held her breath, both afraid and strangely prepared for his answer at the same moment.

"Listen well, daughter. You have prepared for this game of strategy the whole of your life. You are meant to be just where you are. Do not doubt it."

He gestured to the chess board between them, pointing out the white queen. "You've always placed far too much importance on the queen, Edyth. While she is important, do not forget the other powers at play." He picked it up and placed it into her hand, solid and cool to the touch.

Edyth blinked, confused. He wanted to talk about chess? She wanted comfort. Answers. She wanted help. "I don't understand," she said, shaking her head. Didn't he know what she was facing? "Da, I'm scared. I...Father Brewer has accused me of heresy and witchcraft. I need help. What should I do?"

Even as she asked the question, the dream began to fade. The sharp edges of the room melted away as mere reflections on a pond, rippled and distorted. Panic overtook her. Not yet. She wasn't ready.

"*Wait!*" *she pleaded, desperation coloring her voice.*

Her father's image grew cloudy, a meager apparition through smoke. "You know how to play the game, Edyth."

She must have cried out, for the next she knew, Ewan was shaking her awake, muttering his Gaelic endearments.

Mentally clutching the images from her dream to her, she played and replayed the short interaction from her dream. She reviewed the rules she'd been taught, one after another. She knew point values, movements, and patterns, but she did not know how chess would help her here.

"Perhaps he only means you're focusing on the wrong person," suggested Ewan with a yawn. "He said you'd always favored the queen. Who is the queen then?"

"I suppose he means me. It's my word against Father Brewer's, isn't it?" Edyth hadn't intended to focus only on herself. "I'm trying to win with just my word, but Annie wouldn't come," she said needlessly.

"Who else then?"

Edyth bit her lip, thinking. She shook her head. "I can't think of anything that would help us."

After a long moment, both of them lost in their own thoughts, Ewan said, "What about the bishop? Your father said something about the bishop, didn't he?"

"He said I always neglect my bishops." Edyth turned toward Ewan, her head propped up on one elbow. "He took it. In my dream, he won my bishop from me."

Ewan's gaze drew inward as he thought. "I did think it odd that the archbishop was involved before, but with one thing and another, I'd put it out of my mind. It is strange, aye?"

She nodded, the crease between her brows deepening as she considered. While the archbishop governed any number of bishops, his was a role of superior rank. Why not appoint the local bishop to the hearing? Why come himself? "Perhaps the bishop knows something we do not," Edyth suggested.

"Aye," considered Ewan. "Mayhap his priest has drawn too much attention to his dealings."

"Let us hope so," said Edyth. She never did get back to sleep, so muddled was her mind.

Chapter Fifteen

The court was to be held in the chapter house, an adjoining building near the belfry tower. The room, much like a chapel, had rows of pews that usually accommodated monks for their daily general meetings, but today, the benches held townsfolk, interested in the spectacle that was about to unfold.

The layman who had led her through a short hallway and out a side door brought her to her place: a small stage partitioned by a wooden railing where the priests usually conducted assemblies. Today, however, it would serve as her cage, raised slightly to assure that all would see her shame. There was no seat, no comfort however small, for the accused.

The room was close to capacity now, with only a few vacant seats scattered about. A great current of expectation ran through the room and filled the vast space. The bells pealed loudly, proclaiming the start of the proceedings should anyone else care to join.

Edyth wasn't surprised. News spread just as easily as fire jumped from rush to rush. She looked about, searching for Ewan. They had been separated shortly after they broke their fast in the refectory, when she had been brought to the chapel to confess and pray for her soul.

Strangers, all, Edyth hoped that the gathered crowd would not so easily condemn her as her own people had. These people were, after all, not subject to Father Brewer's poisonous words. Mouths moved unintelligibly, speaking over and around one another. Unfamiliar eyes surveyed her, some with curiosity, some with eager anticipation of impending entertainment, and some, she noticed, with frank disapproval.

The door opened, and Edyth, eager to find Ewan's face, felt a jolt of delight turned to apprehension at whom she spotted there instead. She hadn't thought she'd ever see him again, but there he stood, the long bones of his body unmistakable. His brown eyes skittered around the room, skipping here and there, looking for...something.

James was just as she'd left him in Carlisle: pleasantly homely, as thin as a rail, and as long-legged as a stork. At first sight, the excitement at seeing her childhood friend lope reluctantly into the room lifted the heaviness in her heart. She raised her hand halfway into the air without thought, then paused, her fingers closing on air once his eyes met hers. It wasn't difficult to read him. She'd known him all her life, after all, and had spent countless hours in his company.

There was guilt—and perhaps an apology—written on his long face. Clutching his hat in his hands, he wobbled through the narrow space afforded between the pews and sat among the crowd. She stared at him, begging him to look at her, to *see* her as he once had, to recall the bond they'd shared, but his eyes skittered around the room, avoiding her gaze. The heaviness weighing on her heart increased, and she had to look away, lest she lose her composure.

While she'd been busy staring, Ewan entered and took his seat on the front row, forcing one slack-jawed woman to budge up closer to her friend. Edyth already felt better having him there, the flittering of her nerves settling slightly.

It wasn't long before the court authorities entered, elaborate vestments trailing in their wake as they ate the distance from the door to the dais. While she recognized the abbot, with his shuffling, hunched way of walking and his gleaming skull bent for her purview, she did not recognize the other man. He might have been a king for how richly he was dressed, but Edyth recognized his ached miter and knew him as an archbishop, come to oversee the proceedings.

Mouth gone dry, Edyth watched them take their seats at the table to her right and settle in for what was doubtless going to be a very long morning. She shifted her weight, her feet already tired, when the door opened to reveal Father Brewer.

Taking a quick breath through her nose, she tamped down the panic and anger that licked to life at seeing his plump cheeks and black eyes again. The paleness of his skin in contrast to his dark robes, made it appear as though his head was floating in midair, a mere specter intent to haunt.

He bobbed his solemn salutations to strangers down the aisle, his hands pressed together as though praying. Edyth had to force away the sneer that blossomed on her face at seeing his pretense of humble piety. The fear she had felt since the messenger had brought news of the trial burned to ashes, replaced with a revulsion so powerful she had to consciously school her face into passivity.

He took his place on the front pew where she would be forced to endure his black soul in close proximity. He boldly surveyed her, one arched brow of malevolence raised in her honor.

Three monks entered, walking in single file up to the front of the room where they sat behind their ecclesiastical leaders, ink, pens, and parchment in hand. So it was to be recorded. Her shame catalogued in history, chronicled for generations of women not yet born. Do not dare to speak against the church. Do not dare oppose a lie.

The archbishop raised a hand, his glittering rings catching the light from the windows high upon the walls. Silence fell as all eyes rested on him, as eager as a cat for cream. "This is Christ's inquisition," he said, his voice over loud in the breathless room. "Who is this woman's accuser?"

Father Brewer stood and bowed, his face a mask of devoted worship. "It is I, your most faithful servant, Father Andrew Brewer, appointed to the priesthood in Carlisle."

Edyth did her best to keep all emotion from her features, but it was proving difficult.

"What is your accusation?" asked the archbishop, his deep voice carrying easily in the vaulted room.

Father Brewer swept closer to the stand, his black cowled robes making him appear as a smudge against the colorful windows lining the walls. He bowed again, prostrating himself in humility.

"I am, myself, a victim of this woman's cruel malfeasance, Your Excellency." Righting himself, he turned and, in true performer fashion, addressed the crowd, his face a mask of solemnity. "Not only has this woman spread nefarious, heretic lies about myself, a man of the cloth, but she has also worked with her lover, the Devil himself, to bring pain and suffering upon the good people of my flock. With incantations and potions, she worked a strange magic taught to her by her wicked mother."

A tremor of excited abhorrence ran through the gathered crowd; its swift current could be seen in the eyes of the audience as they eagerly lapped up Father Brewer's lies.

"Duty-bound to punish this wickedness, and knowing of her guilt," he continued, a blunt finger pointing at Edyth, his mouth glistening with spittle, "this woman fled justice. She fled to a heathen land, hoping, no doubt, to be well hid. But God will not suffer such wickedness to endure!"

He took a breath, his glittering, black eyes growing bright. He turned to Edyth theatrically, his accusatory finger shaking as his voice rose, impassioned. "There she was discovered, practicing her craft amongst our king's men. God's chosen king!" Tempering his voice as he addressed his superiors, he said, "It was there, dear brothers, that she endeavored to corrupt the minds of great men, to interrupt the king's efforts of bringing peace and conciliation to his people. When her contemptible actions came to naught, this depraved woman fled justice once again, hoping to escape God's law by hiding behind a powerful man, whom she no doubt bewitched through wanton degradation."

The crowd, some shocked, others entertained, followed Father Brewer as he paced and then bowed his head dramatically. "I have prayed for her soul for many years, my brothers in Christ. I have done all I could to influence her for good, but the root of evil her witch of a mother planted within her could not be plucked out. I'm sorry to say that I have failed her."

The crowd stirred, murmuring and shaking their heads. Moved at Father Brewer's acute anguish at losing a member of his flock, one man stood, his hand cupped to his mouth as he shouted, "God willnae suffer a witch tae live!"

"You will remain seated," said the archbishop, rising halfway from his chair, his steely eyes roving over the crowd. Edyth trembled, remembering all too easily her mother's trial, which had started in much the same way. She had no hope of it ending differently.

She looked at Ewan, who had gone white with anger. His hands were clenched into fists on his knees, sitting perfectly erect; his storming gaze was locked onto Father Brewer. She was glad, in that moment, that he hadn't been permitted to wear his weapons inside the room, for she knew he would like nothing better than to run Father Brewer through.

"You have witnesses to these claims?" asked the archbishop, his deep-set eyes hidden under a heavy brow.

Father Brewer nodded solemnly. "Sadly yes. She was discovered beguiling and weaving her spells at the battle of Dunbar by the Earl of March himself."

The crowd stirred once more, heads bent together to whisper their shared shock and dismay. *The marshal of England himself? Then it must be true.* Indeed, the archbishop and the abbot themselves put their heads together, conferring silently. The abbot shuffled through some pages on the tabletop and handed two pieces of parchment to his counterpart.

"The Earl of March could not be here in person, this day," explained Father Brewer for the benefit of the audience, "so he has written his charge in his own hand."

Edyth's hands were shaking. She clutched them together as she watched the archbishop's eyes scan the documents, his stout lower lip moving slightly as he read. "The earl charges you first with heresy and, second, with conspiring to murder himself and the king of England, Lady Ruthven," said the archbishop to Edyth.

Edyth swallowed as the room gasped and muttered collectively, feeling the weight of a hundred glowering eyes.

"These are serious charges, indeed," said the archbishop after the room quieted. "We will start with the first. "Did you or did you not accuse Father Brewer of deceit and rapine as this letter declares?"

She cleared her throat of the knot that had formed there, feeling ill. Her mind touched briefly on that meeting she'd had, cloistered away with the earl, when she'd lost her temper. Taking a shaking breath, she said, "I was taught to only speak truth, Your Excellency. My claims against Father Brewer are true."

Several people stood, shouting angrily. They, like so many others, could not and would not believe a priest could do such things. Edyth did not pay attention, did not want to hear their hatred.

"You see," shouted Father Brewer triumphantly over the noise in the room, "she admits freely spreading such scurrilous charges against a man of the cloth. She would divert attention from her own sins to discredit and dishonor me."

"Heresy is a most grievous accusation, Lady Ruthven, and one the church has endeavored to blot out," said the archbishop, leveling her with his formidable brown eyes. "Do you have any witnesses to speak to your claims against Father Brewer?"

Edyth almost nodded but stopped herself. She and her mother had gone through great lengths to hide Annie away and spread the rumor that she had died of fever. An empty grave had been constructed in the little village near Carlisle, alongside Annie's mother, lending truth to the lie. And since Annie had refused to come, there would be little sense in disclosing the truth now. Edyth only had her word. Nothing more.

"All the witnesses are dead," said Edyth flatly, staring at Father Brewer. He would not meet her gaze, coward that he was. "I am all that stands between the truth and this man's lies. He would have me silenced as well."

The archbishop had to bang his staff on the decking, so loud was the outburst from the audience. Indeed, Father Brewer's face was red with repressed fury, his mouth pressed into a tight frown. "Silence!" the archbishop shouted. "Silence and order! This is a court of God!"

It was with some effort that the crowd regained their seats among the rhythmic pounding of the archbishop's staff upon the wooden planks. Ewan's eyes gleamed with anger, his eyes narrowed dangerously upon Father Brewer's back as he stood and rushed to the table to whisper in the abbot's ear.

The abbot nodded solemnly as Father Brewer spoke. With the slightest raise of a finger, a monk hurried to the abbot's side. Dismissed, Father Brewer returned to his seat, a smug look upon his face that incensed Edyth.

The room fell silent, intent to hear what the abbot would say. Indeed, it seemed to Edyth that the people drew nearer, leaning forward onto their toes so as not to miss a syllable of his wispy words.

"With no witnesses to confirm the slanderous charges submitted to the court by the Earl of March," said the abbot, "we would be forced to put them aside were it not that Father Brewer heard similar heretic words from Mistress Ruthven's own lips ere she left Carlisle." Edyth kept her face neutral with great effort. Father Brewer, on the other hand, looking gratified, bowed before the inquisitors. Never able to hold her tongue, she remembered having shouted at the priest, but she could not recall what had been said.

"Most wise," Father Brewer muttered in approval.

"Which brings us to the next charge against you," said the abbot. "What say you to the accusation of attempted murder at the Castle Dunbar, Mistress Ruthven?"

Taking a steading breath, she straightened her spine. "Only that I am innocent." She looked to Ewan. "I have brought a witness to speak of my innocence, Your Excellency."

"Let them come forward."

Ewan stood and took the place that Father Brewer had occupied at the foot of the stage. Father Brewer's smug demeanor did not change as he passed Ewan to return to his seat, but Ewan ignored him.

"State your name," said the archbishop.

"I am Sir Ewan Ruthven, Lord of Perthshire, Your Honors, and was present at the battle of Dunbar."

"You are of relation to this woman?"

"I am her husband," explained Ewan with a bow.

Scoffs filled the room. *The husband cannot be trusted. A convenient witness indeed!*

"Silence!" The archbishop raised a hand, the sleeve of his robe dragging onto the tabletop as he motioned for calm.

Once the noise quieted to only a handful of breathy whispers, he addressed Ewan.

"What have you to say on behalf of the accused?"

"At the time of the battle, she was not my wife," explained Ewan, a sardonic brow raised at the crowd. "That honor befell me after the chaos of Dunbar ended." He shifted his weight, the long lines of his body hinting at his strength. "I know that Lady Ruthven was not involved in a conspiracy against any person because she was held prisoner at the behest of Marjory Comyn. Guarded always, she had no opportunity to conspire. If ye recall aright," he continued, "Marjory Comyn is a loyal Scot and did not take kindly to Lady Ruthven's presence. She was far removed from all present and under strict guard."

The scritch-scratch of quills on parchment filled Edyth's ears. The archbishop's head bent to the abbot's, his mouth moving silently. "And you were a present witness of the attempted murders at Castle Dunbar?" asked the abbot.

"There was an attempt on lives, aye," said Ewan, drawing breath. "But I cannae say who it was the archer was aiming for aside from a guard. He was all who was witnessed to fall. But this attack was not perpetrated or contrived by Lady Ruthven. She has no authority to command a man killed, nor a desire to harm her king."

His words had been well chosen. As an Englishwoman, it would be assumed she was loyal to King Edward. Ewan shook his head slightly. "Any attempt to malign Lady Ruthven is a lie. She was naught but a maiden, locked away in a tower, and an easy target for blame from conspiring men."

"If so innocent, as you claim your lady wife to be," intoned Father Brewer. He stood, his wobbly chin thrust out defiantly. "Why then did she flee the scene?"

"Why did she nay stay tae be trampled or pierced with arrows do ye mean?" asked Ewan coolly, his brow raised in derision. "Have ye no better questions tae put tae me?"

Edyth wanted to smile at the red-faced priest, his mouth opening and closing in outrage. "You will not speak to me in such a manner!"

"Be seated, Father Brewer," commanded the archbishop, but Father Brewer would not be dismissed so easily.

Puffed up like a great fish, his face glowing, he said, "You claim she was locked away, yet now we hear from your own lips that she was in the presence of the king! Which is to be believed, sir?"

"Is this man now a member of the court?" Ewan asked the abbot and archbishop, his brow raised coolly.

"Tis a fair question," intoned the abbot. "Please answer."

Ewan took a breath, the broad expanse of back and shoulders rising as he filled his lungs. "As ye like. The lady was present at the oath taking because it was demanded of her by the Earl of March, as it was of everyone in the castle."

"You claim, sir," said the archbishop, "that she could not have been involved in any plot to murder, but what of the accusation of witchcraft? What have you to say to that?"

Ewan shook his head and regarded the abbot and archbishop evenly. "If ye call binding wounds and healing the ailing being a witch, then we have two very differing opinions of evil. Let her good deeds speak of her character, instead of what wicked men would have ye believe."

Ewan explained to the court how Edyth had healed his brother using common herbs and how she had, against his wishes, come to help any wounded at the battle of Dunbar. "This is no' a mark of a woman with evil in her heart."

The archbishop and the abbot conferred yet again, the abbot's snowy head bobbing in agreement as he listened to his counterpart. Finished, the abbot asked Ewan, "And do you have anything to say about the accusation of heresy against your wife?"

"Much," said Ewan succinctly, "but I would first put tae ye a question." At the nod from the abbot, Ewan continued.

"Ye condemn murder and the love of evil...of witchcraft and lustful behavior, do ye no'?"

The abbot's perpetually smiling mouth twitched slightly into a frown. "Of course. God's laws are very clear on these matters."

"I'm glad tae hear it." Ewan turned his head and looked at Edyth, speaking a silent language. He addressed the court again. "And yet ye would condemn a witness tae these very things. Lady Ruthven's words against the man ye call a priest are true, and yet here she stands accused."

His words were drowned out by the crowd's outrage. "You dare!" shouted Father Brewer, standing once more, jowls quivering. He swept toward the stand, casting a caustic look at Ewan before addressing the court. "Do you see how her wicked words have poisoned her husband's ear? Do you see how dangerous her evil tongue is? It must be cut out. I demand she be punished according to the law!"

"Be seated, Father Brewer!" demanded the archbishop. "You are not conducting this court."

"This is just further proof that she is what I claim! Heresy in God's own chapter house! Do you not see?" he railed. "She must be punished!"

The archbishop stood, his eyes full of anger. "You will sit and be silent, or you will be removed!"

Father Brewer swallowed air, his mouth opening and closing in outrage. Fuming, he reluctantly returned to his seat, his sallow face blotched red in anger. The crowd was agitated as well, muttering and jostling to better see the commotion.

Seating himself once more, looking agitated, the archbishop addressed Ewan. "Now...are you a direct witness to any claims your wife has made against Father Brewer?"

Ewan's mouth pressed into a thin, white line. "No," he said. It looked as though admitting it had cost him.

Father Brewer smirked.

"But I believe Lady Ruthven," said Ewan, glancing at Edyth. "Spend an hour in her company, and you'll ken as well as I do that she is nae what Father Brewer claims." He then relayed to the court all that Edyth had told him, about Annie's mistreatment and the deaths of Edyth's parents and her narrow escape. "And now this priest would silence Edyth as well."

The villagers mumbled, some shaking their heads in disbelief. Some, though, seemed to consider Ewan's words. "And while I have no way to prove these things to you," said Ewan, "I ask ye tae use the judgement o' yer own senses that God granted ye. I'd ask ye tae consider who it is, exactly, as should be on the stand today. Is it a sin for my wife tae speak the truth, even if it is against a man o' the cloth?"

Ewan sat as the abbot and the archbishop spoke to each other for several moments. Edyth's feet hurt, and her chest ached from her heart's incessant pounding, but she forgot them both when the archbishop stood and said, "Do you have any other witnesses, Father Brewer, to speak of your claims against Lady Ruthven?"

"I do, indeed," said Father Brewer eagerly, quickly gaining his feet. Father Brewer motioned toward the back of the room. People parted like the Red Sea to let James through to the center aisle. Looking awkward as ever, his long face reddened with the attention of so many upon him. He slinked his way to the front of the room, eyes downcast.

She couldn't breathe. She'd vainly hoped that James would come to her aid, but Father Brewer had somehow manipulated him into speaking against her.

When her mother had been charged, James had comforted her. He'd been there in the village square that fateful day, had helped her clean and dress her father's body. He'd helped dig her parents' graves. And now he was here, helping to dig her own.

"Name," asked the abbot, feathery brows raised in question. "My name is James, sir," he said. His voice had deepened to the rich tones of manhood. Gone were the reedy timbres that accentuated youth. His shoulders had broadened since she'd last seen him as well. He looked like a man in truth.

"How do you know Lady Ruthven?" asked the abbot, his head bobbing slightly as though the weight of holding his head upright was taking a great toll on him.

James's eyes darted to Edyth briefly before settling on the crushed hat in his hands. "I grew up with Lady Edyth...sir." He swallowed, the large Adam's apple bobbing in his lanky throat. "My da's the miller there in Carlisle. I'm his apprentice. The lady and I...we spent many an hour in amusement together."

"I see," said the abbot. "And so you've come to know the lady well?"

James nodded solemnly. "Aye. I would say I know her better than any other," he said, his ears gone pink.

"And have you witnessed this lady use herbal magics as she's accused?"

James's brow furrowed, his lips turning white as he pressed them together in thought. "Well, yes," he said after a moment. "She would help her mam in the still room, mixing and crushing medicines and the like. I helped her to gather some of the weeds...so she could be done with her chore, and we could play," he added hastily, should anyone accuse him of anything nefarious.

"Were any of these tonics and potions made by her hand, or was it only her mother who made such things?"

James nodded his head, his downy, mouse-brown hair flopping around his ears. "Yes. Yes, I saw her a time or two, when her mam asked it of her."

The scratching of quills upon parchment filled Edyth's ears as she stared at the side of James's homely face. He was being truthful, nothing more, but she still felt wounded.

"Were these potions, which were made by the accused, given to any person that caused suffering of any kind?"

James's brow knit together, and his shoulders slumped slightly. His eyes darted to Edyth once more, an apology written there. He nodded his head, shuffling his feet. He cleared his throat, his face alight. "Though I cannae say if it were the potion that had done it or sommat else."

"Tell us what you know, and we will judge for ourselves," commanded the archbishop.

Rubbing the back of his neck, James sighed heavily, looking as though he would rather be anywhere else in the world. "Henrick's wife had a difficult delivery...we could all hear her screams. It was... we all felt terribly sorry for her, but there was naught we could do for the woman."

Edyth remembered well that night. The babe had died shortly after being delivered, and a bloody, awful mess it had been, too. Edyth, along with her mother, had done their best to tend to Glenna, but there had been so much blood. Sticky and hot, it had dried under her fingernails and between her fingers so that everything she touched came away soiled. It had taken Edyth four times to wash it all away in the cold stream outside of their hut.

"Henrick's wife, Glenna, had taken a tonic made by Lady DeVr- er, Lady Ruthven's mam, to conceive the babe," explained James. "Glenna spoke about it, and the women gossiped about it for months on end. Nothing seemed amiss until it came time for the babe to be delivered. Glenna lay abed, fevered for many days, with little life to her except to moan and greet for her lost babe. Lady Edyth...she gave Henrick a potion. She said to give it to his wife to help her sleep."

Edyth closed her eyes, feeling the powerless anguish she'd felt at Glenna's suffering once again. She remembered well pressing the vile of mandrake root and hound's berry tonic into Henrick's work-roughened hands.

"Only Glenna did not wake," finished James, his eyes downcast. The crowd grew agitated again, not even trying to lower their voices. "Murderer!" one woman called. People shouted, their angry words swallowing one another.

James said something more, but she could not hear him. The inquisitors were speaking privately again, ignoring the crowd.

Edyth tried to remain calm. She clutched her hands together, wringing them worriedly.

Father Brewer stood, and the crowd's noise lessened, eager to hear what he'd say. "I remember well the sorrow Henrick felt as he first buried his babe and then his wife," said Father Brewer, shaking his head sorrowfully. "Glenna, in her ignorance, came to a witch for help and was cursed for it."

The crowd agreed. Many shouted, faces contorted in anger. It took several attempts for the archbishop to calm the audience. Finally, when the townspeople were quieted enough, he turned to Edyth, his face ruddy.

"Do you deny, Lady Ruthven, these testimonies? Remember, God is watching this very trial. Do not damn yourself."

She could not deny what James had said. He only spoke the truth, and yet it painted her in such a way to make her look as though she'd meant Glenna harm. "I only wanted to help ease her pain," said Edyth. There was nothing in the brew that should have caused harm."

But her words were drowned out. A pleased gleam entered Father Brewer's eyes. He stood, shouting. "A confession of witchcraft from her very lips!" he cried. "She admits it freely! She beguiles and give innocents spell-cast herbs. Only God has the power to heal, Lady Ruthven. You blaspheme at the seat of God's court."

"You will be silent," shouted the archbishop, "Silence!" *Bang, bang, bang* went his staff.

Father Brewer bowed in mock apology, clearly pleased with himself. Edyth's ears began to ring at the crowd's outrage, and then someone started pushing. A shoe was thrown, hitting Edyth in the shoulder. She stumbled at the contact, and then

Ewan was standing before her, his hand reaching for a sword that was not there.

"She must pay for her crimes!" someone shouted.

"Justice!"

"Hang 'er!" someone else shouted.

She couldn't breathe. She was suffocating. The room spun, and tears stung her eyes. It was just as it had been with her mother. She was going to die. She was cowering, and Ewan, standing over her, was taking the brunt of the abuse. All manner of objects were thrown at them while the cries for her immediate death rose to new heights.

Huddled under Ewan's protective body, fear clawing at her throat, it felt like an age before she realized the change in the room. Eyes screwed shut, her arms wrapped around her ears, she didn't notice the door of the chapter house fly open. Nor did she witness the slow dampening of commotion over her tripping heartbeat.

Perhaps it was the look of abject horror that came over Father Brewer's face. Perhaps it was simply the loud crack of the door as it hit the stone wall behind it. Whatever its cause, the crowd's cries and impassioned epithets hurled at Edyth died away as all heads swiveled to view the newcomer.

Light flooded from the open doorway, hiding the intruder's identity. The black silhouette moved more fully into the room, the light shifting to reveal a small but beautiful girl.

Father Brewer's face lost all color at the sight of her, his frozen form turned in question at the interruption. "But you're dead," breathed Father Brewer, eyes wide with dread.

Chapter Sixteen

"Order," said the archbishop unnecessarily, standing to see Annie over and around the heads of the audience. Catching sight of the disruption, his brow furrowed, curious. "What is it, child? Why have you interrupted this court in such a manner?"

Annie twitched as though wanting to run but unable to do so, held in place by some invisible force. Ewan's hand around Edyth's arm was so tight as to be uncomfortable. He helped her to stand, his eyes ablaze with an emotion Edyth could not name, but it was triumphant and proud, and it rested on Annie.

Her chest heaving, her chin quivering, Annie kept her place, her eyes fixated on Father Brewer. Farrah entered then, looking frazzled and out of breath. She hurried to Annie and tugged on her arm. Together, they walked the remaining length of the long aisle cut through the center of the mass of people to stand before the judges. The closer they came to the front of the room, the more courage Annie seemed to lose. Her eyes strayed to the floor, her head bent, face hidden, unable to look at Father Brewer. Nor did he wish to acknowledge her. Any suggestion of victory and satisfaction was now gone from his portly frame, replaced with nervous disquiet.

Rushing past Annie and her guardian to the judge's table, Father Brewer's eyes could not hide his fear. "Pray, Your Honors. Do not allow any further disruption to justice. Do not let your minds be turned from truth."

Sparing the priest a cursory glance, the archbishop motioned Father Brewer away, repeating his question. "Who are you, and why do you disrupt this court?"

"Her mind is gone, Your Excellency," advised Father Brewer. "She is simple-minded. Do not waste precious time questioning her. Send her away and let us commence with sentencing the witch."

"We will hear her," wheezed the abbot, leaning forward in his seat to better peer at Annie. "Speak, child. Tell us why you've come." Annie dared a glance at the abbot but looked away again, her bottom lip between her teeth. Farrah nudged her softly, encouraging.

"Pray. Do not force the child," begged Father Brewer, changing tactics. "It's clear she does not wish to speak but has been forced here. It would be cruel to subject her mind to such goings-on."

"I'm not simple," Annie blurted, daring to look out from under her protector's arm. Some of the color returned to her pallid cheeks. "You said I was simple-minded, but I'm not. Nor was I forced. I chose to come."

"And why have you come, child?" asked the archbishop.

"I came to be a witness for Lady Edyth, sir. Against him." Here she gestured sharply toward Father Brewer, but she would not look fully upon him.

"The witch claimed that all witnesses were dead," complained Father Brewer. "Which is it, then? This is simply more evidence against her. Surely you will not suffer such a mockery of God's court!"

Ewan scoffed, "What could an innocent man fear from her words, Father?"

"Enough," commanded the archbishop. "You will *all* be silent unless spoken to. Be seated, Father. And you, Lord Ruthven. The court will hear what the girl has to say."

Ewan gave Edyth's arm a final squeeze in parting, his hopeful eyes meeting her own. "Do you see, Edie? God or fate or whatever you wish to call it has not abandoned you."

Once left alone to the survey of her examiners, Annie's nervousness dissipated enough to answer simple questions such as her name and her place of birth, but when the abbot asked Annie what claim she had against Father Brewer, her fear returned.

Hands wringing, she moved closer to the two examiners, casting a fleeting, fearful look over her shoulder at Edyth. "Lady Edyth asked me to come, but I couldn't...I was afraid."

"Of what were you afraid, child?" asked the abbot, his soft voice encouraging.

Annie opened her mouth but uttered no sound, her eyes filling with unshed tears. She swallowed and trembled. Not a sound was heard in the room, not even the rustle of clothes or a squeak of a bench as all waited, breathless, to hear what the girl might say.

The abbot's long, smiling mouth turned further upward, his old eyes crinkling as he smiled in truth. "You are free to speak here, child. No harm will come to you. Put your mind at ease and answer the question."

"He—Father Brewer was told I was dead so that I might live in peace. Lady Edyth and her man came for me, to testify, but I was too afraid for Father Brewer to know that I live still. I didn't wish for him to see me, and I...I didn't want to see him."

Annie took a deep breath, her narrow shoulders rising as she paused as though gathering strength. A shaking hand smoothed a curl away from her face that had come loose from her plait. "But I couldn't sleep or eat, and I felt sick always since they left. Farrah said"—she looked up at her guardian briefly— "she said as it was my conscience pricking my heart and that she would bring me here if I wished it. She said I should lay my hurts to rest, and coming here would do that."

Annie straightened her shoulders, standing to her full height. Gathering her courage, she said, "I came for myself and so that Thom could be proud of me. I think...I think he would have wanted me to speak for his lady so that his death might count for something."

"Who is Thom?" asked the abbot, his voice nearly lost in the scritch-scratch of quills as the monks recorded the proceedings.

"Thom is—was—my brother, sir. He tried to help me." Annie sniffed, tears coloring her voice. "Everyone who has tried to help me is dead. All except for Lady Edyth." Annie paused, wiping tears from her cheeks. "Sh-she t-told me he died helping her escape Carlisle. I couldn't let him die for n-nothing."

"And do you know why Lady Edyth fled Carlisle?" asked the abbot.

Annie nodded, pulling her face from her apron, blotched red, eyes swollen. "She ran away because Father Brewer didn't want her speaking the truth. He wants her dead so that she can't tell people what he did."

"Nonsense!" cried Father Brewer, stricken. "The girl has been fed lies by the witch to discredit me! I will not abide such slander!"

"As this is my court, what you will and will not allow has no bearing here, Father Brewer," the archbishop said, leveling him with a steely eye, "you have no authority here. You cannot silence a witness." Father Brewer opened his mouth to retort, looking rather green, but at a thunderous look from the archbishop, he shut it reluctantly and sat back down.

Order restored, the archbishop addressed Annie, his features softening into calm inspection. "What is it that Father

Brewer wants hidden? Do not fear him, child," he reassured her at her worried expression.

"He told me...he said that if I told anyone, I'd be excommunicated. My soul will be lost." Annie rung her apron in her hands, her tear-filled eyes pleading with the archbishop.

Edyth could feel the shift in the room. Scattered whispers wove through the crowd, but this time, their eyes rested on Father Brewer and not on Edyth. An unspoken question burned like live coals in their eyes.

The archbishop frowned, his eyes darting toward Father Brewer briefly. "Is that so? Excommunication is a grievous punishment to be sure, but allow me to put your mind at ease, child. Only the vilest of impenitent sinners are excommunicated, for they should not be allowed to partake in the sacraments that they so easy cast before swine. I cannot think of anything a child might do that could warrant such a penalty."

Annie seemed to sway on her feet as the weight of worry was lifted from her small shoulders. Farrah hugged her tightly to her side, bending to whisper unheard reassurances.

"What charge do you lay against Father Brewer?"

Annie hid her face, unable to speak of her shame. Edyth's chest felt tight, compassion for the girl outweighing her judgment.

"Imagine if you can," said Edyth, watching Annie's struggle, "growing into a body that is valued only for its virtue. Think again, sirs, how difficult the task to remain pure can be, when you are thought of as no more than chattel. And if you are burdened with beauty, your chances diminish further still." Edyth paused, taking a steadying breath. She could feel the weight of the eyes in the room resting on her, but she ignored them. She only saw Annie, trembling with suppressed emotion. And she saw Thom, crumpled and bloodied, at the feet of those whose ears had been poisoned with lies.

"It is unseemly for a woman to speak without being invited to do so," continued Edyth, "so you can see, sirs, how your mothers, your sisters, and this sweet girl lack the courage to open their mouths." Edyth pointed at herself, tapping a finger to her breast. "I was not raised to be meek, nor was I born without means. I was afforded the luxury of protection where this child had none. It is my duty, then, to speak for her when she cannot."

Edyth's finger moved to point at Father Brewer, her eyes burning with fierce anger. "This man. This man who calls himself a priest—a man of the cloth—betrayed his station and violated the trust of his parishioners. He took advantage of Annie's innocence and robbed her of what value the world has placed upon her."

Annie made a sound halfway between a choke and a sob, and Edyth stopped, her heart breaking for the girl. "I will say no more, for Annie's sake, except that Father Brewer's passions have ruined the lives of many."

"Slander! Heresy!" cried Father Brewer, spittle flying from his lips as he leaped from his seat.

"You will remain silent!" commanded the archbishop, looking very angry indeed. "Is this true?" he asked Annie. "Did Father Brewer mistreat you in this way?"

Annie, sobbing, could only nod, her body shaking.

The collective outrage of the people in the room was instantaneous. The tide had turned against Father Brewer, but he fought it, shouting over the crowd.

"She is but a peasant! You will believe her word over my own, a man of godly station?"

Ewan was helping Farrah and Annie into his vacated seat as the archbishop's thunderous voice brought Father Brewer to his knees. "You forget yourself, sir! Peasant or king, we are all God's children. Now is there anyone else who can testify to these charges laid against Father Andrew Brewer? If so, we will hear them now."

"You are not competent judges!" cried Father Brewer, looking around him wildly as though searching for someone who would jump to aid him. "You cannot degrade me in such a fashion!"

The crowd was pulsing with movement, jostling, and hissing. Edyth felt quite undone, the strength gone from her, but she kept her place, watching as Father Brewer gnashed and spat angry words at the crowd.

The archbishop employed his staff again, the booming reverberation echoing in Edyth's feet as it struck the wooden planks.

There was a great surge in the crowd, and James fell forward onto the stone floor. He'd fallen onto his hands and knees, but he stood quickly, straightening his tunic with a disgruntled glance at whomever had spat him out of the crowd.

"I have something to say regarding Father Brewer," said James, his cheeks pink.

At the behest of the archbishop and abbot, he continued, "I'm not one to be bullied, and I sure as h—, and I won't lie for someone either." He cleared his throat, shifting his weight on his feet, a frown on his face. "I came to testify as Father Brewer bade me because I felt it was my duty, which he reminded me of many a time. What I said about Lady Edyth is true. She *does* practice medicine using herbs, and she *did* say some powerful words against the priest, but I know Lady Edyth well. Better than anyone else here. I can say with all assurance that Lady Edyth is no liar. She's got a foul temper at times and is as thick-headed as a mule when she's set her mind to something, but if Lady Edyth tells ye something, ye can believe it."

The mumbling, shocked faces of the crowd continued as James pushed his way back to his seat, elbowing one man who would not make way for him. Edyth's heart, which had been so heavy it ached, seemed to break free of some invisible bond. It floated up into her throat, choking her with emotion.

"This court will reconvene on the morrow," shouted the archbishop. "The accused is to be removed and held until then."

A tall, thin yeoman in a beadle gown promptly moved from the wall to grasp Father Brewer's bicep, which was summarily yanked from his hold. "I am not the accused!" he spat, his eyes wide with fear. "Take the witch away! Unhand me!"

No match for the skinny yeoman, Ewan stepped forward and, taking hold of Father Brewer's robes, lifted the man clear off his feet, their noses an inch apart. "Your influence and power are now at an end," said Ewan through clenched teeth. "You will be stripped of your authority and your robes removed. Look, Priest," Ewan demanded, shaking him. Father Brewer made a strangling noise, clawing at Ewan's fist as it held the man aloft. "Look upon my wife for the last time."

Father Brewer lifted his eyes, watery and bulging. "You have no power over her or any other. She has bested you. And now it is *you* that shall hang."

Ewan loosened his grip, and Father Brewer fell to the floor in a puddle of robes, wheezing and gasping for air. The yeoman lifted Father Brewer with the help of a monk, dragging him to the door Edyth had entered through. His sobs echoed in her ears.

She did not know what to feel. There was no sense of triumph at the sight of her tormenter's fall. There was only exhaustion and a desire to rest her aching feet.

It was a few days later that Annie was giggling as she chased a butterfly from bush to bush in the yard of her home. The sun was high in the sky. Edyth loosened the ties of her robe, letting it fall from her shoulders to the rock supporting her. The warmth she felt had far more to do with the outcome of the trial than the weather, though. She felt a foot taller and a whole stone lighter after her conference with the archbishop and the abbot.

Following Annie's admittance of Father Brewer's crimes against her during the trial, she had been brought to a private chamber where the judges had disclosed their suspicions against the priest.

"There have been whispers," said the archbishop, "for quite some time. I'm sorry to say that, despite the rumors, there was no real evidence against him. No victims came forward, and so, sadly, we took his word for truth. It was only after I received the earl of March's letter that I hoped to finally lay the matter to rest. We are grateful for your valiant effort to bring the truth to light and pray you find peace."

They had then pardoned her of all wrongdoing and had given her their blessing. Edyth didn't know what to do with herself. She felt as free as a bird and just as weightless. She filled her lungs with the earth-rich air, sighing in contentment.

"Will you return to Carlisle?" asked Farrah, reaching to pick a dandelion. "Do you have people there you wish to see?"

Edyth turned her face to the sun, reveling in its touch. She shook her head. "I will only go to see my parents buried as they ought to have been, in the churchyard. Carlisle is no longer my home."

"Will you not stay to attend the priest's conviction and sentence?" asked Farrah frankly.

Edyth considered the matter. Ewan had asked her if she wished to stay, but upon examining her heart, she did not feel the need to see him condemned. It was enough for her and Annie to walk away free, with the knowledge that justice had been meted out. The wicked priest would hang and all would know of his disgrace. She needed nothing more. "I wish only to return to Scotland."

Farrah smiled softly, bringing the flower to her nose. "You find yourself content in Scotland then?"

Edyth nodded and opened her eyes to look upon the woman. "I do." After a beat, Edyth said, "Thank you. Thank you for loving Annie. For giving her a place. I can see she is well loved here."

Farrah's eyes strayed to the girl, who was now twirling in circles, her face upturned to the sky. She fell with a laugh and lay still in a heap, her blond hair blinding white against the tufts of grass.

"I deserve no thanks. It is to you that our gratitude belongs. Thank you for doing what she could not. For giving voice to her pain," said Farrah, her gray eyes somber. She paused, watching Annie with a tenderness that touched Edyth.

"I always wanted a big family," Farrah said introspectively. "I'd prayed for a child of my own for years, but it never happened." She plucked at a blade of grass. It snapped, and she reached for another. "When it did not happen, I grew impatient and angry that I was not blessed in the way that I wanted." She looked at Edyth from the corner of her eye shyly. "But now I can see that my heart had been prepared for *this* child. My prayers were answered in a way I hadn't expected."

A bird twittered gaily in a tree near them, pulling Edyth's eye. "Yes," she agreed, thinking of her prayer so long ago to somehow avoid a marriage to the baron of Wessex. It had been granted in the most unlikely of ways, and not without sorrow. "But would you change it?" asked Edyth. "Would you give back Annie if you could have a child of your own?"

Farrah shook her head, her eyes fixed on Annie as she picked flowers, humming softly to herself. "No. I wouldn't trade her for anything. But what of you? Do you want children?"

Edyth shrugged, an errant hand going to her womb. "Yes." She smiled, looking across the farrowed field to her husband as he bent low to the ground to inspect some plant Benjamin had pointed out to him. "Yes, I dare say I do."

Epilogue

The vibrant colors of summer surrounded them. Emerald leaves filled her vision as their carriage rounded the corner to the MacPherson keep. Here, the view opened, and she could see the dark stone fortress her cousin now called home. A line of MacPhersons waited on the drive, bunched together in a mass. Edyth craned her neck, searching for Meg.

There. She saw her almost at once. Edyth recognized her dark hair and alabaster skin. She looked much the same as Edyth remembered but also changed in subtle ways. She'd lost the roundness of her face, and her lanky form had transformed into the full bloom of womanhood. It also helped that Meg was waving frantically; her broad smile was warm as any welcome Edyth could ever hope for.

Clapping merrily and dancing on the spot, Meg threw her arms wide as the carriage pulled to a stop. As soon as Edyth was free of the carriage, Meg bounded to her and swept her up in a bone-crushing hug.

"Mmph. It's so good to see you again, Edyth. Your hair! What's happened to your lovely hair?"

"Scotland has robbed me of my only treasure," teased Edyth, motioning to her shorn locks, which fell to just below her shoulders. "Look at you," cried Edyth, taking in Meg's changed appearance. "You're with child! How wonderful!"

"Yes, yes," replied Meg, smoothing the fabric of her gown over her swollen belly. "I dare say in a few more weeks, we'll have another mouth to feed. I've got another just there, with his da." She pointed to her husband, who had his hands full with a rosy-cheeked boy of about two, as far as Edyth could guess.

They talked over each other, questions and answers tumbling from them as they touched each other's faces, pulled each other into hugs, and wiped away happy tears.

"It's been an age," said Meg, disentangling herself from their embrace. "I'm so glad you've come! Wait, where are my manners?" She sidestepped Edyth and addressed Ewan, who was watching the reunion with a rather bemused expression on his face.

"Are you my cousin's husband?" asked Meg, openly appraising Ewan.

"I am," he replied, bowing respectfully.

Meg waved his manners aside and pulled him into a hug. "We are family now and are beyond such formalities."

Ewan smiled and patted Meg on the shoulder, his eyes dancing with suppressed laughter.

"I cannot imagine that you could ever deserve her," whispered Meg, "but you can live the rest of your days endeavoring to prove me wrong."

Ewan's eyes met Edyth's over Meg's head, sparking with admiration.

"You are right, Meg," he replied, reaching for Edyth's hand. She took it and smiled up into his face. "I don't deserve her, but do you think she would ever let me forget it?"

"Never," replied Edyth, and stretching up onto her toes, she kissed her husband, feeling a warm contentment settle over her frame. She was whole, and she was free. And she was blissfully happy.

The End

Acknowledgments

No book can be written alone. It requires countless hours of volunteer reading, editing, enthusiastic cheerleading, and endless phone calls wherein loved ones talk authors off metaphorical cliffs. I have been lucky to have had such well-placed and much-loved people in my life. Thank you to Kristal Winsor, who knows my mind and my heart so well. Thank you to Cami Madsen, for reading and offering solutions to my own questions. To my sisters, Valarie Dixon and Melanie Patterson, thank you for your feedback, suggestions, and cheer. And to my mother, thank you for replacing doubt with purpose. Thank you Tresha Beard, Liz Garcia, Shawn Pilj, and Kelsey Renaldo for your excellent opinions and skill. Lastly, thank you to my husband, Bryce, for giving me the time and freedom to test these waters and spread my wings. I love you.

About Author

Jalyn C. Wade is an American author who currently lives in northern Virginia with her husband and three sons. Married to a military man, she has had the great opportunity to move often and fall in love with people of all walks of life. Her works merge multiple genres, featuring elements of historical fiction, romance, and adventure. She has been a public educator—specifically a teacher of the deaf and hard of hearing—for most of her career but has dabbled in creative writing her entire life. Outside of writing, Jalyn also enjoys gardening, painting, and spending quality time with her family.

If you enjoyed reading *The White Witch's Daughter*, please consider leaving a review. If you'd like to receive updates on upcoming works, you can visit the author's website at jcwade-originals.mailchimpsites.com to be added to the newsletter mailing list.

Also By

Other books by J.C. Wade include:

The Fate of Our Sorrows: a prequel novella
Carlisle, England
-1287-

Join Edyth in this prequel novella to its companion piece, <u>The White Witch's Daughter</u>, as she navigates the complexities of self-discovery, only nine short years before her life takes a most devastating turn.

Nine-year-old Edyth DeVries does not know she's different. She does not yet understand what fate has in store for her. But after a terrifying nightmare becomes a reality, she questions who she is, and what her visions could mean.

A Conjuring of Valor: Book Two
1296 Scotland:

In the village of Perthshire, Edyth Ruthven finds that life as the new mistress of the household is not as comfortable as she'd hoped. Rejected by her husband's people as an outsider with a dangerous reputation, Edyth struggles to make a place for herself amid the rampant rumors of her past.

What's more, Edyth struggles to make sense of her nightmares, forewarning of a deadly event fast approaching. When her only friend and good sister Caitriona is forced into an arranged marriage, the full weight of a divided and prejudiced people falls upon her shoulders.

Ewan, meanwhile, walks along the edge of a twin blade, forced to choose between loyalty to his own people or to embrace the English King. When a nefarious sheriff is appointed to their lands, the life the Ruthvens had hoped for unravels before their very eyes, leaving them in a tangle of wicked machinations set forth by the wicked sheriff.

A Storm Summoned: Book Three

From twice nominated Whitney Award finalist, J.C. Wade, the thrilling true history of Scotland's first fight for independence comes to life in this, the final installment of The White Witch's Daughter trilogy.

1297
Scotland

A Storm is coming.

While England's king conscripts Scotland's sons for a war not of their making and his sheriffs tax and repress a burdened people, the seer Edyth Ruthven foretells of an uneasy future. Even as King Edward's fist tightens around Scotland's nobles, a whisper of rebellion spreads.

The world holds its breath as the very fabric of a divided kingdom is held together by conspiring men. Men who know well at what cost freedom is won. For Ewan and Edyth, life has taken a difficult and uncertain turn. But political machinations would be nothing if Edyth was not also navigating a difficult pregnancy.

Iain, meanwhile, is thrust into the midst of a treasonous act all while traversing a new and unwanted relationship. As Iain and his betrothed, Alice Stewart, work toward mutual compromise, their burgeoning relationship is put to the test.

Last, Cait, who has always craved action, learns that getting what you wish for is not always so sweet. With the escaped fugitive, Andrew Moray, in her new home, Cait no longer must listen at doors, but is she ready for what is surely to come? With new alliances comes unfamiliar territory, thrusting the Ruthvens into treacherous waters. Can Ewan navigate his scattered family through the clashing swords and scheming hearts that pervade the political landscape? Can Edyth's efforts keep her men alive and free?

Excerpt from A Conjuring of Valor: Book Two

Perthshire, Scotland
1296

Ruthven Keep

Caitriona Ruthven frowned down at her appearance in the rain barrel, her distorted and rippling features screwed up in anger.

"...bootless, crook-pated, puttock," she muttered under her breath before plunging the hand pail into the icy water. Her brother, Ewan, was all that and more, but she could only say such things out of all hearing, for she was a *lady*, and shouldn't know such indecent and debase words.

She scoffed softly as she pulled the hand pail from the black water, her mouth twisting mockingly. If her mother had wished to raise Cait as a lady, she ought not to have had any sons. From where did the woman think she'd learned such words in the first place? No, Ewan deserved her sharp tongue. What was she to do? Step aside and meekly let him plan her life with no consideration to her feelings?

Yes. Exactly that, she thought sourly, her mouth pressing tightly with a fresh wave of indignation. That's precisely what her mother and brother expected of her. She'd told her brother —that droning, flap-mouthed clot—just what he could do with his plans. Granted, she ought not to have said it within her mother's hearing, but she stood by what she'd said. He *was* meddling. She sighed forlornly as another cold stream of water trickled into her shoe. Still, in all her seventeen years of life, she should have learned by now to hold her tongue in front of her mother.

For her impudence, she'd been punished, as always, with menial chores. You'd think her mam, a canny and otherwise astute woman, would have noticed by now that no amount of scrubbing, digging, washing, or carrying would motivate Cait into meekness. By the Saints, she'd tried to please her mother. She really had. But one can only be submissive and gentle for so many hours in a day before nature took hold and her true character could be suppressed no longer.

Today's task was to keep the kitchen pots full of water and the fire constantly stoked. It would be hours of work that would hurt her hands and back, but it could have been much worse. She shuddered, thinking of the time she'd been tasked with scrubbing chamber pots clean.

Water continued to slosh over the rim of the pail with each step she took on the way to the kitchen; the side of her skirt was damp and her shoe squelched with each step. *Damnation!* She trudged around the corner of the kitchen, careful to step squarely on the wet stone step at the door, and into the blazing hot room.

The kitchen boasted two hearths and a baking oven for bread, which was all fine and well if you weren't tasked with keeping them hot all the day long. Cait moved to the second hearth, on the far side of the room, and dumped the pail of water into the simmering pot the household used for daily tasks.

"Done," announced Cait, turning expectantly to the cook. Alban was a spindly, sullen man, who'd had the run of the kitchen since her other brother, Iain, had been born. For the twenty years Alban had served the Ruthven family, she doubted he'd ever cracked a smile, which is probably why her mother tasked her to work under him so often. Cait could not charm him, no matter how hard she tried.

"Mmmph," he grunted not even sparing her a glance. The cleaver in his hand fell upon a sheep's leg joint with a wet *twhack*, spraying his apron with tiny speckles of blood. "Dinnae ye doddle, lassie. Tae the woodbox, and quick. When ye're done there, I'll need more water. The lassies are scrubbing the tiles today."

"Aye," sighed Cait, curiously eyeing the grotesque sheep's head that laid upon the table as she passed. She swung the large linen sacks used to cart wood into the kitchens over her shoulder and set off, looking to the sky in hopes that the sun was further along in its journey across the sky than when she'd last checked. She grumbled slightly, seeing it wasn't even past noon yet. At this rate, her blisters would have blisters.

There was space dedicated to chopping wood for the kitchens not a far way off, clustered amongst spindly alder trees. Someone was already industriously chopping blocks from the sound of it.

Making her way down the dusty path, she felt the weight in her chest lighten marginally when she saw Ewan's squire there, splitting logs with powerful strokes. He was partially turned away from her, so he did not notice her at first; his sweat-soaked liene outlined the broadened expanse of shoulders and muscle that was usually hidden to her. What luck that her friend was here to lift her spirits on such a sullen day. When he turned as he tossed the split logs into another pile, his brown eyes found her with a look of happy surprise.

"'Lo, mistress."

Alec was fun and loved to tease, which she thoroughly enjoyed. The only thing she didn't care for, was his rather worshipful obedience to her overbearing brother. She supposed she couldn't be too judgmental of him; being a squire had a way of forcing such blind adoration. She supposed her brother wasn't all that bad. He was no villain, but still, she could think of no woman who would welcome a man planning her life for her.

Alec's sweaty face was open and friendly, and not a little hopeful. She felt her cheeks warm at the look on his face. She'd kissed Alec last winter at the Yuletide celebration. He'd been rather dashing in his green surcoat and dark hair and she, overcome with the cheer of the day and the wine, had pulled him into a darkened corner and pressed her mouth to his. It had been quick and chaste, but it had been her doing, which she supposed she should be ashamed of. She was a maiden. A lady. And ladies were not to kiss their brother's squires, no matter how winsome or witty. Or anyone, for that matter. She could never quite conjure the remorse she should have felt for her actions, however. It was a good thing her mother hadn't learned of it.

Ever since that kiss, they'd been engaged in a strange dance, where flirtation existed, with hope of more, though they both knew it was forbidden. Still, this dance was diverting, and she could use some entertainment at present. Haps she would kiss him again. It would lift her spirits in no time.

"Good e'en," she replied, unable to hide a coy smile. Alec was tall and sinewy, dark haired and long-limbed. He had the awkward grace of a boy who'd woken to discover he'd grown into a creature he'd never before considered. Like a caterpillar changed to a moth. He would soon be knighted, she thought, and wondered if Ewan would grant him a parcel of their lands to work, not that she would be there to watch him care for it. No. She would be married off to some stranger and only return home when allowed. Sourness returned to her belly at the thought.

Sometimes she hated being a woman of station. How lovely it would be to have the freedom of choice! Instead, she must marry a groom who presented the best advantage for their family. Her sullen mood settled over her once again, making her shoulders droop slightly.

"What'd ye do this time?" Alec asked, leaning against the handle of the ax as it rested on the chopping block. His winsome smile did not mock, but still she could not help bristling.

"What makes ye think I've done aught tae be punished?" *What a stupid question.* She felt her face blush despite herself.

He scoffed and bent to the pile behind him for another log. It *thunked* dully as it hit the block. Nodding toward the sacks that hung limply just below her hips, he said, "Then I'll have tae assume ye enjoy carting loads o' kindling for Alban or is that ye're just looking fer any excuse tae find me alone." He wagged his thick eyebrows at her flirtatiously, making her blush deepen.

Effecting a visage of superiority, Cait mocked him. "Ha! If I wanted ye alone, I wouldnae come here, where the very stink of yer labors mists my eyes."

Without warning, he exploded forward, his ax falling to the ground unheeded, and caught her around her middle before she could even take two steps. She squirmed and screeched against him as he rubbed his sweat-drenched cheek against her own.

"Och! *Gu leòr!*"

He let her go quickly and, laughing, said, "So I was right. Were ye late tae Matins again?"

"Ew!" she panted, wiping the wet patch of his sweat from her face with her sleeve, but she smiled grudgingly. He retrieved his ax, not apologetic in the least, and looked at her expectantly. She sighed and sat down on an upturned log. "I told Ewan I wouldnae do as he bid."

Alec gifted her with a look that communicated his lack of surprise. "And why should this time be any different. Ye've made it a sport tae disobey him all yer life, so far as I can tell."

She tossed her dark braid over her shoulder and said, "Aye, weel. I...may have cursed at him. Within Mam's hearing."

"Ah." His smile widened as he swung the ax up over his head, then forcefully down and into the oak log. It split easily, splintering satisfyingly into three pieces. "What does he bid ye do that ye find so distasteful?"

Cait frowned mightily. "He wishes tae set my betrothal."

Alec faltered only slightly in tossing the split pieces into the pile. His smile had gone, replacing his levity with the proper amount of gravity she felt the news deserved. "Aye, I heard him speak o' it tae Iain last week in the lists. Has it been decided?" He looked at her then, and she thought maybe he understood her anger. And fear.

"He's received some letters. Inquiries as tae what's tae be done with me." She forced herself to move, to stand and remove the bags from her shoulders and start to fill them with the split pieces littered between them. "As if I'm a problem tae be solved...a bundle o' goods tae be sold and delivered. If the idea hadnae been put into his mind by my uncle, I doubt he'd given my future much thought, which is how I wished it.

Alec frowned. "Did ye think he would forget the future of his beloved sister?"

Cait scoffed lightly but felt herself deflate slightly. "Nay. I just...I wanted tae wait a wee bit longer, aye?" "My Uncle Niael, the Caimbel –that's me mam's brother—says he's got someone in mind for me, but I forbade Ewan from even considering the prospect. And then, suddenly, he recalls a letter from the

Stewarts he received months ago. They're keen tae match me tae their middle son. Robert, I think his name is. Can you believe that he's nearly thirty? And they want Ewan tae agree tae it! Ouch!" Cait dropped the kindling she was holding to find a splinter in her palm.

She plucked it out neatly and sucked on the wound briefly.

"So ye told him ye wouldnae do it."

"Aye," said Cait, standing up. The bags were full and so she carefully slung them over her shoulders and across her chest so that a bag hung on each side. She looked at Alec, sweating, with sympathetic eyes in the summer sun, and she knew she could not fight what was to come. His face said it all: she was doomed. She had no choice, despite her words to the contrary. Her own powerlessness threatened to overwhelm her so she turned to flee before Alec could see her weakened spirit.

She turned to go and was almost out of the small clearing before Alec spoke again. She paused just long enough to hear his conciliatory, yet empty words. "My laird has a soft heart for ye. Perhaps he will delay yer betrothal if ye ask it o' him."

Delay it, perhaps. But for how long? And what did it really matter if she was a free maiden for another six months or for only another six weeks? Nothing would change the fact that she had no real power to choose her path. She cleared her throat and shrugged the weight upon her shoulders into a better position, keeping her eyes turned away from her friend.

"Aye. Perhaps he might at that."

The walk to the keep's kitchens seemed over-long in the summer heat and she wondered what it had been like for her sister, or her mam, when they'd been betrothed. She'd never bothered to ask.

***

Cait's hands were slippery with sweat, even in the cool late afternoon. She gripped the dulled short sword in her hand tighter, her forearm muscles quivering, and blocked the attack from her good sister, Edyth.

Ewan's English wife had turned out to be quite the ally; Cait had loved her quickly and fiercely. Both cut from the same cloth, they enjoyed spending their free time out of doors, and far away from needle and thread or comb and shuttle.

Edyth smiled brightly, her red hair glinting in the dappled sunlight of the orchard. They'd chosen the upper orchard as their practice yard, as it was out of sight and would require less explanation. No questions would arise from the ladies of the manor taking air in the leafy canopy in the north parcel, for instance, but they would quickly notice them sneaking into the lists.

"I thought I had you that time," breathed Edyth. She thrust her sword into a grassy lump of sod and sat on the ground, her back against an apple tree. The dappled light painted her with gold, making her hair shine bronze and copper.

"Aye, I thought so too," agreed Cait. She'd grown stronger since Edyth had shown her how to stand, how to find her balance with a sword in hand, and parry a thrust these last few weeks, but she didn't pretend she was talented.

Cait deposited her own sword in its hiding spot —amongst the branches of one of the larger trees—and picked up the basket she'd brought on the pretense of gathering flowers or mushrooms, or whatever else they could find in a hurry to excuse their absence. "What shall it be today, Edie?"

Edyth shrugged and stood, pulling apart the knot she'd tied in her brown skirts to keep her feet unencumbered. "Acorns for the pigs, perhaps? Or flowers. The meadowsweet is in full bloom."

"Aye, but I picked meadowsweet the last time we met." Cait pursed her lips in thought. "Haps we should go tae the village and seek the spun wool Mam requested. She's wanting tae make a new tapestry for the hall." Cait pulled a face, knowing that her role in this endeavor would be paramount.

Edyth smiled pityingly. "Yes, I heard her tell of it yesterday."

After washing their hands and faces in the brook, they made their way down the hillside and onto the road, passing through the stone fences that separated the land parcels. People dotted the landscape, industriously tending to their animals and fields, all of whom, when they passed, waved in their direction then summarily ignored them.

"Did Ewan tell ye that the King of England has laid siege tae Edinburgh Castle?"

Edyth nodded and filled her lungs, the preoccupied look Cait had noticed earlier returning in full force. She chewed her bottom lip, her eyes far away. "He did, though I confess he did not go into detail. He fears that soon Perth will be met with such a fate, should he resist.

Cait nodded, feeling the weight of her brother's concern, for she felt it too. Having a great talent for listening at doors, she had overheard the private conversation between her brothers and his captain, Rory, that morning. "King Edward bombards the castle with Greek fire with his trebuchets. If he should succeed, he will be the first ever to take it."

"What of Iain?" asked Edyth. "What is his opinion?"

Iain was the second son, just three years her elder. While he was far less serious than Ewan as a rule, he took his responsibility as older brother far too seriously for her taste. "Iain doubts the King will win such a prize, but Ewan, who has seen more of war, kens no keep is without its weaknesses."

"What do you think will happen?" asked Edyth, her large, green eyes betraying her worry.

"I am but a lass," said Cait on an exhale, "who has n'er seen war. I can only guess."

"A woman, yes, but not a stupid one. I would hear your speculation."

The compliment made Cait's mouth twitch upward, but she shrugged humbly. "I dinnae wish tae injure ye with my thoughts on yer English King."

With a scoff, Edyth said, "You know I do not love him, nor claim him as my sovereign. I am a Scotswoman now, thanks to your brother. Speak your mind."

Cait swooped to pick up a rock from a rut in the road. "I dinnae ken what tae think. I hope he doesnae take Edinburgh, for it would rally the Scots who oppose him tae unite." Cocking her hand back, Cait threw the stone down the road and watched as it bounced twice then ricocheted into the tall grass lining the path. "If he takes it," she added, "I think Ewan has the right o' it. Edward will have none tae stop him, then. The clans will submit."

She looked to her sister-in-law for any telling sign that she might know more. Edyth was *bana-bhuidseach geal*. A white witch. A seer, more specifically. She'd *seen* her brother Ewan's death at the battle of Dunbar only a few months previously and had moved heaven and earth to prevent it with some help from herself.

"Mmmph," agreed Edyth, her eyes far distant. "King Edward is a greedy man, who would devour his mother's soul if he thought it would sustain his own."

They walked in silence for a time, listening to the birds and the grass shuffle in the breeze. Cait hesitated briefly, then asked, "Have ye seen such visions, then? Is my speculation true?"

Edyth shook her head, her pretty mouth turned down into a frown. "I'm not sure. I've had a few dreams, but I can't make sense of them. Just shapes and shadows, but always with a feeling of disquiet. I cannot say as yet. It could be nothing."

"Or it could be something," said Cait. They walked in silence for several minutes, each lost in their own thoughts before Cait had the nerve to ask the question foremost in her mind.
"Has Ewan telt ye of his plans tae arrange my future?"

Edyth's eyes, distant and clouded with thoughts Cait could not see, darted ashamedly toward Cait then away, an apology written on her face. "Yes, he's told me a very little." She took Cait's hand then and gave it a squeeze. "I don't envy you. I was blessed to find your brother and to have found happiness here, but I know well what you feel. It's a frightening prospect, to be bound to a stranger."

"Aye," Cait agreed. "I think I trust Ewan tae find me a good match, but.... How can he be sure? He cannae know with any certainty what kind o' man he chooses for me."

Edyth signed and nodded. "Yes. Yes, I know."

Cait slipped her arm through Edyth's and asked, "Do ye think that yer dreams may have sommat tae do with my future husband?"

The look of surprise on Edyth's face gave her some relief, though it was small. "No. I...we can't be certain my dreams mean anything at all."

"Mmph," Cait muttered uncommittedly. "Ye'll tell me though, if ye think they might."

"Of course I would," Edyth said as they crossed the stone bridge over the river and entered into the sprawling village of Perthshire. It didn't take long for Cait to realize that something was amiss. Shouts were heard from the square and a milling crowd of people were gathered there, hiding whatever spectacle was taking place.

Cait hurried forward and, coming to the edge of the crowd, stood on her toes to see what was happening. Through a gap between two women, she saw that a wheel had come off a wagon, spilling its contents all over the ground, and —somehow—entrapping a child. It was a lad, his legs visible from under the axel, still and lifeless.

"Hurry, *Piuthar*. A child is hurt!" Her hand fumbled for Edyth's forearm, her heart seeming to quit altogether, but the woman was already pushing through the crowd, her skirts billowing out around her as she fell to the ground to assess the damage.

Cait watched, breathless, as Edyth's hands traversed up the boy's body, disappearing into shadow. A woman, the boy's mother, Cait presumed, was weeping volubly, frantically removing the remaining vegetables from the cart along with several other people. Cabbages rolled around their feet, ignored, as men came running, carrying farming tools long enough for prying.

"Hurry!" shouted Edyth from her place, "He lives still!"

The men thrust their long handles under the wagon and pushed against them, their faces screwed up with the effort. Hands, Cait could not tell to whom they belonged, pulled on the boy's legs, slipping him from the undercarriage of the cart smoothly.

The ground shook her feet when the men let their burden go and Cait's worry increased. It had been very heavy indeed. Blood and bone blossomed forth from the boy's upper arm, where he'd been pinned. His face was wan and lifeless. Cait would have thought him dead, had Edyth not said he still breathed. She could only watch with the quieted crowd —collectively holding their breath—as Edyth took command. She tied something around the boy's arm and shouted orders to a man, who cradled the boy and whisked him away as quickly as possible without jostling him, his mother rushing after them. Her cries made Cait's skin pebble to life and her chest tighten in grief.

Edyth found Cait with her eyes, her mouth moving. She couldn't hear what Edyth said over frantic cries of the boy's mother, so she hurried forward.

"I will need Alban's saw," said Edyth calmly, quietly, though Cait saw her hands were shaking. "I will need my herbal tome and my box of herbs. Go, Cait. Run as fast as you can and return to me at once."

Cait did as she was bid, running so fast that she lost a shoe as she crossed the bridge, but she did not stop to retrieve it, nor did she stop when she thought her ribs might split open from the pain in her side.